MINA IKEMO
Hyo
THE
HELLMAKER
SCHOLASTIC

Published in the UK by Scholastic, 2024
1 London Bridge, London, SE1 9BG
Scholastic Ireland, 89E Lagan Road,
Dublin Industrial Estate, Glasnevin, Dublin, D11 HP5F

ISBN 978 07023 2895 4

A CIP catalogue record for this book is available from the British Library.

Printed and bound in Great Britain by
Clays Ltd, Elcograf S.p.A
Paper made from wood grown in sustainable forests and other controlled sources.

1 3 5 7 9 10 8 6 4 2

www.scholastic.co.uk

To my family, because damn.

And to you who picked this up – thank you, and I hope this en is a good one.

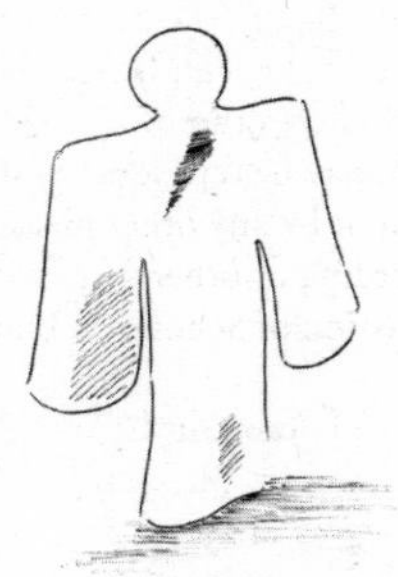

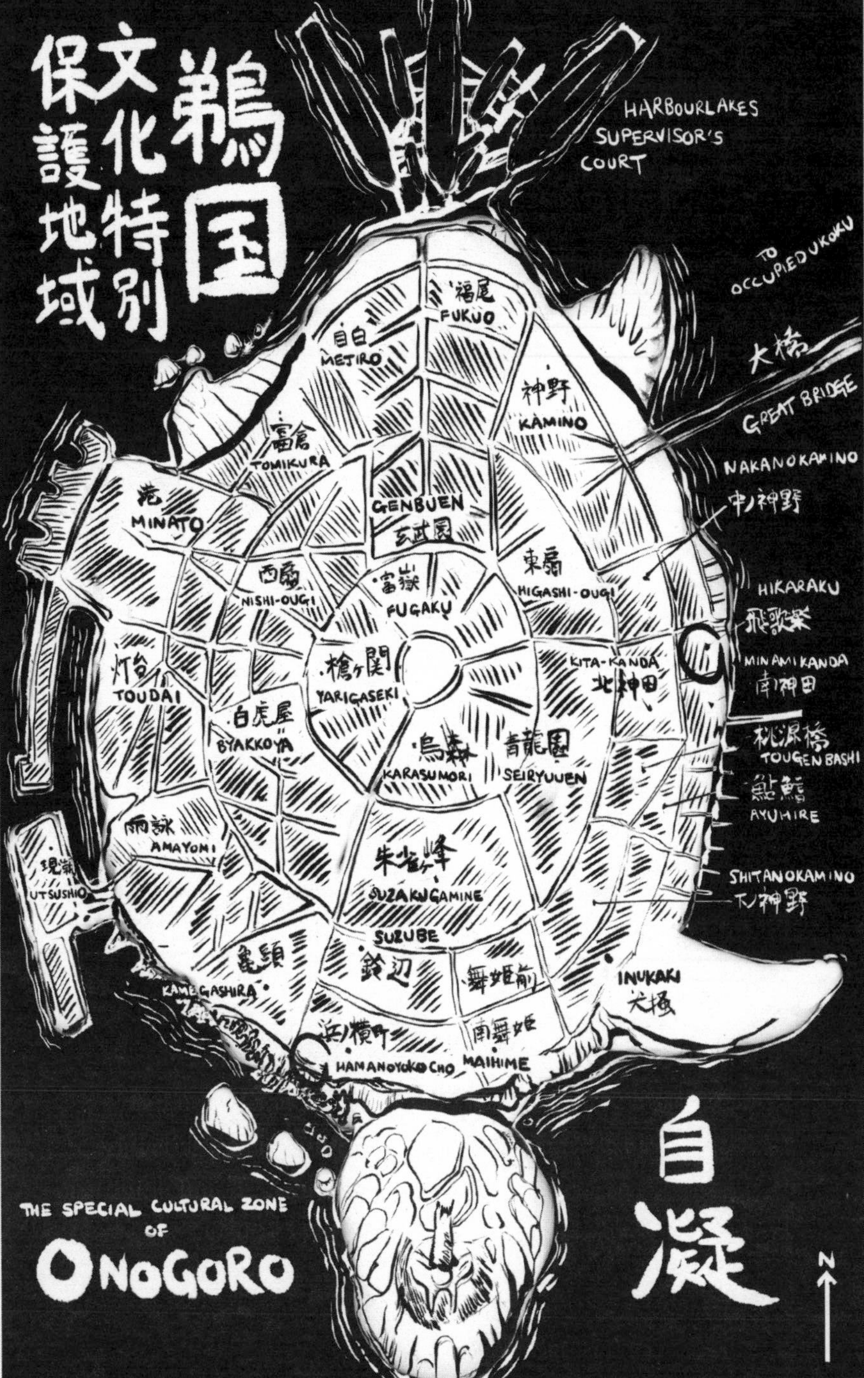

鵜国
文化特別
保護地域
HARBOURLAKES
SUPERVISOR'S
COURT
TO
OCCUPIED UKOKU
大橋
GREAT BRIDGE
福尾
FUKUO
目白
MEJIRO
神野
KAMINO
富倉
TOMIKURA
NAKANOKAMINO
中ノ神野
港
MINATO
GENBUEN
玄武園
西扇
NISHI-OUGI
富嶽
FUGAKU
東扇
HIGASHI-OUGI
HIKARAKU
飛歌楽
MINAMIKANDA
南神田
KITA-KANDA
北神田
灯台
TOUDAI
槍ヶ関
YARIGASEKI
白虎屋
BYAKKOYA
烏森
KARASUMORI
青龍園
SEIRYUUEN
桃源橋
TOUGENBASHI
鮎鰭
AYUHIRE
雨詠
AMAYONI
現潮
UTSUSHIO
朱雀ヶ峰
SUZAKUGAMINE
SHITANOKAMINO
下ノ神野
SUZUBE
鈴辺
亀頭
KAMEGASHIRA
舞姫前
INUKAKI
犬掻
浜ノ横町
HAMANOYOKOCHO
南舞姫
MAIHIME
自凝
THE SPECIAL CULTURAL ZONE
OF
ONOGORO
N

Hakai Family Hellmakers, Est. Taiwa 134
Purveyors of Artisan Hells & Unlucky Days
to Inflict Upon Your Enemies
We Will Make It Personal
Prices Upon Consultation

"Hellmakers, eh?" said the demon, who was following the scroll's cursive script with the Hakai family business card. "Is this story literally true, or a mythical retelling?"

Hakai Hyo, Thirty-Third Hellmaker, like all Hakais before her, knew the Record in the demon's claws by heart, and she knew that the story was true enough to matter.

Hyo said nothing. The shock of finding a demon just seconds ago – *the* demon, the very one who had caged her village in endless loops of cruel winters – in her own study, at her own desk, had killed her words. The demons of stories were man-eating monsters, mad from the bottomless hunger that was their price for eating the hitodenashi fruit. They weren't supposed to be quietly leafing through the Hakai family archives and fluent in ancient scripts.

Hyo took the demon in – her eyes, teeth, her lithe movements, the inhuman shine of her hair. Had something changed? What fresh hell had Hyo to fear?

"*The gods of fortune punished the First of Us for killing the gods of sickness, poverty and rot – of misfortune,*" the demon read aloud. "*She learnt too late that fortune cannot exist without misfortune. In killing the gods of misfortune, she'd threatened the lives of the gods of fortune too. Fortune cursed her to be the First of Us – to be a source of misfortune in the place of the gods she destroyed. Her daughters would inherit her curse. Her sons would inherit her weapons. Daughters and sons together, the Hakai family is never to be free of her crime and must bear its memory with the duty of guilt.*" The demon looked up from the scroll. "Making a family business of this supposed curse doesn't seem especially penitent to me."

"There's nothing 'supposed' about it." Hyo found her voice at last.

The demon regarded her coolly. "All the power of the

old gods of misfortune sealed in you – yet you haven't used any of that power against me."

"Hellmaking doesn't work like that."

"No. I guess it wouldn't be a *curse* if it was that convenient." The demon placed the scroll in its box. Curdled smells of old blood and rotting blossom wafted from her shimmering hair, and Hyo bottled down the urge to run. "A shame your neighbours don't remember what's about to happen to them. Otherwise, they could've commissioned you to avenge them on their behalf by now, hmm?"

Outside, the villagers were breaking ice, winching open frozen shutters and greeting each other with the dawn. No one knew that they'd lived this day before, that Hyo could predict every snapping icicle, every turn of the crows in the skies – that she knew what each of them looked like in their moment of death.

The demon cocked her head. "How many winters has it been now, Hakai Hyo, that I've turned this village of yours into my orchard? That you've watched your people suffer by the hitodenashi curse? Five winters? Six?"

Eight. "Shut it."

"You know, I've never killed your villagers. Not one. In any of these winters." The demon picked up a brush and played with its end. "Hitodenashi pear is a parasitic curse. It *wants* to keep its human hosts alive, to feed off the curses in their hearts. My sowing the seeds, to turn

呪詛百科
万縁起其ノ参・上
万縁起其ノ弐
万縁起其ノ壱
式神術②
式神術①

your friends into my hitodenashi trees, gave them eternal life. Burning those trees to the ground, that's what kills your villagers each time – and that's all yours and your brother's doing. Not me."

Hyo bunched her hands. Her nails sank into her palms. "What did *we* ever do to you to deserve this?"

"I asked the same thing eighty years ago, back in the Hell-on-Earth War. What did I ever do that meant no one thought my human life was worth just ... leaving alone?" She scratched her head, then shrugged. "Sit, Hakai Hyo. I've a proposal for you."

"Will you let the villagers live?"

"Too late for that – they die in one loop, they're dead for good. But you and your brother..." The demon's black and gold eyes were unblinking. "Every loop I've tried to infect you both with hitodenashi and it's never taken root. The irony of it, really. I came all this way to see the two of you learn how hitodenashi's eternal suffering feels, and it's the two of you who are immune to it. Ha!"

"You came here for me and Mansaku?" Hyo couldn't hold back her laughter. "I don't understand you."

"Call it a blood feud." The demon nudged the chair opposite her. "Didn't I tell you to sit down?"

"Or?"

"Or I'll go and find Mansaku to rip off his jaw. See if that gives me the satisfaction you've denied me. I won't know till I try."

Hyo sat.

The demon smiled, baring golden fangs. "What do you know of the island of Onogoro?"

"It's a Special Cultural Zone of Ukoku." Hyo wrung her mind for everything she could recall. "Ukoku's gods of fortune retreated there during the Hell-on-Earth War, taking enough of us Ujin to survive. The gods haven't left it since and Onogoro-Ujin can't leave the zone unless on approved Cultural Expeditions."

"And what's Onogoro renowned for?"

Hyo's heart thudded in her ears. "They make shinshu – hitodenashi's only known cure."

Onogoro's prized pitch-black rice wine, shinshu, was medicine for the hitodenashi-infected, weedkiller for its sprouts, and poison for the demons born from the humans who ate its fruits. As far as the world knew, it could only be made on Onogoro. Nowhere else had succeeded.

That was why everyone said that, after the Hell-on-Earth War, shinshu had bought Onogoro's freedom. The whole world was dependent on Onogoro's shinshu to keep the hitodenashi curse at bay. Ukoku was officially under Harbourlakes' occupation, but Onogoro alone had been able to negotiate special privileges, using the threat of stopping shinshu production in exchange for near self-rule.

Onogoro had its own assembly. They had banned foreign gods. They refused to teach in four languages as the rest of Ukoku did. They isolated themselves to "preserve their endangered culture and protect their gods" – which had been permitted, because Onogoro's official story was that Ukoku's gods were essential for shinshu. Only *these* gods, they said, could make the blessed rain that was shinshu's key ingredient, and the rest of the world hadn't yet proved them wrong.

Hence Onogoro, the Special Cultural Zone, was born.

"Here's my proposal, Hyo. I can't get on to Onogoro. Wards prevent demons from even setting foot in the gateway. I'll set you and your brother free of my winter." The demon pointed a claw at Hyo. "And in exchange, you two will go to Onogoro for me."

Light caught on the tip of the claw. "To do what?"

"I heard that someone's growing hitodenashi pear there – an orchard all to themselves."

Hyo stared. "On Onogoro?"

"You don't believe it?"

Hitodenashi needed humans to grow on – to make an orchard of it, to even wish to do so! And for Onogoro to do it! "Why would they do that?"

"Because it's been long enough since the Hell-on-Earth War that someone's forgotten why they shouldn't." The demon let out a bubbling laugh. "You're wondering what this has to do with you. Very well. You could say that we ... share an inheritance, and what that means is that you've a duty of guilt, as you called it. It has to be you to find the hitodenashi on Onogoro, Hyo the hellmaker, and then, when you do, you can do as you were cursed to."

She pointed a claw at Hyo. "You're going to make hell on Onogoro for me."

ONE

到着

Onogoro was the island of beginnings. As the world-builders finished stirring the swamp of Earth's chaos with their spear, a drop of silt fell from the spear-tip. It settled on the world's new surface in a shape of its own choosing. This drop was Onogoro, meaning "that which set on its own".

FU-NO-MONO,
Third Hellmaker

Beyond the Gateway Terminal's arrival counters, the island of Onogoro was sunlit, green and basking in smooth water, all framed by a great glass window.

Onogoro was shaped like a turtle. The domed rock at the southern promontory was its head; the skyline of

its lush green skyscrapers was its shell. On its nose was a statue: a dancing woman with her face worn away by wind and water, and the stubs of her forearms lifted heavenwards. At its tail were the black masts of the Harbourlakes Supervisor's Court.

"It looks just as Jun told us," Mansaku said, gazing at the island. A chill clung to his clothes from the disinfecting cubicles. "Whoa, is that the statue of the Nakihime? Of the Three-Thousand-Year Kagura? She's bigger than I thought."

"Whole island's bigger than I thought," Hyo said, then felt immediately silly. Why would the demon have made this easy for them?

"Hi there!"

Hyo startled. The official who had stopped by them was dressed as a giant pear. Green and bobbing, her huge cartoon eyes were filled with angry red swirls. The sash across her front read, "Make sure Pear-chan stays at the Onogoro Gateway Terminal! Please comply to stop the hitodenashi!"

The pear said, "Would you like some pamphlets?"

"Are you serious?!" Hyo blurted, then shrank as heads turned their way.

"Thank you so much – yes, please," Mansaku said smoothly to the pear. Once she had bowed and bounced away, he nudged Hyo in the ribs. "You all right?"

"Mansaku, she's dressed as a *hitodenashi pear*." Hyo switched to Harboursigns, keeping them low and hidden. "Who makes a *mascot character* out of hitodenashi pear?"

"Onogoro, apparently," he signed back. "You remember what Jun was like. He was clueless. He didn't even totally believe that hitodenashi pear was real."

Makuni Junichiro – Jun to his friends – was the only born and bred Onogoro-Ujin that Hyo and Mansaku had ever met. He was a reflectographer and poet; five years older than Hyo, the same age as Mansaku. Two winters ago, Jun had separated from the rest of his Cultural Expedition and arrived at Hyo and Mansaku's village, lost and utterly thrilled about it – even as they'd had to haul him out of a snowdrift.

The snow meant Jun had stayed with them all winter and they'd got to know him well. Hyo had chalked many of their differences up to him being *Jun* rather than being from Onogoro. They were all of them Ujin, people of Ukoku – even if Jun had spoken a dialect he called "Standard" and sometimes said things like "you Occupied-Ujin" as if Hyo and Mansaku were from a different country.

Perhaps, they may as well have been. Eighty years on from the war, Onogoro-Ujin had prospered, carving a story of post-war "redemption" for themselves through the making and selling of shinshu. They could put aside the inconvenient truth that Ukoku's own scientists had created the hitodenashi, during the war, in the first place.

The same could not be said for the rest of Ukoku, upon whom the Harbourlakes had done everything they could to impress the horror of hitodenashi's creation. War winners got the privilege of deciding what war losers were allowed to forget, and Ukoku had very much lost – except, Hyo felt, on Onogoro.

With wartime lived memory disappearing and isolated from hitodenashi in the present, if anyone was to grow hitodenashi, perhaps it *would* be someone on Onogoro, simply out of curiosity.

To learn, just as Jun had asked, about the pear: *"Is it really as horrible as everyone tells us?"*

Hyo held out her hand. "Let's see those pamphlets."

She'd skimmed through "So You've Made It to Onogoro, Last Home of Ukoku's Gods – Congratulations!" and "Don't Worry, They Can't Kill You Unless You Ask for It: A Guide to Co-existing with the Earthbound Divine" when a voice called from a counter.

"Hakai Hyo and Mansaku?"

Mansaku signed, "Best feet forward."

Six shaku back from the counter was a rope adorned with twists of paper. An Onogoro official in the white and red uniform of a shrine attendant approached them with a cup in one hand and a basin in the other.

"Wash your hands and rinse out your mouths, please," she said in crisp "Standard", like Jun's.

Hyo took the cup, tipped a portion of midnight-dark shinshu over the back of one hand then the other, over the basin, then rinsed her mouth with it. She gave Mansaku the cup to do the same.

"It didn't taste of anything," he said with disappointment.

It had tasted to Hyo of winter mornings, which had made her stomach lurch, so she focused on the counter and the official behind it.

The official had the hooded eyes of a sleepy turtle. Around the concertina wrinkles of her neck she wore strings of jasper and agate beads, upon which hung the curled teardrop of a green jade magatama.

"Your papers, please."

Hyo handed them over. Mansaku fidgeted with his kerchief.

"'Relocation of residency to the Onogoro Special Cultural Zone from Tsukitateyama, Koura Prefecture, of Harbourlakes-occupied Ukoku.' Urgh, what a mouthful." The official licked her thumb and turned a page. "You both know that once you move to Onogoro, no further relocations are permitted? On the chance you *do* leave Onogoro for short visits elsewhere, you'll be subject to all silencing curses judged necessary?"

"We do," Hyo said, and Mansaku nodded.

The official squinted at their papers. "Reason for relocation: 'hitodenashi'."

"Our whole village caught it in the winter."

"Caught it?"

"It was spread there by a demon." The official nodded sleepily, as if she heard such vicious stories every day.

Hyo had no idea what she was thinking. "She turned my village into a hitodenashi orchard, so that she had the pear to feed on."

"Ah, yes. Demons do that. Poor things. It's either that, or they have to hunt humans. Some never forget their humanity enough to manage that." The official hummed. "You two must have been very lucky to have survived her – that, or you're in possession of some special, secret, possibly troublesome quality up your sleeve, eh?"

Something wasn't right. Hyo studied the official in silence, then she glanced at the counters to their left and right, and realized what it was.

"That's right. We do have a secret," Hyo said, making her decision. "Mansaku and I are the last of the Hakai family hellmakers. It's because of this that the demon let us go."

The official looked up.

A strange *pressure* which Hyo didn't so much feel as taste – as a sea-breeze gathering salt off a wide expanse of waves – unfurled between them.

The official set aside their papers. Her thin lips stretched wide. "So you do know a god of fortune when you see one. What gave me away?"

"Your fingers."

"Ah, yes. *These*. Well spotted," said the god, holding her fingertips up to the light. They were polished perfectly smooth. The ancient divine had no fingerprints. Even for those who had been human once, they had been worn away with time. "A wise choice not to hide that *very* special quality up your sleeve! That seal on your powers may be invisible to the other humans, but *I* and the other gods have no trouble seeing it. Well, I never! A hellmaker on Onogoro. Let's have a look at your seal then, dear. May as well check it's the genuine article."

She meant the seal locking the powers of the gods of misfortune in Hyo – the one she'd been born with, like an elaborate birthmark.

Hyo held out her hands and turned them over. Dark red symbols crowded the underside of every digit, racing along the creases, cramming her palms with the scrawling talismanic charms of the curse that was written into her blood. Only she and Mansaku had ever been able to

see the seal; there were no Ukoku gods of fortune left on the mainland to appreciate their own craft.

The god cooed and snatched up Hyo's hands. "Look at that cursework – it's exquisite! Oh, you *are* the real deal." She glanced at Mansaku. 'And that makes you the last of the hellmakers' weapons, does it? Which one are you? The pole-arm? Or the mallet, maybe?"

"I'm not a weapon, madam." Mansaku pasted on a smile. "I'm *hosting* the spirit of Kiriyuki the nagigama."

"Ah, the water-scythe. Lovely. You be careful about swinging that blade around where any Onmyoryo officers can see it. The official line is the public don't have weapons here, including weapon-spirits." The god rubbed at the symbols on Hyo's palms as if they might come off. They wouldn't, of course. "I take it your demon sent you here to give us the hells we deserve for something it takes umbrage with?"

Hyo said, "The demon believed there was hitodenashi growing on Onogoro." The god's smile slowly shrank. "She was sure of it."

Mansaku sucked in a breath. They braced for the god's reaction.

The god nodded in that thoughtful, unflappable, ancient-turtle way. "Oh, that won't look good for us at all, will it? The world might think we're now working to keep the sickness alive, just so that we can keep selling them all the cure." She patted Hyo's hands and chuckled.

"Best go about your search *quietly* on the island, or the ghosts you're looking for might hear you coming and make themselves scarce."

Hyo wasn't sure she understood, but she sensed that she wasn't meant to. "You're not going to stop us entering Onogoro?"

"That depends." The god squeezed Hyo's hands. The gesture was almost grandmotherly. "Long ago, I was told that hellmakers were paid for their services in lives – that they needed the warmth of someone's living spirit to melt their seal open. Is that true?"

"It's true," Hyo said. "But, unless it's a special commission, I don't need to be paid in whole lives. Months, days, even minutes can do."

"Money works as well," Mansaku added. "Because money's, like, life tokens."

"Unless, so you say, it's for a 'special commission'." Hyo's heart sank. The god knew more than she was letting on. "Can you tell me what exactly happens then?"

Be honest. This is a god, and our last obstacle on to Onogoro.

Hyo swallowed her fear down and straightened her shoulders.

"I can't tell you exactly because I've never done one," she admitted. "I know that bodies come my way, and some people will die before their natural time, but not *because* of me. The hellmakers' en just brings me the bodies. And then … I'll take whatever the special commissioner has to give me."

The god was silent, eyes on Hyo.

"You're full of fears. I like that. Well, now, Onogoro's vengeance management sector *could* do with new blood. Yes, I could see you providing a vital new service to this densely populated, fearful and jumpy little island." The god sat back and cracked a wide grin. "I'll let you both on to Onogoro."

Mansaku clenched a victorious fist under the table. Hyo bowed her head. "Thank you, divine madam."

"Oh, no need to thank me. I always felt that fortune and misfortune would do better in this world if we helped each other." The god took a white jade seal-stamp and pressed it into a cup of vermilion paste. "Hold out your hands, dears."

The stamp left a vermilion magatama shape on the backs of Hyo's and Mansaku's hands. A soft summer-wind heat blew over Hyo's knuckles, then the magatama shimmered, and disappeared into her skin.

"All done!" The god shuffled the papers and held out a selection to Hyo. She winked. "May you be blessed with all the en you need – the good kind and the hellmakers' kind."

*

When the hellmaker and her brother had passed through the gates, the god of the Onogoro Gateway turned in her seat and cackled.

"Some people will die before their natural time," she wheezed. "You think only *some* people? Oh, my days. Next group, please!"

TWO

留守

Before the war, Ukoku called Eleventhmonth "No Gods Month". On Onogoro, however, they called it "All Gods Month", for that was where all the Ukoku gods went – once a year, to weave the nation's en for the year to come.

TSUYU,
Thirty-First Hellmaker

As a hellmaker, for as long as she could remember, Hyo had been trained to think of the world in en.

An en was a fateful connection. It could be had between people, between a person and a place, or a person and an object, such as a cancer, a colour, a vacancy, or a joke in a book found at the right time.

People went through life making en at every moment, dangling the potential to connect in threads that grew from their spirit, stretching out into the world and seeking other threads with which to tie. Some said these threads of fate were relics of past lives, of connections so strong that they survived the rinse of death before the repeat of life. When they tied together, they made a great invisible network, as integral to people as the roots beneath a forest. To belong to a place and a moment was to be part of its en-network.

A good en was a meaningful connection that brought positive change with it.

The hellmakers' en was the en between the hellmakers and those who'd pay for the misfortune they could spread. It drew people to Hyo and her to them, tugged by the pull of a tightening tie.

For special commissions, it would bring her the dead and the dying who would, otherwise, never be avenged, whose truths would stay buried and whose killers would walk free.

The hellmakers' en had made Hyo wonder, once,

if the hellmakers weren't a kind of en-musubi god (an en-connector), or an en-giri god (an en-cutter), but her mother Hatsu had assured her that wasn't so. Hellmakers had no conscious abilities for manipulating en like those gods did. Their work was to follow the trail as the hellmakers' en led them, not lay down trails themselves.

In a place as full of people as Onogoro, the en-network would be denser than Hyo had ever lived with, and the trails the hellmakers' en pulled her along more complicated and unpredictable for it. One fateful connection tying fast in a corner of the network would have an extensive cascade effect.

It might've been intimidating, if, despite how complicated, lively, busy Onogoro was, there wasn't a strange familiarity to the island. Onogoro may have diverged from the rest of Ukoku but much was recognizable.

The monorail – the dangling "buraden" – may have hung from a steel and ceramic spine, snaking through clouds of shinshu-brewery vapour and between shinwood-timber-core skyscrapers, but it also passed rice terraces and subsistence allotments. Rooftop gardens grew beans in light channelled down the towers by giant mirrors and solar-powered lamps. The clothes on Onogoro were clearly related to what Hyo and Mansaku wore, with the Ukoku cut of layered robes that could be tucked and tied into shape, but with bolder patterns and in recycled threads. Signs were written in "Standard", but without Harbourspeak, Lingyu or Para-Genera translations below.

What Hyo had never seen in a town before was the blatant, open practice of Ukoku spiritual techniques. In the mountains, the hellmakers had got away with it, but never in the towns.

Flightcraft had anti-traffic-accident amulets in their windows. Talismans were stuck over doors to ward off misfortune. Paper slips were pasted near hydrogen veins to stop sudden fires. At the first stop the buraden came to, a shikigami – an animated paper man the size of Hyo's hand – had darted into the carriage, and the passengers had only shifted to give it space. There were wards everywhere. Hyo could feel these spiritual shields as a light pressure against her souls.

Talismans, amulets, wards, shikigamis – this was Hyo's world, her techniques, the language that hellmaking was made from, and it blindsided her to see it as common and everyday as the pot plants and adverts on the bridge columns.

But appearances were just that. Hyo didn't really know yet what was common or everyday on Onogoro. For all its familiarity, she'd heard enough from Jun to understand that Onogoro-Ujin thought their differences from the rest of Ukoku mattered.

Jun, their first port of call on Onogoro, was the only truly familiar thing here.

A cold flask of barley tea landed in her lap, tossed there by Mansaku, who was lowering his luggage from the rack overhead. "Pause the thoughts for a moment. It's our stop."

The sign on the platform read Hikaraku: 飛歌楽.

The Fifthmonth evening breeze sifted through Hyo's hair, briny with the sea and touched by the winter breath of shinshu. Hikaraku was the theatre and artisan district of Onogoro, and the easternmost. As Hyo set foot on the platform, the wind shifted, blowing in from the east and the shore where Onogoro's Gateway Terminal stood. Ever since the war, the coast around Onogoro was a sulphurous, glass-glazed wasteland, the result of the Ukoku gods diverting one last barrage of Harbourlakes' god-killer bombs back on to Ukoku itself, announcing simultaneously their abandonment of the Emperor and their surrender.

Now windows closed and doors slammed shut against the foul-smelling wind, chinks in the walls and shinwood planks quickly stuffed with newspaper, as Hyo and Mansaku made their way to Jun's home.

Jun's apartment was a tatenagaya, as most of the apartments in Onogoro were. Sideways space was precious, so the apartment was one-room wide and three floors high. In the tower opposite was Onogoro's oldest theatre, the Shin-Kaguraza, spanning six floors. Its sloping eaves and polished grey tiles were lit up with strings of lilac lanterns. Jun had a younger brother, Koushiro, who worked with the theatre's shin-kagura troupe and lived in the troupe dorms.

Everything was as Jun had described it in his directions, down to the whole-body skin-shedding of a white snake nailed over the doorway.

Except for one thing.

Jun had said that he'd be waiting for them.

"Jun?" Mansaku called. The lights were out. He gave the door a tug. It was locked. "Are you sleeping or dead in there? If you're dead, don't be shy. We can still work with that."

Empty slats of darkness stared back at them through the cross-ribbed glass.

The metal lid of the postbox lifted with a squeak, flicked open from the inside. Something white slipped out.

Hyo jumped back as the white snake wriggled towards her, but all it did was touch her boot toecaps with its tongue then slip away into the walkway drain, leaving a blue-grey envelope where she'd been standing.

"O'Hyo!" Mansaku said with excitement. He'd recognized the charm on the envelope's back. Unlike the other charms they'd seen on Onogoro, this was one that Hyo had invented herself. Drawn on an envelope, it prevented all but the intended recipient from opening it.

Hyo quickly snatched it off the ground.

葉堺 萬咲
漂

Their names were on the front. It was nothing like Jun's usual brushwork. Jun's *usual* writing was so neat every symbol looked stamped. These symbols were blotchy and sprawling.

Hyo tore open the envelope. A key dropped into Mansaku's waiting palm, along with a note.

Fifthmonth 13th

Mansaku and Hyo,

Welcome to Onogoro! I'm sorry I'm not there to say it in person. I have to be away for a few days. Feel free to use my place as a base. Eat the rice.

Found a room you guys might like – near me! See back for details. What's the point of you being in Onogoro if we don't get to be neighbours? At least till you're sick of me.

Don't worry. I am absolutely fine. Be back soon.

Jun

On the back was an advert for a tatenagaya in the same tower. A tiny newspaper clipping described the previous occupant's nasty death, which meant it had a "probably haunted" discounted rent. It didn't need references, guarantor, bank account or certificate of residence, or charge key money. Jun had clearly picked it out with a lot of care, knowing that a "probable" haunting would be no problem for the Hakais.

Mansaku tried the key in the lock. There was a click. He slid the door aside, and that was when Hyo felt the tiny *flick* against her spirit, like a fine hair broken beside her ear.

Blue light flashed from behind them. Flames crackled, and a white horse in a red tasselled harness plunged down between the towers, appearing from nothing.

It was headless. Blue fire streamed from the stump of its muscled neck down to its withers where the boy riding it clutched its braided red and white reins.

"Makuni Junichiro, when I tell you to STAY at my shrine, why don't you do as I say?! It's *for your own sake...* Wait." The booming resonance in the boy's voice faded. When Hyo blinked away the glare of blue fire, she saw that the boy was squinting at her and Mansaku with suspicion. He looked her age, maybe younger, and wore a high-collared purple uniform. "You're not Makuni Junichiro."

"Neither are you, kid, so the surprise is mutual," said Mansaku nonchalantly, but Hyo sensed the invisible edge of the water-scythe slide between them. "If you're looking for Jun, he's gone away for a few days."

"I *KNOW* THAT! But he's not at my shrine where he's

店!!
吉
を知
毎

supposed to—" The boy seemed to realize he was giving too much away. He cut himself off with a snap of teeth and pinched the bridge of his nose. "Who are you, and what are you doing at Makuni's home?"

Mansaku waved the key at him. "We're friends of Jun – he's letting us house-sit a little whilst he's gone."

"House-sit," said the boy weakly. "I've heard nothing about this. When was this arranged?"

"About a month and a half back. But the plan then was that he'd be here too."

"You put a charm on the door to tell you when someone opened it," Hyo said, still feeling that *flick* against her spirit. The boy's attention snapped to her. "Why?"

"Why shouldn't I? I'm his curse-mediator! I'm meant to be helping him, but he insists on being as uncooperative as possible!" Silver flames flashed at the boy's mouth and the headless horse bucked, almost flinging him off. When he'd scrambled back into the saddle, he coughed. "You haven't seen Makuni this evening?"

"No," said Hyo. *Why does Jun need a curse-mediator?* "Maybe he's at his brother's?"

"I didn't ask for suggestions!" The boy rummaged in the front of his uniform and found what looked like a talisman slip. "If he comes back here, burn incense in front of this and say my heavenly name. Damn human, I don't have time for this!"

He flung the slip over the walkway rail, the piece of paper flying fast like a weapon before it slowed in front of Hyo's nose and drifted down. She caught it.

It read: 留眼川大明神

Todomegawa Daimyoujin.

On the back it said in smaller calligraphy: 陰陽寮呪解師 3級

Onmyoryo curse-mediator Level Three.

Hyo recalled the word "Onmyoryo" from the warning of the god at the Gateway. *That's right – gods and humans can both work at the Onmyoryo.* Jun had said so. It was a force that worked alongside the police, specializing in issues that came about between gods and humans, leaving human–human problems to the police alone.

With a start, she realized that this boy with heavy bags under his eyes and smoke between his teeth was a god. Maybe him riding a headless horse should've clued Hyo in faster, but she'd only been on Onogoro a few hours.

"Thank you for your cooperation!" Todomegawa barked, then he dug his heels into the headless horse's sides and it jumped away into nothingness, the two of them vanishing like mist.

Mansaku took the slip with the god's name on it, muttering, "Jun, you idiot! What've you got into that a curse-mediator's looking for you?"

Hyo turned to Jun's apartment. "One way to find out."

They dropped their baskets in the entranceway, pulled

off their boots, and once they'd hand-cranked the power to the lights, they did what the Hakai family did best after hellmaking: investigating.

The room on the ground floor was a study cum living room. Mansaku went to the chest of drawers in the corner, Hyo to the table. As she knelt by it, something crunched at her knees.

White grains of crystal were caught in the tatami weave, and as soon as she noticed that, she saw the smear on the polished surface of the table – a patch of white dust where a liquid had been wiped away, like the chalky trail of a sweat stain.

Hyo dabbed her finger in it and licked. *Salt.*

Mansaku let out a whoop, holding aloft a sheet of blue-grey paper. "Got an interesting letter from Koushiro here. Take a look."

Fifthmonth 11th

Niisan, do not come to the Shin-Kaguraza.

I've been checked by the Wavewalker. Result: I'm not cursed. But bad things happen around me regardless, and so much bad luck is concentrated on me, I can't risk you here. My bad luck could spread through our en, and the stronger our en, the more you'll suffer. I'm too unlucky to chance it!

I wish I was cursed. Then I could go to the

Onmyoryo and hire a curse-mediator to sort it out between me and whoever's cursed me, and I could find and give them a good kicking.

But I'm not cursed by anyone. I'm just unlucky.

Don't come to the Shin-Kaguraza until I say so. Write to me if you've got something to say.

The letter was dated Fifthmonth 11th. The letter for Hyo and Mansaku had been left on 13th. Today was Fifthmonth 15th. Jun had been away from his apartment for two days.

"What do you think?" Mansaku prompted Hyo.

She shook her head. "This won't help us find Jun-san."

But unluck was her speciality, so she made note of Koushiro and his 'bad luck' for later.

Something glinted above her. Hyo looked up. Against the ceiling corner was a shrine shelf.

The three god cabinets on it were framed in dark branches of sakaki. Each had its own gateway arch and vessels for offerings. The centre had a round mirror, which was what had caught the light. In each cabinet was enshrined a slip carrying a name and a promise of protection from a god, but Hyo couldn't see them from below.

Mansaku smiled uneasily up to the shelf then waved. "We're not breaking and entering. Promise."

There was a watchful air about the shelf, nothing like

the bomb-burned and god-stripped cabinets and shrines that could be found in the forests of Koura. God-killer bombs worked through a radiation that erased gods' heavenly names from human memories and writings. Just before the war's end, the Harbourlakes had carpet-bombed Ukoku for the gods who hadn't gone to Onogoro. The unnamed, nameless shrines were all Hyo had known.

She felt a touch, not quite a pluck, like a finger alighting on a bowstring. "Mansaku, can you help me up there?"

She only needed a little more height, enough to see on to the shelf. Grumbling and legs wobbling, Mansaku picked her up by the waist. Amidst the dried sakaki leaves and dust, she spotted something white sticking out from beneath the left-most cabinet – a glossy white corner.

Hyo planted a finger on it and tugged loose a small stack of stellaroid reflectographs, scattering them over Mansaku below, who dropped her with an unceremonious yell.

He scooped them off the floor, then let out a sharp laugh. "'Absolutely fine,' he says, that lying rat."

Jun's face stared out of every picture, and in each were the molten colours of a curse.

THREE

反運子

There are two types of curses. Humans cast noroi. Noroi turn people's bodies or minds against themselves or both. Gods and ghosts more often cast tatari. Tatari turn the world against people, distorting their luck and en-networks.

NOE,
Twenty-First Hellmaker

When Jun had come to Koura, he'd brought with him a stellaroid camera. Of all his cameras, it had been his most treasured – because this model of stellaroid had been able to capture curses.

Curses appeared in Jun's reflectographs as bands of an eerie, twisting colour. Purple in the corner of Hyo's right eye, and green in her left, it was, at once, both colours simultaneously and neither. It slipped between human words like smoke through fingers. Looking at the curse-colour directly had given Hyo an uncomfortable sensation, as if her ears were ringing without any sound. Jun's stellaroids had entertained the Koura villagers immensely, showing up small smears of curses still lingering on some family heirlooms, on the threshold of an abandoned building, on an old stone near a crossroad they'd all suspected was slightly cursed but had never dared to touch and find out.

In Jun's stellaroid pictures of Hyo, she had breathed the weaving colour from her lips, caught it in her fingernails. They'd shown the hellmakers' curse in her skin, her eyes, her teeth, inseparably a part of her.

Now, she and Mansaku looked down at the stellaroids that captured Jun – cursed.

That same colour burned in Jun's eyes and streamed down his face in watery lines. He'd wept it as he'd gazed into his camera, recording his curse one day at a time.

"Fourthmonth first," Hyo read the date stamped in the image corner of the oldest stellaroid, setting it on the floor. In it Jun was slightly pale, a glow of curse colour in his eyes. She set down the most recent. "And Fifthmonth the thirteenth."

The day Jun's letter to them said he had left the apartment.

In that final one, the camera was so shaky his face was an explosive, blurred cloud of curse colour. Silently, Hyo and Mansaku laid out the rest of the stellaroids by date and watched Jun capture the daily progress of his own curse.

"Guess this explains why Jun went to a curse-mediator," said Mansaku faintly. "Koushiro didn't say anything about Jun being cursed in his letter."

"Maybe Jun-san hid it from him." Hyo recalled that when Jun had spoken of Koushiro, he'd been deeply protective of his brother. He probably wouldn't have wanted Koushiro to think his bad luck *had* spread to Jun, as Koushiro had clearly feared would happen.

Another finger on the bowstring. "Let's find Koushiro and ask him. Then we can be sure."

"Good plan, but for tomorrow, not now," said Mansaku firmly, planting his hands on Hyo's shoulders. "Koushiro can wait. You never know – Jun might come back in the night. Then we can call up that curse-mediator god, to give Jun a grilling for making us worry, and it'll be sorted. Besides, you think you can make your way to the theatre without falling asleep standing?"

Hyo grimaced. All the tensions and the newnesses of the day were catching up with her, and under the simple gratitude for safe shelter in a strange new place, exhaustion had slipped in. Mansaku squeezed her shoulder. "You're going to be busier with the hellmaking here than you were in the village. Give yourself a break whilst you can?"

Reluctantly, Hyo had to admit defeat.

"Koushiro tomorrow," she agreed. Mansaku relaxed.

He gathered up Jun's pictures into an envelope whilst Hyo went to the kitchen to find offerings for the gods. It seemed only polite. Salt, rice and water. The villagers in Koura had sometimes left the very same on the Hakai family doorstep when times were rough. The Hakais weren't gods, but they were the closest the village had.

The kitchen had its own god cabinet for a god called Koujin-san the Hearthwatcher. Hyo was laying out offerings for them when Mansaku entered with the vases and vessels from the living room for cleaning and refilling.

Once everything was restored to the living room shelf, Mansaku bowed, twice. Hyo stared. "What are you doing?"

"Making a good first impression." He had a point.

Hyo stepped up as Mansaku straightened and clapped his hands. "Thank you to Ohmononushi'no'Ohkami, Sayo'no'me and the Nameless World-builders for your hospitality tonight. Sorry for disturbing you. We really hope you, you know, watched over Jun carefully, with his curse and all, and appreciate that."

They bowed their heads. Hyo wondered if they were meant to expect any sign that they'd been heard.

Gods needed humans to call their heavenly names in worship to survive. Every time a human did so, they were making a wish for the god to exist. That wish offered gods musuhi, the raw creative energy that sustained their bodies. Without it, the gods would disperse away to be forgotten, faceless, nameless natural forces again.

Hyo went upstairs to sleep. Mansaku stayed a little longer, forehead to his hands.

It wasn't surprising he'd be more sympathetic to the gods. Their mother had named him Kiriyuki at birth, the very name of the water-scythe bound to his spirit. She'd tried to drum into him that he was a weapon, rather than a human, and when she had died, he'd named himself Mansaku, his way of reclaiming his humanity. Mansaku understood better than most the power of naming things for making things *be*.

Hyo took the slip with Todomegawa Daimyoujin's name with her, along with a gas burner and stick of incense, just in case Jun returned in the night.

She wondered, briefly, as her eyes closed, what a god's flame of life might look like, fed by the musuhi of all the humans who'd named them into existence.

In the morning, Hyo knew something was wrong because there were particles of unluck drifting through her vision.

The particles looked like the shadows of snowflakes and glistened with a greasy sheen. Hyo checked her hands and pulled a face. Half of an index finger's seal on her powers had faded.

A hellmaker existed as a source of misfortune, to balance the gods of fortune. The seal locked in her the powers of the old gods of misfortune, and if Hyo didn't use them, they would wear away at her seal and use *her*, stealing from her the choice of when and where to wield them.

To be able to see unluck was one of those powers. Hyo needed a commission – soon. Hyo let out a heavy sigh, and went to join Mansaku, who was already awake and battling the stove. She spotted a set of glowing red eyes peeking out of the Hearthwatcher's cabinet on the shrine shelf, which vanished once they were sure that Mansaku wasn't about to burn down Jun's apartment.

"No sign of Jun in the night," said Mansaku, then he froze, hand jumping to his chest. "Whoa, O'Hyo! Eyes to yourself!"

"Sorry." She'd stared through a patch of unluck and ended up focusing too hard on Mansaku's flame of life.

Nobody reacted well to having their life seen. It was too much of a reminder that they had a life that could be lost. "The seal's worn through a bit."

"Let me see." Mansaku took her hand in one of his, stirring a saucepan of clear pickled plum and salted shiso soup with the other. He pursed his lips at the faded seal. "You should repair that. We can save seeing Koushiro for after lunch..."

"I can sort this out myself." Hyo closed her hand. "You go and see him, Mansaku. Find out if he knows anything about Jun." She paused, remembering Todomegawa Daimyoujin, the curse-mediator god, charging off into the night with a sort of desperate urgency, as though afraid he was short for time. "I've a feeling we need to know what's going on as soon as possible."

"A feeling?" It was Mansaku's turn to pause. "Is it the hellmakers' en?"

She shook her head; she couldn't say for sure yet. "That bridge leading to the front of the theatre, I'll meet you there when I'm done."

"All right," said Mansaku. He picked up Jun's letter to them, the one with the haunted apartment address. "I'll check this out first then head to the theatre. You get that seal sorted."

After clearing breakfast, Hyo sat at Jun's table with a pad of blue-grey paper and stick of white ink, then got to scribing Oblivionist sutras.

In Koura, Hyo had done this every morning on rising. It wasn't the sutras themselves that repaired the seal, but the willpower and focus she packed into every symbol as she copied them out. It was a temporary solution only, effectively forcing the cracks and holes in the seals shut, but it worked to tide her over between commissions.

When her mind began to drift, Hyo set down her brush and checked the dark red marks on her palm. The faded seal was mostly restored.

But not entirely. She opened the front door, looked out at the Shin-Kaguraza Theatre opposite and sighed. The cloud of unluck shrouding the theatre floors was so thick that Hyo could barely see the colourful banners at its front. If that was centred on Koushiro, no wonder he thought he might be cursed. There was so much unluck clinging to the building it made Hyo's head spin to look at.

Ukoku's gods of fortune were supposed to manipulate *luck*, whilst hellmakers manipulated its opposite particle – *unluck*. Luck was the light particles emitted by the flames of lives, and unluck was the soot from their burning wicks. Luck carried the energy to melt away obstacles and change the world, and unluck smothered people's efforts and blocked their way.

Both were natural to the world, neither inherently good nor bad. It was humans who decided to call their effects 'good luck' and 'bad luck'.

Hyo closed the door on the Shin-Kaguraza Theatre and turned to the shrine shelf.

The centre cabinet's mirror gleamed.

"Bad things can still happen to people here, then," Hyo said to the shrine shelf, not expecting an answer. "Even on Onogoro, with all of you watching, people can still end up being in the wrong place at the wrong time.

"My great-great-grandmother, Fuyu, said that we're meant to give the gods the same respect as anyone who's older than us and have had the time to be disappointed by more people," Hyo continued. A faint breeze lifted her hair. "I'll do my best with that – but you won't get any worship from me, and if you expect to have front row seats in the Hakai family house, once we have one, you can think again."

Feeling that she'd made herself clear, Hyo finished the last of her sutras and rose to search Jun's study. Daylight and a full stomach might help her see things differently.

There were notes for a libretto he'd been writing – about a year on Onogoro through the seasons – and tourist guides and local histories to go with it. Hyo opened up a couple, looking for a hint as to what Jun had been up to before their arrival, but as she skimmed the pages, she noticed something.

Everything beyond Onogoro was called the "outside", and there was little mention of the way hitodenashi had tormented the "outside" since the war, and even less on

Ukoku being responsible for unleashing it. It made a twisted sort of sense. Onogoro had moved on from it, relishing in shinshu's success and in their own confidence that they'd never be short of shinshu to fight it, should hitodenashi arrive there. It was the only place in the world that could.

In the war, Ukoku scientists had made the hitodenashi to be a weapon. It was said to have been born from a deification experiment gone wrong.

Hyo thumbed through a few more pages. There was precious little in Jun's books about deification too, even though Ukoku had once been renowned for it. They'd made gods from humans many times over the centuries. The most recent human to nearly be deified was the last Emperor, who was destroyed at the war's end.

And then convenient stories emerged, blaming Ukoku government deification efforts for a national madness; that the forced, dishonest harvesting of musuhi from the people to deify the Emperor had warped Ujin spirits and judgement; in their right minds, Ujin, so the stories said, would never have tried to imitate the empire-building efforts of the Harbourlakes or Paraisium States, invade the Grand Continent, or catalogue its peoples as theirs to exploit and destroy.

In their right minds, so the story reassured them all, Ujin wouldn't create something like hitodenashi again. The bullshit of it made Hyo's teeth itch.

But this seemed to be Onogoro's favoured narrative, optimistic and upbeat, where they could sweep hitodenashi into the past and focus on the present's bounty of shinshu. Meanwhile, people like Jun would come to Koura, hold up his camera to the moon rising between its blue-tinged peaks and still tell Hyo the "outside" was "the land of the 3-Ds" – dirty, dangerous and dying.

Finding no hint as to Jun's curse or his whereabouts, Hyo closed the books. She collected her and Mansaku's most important documents, and left to meet Mansaku on the bridge.

Hikaraku walkways on an Earthday afternoon were very different from evenings on which the east wind blew. Hyo had to use her elbows to make her way. The First of Us had had seven brothers, hosting the spirits of seven weapons, and one of those weapons had been a sasumata – a pole with an oxbow-shaped end for shoving people aside. Hyo could see the benefits of one now as she tried to pick her way through the crowd on the bridge.

The sasumata, the pole-arm, the battle-axe, the kumade, the mallet, the saw and the nagigama. Over the centuries, the seven original weapons had worn away at their hosts and killed them before they could be passed on, until there was only Kiriyuki the nagigama left, fused to Mansaku's spirit.

It had been a while since Hyo had taken a good look at

Mansaku's flame of life. Unlike other humans, Mansaku's candle had two flames – one for his human spirit, and the other for the nagigama – on a wick stuck fast and spiralling up his candle's sides.

Hyo had been trying so hard not to look. If she had her way, she'd keep track of it daily, hourly, to know how much time for Mansaku they had left; but Mansaku had told her not to. She was meant to be able to respect that.

Hyo gripped the bridge handrail, just in time to stand firm against a sudden surge of movement towards the Shin-Kaguraza where the doors had opened and figures appeared on the steps.

An old woman stood at the top. She was in her seventies and had a square jaw. Her grey hair was pulled formidably back into three parts.

Flanked by two glowering men with prop spears, she raised a megaphone. "If you magazines are going to be spreading malicious rumours about Kikugawa Kichizuru, you can all clear off! And I'm giving you five drum beats to do it in! Five!"

A drum sounded out behind her.

"Hey, Onoue-san! Is it true that the Kikugawa troupe leader almost died at last night's show?" shouted someone from the crowd, of which many were armed with cameras and notepads. "Any comments regarding the rumours that the Shin-Kaguraza Theatre bought up all talismans against bad luck available from the Pillar Gods' southern shrines?"

"Four!"

"Will there be compensation for those who attended Kichizuru's performances these past two weeks in case of bad luck transmission?"

"Three!"

"Is Ukibashi Awano going to withdraw her patronage for the season? Will Kichizuru's remaining shows be cancelled?"

"Two!"

"How unlucky is Kikugawa Kichizuru *exactly*?"

"One!" The old woman brandished a hair-setting iron over her head and bellowed into her megaphone, "Clear off, you vultures and grease-rags!"

Hyo clung to the bridge, tucking against a column as the troupe members with prop weapons charged the crowd of reporters, fans and over-interested bystanders, chasing them away.

When the dust cleared, the crowd had thinned. The old

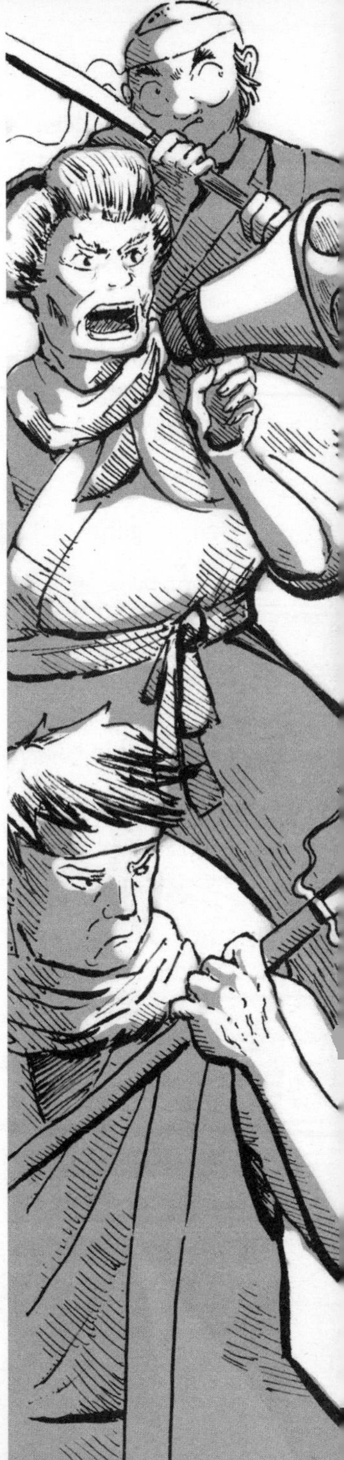

woman nodded with satisfaction and retreated into the theatre, and Hyo finally spotted Mansaku near the theatre steps.

"O'Hyo!" Mansaku came running as she climbed back on to her feet, thankful that the flood of people was gone. "Are you all right? I couldn't see you for that crowd."

"What was going on there?" Hyo asked, as Mansaku checked her over, finishing with her seal and the fainter

than usual marks. "They were talking about some Kikugawa Kichizuru, and his bad luck?"

"It's Koushiro, O'Hyo! Jun's baby brother! Kikugawa Kichizuru's his stage name." Mansaku sighed and rubbed his face. "Trust Jun not to tell us that his brother's actually *famous*. I only just found out myself the hard way – after getting booted out of backstage when they thought I was press. Almost literally. Someone

threw a geta at me. It missed, but then I had to go and walk face first into a prop bell anyway…"

"Did Jun go to the troupe dorms last night?"

"They wouldn't tell me. Nobody's talking to strangers today." Mansaku breathed in deeply then tilted his face up to the sun. "But somebody did mention a curse-mediator on a headless horse, so it sounds like *he* dropped by. Anyway, I left one of Jun's stellaroids at the box office for Koushiro, with our names."

"And a note at least?" Springing pictures of a family member battling a curse on Koushiro didn't strike Hyo as an endearing first impression.

"I spelt it out that we're not press, that we just want to know if Jun's all right, and that I'll be back at the box office in five days for a response if Koushiro has one. Whether he believes me or not is out of my hands. If you want to retry the stage doors later, O'Hyo, do it alone. I'm not risking my handsome nose against a well-aimed Taiwa clog."

"And my nose is worth risking over yours? Sure."

Mansaku looked out over Hikaraku. "This is some view."

Hyo followed his gaze. Hikaraku streamed with advertising pennants and banners. Willow branches hung off walkways with their swaying branches tied with fortunes, and the white front of the Shin-Kaguraza, with its slate-blue tiles and purple lanterns, was a striking, vibrant face in the sea of otherwise green towers. It was the only district of Onogoro without shinshu distilleries or vertical rice farms, set aside for Onogoro citizens to escape their cares and fears. Hyo could still smell shinshu on the breeze though, frost-clean whispers of it amidst the sweet wisteria and soft greens of springtime.

If it wasn't for the demon's words in Hyo's ear, insisting that somewhere under this skin was hitodenashi, like a hitodenashi needle-spore burrowed into the lungs, her heart might have lifted a little, buoyed by Hikaraku's hopeful sunlit beauty.

If Hyo could prove that there wasn't hitodenashi on Onogoro, that the island wasn't dealing in both the sickness and the cure, then she could forget everything the demon had asked of her.

"How was the haunted room?"

Mansaku looked up from his own contemplations. He'd been watching a shikigami doll scamper along the walkway below. "It's creepy enough that it's been killing the landlord's teashop business next door, so they're desperate. We can move in as soon as they exorcise it. It doesn't actually need an exorcism, but they seemed keen to try, so I couldn't kill that spirit." He nudged her in the side. "Get it? 'Kill that spirit?' Like, 'I didn't want to crush their morale', but also like 'exorcise', right?"

Hyo groaned, and in her moment of weakness, Mansaku gave her a kick in the shin, which she returned in kind, then they hugged, earning looks from passers-by.

"We're really doing the hellmaking here together." Mansaku's voice wavered slightly, and Hyo knew what he really meant was both the hellmaking and what the demon had asked of them. *To make hell on the island.* "Still can't believe we made it out of that winter, and down the mountain, and that this is all real."

"It's real, Mansaku," said Hyo quietly. "It'll be easier to believe as soon as we see Jun again, you'll see."

"I'll see and give him a piece of my mind for getting cursed, running off when his curse-mediator's looking for him and making all of us worry that he could've dropped dead somewhere in the night with no one there to chase the scavengers away from his body."

... which was naturally the perfect moment for a man to stumble over the bridge, heave a gasping, rasping breath and drop dead at Hyo and Mansaku's feet.

And the bowstring of the hellmakers' en plucked.

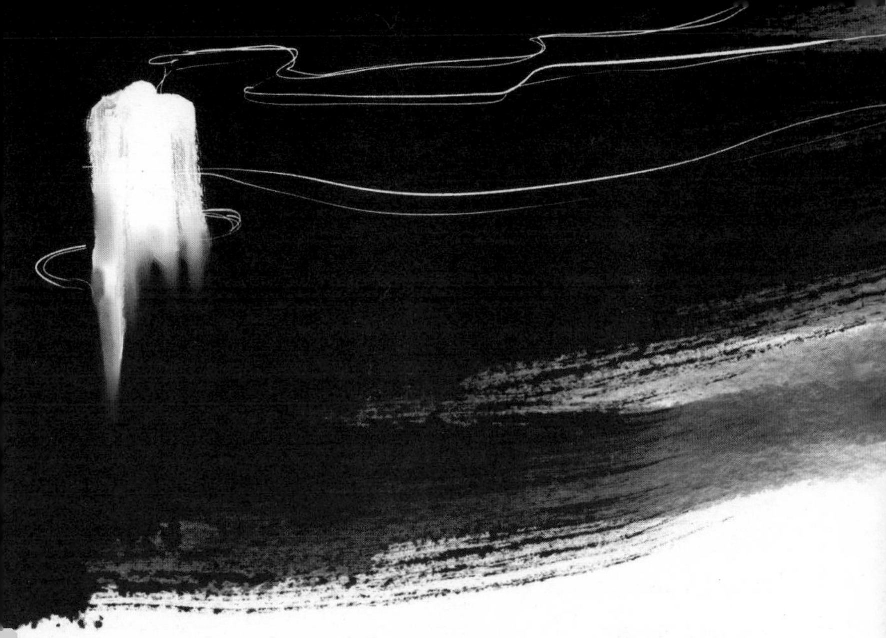

FOUR

結晶

When the special commissions come to us, we thank them for entrusting us with their deaths.

NOE,
Twenty-First Hellmaker

No, not dead.

The man was breathing hoarsely. His right hand stretched shakily towards the Shin-Kaguraza Theatre. His head was covered in a folded newspaper, which hid his face and neck.

Some passers-by glanced his way then hurried on, but most didn't even do that. They gave the man twitching on the planks a wide berth as if he were behind a glass wall, gazes sliding over him to avoid eye contact.

En. Even a glance could form that connection. They were an avoiding an en with him, and whatever trouble it might bring.

Hyo pushed past Mansaku to the man's side. Keeping her focus light, she looked at his flame of life.

The flame was guttering, the candle-wick was crumbling and pearly wax had been blown sideways in long sweeping lines. Hyo knew that windswept look. That winter, when the demon had sown the hitodenashi in her village, she'd seen every which way a life's candle could be bent and warped under the wearing wind of a curse.

This man's curse wasn't hitodenashi, though. It wasn't so deeply rooted – and it wasn't interested in keeping him alive.

His flame of life was going out. The wick was exhausted from bearing a light.

She turned the man over and rested his head on her lap.

"Ah ... ah..." The thin noises from beneath the paper

raised Hyo's hairs. He hadn't cut any eyeholes, only torn the barest, narrowest of slits. He breathed with an odd high-pitched stutter and leathery creak with every inhale.

Hyo touched the newspaper. "I'm going to take this off."

The man caught her wrist, stopping her short, and suddenly Hyo felt as if the east wind had swept through and blown her candle bare.

There was a pale scar between his first finger and thumb. A ridiculous swirly flower that Mansaku had cut – because Jun had dared Mansaku to prove his invisible scythe's edge really could cut him from a two-ken distance, and Mansaku had been drunk enough to actually do it.

Hyo had bandaged this hand. She'd seen the life of the Onogoro boy it belonged to through a winter, and now that warm and vibrant life was at her knees, strangled short.

"Jun-san?" she said. Mansaku froze, but didn't turn. He stayed where he was, blocking Hyo and Jun from the view of the few nosier passers-by. "Jun-san, it's Hyo from Koura. Do you recognize me?" Jun's masked head lolled to face her. An awful, dry rasp issued from under it. "Mansaku, help me get this off!"

Mansaku crouched and touched a finger to the newspaper hood.

It shattered, exploding into a paper blizzard that the wind scooped up and swirled away. Mansaku choked and sank down next to them as Jun's choppy mess of hair emerged from under the newspaper, and then his face...

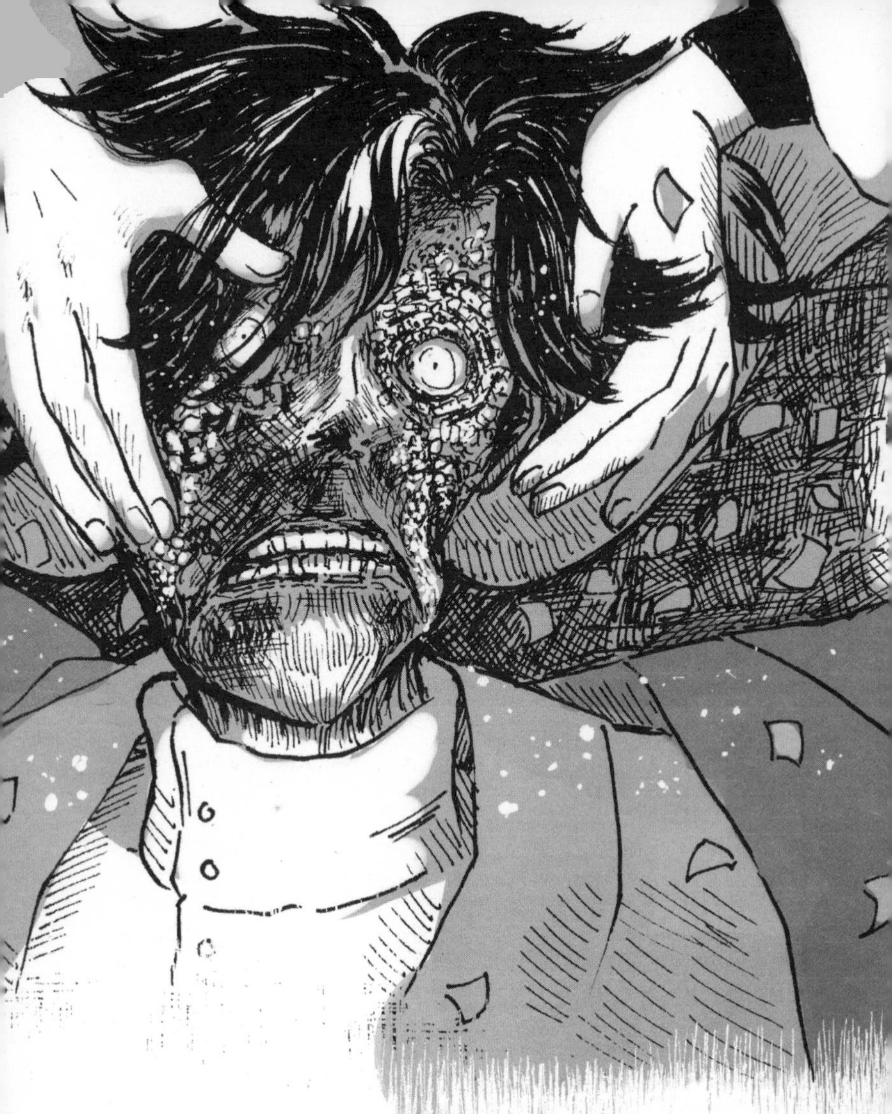

Jun's face was a shrivelled, parched grey-brown. His skin clung to his skull. His lips were stretched into a thin white band over dead gums. His eyes were crusted with dried pus. White crystalline stripes of salt ran down his cheeks, and a thick rime lined his eye sockets. Crystals glittered in his hair.

The salt stripes matched the curse colour flowing down Jun's face in the stellaroids. Tears. Jun had been wrung dry of water from his eyes, and when all the water had been drained from his sockets, the curse had moved on to his face, head and brain.

Why? What could Jun have done to deserve this?

"Who did this?" Hyo took his hand and gripped it. She could feel the memory of that bright young adventurer slipping from her. "Who cursed you, Jun-san?"

Jun whimpered. He had no eyelids, and the sunlight had landed on his face.

Mansaku shifted to shelter Jun in his shadow. "'Absolutely fine', you magnificent idiot. That's more than pattern baldness you've got going on there." He lowered his voice, for Hyo. "Is this a special commission?"

Hyo nodded. She could feel it, in her skin, the tautness of a knot that had been tied, the tugging in the threads of the en-network that would bring her to a special commissioner. Jun was dying, and right then, the hellmakers' en had tied her to someone, somewhere in Onogoro, who would commission Hyo to avenge his death for a special commission.

One where the living would pay on behalf of the dead.

Paying maybe, even, with their own life.

Hyo said, "Here goes our very first."

Mansaku nodded slowly, then took Jun's other hand. "You hear that, Jun? O'Hyo's got you. Whoever did this, they'll get what's coming."

The corners of Jun's lips cracked. His shrivelled tongue waggled – up, down, like a lever. Hyo pressed her forehead against Jun's. Salt crunched.

"You withstood so much." She could see it in the violent explosions of wax, where his flame had fought the winds, his determination to hold on burning true. "Well done, Makuni Junichiro. Thank you for bringing your death to me." She braced for the loss and forced out what needed to be said, because to live was to burn, and to burn was so difficult to endure. "Thank you for living, Jun-san."

His candle gave out with a sigh that smelled of dust.

Hyo lowered Jun to the bridge. The sun shone on his face. Without thinking, she reached down to close his eyes, before remembering he had no lids to close.

A dead body wouldn't know if its eyes were open or shut, but it didn't feel right. Hyo looked about her and, finding nothing, she reached into her waist-pouch for the only thing she had that could serve her purpose.

Mansaku stiffened at the sight of the band of yellow-mountain-rose silk. "That's—!"

"From Mum's hellmaker haori." Hyo looked guiltily away from Mansaku. "I know she was awful to you, and I'm sorry I couldn't leave it behind."

He reached over and gripped her arm. "All I'm hearing is that you chopped up Hatsu's coat. Go on. Do something good with it."

Hyo laid the silk over Jun's eyes then tied it in place. It covered the worst of the curse. A curse as ugly as this one, it would be so easy for people to forget the person and remember only how he died. No one deserved that. Everyone should be more than how they died.

She looked up, feeling eyes. They had an audience. On the steps of the theatre, the old woman had reappeared at the doors, along with someone behind her with their face wrapped in a scarf.

"I take back everything bad I've ever said about the hellmakers' en." Mansaku folded Jun's flower-swirl hand over his chest. "It brought Jun to us and us to Jun. I love the en. I'm its new convert."

Hyo dusted salt from her knees. "We're done here."

Mansaku put his hands over Jun's one last time, bowed his head, then stood. They faced the few curious onlookers, who shuffled back, averting their gazes.

"What?" Mansaku tossed at them. "Afraid you'll catch his curse from us?"

"It's been known to happen," said one.

"Oh, yeah?"

"You know what I mean," they said. "Bad en. And death comes with taint."

"Bad en and taint, eh? So, if I come at you like this..."

Mansaku advanced on the onlookers, his hands raised, but then he stopped and looked up quickly.

He dropped with Hyo to shield Jun's body as the headless horse slammed into the bridge, a plume of blue fire blazing at its neck and travelling so quickly it flung off its rider on impact.

Dust exploded. The bridge's exposed hydrogen veins hissed, cut off sharply by an automated system.

Todomegawa the god curse-mediator clawed his way out of the crater in the bridge planks, coughing up a luminous liquid like molten iron, dark purple uniform paled to lilac by the dust.

The headless horse pawed at the shattered boards and snuffled.

Todomegawa spotted Hyo and Mansaku with Jun, and his eyes immediately widened. "You!"

"Nice to see you. Anything broken?" said Mansaku conversationally. "Beautiful belly-flop off your horse there."

Hyo said under her breath, "Too bad you couldn't get here any faster."

"I came here as soon and as ***quickly as I was capable of***!" The snap of the god's voice filled the space between the towers. The hairs on the back of Hyo's neck stood on end. Silver flames jumped from Todomegawa's eyes. "Now move away from the body. Now, I say!"

"All right, all right, no need to combust at us."

Mansaku rose slowly, stepping back and away from Jun. "O'Hyo, come on. Let's leave this to the professionals."

"Buru-chan!" Todomegawa called the horse, and the fire plumes at its neck shimmied. "See that these two stay. I'm not done with them yet."

The headless horse's neck turned their way. Buru-chan swished its tail, and the next moment, Hyo was crowded against the railing with Mansaku, trapped there by the bulk of a horse flickering with ghostly fire.

They watched Todomegawa tweak his nose straight then hold his hand over Jun's body. Briefly, Hyo felt tension, like fabric had been bunched together.

"What are you doing?" she asked.

"At the moment of death, when the en between curser and cursed breaks, there's a brief recoil. An echo of the curse goes back to the curser. Sometimes I can follow that and find who cursed him." Todomegawa lowered his hand. "But it's no use. It's just the same as when Makuni was alive. Whichever god cursed him, they're untraceable in the network."

"How do you know that Jun-san was cursed by a god?" Hyo asked.

"Makuni was silenced from telling others about his curse. Only a god could have arranged that."

"Are you sure?"

"I have been on Makuni's case for a month! Yes, I am sure! I'm a professional; I've done all the tests! A god is responsible. One with a clear disregard for the rules for cursing!" There was a *crack*. The horse jumped. Todomegawa lifted his fist from where he'd punched into the boards. "I apologize, Makuni Junichiro. I failed to discover the reason for your cursing and your curser's identity. As penalty, I accept the taint of our failed contract." Luminous red blood dribbled out of Todomegawa's nose. He sniffed. Hyo almost felt sorry for him.

She asked, "There are rules to cursing?"

Todomegawa shot her a severe look that reminded Hyo of the most anally retentive classroom reps. "When a god curses a human, they must step forward, confess that they did so in a General Declaration of Cursing and lay down the terms for breaking it. It's only good divine practice. The god who cursed Makuni Junichiro ... has been lax in that."

"So, what we're saying is," Mansaku broke in, "Jun's curser didn't leave a receipt."

Todomegawa's eyebrow twitched. "In essence."

"Making your job as a 'mediator', between them and Jun, difficult? You actually had to figure out who they were, for once, and Jun couldn't tell you outright who did it to him because he'd been –" Mansaku mimed stitching his lips – "silenced?"

"Exactly!" Todomegawa thrust a finger at Mansaku. "So let this death be a reminder to you humans of what the gods can do when crossed!"

"Did Jun know who'd cursed him then?"

Todomegawa frowned, as if Mansaku had asked a trick question. "The cursed always know who cursed them, do they not? The Declaration is a formality. Instinctively, the cursed *always* know."

"Right." Mansaku nodded. "Course they do. Silly me!"

Todomegawa narrowed his eyes. "How is it that you two came to be here exactly when Makuni died? Did you summon him here? Did he say anything? Speak, or else I've good reason to enact divine punishment upon you!"

Hyo replied, "He didn't say anything."

"Really? Not a word to hint at who did this to him?" Todomegawa looked back at Jun as if any moment now a culprit's name would spill out of those dried lips. "Stubborn, uncooperative idiot. He could have at least tried to leave *something*." Swaying slightly on his feet, Todomegawa stood. "You two will return with me to the Onmyoryo to give a statement. Your en with Makuni is more complex than solely friendship. This ... *coincidence* of you being here concerns me."

Mansaku stopped petting the horse. "You're not giving us a chance to refuse?"

"Why would you refuse? Do not be afraid. You will not be tormented. There will be tea."

Buru-chan the headless horse suddenly stamped its foot, drawing their attention to where the old woman from the theatre had come to the end of the bridge.

She raised her megaphone. "Greetings, divine sir of the Onmyoryo. My colleague wishes to retrieve that body from the bridge. Is it safe for him to do so? Are you feeling peaceful?"

"Peaceful? Retrieve?" Bristling furiously, Todomegawa limped away from Hyo and Mansaku. "This case is unresolved! Why would I be 'peaceful' about it? And who does 'your colleague' think he is?!"

"My colleague, divine sir, is family." The old woman caught Hyo's eye, and Hyo got the message: *Go*. "And so has every right to his request."

Hyo gave the horse a light shove. It stayed firmly in place, a wall of muscle, one back hoof resting on its tip in a picture of relaxation. Hyo looked to Mansaku, who pushed up his sleeves. "Sorry, Buru-chan."

For a slice between seconds, Mansaku's edge was there, invisible but present, in a *gleam* that Hyo felt rather than saw. A cold, vibrant sharpness scraped over her and the headless horse, and it jumped, suddenly and sideways in a spray of sparks, as a bright red mark appeared on its flank.

Buru-chan bolted. Galloping off into nothingness, it disappeared from the bridge.

Todomegawa spun round. "Buru-chan! What did you do to my horse?"

"Split up, and I'll see you at the buraden station later?" said Mansaku as Todomegawa strode towards them, billowing smoke, his eyes exploding with licking tongues of fire.

Hyo nodded. "Got it."

They turned – and ran.

"I said, ***STAY where you are!***"

Without his horse, Todomegawa followed them at a lurching, clumsy run. Still, he *did* run wreathed in flames that grew increasingly violent with every frustrated step.

There were no dead ends on Onogoro. Bridges flowed into walkways, into flying arches, into hollow buttresses. Hyo and Mansaku ran. Fire thundered behind them, sending Onogoro's people, human and divine, leaping out of its way.

At the first split walkway, Mansaku took right, Hyo left. When Hyo had cleared a good distance from the junction, she looked back. She saw Todomegawa pause, then move as if to follow Mansaku down the right.

Not good. Between the two of them, Hyo wasn't the one carrying an incriminating weapon spirit welded to her souls. If one of them should end up at the Onmyoryo, it should be her, not Mansaku.

In a flash of panic, she looked hard and close at Todomegawa's flame of life.

The god stumbled, sliding to a stop, hand jumping to his chest.

Gods, it turned out, didn't have a candle. Their flame burned in a bowl of glossy oil so dark it looked like shinshu. That oil ... it had to be musuhi, dripping into the bowl, constantly replenishing their life.

Todomegawa's gaze met Hyo's from the other walkway. She couldn't see his expression, but she could imagine it, young and frightened, and then he was doubling back to the split. He was coming after her. Good.

That's not good either!

She ducked into a side-alley as Todomegawa's voice boomed behind her, **"COME BACK. EXPLAIN YOURSELVES. YOU WILL NOT BE HARMED."**

"Oh, heavens, he *is* having a bad day!" Too busy looking backwards, Hyo hadn't noticed the figure who'd stepped out from a nearby hut, and nearly ran straight into him. "Er ... I apologize in advance for the manhandling! Quickly, in here!"

An arm wrapped around her, wrenching Hyo back into the hut and setting her down preciously, like something that could break, in its darkest corner.

Then the young man closed the door and ducked below the cross-ribbed window.

Todomegawa blazed past, flames and smoke pouring off him, boots kicking up molten drops from the shinwood planks. Hyo waited, crammed into the corner, for one minute, then another, until her companion shuffled on hands and knees back to the door, and opened it just enough to peep outside.

He closed it. "He's gone."

Hyo exhaled. "He didn't even look this way."

"That's because of where we are. See that talisman up there?" Hyo followed his graceful hand gesture to the slip of paper pasted against the ceiling's edge. "It's a ward against en-giri gods like Toki. Notice huts like these are for connecting people, bringing people together. He's not welcome in these spaces, so they're, er, often blind spots for him."

En-giri. *A god specialized in cutting en.* "Toki? Is that Todo—?"

"No, no, no, don't!" Her companion hurriedly raised his hands, cutting her off. "Don't say his heavenly name. He'll sense where you are when you speak it. Then he'll find you, and find me. Call him the Bridgeburner, if you want to talk about him and not get his attention."

Hyo raised her eyebrows. "You're hiding from him too?"

"I'm not hiding," the man said carefully. "I'm taking a temporary break from his presence."

The moment caught up with Hyo. Suddenly she was aware that she was in a small hut with a stranger, who was evading an Onmyoryo curse-mediator.

He was a waist-high mound of black hair.

No, that wasn't it. He was kneeling. It was just that his hair was so long, thick and unkempt that it hid the entirety of his face, body and hands. There was a glimmer of glasses, a glimpse of dark, intelligent eyes looking out at her.

He went on, "I would like to apologize on the Bridgeburner's behalf. We're, er, acquainted. Somewhat. I'm not sure what you did, but I can't think it deserved being chased by him in that state. He must be feeling very emotional today."

"How do you know he wasn't after me for a good reason?" Hyo asked, genuinely curious.

"I like to assume the best in people. Unless they're the Bridgeburner, in which case, I know he can do better." His voice was soft in that way of the corners of old books turned too often, if a little prim. Then: "Perhaps you should leave now, whilst he's looking elsewhere."

That was an idea, but something in his tone made Hyo hesitate. "You want me gone?"

Glasses glimmered, then the hair nodded. "People don't stay to talk with me long lately – and I think it's better for them. Safer for them, even. But thank you for the brief company. I've missed friendly conversation."

Loneliness – it rested on him like a feather cloak, but if there was a chance to leave, Hyo should take it. She bowed. "Thanks for helping me."

"You're most welcome."

Hyo opened the door, looked out into the walkway, then thunder clapped.

FIVE

荒雨

En-musubi gods. Fate connectors. You think they're nice then they'll tie your fate to some drunk bum whose fate has been tied to a smelly death in a cesspool.

TAMA,
Twenty-Second Hellmaker

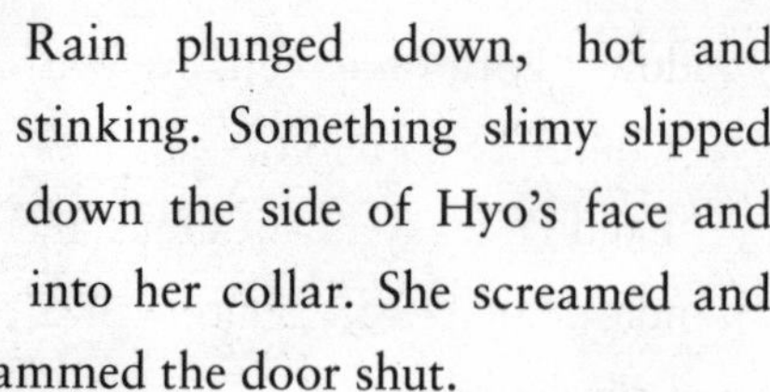

Rain plunged down, hot and stinking. Something slimy slipped down the side of Hyo's face and into her collar. She screamed and slammed the door shut.

"Guts?!" Quivering globs glistened in a flash of lightning, splattering against the window. Thunder boomed. "Are you kidding me? Fish guts?! In the rain?"

"It wasn't in the divine forecast for today, was it?" noted the hair mildly. He unfolded from the floor as Hyo clawed at her face, trying to clean off the slime. "Here. Use this."

A sheet of manuscript paper entered her vision, its grids crammed with writing. He'd pulled it from the battered satchel at his side. "I can't use that."

"It's nothing important. Well, not any more. I'm a writer, you see. Or was. My serialization was cancelled today, so this chapter's worthless now. You've, er, a flotation sac by your ear."

Hyo took the offered page, not looking at the text. "Thank you. Is this normal on Onogoro? For it to rain guts?"

"Not guts specifically. You never know what you'll get with wild rain." A hard blob splattered against the window. "Forgive me, but are you new to Onogoro?"

"Couldn't you tell?"

"I didn't want to presume. Plenty here don't speak 'Standard' in private, but, well..." His hands emerged from the hair curtain to gesticulate. From fingertips to wrists, they were striped in long pinkish scars. "What I'm saying is, divine phenomena like wild rain is perfectly natural, and there's no need to worry. Are you familiar with taint?"

Kegare. Taint.

"It's like a dirt that sticks to the spirit," said Hyo. "You can pick it up from death and things that are wandering close to death, like people who are sick or in childbirth." Ideas about taint had never been kind to women, or anyone associated with blood, butchery, and flesh and bone things. "But what's that got to do with the wild rain?"

"It happens whenever a god needs to burn off taint. Gods exist because humans wished that they could bargain with an otherwise faceless natural world for their protection," he replied. "So when a god does anything to hurt a human, even unintentionally, they reject that wish which gives them life. Ergo, it brings the god closer to their version of death."

"Then every single time a god fails to protect a human...?"

"The god picks up taint." Hyo thought of Todomegawa punching the broken boards of the bridge. *As penalty, I accept the taint of our failed contract.* Her companion stood alongside her to peer out of the slime-smeared window. "So you can imagine, it's easy to accumulate – inevitable, even. Humans can be so easily hurt. That's why festivals are so important and we have so many. They cleanse the gods of taint through the year. But, in between festivals, sometimes the gods burn it off themselves by going a little 'wild'. Wild rain –" he traced the greasy trail of something slippery and grey with a finger – "is just that. A god burning off a little taint. You'd think this would count as harm to humans, but it doesn't. Just about."

"How so?"

"Gods have their four souls just as humans do. Roughly, they're split into their two 'faces'. The face that we see on Onogoro streets – the one humans wish to talk to – is the nigimitama. That's the 'humanish' god – the face that's peaceful and welcomed in Onogoro's human en-networks. The other face is the aramitama. That's the 'wild' god – the god outside of human en-networks. Untied from human convenience, they're not there to protect anyone. They're simply raw natural power, so they don't accumulate taint, even if they're destructive. Going slightly 'wild' lets the god slip, briefly, out of the en-network, just enough to burn off the taint without picking up more."

Hyo stared. If "going slightly 'wild'" meant dropping

guts from the sky... "What happens if the god *keeps* picking up taint?"

"Then the poor soul will naturally slip into the 'wild' state. No choice. They'll fall out of the human en-network and indulge the aramitama completely, humans be damned." Her companion twisted his scarred hands. "We call it 'falling'."

"Do gods pick up taint when they curse humans?"

She felt his gaze on her. "They should do, but not always."

Hyo clicked her tongue. "Loopholes?"

"Just the one. The 'Good Reason' loophole. With capitals. If the god had Good Reason to curse the human, the taint from the cursing will be lower."

"Who decides what's Good Reason?"

"The humans do, although not consciously. In the rules of cursing, it's written as the 'collective Onogoro human spirit'. Vague, isn't it?" he said, when Hyo grimaced. "It changes all the time. The gods are never sure what Good Reason is, so they'll curse first and find out if they had Good Reason later."

"Then why risk cursing humans at all?" *What could Jun have ever possibly done to count as* Good Reason *that a god would curse him so cruelly?* Hyo wondered.

"They might think a little taint is a small price to pay for vengeance," came the reply. "Or in their anger, they might very easily forget."

Guts rotted to a thin grey slime on the hut's window.

Hyo turned away to look around the hut. The walls were covered in bamboo slats. Adverts, fliers and even letters had been woven into them. "What is this place?"

"It's a notice hut," her companion said softly. "It's for leaving messages for people you don't know the whereabouts of."

Hyo moved closer to study the blue-grey patchwork of paper. Something crunched under her boot. She lifted her foot.

Crushed salt clung to the sole.

She felt a cold *pluck*.

Jun. Jun had been here. In this very hut!

She shouldn't jump to conclusions, but it made sense – and Hyo could feel it; the tug of the hellmakers' en, a fateful connection pulling threads taut. "Are there any other huts like this closer to the Shin-Kaguraza Theatre?"

"To the Shin-Kaguraza, this is the closest."

If Jun had been hiding here since the night, in the en-giri god's blind spot, it would explain why Todomegawa had failed to find him. Hyo squatted to check the floor. More flakes of salt glittered in the shadow of the bench.

Her companion cleared his throat. "Are you looking for something?"

Hyo straightened. She turned to the letters along the walls. "A letter, maybe."

Jun hadn't been able to talk, but maybe he'd been able to leave a message. Even if it wasn't for Hyo, it wouldn't matter. Any clue about what he'd been doing and what had been on his mind before he'd headed to the Shin-Kaguraza Bridge would bring her one step closer to figuring out what was going on, and one step closer to her special commissioner.

The one who'd buy revenge on behalf of the dead, for Jun.

"I can help, if you wish." The stranger had come to look at the wall too. "I come here every week. I know which of these notices are new."

"It might not be a letter," Hyo amended, her stomach sinking as she realized just *how much paper* there was, enough that the hut's insides looked smothered in blue-grey ivy. "I'll know when I see it."

He snorted softly. "You don't sound so sure."

"I've got this … en that directs me to people who need me." Hyo scanned the wall for Jun's handwriting – the more recent blotchy calligraphy. "Sometimes the en will bring me a dead body that needs someone living to … make sure they're not forgotten. Then the en helps me feel out the clues for how the body ended up as one, and find the person who'll pay for … my skills. At least, I hope so."

"I'm sorry – did you say you've an en with dead bodies?"

"No, but close enough. More like, the dirty laundry from other people's cruelties."

"But that's a terrible en to live with. Think of all the taint you'll invite. And everything you'll see!"

"Yeah, tell me about it." She thought of Jun – broad smile shrivelled dry, a boy who'd been so full of feeling drained of tears, his bright mind a dehydrated husk. "It's all right; it's just part of me and my life."

"*Part of your life?*" The stranger lifted a hand as if to reach for Hyo's sleeve but lowered it before he touched her. "You should pray to an en-giri god to have this broken at once! What a life you must've had because of it. Heavens, I'm so sorry."

"I'm not interested in breaking the en," Hyo intoned, because that was that. "And what are you apologizing for? It's nothing to do with you."

"But it's everything to do with me," he said forlornly. "I'm the god of en-musubi and fateful connections."

Oh.

Belatedly, Hyo recalled that Ukoku's gods were known as "Yaoyorozu-no-Kami" – the Uncountable Gods – and made up possibly more than half of Onogoro's population.

Hyo's companion had neither Todomegawa's flaming eyes nor the Gateway god's press of power to give him away. Maybe, if she trained her senses to pursue it, she could feel a heaviness in the shadows, as if each were a wet robe hung out to dry and when the wind blew just so, they clung to something vast and watchful crouched just behind them.

Hyo bowed so quickly her neck cracked. "I apologize for any disrespect in my words or actions that might've given good reason for cursing."

"Oh, don't. Please. Look up. There's no need for formal language either. We've been doing very well without it." The en-musubi god waved his hands frantically. This time, Hyo noticed the polished sheen of his fingertips where the fingerprints had been smoothed away. "That was a slip of the tongue... I'm not 'the' god of fateful connections, ha ha. I'm *a* god. There are so many others in my field, who do such good work. I've no followers, so no power. Can see the en-network but can't touch it. As far as I know." He laughed again, but trailed off when Hyo stayed silent. "I swear I haven't taken offence. Please look up, then let's continue, as we were. Just two strangers in the wild rain, looking for a maybe-letter. Who won't ever meet again."

Hyo looked up, and found that her companion's hand movements had been so wild that they'd parted his hair, and she finally saw his face. The ragged scar-stripes of his hands covered his face too. They crossed from a torn ear to a fine chin, over high cheekbones and a low nose. They fanned about the corners of his mouth. They were raked over each eye as if someone had tried to scratch them out, perhaps some terrible mob that had tried to tear him apart with their bare hands.

He looked younger than Mansaku, maybe not much older than Hyo. He blinked quickly and stared, wide-eyed behind his round-framed glasses, as if he couldn't believe that someone had dared meet his gaze. But his expression was gentle. It had the feathered edges of a treasured letter. The overall impression subtly opposed that of Todomegawa the Bridgeburner.

He tried to hide behind his sleeve.

"Wait." Hyo stopped him with a hand, but didn't touch. He'd held back, after all. "It's nice to see a friendly face. If you don't mind."

"Friendly? This face?"

"You helped me get away from the Bridgeburner; you gave me paper to clean up with. It's the face of someone who's been kind to me twice." That sheet of paper was still scrunched in her fist. One unsmudged corner of elegant calligraphy read: "... *and so ended another strange tale in the lanterned streets of Hikaraku where dreams come to life and their dreamers die.*" The lines struck Hyo as vaguely familiar but she couldn't think from where, so she set all that aside and focused on the notices. "Why are you so sure we won't meet again, anyway? We might have an en."

"We might – but it's unlikely."

"Why?"

The en-musubi god smiled. "I find it near impossible to make an en with anybody I meet lately. I wish I knew

友達に
社会のため
私

why. So, this maybe-letter you're looking for. Anything else to go on?"

Hyo thought about it. What would Jun put on a letter he'd leave in a public notice hut? His name, maybe, but better still: "A talisman."

"Right, a talisman." The god bent his knees a little to look at a row of notices. "Unusual. What kind?"

"A protective one that stops everyone but the intended recipient from opening it. It looks like..."

Hyo drew it in the air with a finger.

The god was silent, then he pulled a narrow blue-grey envelope out from the front of his robes. "You mean, like this one?"

He turned it over.

The talisman Hyo had taught Jun faced her.

The string of the hellmakers' en sang.

"Yes, like that." Hyo felt abruptly breathless, like she'd tripped over a thread strung across the floor and just picked herself up. She looked from the envelope to the god. "Why do you...?"

Why do you, an en-musubi god with no power, have a letter from Jun?

The god's long, brush-stroke eyes darted around the room. He was looking for an escape. Hyo didn't blame him. She'd search for a way out too, the way even she could feel the stranglehold of fate and en in that moment.

"Natsuami," he blurted suddenly.

"What?"

"It's my earthly name. My editor moans at me with it. My brother chastises me with it. Jun writes to me by it." His soft voice cut through the slaps of gut on the roof. "Knowing a human's name and face gives a god the ability to curse them. I know your face – and I think I already know your name. It's only fair then that you know mine. You're Hakai Hyo, am I correct?"

"You are." Hellmakers shared their rules for cursing with the gods. Hyo, too, needed the name and face of those she'd be cursing. "Who are you to Jun?"

"A friend. Well. A pen-friend, to be precise. We met once, by chance, and got along. But with my en with people being as it is, pen-friend was the best I could do for him. Every sixteenth of the month, he leaves me a letter here, and every thirtieth, I leave my reply." Natsuami gave her a small, uneasy smile. "He told me to look out for you and your brother when you arrived, and be a friend for you in his place."

"When did Jun say that?"

"In his letter from today, although why he's asked *me* of all people on Onogoro, I don't understand. He *knows* I struggle to keep ens." Natsuami turned the envelope in his hands, seeking clues too, maybe, in the blotchy calligraphy. "And you, Hakai Hyo? Who are you to Jun? With your en that draws you into investigating the deaths that come your way..."

Even as he spoke, Hyo saw the realization washing dark and heavy over Natsuami's features.

"No."

Hyo swallowed. She nodded. "Jun's dead."

Natsuami's smile was desperately polite. "No, he isn't."

"He was murdered."

"No."

"He died right in front of me, tying me to his case, and there's something in your letter –" Hyo pointed at the envelope, felt the hellmakers' en hum as if she'd touched a wire – "that's a clue, however small, as to why someone wanted Jun dead."

"There's nothing in it at all like that."

Hyo held out her hand. "Let me see it, then we'll be sure."

"No, you don't understand." Natsuami stepped back, pulling the letter close to his chest as if Hyo would snatch it from him. "I tried to keep him safe! We wrote, but I kept my distance! I never agreed to meet him! I did everything I could think of, so that he wouldn't end up like the others! But if even this fragile en could be enough for him to... Oh, heavens, I should never have let him write to me."

"What do you mean 'keep him safe'?" Hyo's breath hitched. "Are others dead too?"

Natsuami's eyes were wet. He dragged his hair over his face, hiding it in shadow. "If Jun's as you say, that makes him the fourth of four humans who had an en with me, who were *dear* to me, who've..." Natsuami shuddered, unable to seal reality into words. "I'm sorry, Hakai Hyo. Jun asked me to help you and I will. The first thing, and the last thing, I can do for you is to leave now and take this letter with me, before any en you have with me might strengthen. And then never see you again."

"No, wait..." Hyo caught hold of Natsuami's sleeve as he tried to move past her. She felt a strange pressure against her skin, or the opposite of it. If the Gateway god's power had felt like the touch of a wave, this was a sharp receding of the tide, a sudden void, the opening of a cavernous mouth. "Jun was my friend. Jun ... he was supposed to be *here* for us, on Onogoro. Fine and happy. He was the only person alive who still remembered my hometown

as a *happy* place. Not even my brother can do that any more. We lost *so much* with him. We've lost so much!" Her voice was too loud and too fraught. "Just let me see what Jun wrote to you then you can disappear, if that's what you want."

And then she was crying in front of a strange, scarred god whilst the sky spat blood and fish guts down the window.

"I *can't.*" Natsuami sniffed. "If I share this letter with you, the risk is we'll share a turning point – an event that will tie our fates together, and that's a powerful en. And an en with me..." He bowed. "Please excuse me. I'm so sorry. If it wasn't for me, if it wasn't for Jun's en with me..."

He pried Hyo's hand from his arm, then in a blink of an eye was at the door.

Outside, rotting offal was ricocheting off the walkway boards. A large white aircraft – a windturtle, one of the sturdier solar-powered vehicles – flew by, a blue lamp flashing on its belly.

Snatches of an announcement drifted down.

"*... all citizens please remain in shelter until further notice ... remain calm ... do not go out ... the Onmyoryo apologizes for this unforecast divine phenomenon ... inconvenience to your day...*"

Natsuami pulled the door open. The cloying smell of the fetid rain swept into the hut. He choked, stopping on the threshold and swaying back inside.

He looked over his shoulder, meeting Hyo's gaze.

She saw his resolve solidify. Covering his nose with a sleeve, Natsuami jumped out into the rain of fish guts – and was gone.

Thunder rumbled. There was no use following. Natsuami had fled with a god's speed and a local's knowledge, taking whatever it was that might have been Jun's final thoughts away into the rains of Onogoro.

Hyo closed the door. The rain's smell wasn't unlike the orchard her village had been turned into. Whatever reflex had made Natsuami gag, she didn't have it any more.

The tension that had been keeping Hyo moving, thinking, running, ever since Jun's candle had gone out under her hands, snapped. She sank on to the bench and sighed.

Ah. Sitting down. An amateur's mistake. She should've known better. Hyo focused on the coolness of the tears sliding down her face, and wished they'd soothe away the dismal ache of failure.

SIX

水神様

If you're stuck for a god to whom to offer your musubi, why not try one of the Pillar Gods? Our top three gods and "pillars" of Onogoro society, the Paddywatcher, the Wavewalker and the Harvestlight, can be found at shrines in all districts.

From "So You've Made It to Onogoro, Last Home of Ukoku's Gods – Congratulations!"

"Hey, you!" Hyo woke to the shout of a woman in the hut doorway, then woke up *properly* when the woman threw a shovel at her. She caught it before Mansaku became the only Hakai child. "No time for napping. We need all hands here!"

The wild rain had cleared, giving way to yellow evening light. People were emerging from shelters to take out cleaning tools from hidden cabinets in the walls. Mops and folding hand-carts were handed out as Onogoro got down to clearing up a god's mess with a day-to-day weariness.

Right. Hyo was a god-approved Onogoro citizen. She had to act like it. She tied a kerchief over her face, and got down to shovelling innards into the carts.

It was repetitive, slippery and stinking work, and it helped clear her head. So what that she'd let Natsuami disappear into the rain? Hyo was a Hakai hellmaker. So long as the hellmakers' en had connected her to Jun's letter and to Natsuami, they were all of them caught together in the same spider-web of Jun's death. Natsuami couldn't escape her.

Hyo turned her ears to the conversations bubbling up along the walkway. She picked out a group of local traders and their regular customers, and sidled closer to shovel with them.

"Excuse me," she said. They looked her way. "I was looking for someone in the area before the rain hit. Have any of you seen a tallish guy with scars all over and a load of hair, like...?" She mimed a cross between chaos and seaweed. "He said he comes to this walkway maybe once a week to check the notice hut."

"Big, scarred and hairy?" The locals conferred with each other.

An old man said, "Could be the Ohne gang's new strongman – you know, Meatfist Kumataro?"

"No, that's not it. He's more –" Hyo racked her brains – "big deer than bear?"

Another conference, then the old man replied, "Sorry, young lady, never seen anyone like that around here."

"That's all right," said Hyo quickly. Natsuami hadn't been exaggerating when he'd said his ens failed to last. Anyone of Natsuami's appearance should have been very memorable. "Then what about a young man, about my height, in a high-collared shirt and hakama? He would've gone to the notice hut sometime yesterday. Maybe with his face covered?"

The old man scratched his head. "In newspaper?"

"Yes! When did you see him?"

"I saw him leaving that hut at about half to noon today, staggering like a drunk."

Forty minutes before Jun had arrived at the Shin-Kaguraza Bridge. It was doubtful he'd gone anywhere else in between. "Did anything else seem off about him?"

"Oh, lots. The newspaper, for one. And he'd stuck one

of those divine privacy talismans down his front – the ones the Onmyoryo use to keep their business unseen to gods' eyes. But it was smudged up and near useless. It was obvious he'd gotten in trouble with the gods, so I left him be." The old man leant on his shovel. "Young lady, you a plainclothes Onmyoryo officer or something?"

"I'm a hellmaker."

"Ah, right, a bell-maker. A proper trade! It's not a proper taint-cleansing festival without some bells! Well, bell-maker, if you're asking out of concern for a friend of yours, it sounds like it's time to cut all en with your friend." He held out a wheelbarrow for Hyo to dump her shovelled guts into. "Let the Onmyoryo handle whatever they've gotten into. That's their job after all – keeping the passage of gods and humans' relationships clean, clear and *smooth*."

"Although the Onmyoryo haven't been much good with their divine forecasts lately, have they? Wasn't a peep about any flesh rain in today's one," the woman who'd woken Hyo grumbled. "What happened to all that 'investing in better atmospheric taint-detection technology' that was in the papers after Three Thousand Three Fall?"

The old man nodded. "True. If another god falls like that one did, we won't be warned any earlier."

"What's Three Thousand Three Fall?"

Shovels paused.

Then a voice piped up at Hyo's ear, "I'll take it from here. Everyone!" Hyo felt a playful buoyancy, as if she were an acorn fallen into a stream and the water had lifted her to its surface to bounce along. "Cleaning's over."

A drop splashed on Hyo's forehead. It wasn't gut-slime but simple rain. A second drop fell, then another, and another, until they were all standing in a sparkling downpour that was falling out of a cloudless sky.

It dissolved the remaining sludge from the boards, melting the viscera to wisps of steam.

"Thank you, Wavewalker," said the woman, dropping to her knees in the lowest of bows, and the others followed. The old man was helped down by a partner. "Fuchiha'no'Utanami'Tomi-no-Mikoto, thank you!"

The water danced. "You're all very welcome!"

The woman took the shovel from Hyo's hands. "Go on now, dear – and take care."

"Now, little darling! Let's have our chat. How about we go ... that way?" A pincer slipped into Hyo's vision, pointing to the right. She glanced down. A little blue crab was perched on her shoulder.

At the same time, she felt an enormous presence, not unlike Natsuami. The crab she saw was only the tip of an enormous iceberg.

"As the god asks," Hyo said deferentially.

"No need to be so reverent. You're a hellmaker, after all." The crab's legs pricked her neck. "Allow me to introduce myself. I'm the Wavewalker, Chief of the Water Gods. I'm rainmaker, healer, friend to the blood in your veins and watcher over the sea of the womb. Onogoro drinks from the rain barrels I fill and makes its shinshu from the same. Taints, sicknesses and curses are my special side interests. You may call me Fuchiha, if you want my special attention, and Wavewalker if not. And you, little darling? Gift me your name, hellmaker."

The back of Hyo' nose and mouth tingled like she'd breathed lightning. "Hakai Hyo, Wavewalker."

"Hyo-chan. Mm, there's a touch of water in that name. I like it." Something invisible patted Hyo on her head. Her hair stood on end. "Let's see now – you were asking about Three Thousand Three Fall..." The crab tapped its mouthparts in thought. Hyo moved her feet down the walkway it had indicated. "It's been three years since the incident, and we all remember it keenly still, gods and humans alike. Three Thousand Three Fall, little darling, was the last far-fall event on Onogoro."

Natsuami had talked about 'falling', but this sounded like something different. "What's a far-fall?"

"It's when a god accumulates so much taint that, when they fall, they fall so far it cannot be reversed. They're not merely a 'wild' god. They become a god of destruction," said the crab. "Three thousand and three humans died that single night."

"How many?!"

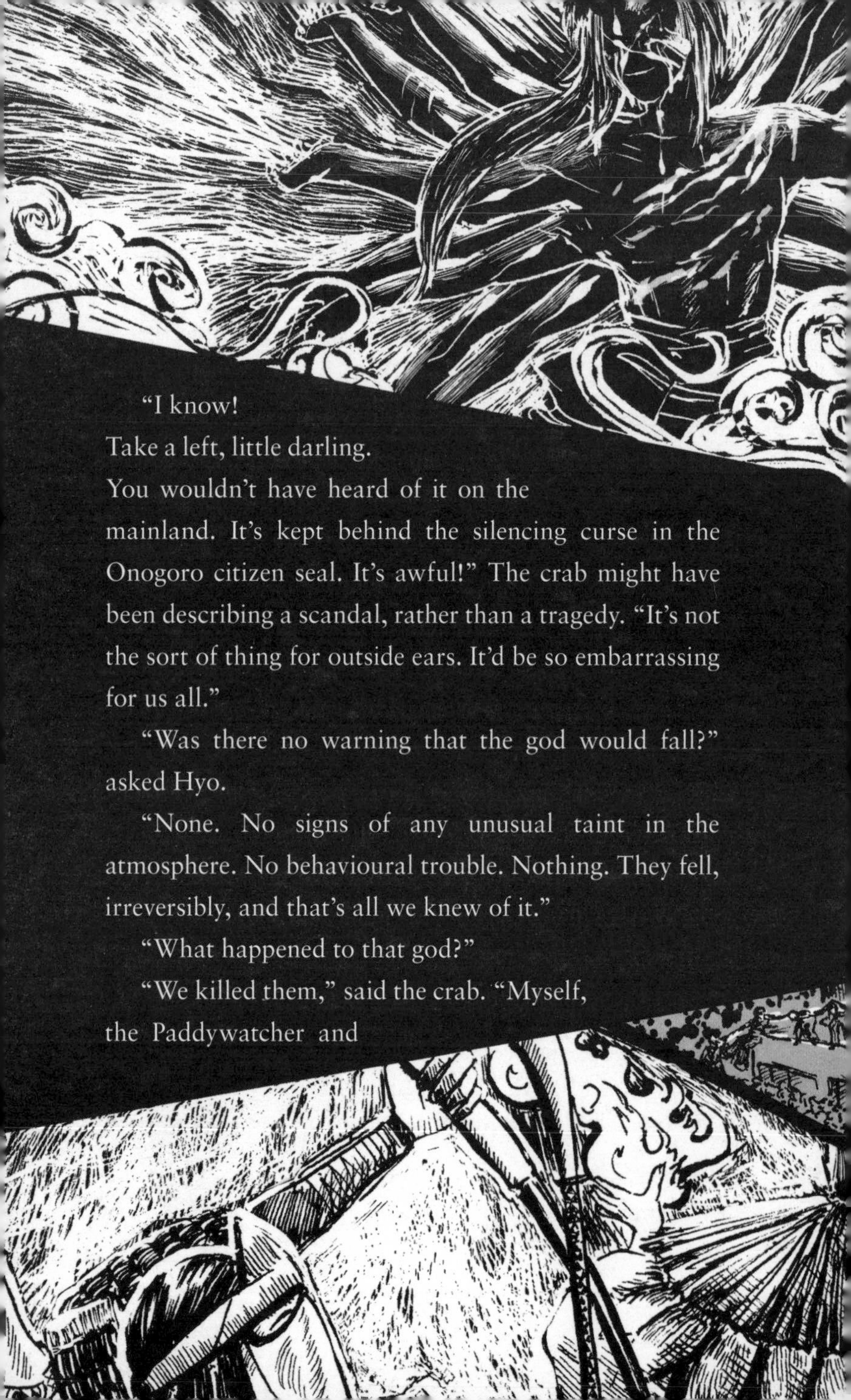

"I know!
Take a left, little darling.
You wouldn't have heard of it on the mainland. It's kept behind the silencing curse in the Onogoro citizen seal. It's awful!" The crab might have been describing a scandal, rather than a tragedy. "It's not the sort of thing for outside ears. It'd be so embarrassing for us all."

"Was there no warning that the god would fall?" asked Hyo.

"None. No signs of any unusual taint in the atmosphere. No behavioural trouble. Nothing. They fell, irreversibly, and that's all we knew of it."

"What happened to that god?"

"We killed them," said the crab. "Myself, the Paddywatcher and

the Harvestlight –
we're known as the Pillar Gods. It's our duty to ensure that Onogoro society stays standing. The three of us fought them and destroyed their shrines, erasing their heavenly name from this world, and erasing them."

"But wouldn't the god's followers remember their heavenly name, keeping them in existence?"

"They would've, if the god hadn't already killed their followers themselves. Those *were* the three thousand and three. A suicidal thing for a god to do. But when gods fall to destruction and indulge the aramitama, we tend to forget we're *gods*, as humans wish us to be, and not storms, or typhoons, or other forces of nature that could exist without human musuhi. Turn left here, then take that little alley by the knife-grinder on the corner." The crab jumped. It landed in Hyo's hands with light pinpricks of its claws. "Are there *really* no surviving Ukoku gods on the mainland?"

"None."

"But the Harbourlakes' god, the Pater-in-Pieces, are they so different?"

"I don't know. The Harbourlakes were stopped from force-feeding their god to us thirty years ago." Hyo held up the crab to eye level. "You gods are all new to me."

"But we're far from strangers to you, hellmaker, with that curse of yours." Hyo opened her mouth to reply but the crab had already continued. "Oh, yes, you were asking those humans earlier something about a tall, scarred individual who frequents this area?"

"Natsuami? Do you know him?" Hyo pressed.

"Not so loud with his name. Down this alley, please! But how curious, that his name's not faded from you yet." The crab probed the hellmakers' seal on her palm thoughtfully. "Did you want anything from him in particular or was he ... just interesting?"

"He was interesting," Hyo said with confidence, because it wasn't a lie.

"Hmm, he is, isn't he?" The crab's voice popped against her ear like foam. "Well, give it three days, little darling. If your en with him hasn't broken by then, we'll have to consider ... measures. For your safety."

"Could an en with him ... kill me?"

The crab let out an amused bubbling noise that Hyo took as affirmation. "Wavewalker, sir, where are you taking me?"

"Ah, did I fail to mention that I'm also the most senior of curse-mediator gods at the Onmyoryo? You met my subordinate earlier. The Bridgeburner – he's one of my rivers. Practically a child of mine."

Hyo stopped walking. The Wavewalker's cleansing rain pattered around them, evaporating from her clothes rather than soaking into them and filling the air with fine mist. "Am I under arrest?"

"Don't be silly. I've enough to do without doing my subordinates' jobs for them. But I am responsible for their behaviour, and I'm not at all impressed by the Bridgeburner's today. It's one thing to be frustrated if a case doesn't go your way, and quite another to be running around Hikaraku on fire." The crab snapped its pincers viciously. "He will be disciplined exactly as he should've expected to be! Please accept my apologies and allow me to reunite you with your brother."

"You're taking me to Mansaku?"

"Shhh, be more precious with names, little darling," the Wavewalker warned, and despite seeing only a crab on her shoulder, Hyo felt the press of a cold and invisible finger to her lips. "You know what it takes to curse a human – knowledge of their name and face. I found him sheltering from the rain in one of my shrines and took the liberty of guiding him to the Ujigami Info-point, just around … here."

They came out of the alley to a sunlit terrace. What looked like a newsagent or general store was painted in what Hyo thought were leaf greens. Closer inspection showed it to be covered in moss and curling trellises of bean-plants that nearly obscured a sign at the shop's front.

氏神相談窓口

安全な暮らしのために、あなたを守る情報を！

Ujigami Info-point

Information is your best local protection!

Mansaku was sitting outside it, next to a telephone box, eating something charred on a stick in one hand and clutching a half-finished onigiri in the other. He was reading a magazine opened on the bench.

A hand landed on Hyo's shoulder where the crab had been perched. "Shall we?"

Hyo looked round quickly. The Wavewalker was now a man in the white and blue of a male shrine attendant's robes, a cloth mask hiding his face but for a sharp-toothed smile of sea-green teeth. Before Hyo could respond, he was guiding her to the Info-point.

"Mansaku, is it?" the Wavewalker called out, and Mansaku scrambled to tidy away his food, knocking the magazine to the floor. "Here's your little sister, water-scythe, just as I promised."

"Thank you, Wavewalker." At "water-scythe", Mansaku's smile had chilled to a grimace. He kept his eyes on the Wavewalker and pulled Hyo closer to him by the first fistful of fabric he could reach. "You said, er, there was something you wanted to ask us?"

"Yes, now that the two of you are here!" The Wavewalker sat on the bench that Mansaku had just vacated, hummed cheerily and picked up the magazine, directing his hidden gaze away from them. "You were both there on the Shin-Kaguraza Bridge when the Bridgeburner's client died upon it. A great shame, that, to fail a client. Anyway, I happen to be the current patron god of the Shin-Kaguraza Theatre – it comes with being the Chief Water God, as one of my predecessors had strong associations with music and the arts – and I noticed that the client was pointing at the theatre before he died. Did he, perhaps, direct any last words or curses towards the theatre or persons related to the Shin-Kaguraza, which I need to be concerned by?"

Hyo and Mansaku looked at each other. She recalled Jun's outstretched arm, flung in the direction of the theatre, as if he'd have dragged himself over the bridge if he could.

Hyo shook her head. "He didn't say anything about the theatre."

"Absolutely nothing," said Mansaku firmly. "He didn't leave any last words or messages, or vent any grudges, or have a single thing to say relating to the theatre, or to anybody theatrical, or even slightly dramatic whatsoever."

"Oh. Really?" The curve of the Wavewalker's smile didn't change as he turned the page of the magazine, but something loosened in the air, felt freer. "That's a true relief to hear. Kichizuru-kun's luck is terrible enough for the Shin-Kaguraza as it is— What is this?!"

He'd stopped on a double-page spread. Hyo craned her neck to see the black headline splashed across the top:

FIVE MONTHS ON SINCE UKIBASHI AWANO KIDNAPPING: NEW DEVELOPMENTS!! CLUES!! HOW DID THE WAVEWALKER REALLY HELP THE UKIBASHI HEIRESS ESCAPE?

DID ERASED POLICE RECORDS SHOW BLOOD ON THE BOAT?

BEHIND CLOSED DOORS: SCOOP ON AWANO – SHINSHU PRINCESS, INCAPABLE OF LEAVING UKIBASHI ESTATE ALONE SINCE

"And they call this journalism?" The Wavewalker's fingers traced the reflectograph of a young woman, black hair curled over her ears and stylishly short, turning smilingly towards the camera.

Something, distantly, grazed the strings tied by the hellmakers' en. It made Hyo ask, "Who is she?"

"Ukibashi Awano, heiress of the Ukibashi Shinshu breweries." His tone was the warmest Hyo had heard it. "They say I'm her guardian god – but she's the one who saved me first. After the war, when I was nothing but a small god with a rotting shrine, she found me and spread my heavenly name, sparing me from dissipation. I'd call her my guardian human," said the Wavewalker reverently, then his lips peeled back, "and they dare to speculate about her rescue!" He'd flipped to the magazine's back cover, revealing a talisman printed on the inside, and clicked his tongue. "And the writer has used an anonymizing charm! How typical of a weekly rag. Cowards. Insects of the gutter. Well, I'm going to get to the bottom of it. These scurrilous rumours must be stopped. Goodbye, hellmaker and scythe. I'm sure we'll cross paths again, little darlings. If you'll excuse me."

The magazine dropped on to the bench where the Wavewalker had been sitting ... and he was gone.

SEVEN

伝言

Our bargain with the rest of the world is simple. We give them our shinshu, and in exchange, they let the Ujin on Onogoro live as we please and keep our Ukoku gods. Should someone interfere, we've only to limit their shinshu supply – and see how long they last against hitodenashi's bite.

From "How Shinshu Keeps Onogoro Free: The Shinshu Economy of Onogoro", essay by Ukibashi Awano of the Ukibashi Shinshu Company

"So that was a Pillar God." Mansaku held up his half-eaten onigiri. "This was supposed to be yours, but I got hungry."

"Then who's that one for?" Hyo pointed to a fresh onigiri on the bench, still wrapped in algacell. Mansaku made a show of surprise then pressed it into her hands. "How'd you end up at the Wavewalker's shrine?"

"I doubled back when I realized our fiery friend had gone after you rather than me, got lost, found this little shrine down one alley and figured it wouldn't hurt to ask for directions."

"You couldn't have just asked ... a pedestrian?"

"It was such a small shrine, I didn't realize he was a Pillar. But the Wavewalker's got hundreds of these little shrines, all over the island. I explained I was running away from his junior, and, apparently, gods can't get or even see past the shrine gates of another god's shrine, so the Pillar God let me hide there until the Bridgeburner cooled his head. Then, it started raining anatomy." Mansaku let out a loud groan and flopped back on to the bench. "I ache everywhere, dammit. What happened to you? How did you lose the Bridgeburner?"

Hyo let out a long breath, and told Mansaku everything about her meeting with Natsuami in the notice hut and Jun's letter.

"Natsuami wouldn't show it to me," she said. "He thought that people with strong ens with him were getting hurt because of it, and if I saw that letter, we'd connect too strongly."

"So he ran off to cut your en with him whilst it's weak to keep you safe – basically, what he should've done with Jun, before they got too close." Mansaku chewed his rice slowly. "If what he said is true, this Natsuami guy sounds … kind of guilty, O'Hyo."

"He'd probably agree." Hyo thought of the shock that'd filled those gentle eyes, the horror Natsuami hadn't been able to hide even behind that curtain of hair. "But I'm not guilty of murder when the hellmakers' en brings me a body. Maybe it's something like that for him too."

"Well, we can find out when we see him again – which we will. If Natsuami visits that notice hut that often, he's probably local." Mansaku picked the last grains of rice off his fingertips. "Speaking of notice huts and god blind zones, did you know that, as this is an Ujigami Info-point, that phone box over there counts as a shrine? It's a direct line to Hikaraku's Ujigami, the local guardian god."

Hyo followed Mansaku's gaze to a phone box with clear resin walls. The twist of rope hanging over it was adorned with shide and straw tassels, and an arrow was buried in the thatch above its door. "So?"

"So, in there, other gods won't be able to listen in on us."

"But the Ujigami could."

触らぬ神に祟りなし
氏神電話

"Nah, actually. I asked Ikushima – she's this Infopoint's shrine attendant – but apparently, the Ujigami won't hear you *in the phone box* whilst the phone is down. It helps keep her line clear." Mansaku stood, taking Hyo's rubbish too. "When you finish eating, I want to show you something."

Inside the phone box was a little fountain for them to wash their hands and mouths. The bright-green corded telephone was framed on each side with sakaki, just like the god cabinets up on Jun's shrine shelf.

Mansaku closed the door behind them. "I might've told the Wavewalker a preferred truth earlier, rather than an actual one, about Jun and messages." He withdrew a blue envelope from his sleeve. "When the Bridgeburner crash-landed, this shook loose from Jun's robes."

The hellmakers' en sang. It took everything in Hyo not to rip this envelope from Mansaku's grasp. This was something she needed to see, to touch, to know more about.

On the front there was only one large and streaky symbol: 光.

"Light?" read Hyo. Then it clicked. "'Kou' – this is for Koushiro."

Mansaku nodded. "Jun was heading to the Shin-Kaguraza Theatre to give this to Koushiro."

Jun's last message to his little brother. What would it be? A warning? A confession? An accusation?

"Give it to me."

Mansaku handed it over. "I knew it'd be useful."

Jun's talisman to block out unintended recipients was so badly drawn that it offered no protection at all. As useless as a child's scrawl. Hyo opened the envelope without trouble, and unfolded it so that both she and Mansaku could see.

Jun had been running out of ink. The last symbols were scratched on to the paper. They had been written large, Hyo guessed to make up for a clumsy hand.

全部燃やせ!!!

BURN EVERYTHING!!!

Mansaku paused, then said quietly, "That's a nice, calm statement from someone having a really great day."

"This was Jun's last message to Koushiro." Hyo folded up the letter, placing it in its envelope. "We have to make sure Koushiro gets it."

By the tug of the hellmakers' en in her spine, Hyo felt something, somewhere, falling into place. The real clue wasn't this letter – it would be how Koushiro responded to it.

She turned to the Ujigami's green telephone and clapped her hands twice to pray.

One clue had come to Hyo's hand. *May the next follow soon.*

*

They had two days until the "probably haunted" flat was exorcised and theirs, and since neither wanted another run-in with Todomegawa – who seemed persistent enough that he'd probably be waiting for them at Jun's – Mansaku asked Ikushima, the Info-point shrine attendant, for advice on somewhere to stay nearby.

Before Ikushima could reply, the green phone rang in its box. Ikushima went out to it then returned moments later looking unsettled.

"The Ujigami-sama says to stay here for the two days. You're both too much potential hazards to let roam about Hikaraku without her knowing where to find you." Ikushima was a large woman with glossy braided hair and a round, friendly face, but in that moment she looked severe and suspicious. "Who in the world *are* you two?"

"The couch-surfers who are going to clean your Info-point," Mansaku replied, picking up a broom.

Ikushima beamed. "Of course you are."

A narrow ladder from the Info-point's newsagent floor took them up into the Info-point office, where a manoeuvring of folders gave them room to lay down bedding. Ikushima lived above the Info-point office in a tiny one-room apartment. It seemed she took the Hakai's "potential hazard" label to heart, and asked no more questions about their situation. When she spotted Hyo copying out sutras at the crack of dawn – fixing the seal that had faded two fingers' worth on Hyo's left palm – all she asked was if Hyo needed more paper as she peeled back the calendar for Fifthmonth 17th.

The day after Jun died, Mansaku tried to reach Koushiro at the theatre again, letter for him in hand. He failed thanks to the crowd of reporters accosting everyone who looked remotely interested in entering the Shin-Kaguraza, asking if they'd seen the death on the bridge, who they thought had died and if they believed it was connected to "Kichizuru's luck".

Hyo made use of the Info-point's newsstand and Hikaraku's library to read up on Ukibashi Awano. Something in the heiress's story, however unrelated it seemed, was important. The spider's claw touch of the hellmakers' en when the Wavewalker had shown Hyo Ukibashi Awano's picture had told her as much.

Heiress to the Ukibashi Shinshu Company, the biggest of Onogoro's 'Big Three' breweries. Graduate of both the university on Onogoro and another somewhere in the Harbourlakes. Licensed solarcrane pilot, who'd twice rescued Onogoro fishermen from the Jade Sea.

On New Year's Eve, Ukibashi Awano had been kidnapped from the annual Ukibashi New Year Party, taken out to sea and ransomed for "shinshu's secret recipe" by an unknown group. Speculation and sensation had followed her since. The idea that shinshu had a secret recipe, which Onogoro was withholding from the "outside", wasn't uncommon. Hyo's mother Hatsu had thought it more plausible than Onogoro's gods producing just the right, perfectly blessed rain.

"But the Ukibashis refused to hand the recipe over," Hyo told Mansaku, when they reconvened at the Infopoint for lunch. He'd had no luck getting through to Koushiro that morning. "Either there really isn't a secret recipe, or..."

"Ukibashi Awano's family chose the shinshu monopoly over her," Mansaku filled in. "Brutal. Then what happened?"

Then Awano, miraculously, escaped her captors.

The Wavewalker found her swimming back to shore, terrified from her ordeal but free. A day later, the coastguard found an empty fishing boat drifting in Onogoro waters. Awano identified it as her captors' vessel but, of its crew, there was no sign. Rumours abounded that early witnesses had seen blood on the towed-in boat, but these were quickly retracted and apologized for. No retraction, however, could succeed in dampening Onogoro's appetite for mystery.

Everyone was still asking how it was that Ukibashi Awano had escaped. She had given one interview two months later, but it had only given the gossipers more fat to chew on.

"The Wavewalker helped me escape," she'd said. "He sent me a gift on the waves. Even though I was beyond the reach of his powers, beyond Onogoro's sea borders, the

Wavewalker was still my guardian god. Where he couldn't save me, he gave me the means to save myself."

What that gift was, however, Awano refused to say.

The best the weeklies had cobbled together was that it had something to do with her left eye, which on her return had burned phosphorescent blue, and that, ever since her return, the Wavewalker's shrines had been delivering medicinal pills to the Ukibashi residence. Perhaps, the articles whispered, such a divine gift had been too much for an ordinary human body to bear.

All that was very well, but nothing explained why a five-month-old kidnapping case would have any connection to Jun's death on the Shin-Kaguraza Bridge. Hyo left the library as it closed, feeling over-informed and underequipped to understand any of it.

When she returned to the Info-point, Hyo saw Ikushima coming out of the Ujigami's phone box and had an idea. Traditionally, "Ujigami" was the title for a god who protected a clan or community within a bounded territory, but their role had evolved on Onogoro. "Protection" now meant "information", and the Ujigami had become the district residents' source for information on-demand.

All they had to do was call her on the Info-point's green phone.

It was unlikely that Hyo could just ring up the Ujigami to ask for the truth behind Ukibashi Awano's eye, otherwise countless others would have already done it, but she went to Ikushima anyway.

"How does calling the Ujigami-sama work?" Hyo asked her. "Say I wanted to know about the truth of Ukibashi Awano's eye, or Kikugawa Kichizuru's bad luck, could she tell me about those things?"

"Oh, no, dear. The Ujigami-sama only gives *local* information, about the local community's businesses and residents – and nothing private." Ikushima, to her credit, didn't laugh at Hyo's obvious disappointment, but did look as if she could spit out a frog. "She answers simple questions, like the wheres and the whos, and when events are happening, that's all. And always for a price! A small donation, or an offer of services. Or secrets, of course. Human secrets are like honey to gods."

Hyo pricked her ears. "Did you say she gives out ... information about local residents?"

"That's right. *For* local residents, mind. If you're not registered at an address here yet, you might not qualify for the normal rates." Ikushima propped her chin on her elbow and smiled at Hyo over the black-sugar throat candies at the till. "But sometimes the Ujigami-sama's in a generous mood even to non-residents, and she *might* offer you the resident's rate. Or she could double it, and add a month's basic rice portion, or a limb. Want to try your luck?"

"Can I know the price first then back out?"

"Sure – ask me what you need, and I'll check today's prices for you."

Hyo chewed her tongue, then took a discarded receipt and wrote the "summer" and unusual "畢" she'd seen on the envelope from Jun. She showed it to Ikushima. "I want to know where I can find a god called Natsuami."

The green phone rang.

Ikushima's eyebrows leapt to her hairline. "That's for you."

Hyo went to the phone box, closed the door behind her and picked up the phone. Yellowish smoke was issuing from the handset.

The Ujigami spoke: "Hakai Hyo."

"Yes, Ujigami-sama?"

"I'm required to inform you that any searches for 'Natsuami' or 'Ryouen Natsuami' at the Info-points result in an alert being delivered to certain interested parties. And, er … give me a moment, I'm reading off a card…" There's a pause, some shuffling. "Basically, you've been warned, hellmaker. Don't do it again."

Hyo changed ears. The handset was like a hot rock. "But I didn't even ask you anything!"

"Listen, the alert's gone. It's meant to make you feel stressed enough to question your life choices and think twice about prying where you shouldn't. Call it tough love."

"Right. Thanks a bunch."

"Don't mention it." Smoke jetted out of the earpiece, acrid with sulphur. "Do me a favour, Hakai Hyo, and keep out of my phone boxes, will you? You're making me itch just talking to you, with all that hellmaker unluck and taint and malevolent energy *stickinesses*."

The Ujigami hung up. Hyo left the phone box feeling like she'd stuck her face over a firepit, cheeks too warm and forehead sweaty.

"Huh, she must've liked you. You've got your ears still," said Ikushima. Hyo shot her a look. Ikushima handed Hyo a form. "Sign *here* to acknowledge that the Ujigami of Hikaraku, Sayo'no'me the Mothmouth, has warned you to back off, and *here* to say you've understood."

Hyo took the form glumly. "Does this happen often?"

"Not in Hikaraku. Your Natsuami must've paid for the extra privacy. Or someone has."

And now an alert had been sent, and someone, maybe Natsuami, would know that Hyo had wanted to ask the Hikaraku Ujigami about him.

But wait... *Stay calm and think, Hyo.*

What the Ujigami had said was meant to rattle her, but Hyo hadn't lost anything – she'd gained.

Ryouen Natsuami. It might've been a slip of the tongue, but Hyo now had his full earthly name. She'd confirmed that Natsuami lived in Hikaraku. She'd learnt that Natsuami, or someone related, wanted to know when people were looking for him, and was actively discouraging it.

Hyo returned the form to Ikushima with a smile.

The second day at the Info-point, Hyo went with Mansaku to the Shin-Kaguraza Theatre.

Upon approaching the building, Hyo narrowed her eyes. The sutra-copying hadn't fixed the seal as much as she'd liked, so she could still see unluck floating in the air. If unlucky Koushiro was at the Shin-Kaguraza, she'd expect to see a silvery pall of unluck coiled tightly about the theatre floors, but it wasn't there.

Like Mansaku had described of the previous day, there were reporters loitering around the front of the Shin-Kaguraza, although their numbers had thinned. They'd been replaced by a small army of shrine attendants and Oblivionist priests, their haoris emblazoned with the crests of various shrines and temples, who were shaking bells, chanting sutras and sticking talismans on the theatre doors.

"If you're looking for Kichizuru again," said the box office assistant, when Mansaku approached, "he's out."

Mansaku nodded. "Out is healthy. Good for him. When will he be back?"

The assistant flicked his fingers at them. "'He's out' is all outsiders are getting."

They moved off together. Hyo and Mansaku were at the edge of the plaza when a voice stopped them.

It was the old woman who'd had the reporters chased off the steps, and given Hyo and Mansaku their chance to get away from Todomegawa.

"Kichizuru-san is at a funeral today," she said. "For those killed by curses, they tend to be done quickly and quietly. I think you might have an idea as to whose funeral it is?"

Hyo nodded numbly. Mansaku's hand curled around her wrist. *Jun's.*

A long ruler was stuck through the old woman's monpe like a sword. She seemed satisfied by their silence. "Kichizuru-san's luck really isn't on his side. I know him, and he's been hoping to see the two of you – Hakai Mansaku and Hyo, isn't it?"

Hyo glanced at Mansaku and nodded. "That's us. How—?"

"You're in Jun-san's reflectographs from the Cultural Expedition. I'm Onoue Ritsu, a robe-folder at the Shin-Kaguraza. Mansaku-san, Kichizuru-san would like to know more about the stellaroids you left at the box office. They've deeply troubled him. Hyo-san, there is something he'd like to give you. Where can I find you two again?"

"Here." Hyo found one of their old business cards from Koura in her waist-pouch. She scrawled the address of the apartment that'd be their new home from the following day. "We'll be here."

Ritsu took the card in both hands and read it, lips moving silently. "I'll come by soon."

Then she brushed past them both and strode out into the plaza, raising a megaphone. "Anybody here from the press, waiting for gossip like the pigeons wait for vomit on Skyday evenings, you can CLEAR OFF!"

EIGHT

New residents will be greeted by their hancho – your local civic unit leader. These volunteers are there to keep you on the straight and narrow in your local neighbourhood.

From "So You've Made It to
Onogoro, Last Home of Ukoku's
Gods – Congratulations!"

After the usual gift-giving and meeting and greeting their neighbours, the first thing Hyo and Mansaku did on settling into the "probably haunted" apartment was burn incense for Jun. The only pictures they had of him were the stellaroids showing his deterioration under the curse, but that afternoon, in a second-hand bookshop, Hyo chanced upon a copy of *Hikaraku Bara Bara Case Files 7: The Human Sideboard.*

Jun had loved the novel. He'd brought it to Koura on the Cultural Expedition and terrified (delighted) the children with dramatic readings from it. He'd kept it always close like a precious keepsake.

"What's wrong?" asked Mansaku, when he found Hyo staring at the prologue's final passage.

"... *and so ended another strange tale in the lanterned streets of Hikaraku where dreams come to life and their dreamers die.*"

Hyo had seen those very lines the other day, on a page she'd used to wipe her face.

She remembered Jun saying that every *Bara Bara Case File* began with the same prologue. It was a series trademark. "Nothing."

They set their incense bowl on their makeshift altar. A thought crossed Hyo's mind that they were being distracted, that following the pull of the hellmakers' en for Jun was an excuse to forget the demon's task for them, and forget hitodenashi on Onogoro.

But Hyo was a hellmaker. Where the hellmakers' en drew her, she had no choice but to go.

"*Gomen kudasai!*" The front door flew open, and two women in orange armbands stepped into the shoe-space. Hyo and Mansaku were just finishing their breakfast. The taller of the two women broke into a wide, sunny smile. "Welcome to Hikaraku Iris Hill!"

"Oh, no, it's an extrovert," said Hyo under her breath, earning a look from Mansaku.

"Hakai Hyo and Mansaku, is it?" The taller one was already tying back her sleeves for work, showing the pot-bellied tattoo of a wind god on her forearm. "I'm Nagakumo Masu! I'm your hancho, of the Sixteen-Nineteen-Nine Han."

"Our ... han?"

"Your local community squad. We do neighbourhood clean-ups, organize for festivals, do our bit in the allotments, that sort of thing. Let's get you two settled in quick." Nagakumo snapped her fingers. "Tsuda, where's their welcome rice portion?"

The second woman pulled a loaded trolley into the porch. Bewildered, Hyo and Mansaku leapt up to help.

Sacks of brown rice, jars of miso, nukadoko for rice bran pickling, a box of eggs, a doorstopper wedge of tuna and a bag of dried persimmons quickly filled the kitchen. Hyo found a "welcome pack" crammed into her hand, including a han rota chart, a pocket telescope, emergency torch, three kerchiefs, a protection talisman from the Ujigami and half a dozen paper forms.

"Now, let's get the dark stuff out of the way." Nagakumo sat down cross-legged. "Your landlord tells me you're going to be running a kind of private diviner business here."

"Hellmaking," said Hyo straightforwardly.

"That's a new one. Let me tell you a bit about me and my han." Nagakumo looked from Hyo to Mansaku. "Specifics aside, I'm sensitive to ghosts and taint on humans, and everyone assigned to my han has a job or lifestyle that's likely to attract ghosts or gather taint to this tower." Tsuda finished putting things away in the kitchen. Nagakumo gave her a thumbs up. "Alongside the usual han duties, we've an extra one. We keep an eye on each other to make sure our taint levels and area ghost numbers stay low, so that we don't become nuisances for our neighbours. That sound all right with you two?"

"Sounds about what we'd expect," Mansaku answered for both of them. He handed back his completed forms for the han membership. "Good to know we'll be watched."

"It's a mutual watching. Friendly and neighbourly. And I don't think you'll be too much trouble. You wouldn't be in this apartment if you weren't spiritually sensitive enough to recognize that this 'property with history' wasn't actually haunted. No, it's the people who attract ghosts and don't notice who can be a handful." Nagakumo pointed to the front door. "Although I'm guessing that one over there has been a bit quiet for even you two to spot, huh?"

Hyo almost dropped her form. "Which one?"

"Him looking in through the door. He's a fairly fresh ghost. An unanchored drifter. Seems harmless." Nagakumo cocked her head, listening to something only she could hear. "Although he says something about a letter to get to his brother? Ring any bells?"

Hyo jumped to her feet, but just as she'd stepped into her boots, Nagakumo called out, "He's gone. Sorry, that tends to happen when I've passed on the message they want heard."

"Gone, as in joubutsu gone, or just…?"

"Just drifted on." Nagakumo untied her sleeves. "He might come back, but you can't force 'em. I think he wanted to see you two settling in. And check in on his letter." She looked at the two of them slyly. "I might come by and see if you've sorted that out by the end of next week."

Hyo pulled a face. "You don't have to."

"Oh, I do. Like I said, we han members watch each other." Nagakumo waggled her eyebrows. "You might turn out to be a foreign agent, you know? Someone looking to steal shinshu's 'secret recipe' to sell to the outside. Look at Ukibashi Awano's kidnapping. Help from the inside would've made it way easier to pull off." She took Hyo's completed form. "We've all been a bit on edge after that, so it's nothing personal to the two of you."

As new members of Nagakumo's taint-prone han, they were taken on a tour of all the local shrines and temples, Nagakumo pointing out malevolent energy sinks, power spots and ghost hang-outs, and ending at the Hikaraku branch of the Onmyoryo. It was an unimpressive turret jutting off the neighbouring tower, its entrance emblazoned with the five-point star of its bellflower crest. Hyo combed her hair hastily over her face but Todomegawa did not gallop out on Buru-chan to drag her inside for "tea".

The ghost at their door did not reappear.

Hyo had never been afraid of ghosts. The most she'd seen in Koura had been a shoal of ghost lights flitting between the houses, but the mountains had always been a little bit haunted.

When they returned to the apartment, Hyo set a ghost detection talisman over the doorway. Just in case.

"You want to be haunted or something?" Nagakumo laughed, as Hyo smoothed down the paper.

"Yes," said Hyo stonily.

"You're a funny one." Nagakumo's face softened. "I'll show you the allotments then leave you be. The view's nice up there."

The rule in Onogoro, according to Nagakumo, was that every citizen who could had to offer time to the allotments or rice. Onogoro's assembly said it was to keep reliance on imported foods lower, so that outside nations couldn't barter Onogoro's food security for cheaper shinshu.

"The reality though, it's probably just another way for us to keep eyes on each other. It forces us to come out and show our faces," Nagakumo explained. She waved at another han, their members dressed in blue noragi, gloved to their elbows and busy tying stems and plucking away low-growing aubergine buds. "The rest of the world has its problems – its politics, its wars, the hitodenashi – but those aren't our problems. They can't hurt us. What will hurt Onogoro most will come from inside, so that's what we've got to focus on: each other, so that nobody falls, human or god."

The sun warmed Hyo's back. She smelled turned earth and insect-repelling incense. "You don't think hitodenashi's your problem?"

Nagakumo shrugged. "On Onogoro, why would it be? It's near impossible to grow here. I should know. I've met people who've tried."

Hyo stiffened. "You have?"

"We get the occasional bright spark. Don't look so alarmed. Everyone knows this. They'd have heard that the humans who eat hitodenashi pear become immortal and gain abilities not even the gods have. Special powers that'll help them attain their deepest desires. The part where 'immortal' and 'special powers' makes that human a demon doesn't figure in their maths." Nagakumo raised her hand in greeting to another person across the beds. "They'll sail out to the sea border, pick up a bag full of seeds where the gods can't reach them to stop them, then come back. It's kind of an open secret. Nothing happens, obviously. Trace shinshu in the water, soil and air makes any little hitodenashi seedling they might get to germinate shrivel up and die."

"But hitodenashi doesn't *need* water and soil to grow, or even light!" Hyo snapped. "It's not like other plants, because it *isn't* one. It's a curse that *looks* like one. It..." Mansaku touched her gently on the elbow. Hyo broke off, feeling out of breath, her chest tight. Nagakumo was eyeing her with a sly look of interest. "Fine. Nobody's managed it yet. As far as you know."

"I know about enough." Nagakumo crouched by a low trough with a lid and opened it. "Oh, look, we've got some worms to sow here. Want to give me a hand and just think about some *real* plants for a bit?"

And before Hyo's thoughts could spiral off into her cold memories of hitodenashi, she and Mansaku both had a scope in one hand and a bucket of earthworms in the other, and a grudging respect for Nagakumo's perceptiveness.

The smells of earth and greens were vibrant and comfortingly familiar. The white swaying globes of the onion flowers, the glossy leaves of the yuzu trees with their hidden thumb-long claws, all could have been sights from home. Their old home.

If Hyo closed her eyes, she could, for a moment, forget about ghosts, pears and islanders.

Hitodenashi wasn't really a plant. It was a curse with a life of its own, one that could cast itself. Spreading by airborne needle-spores or by the teeth-seeds of its pears, hitodenashi needed only two things: human bodies and a bed in which to root and anchor.

Then, sometimes slowly,
sometimes quickly,
on the rare occasion
in an instant so quick
that the curse killed
its host, hitodenashi
would armour their
human hosts in bark
and turn them into a
mockery of trees.
They'd be blessed with
a tree's long life, if not
eternal one.

They'd blossom from branches that had burst from the crowns of their heads, and then be laden with fruit not long after
– the infamous "pears" – the fruits which were designed to tempt humans into demon-hood.

On Onogoro, if grown somewhere dark, where no one was looking, hidden from the gods and shielded from shinshu vapours, there was no reason hitodenashi couldn't be cultivated. It'd be difficult but not impossible.

Hyo tipped the last of the worms into a tray of new soil, then stood and stretched. Around her, the timber and ceramic skyscrapers soared up to a clear blue sky.

"What do you think?" she said, when Mansaku joined her. "About what Nagakumo said."

He did her the favour of actually thinking about it. "People here live pretty much on top of each other. Nagakumo's probably right. She'd hear about hitodenashi if it was here. But if Onogoro people really kept an eye on each other like she says, what happened with Jun? Except for the Bridgeburner, he was dealing with that curse on his own." Mansaku put away his scope in the tool cupboard, and looked to where Nagakumo chatted with the other Iris Hill residents by the railings. "Maybe they're too worried about bad en to *really* catch the people falling out of the network."

"Hyo-chan! Mansaku-kun!" Nagakumo beckoned them. "Come over here and see this."

The crowd at the railings was looking down between the buildings and pointing at a sleek white flightcraft parked by the Shin-Kaguraza Theatre's plaza, its wings folded elegantly over its body.

Nagakumo passed her telescope to Hyo. "That's

Ukibashi Awano's solarcrane down there. Look at that fancy thing! Damn, I'd love to fly it."

The kidnapped heiress's flightcraft? Hyo took the eyepiece and adjusted it. "What's Awano doing here?"

"She probably came to cut ties with Kichizuru. She's basically his patron. The Ukibashi Shinshu Company is sponsoring his shows this season, but bad luck like Kichizuru's would be hell if it spread to the company by association." Nagakumo clicked her tongue. "Best to cut en with him now before it hurts Awano or them."

"Is Awano a shin-kagura fan?" Mansaku asked.

"The Wavewalker is – and the Shin-Kaguraza is the Wavewalker's favourite theatre, and Ukibashi Awano's his favourite human. He's her pet god," Nagakumo said with glee. "The story goes that Awano found him near-dissipated when she was a kid and raised him up to be the Ukibashis' guardian. He was a sad little god from the north-west who couldn't bring down enough of his followers to Onogoro before the war's end. Now he's a Pillar God, with the Ukibashis' wealth behind him, and the Ukibashis have built him into their whole company myth. For how the gods chose them to make shinshu for the world."

A group emerged from the theatre doors. Hyo focused the telescope. Dressed in dark haoris and repelling the odd reporter and cameraman like water droplets from leaves, thick-set figures huddled about a young woman in silver.

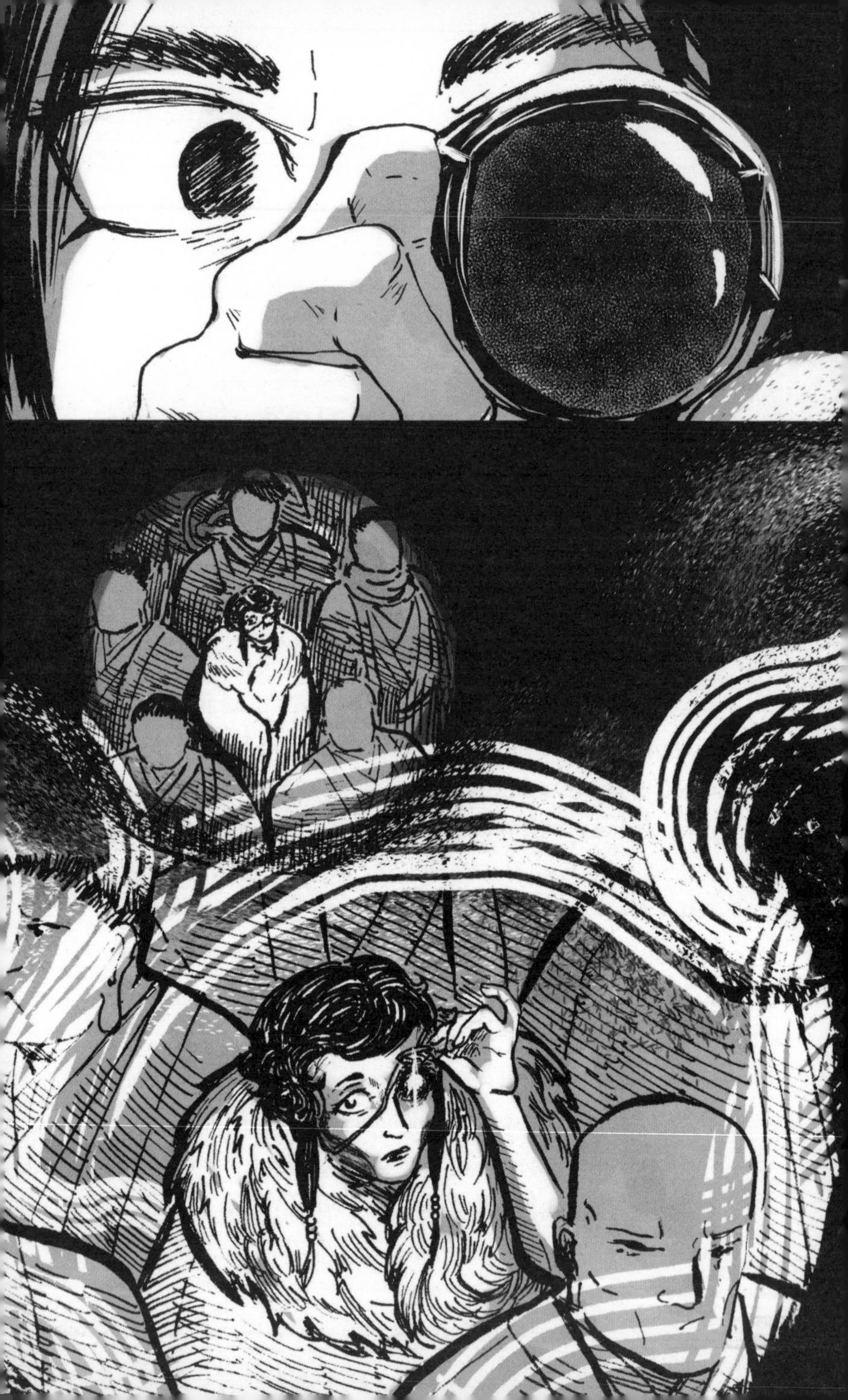

Ukibashi Awano. She looked much like her reflectograph in the article. Her left eye, the object of so much speculation, was covered in a scallop-shaped eyepatch. She laughed at something an aide said, then turned her face up to catch the sunlight.

Impossibly, her gaze, from fifteen floors below, seemed to catch Hyo's. Ukibashi Awano flinched, blinked, looked straight up into the telescope with something like confusion, then shyly lifted a corner of her eyepatch.

Cool blue glowed beneath it, and briefly Hyo was transparent. The sea of her had been exposed to its ocean floor and the sand sifted through, and just when the feeling was almost too much to bear, Ukibashi Awano lowered her eyepatch and ducked her head to enter the solarcrane.

Mansaku tugged the back of Hyo's belt, pulling her back from the rail. "O'Hyo? You all right?"

Hyo handed the telescope back to Nagakumo. "That eye..."

"It's something, isn't it? With that jellyfish glow?" Nagakumo said, only too happy to gossip. "And whatever it does that got her away from her kidnappers is a secret between just her and the Wavewalker."

"Did you hear about the *Weekly Bunyo* writer who wrote that piece the other day?" said one of the residents in low tones. "Apparently he woke up yesterday with crab pincers instead of hands."

"No!" Nagakumo gasped, turning to the newcomer. "Really?

"They'll be cursed like that until the next full moon." The resident smiled, flashing sea-green teeth behind the insect mesh hanging from the brim of their straw hat. "Let's see them try to write their bottom-feeding drivel like *that*."

Nagakumo turned to spread the new gossip, whilst Hyo kept her eyes on the resident. Or, rather, the Wavewalker.

"Hello, little darling," said the god. "Do you remember what I said three days ago?"

Hyo thought back to it. "You said 'give it three days', about my en with Natsuami."

"Ah. So it hasn't faded." The Wavewalker's smile widened. "Usually, a human would've forgotten his name by now. Well, well, you *do* have an en with him."

"Care to explain more or are we keeping things cryptic for fun?" Mansaku broke in from the side.

The Wavewalker laughed and disappeared, and Hyo shuddered, suddenly cold despite the sun.

NINE

代理人

It's common for dancers, actors and anyone on the altar of a stage to take on multiple names – stage names, nicknames – to protect themselves and their loved ones, and evade the gods who might think to put them in their place.

NOE,
Twenty-First Hellmaker

A comb was running through Hyo's hair, over and over, teeth teasing apart tangles as if raking through ashes.

"To know the shape of someone's hell, just shine a light on their most-feared truth."

That was Mum's voice. Or was it? There was the rasp of a long tongue covered in steel needles. Maybe the eyes and fangs burned gold, and maybe the hands holding the comb had golden claws.

"It'll be there in the truth's shadow."

There's a ghost at your shoulder,
It stands at your hair
And it asks you to name it
And tell it it's there.

"I dreamt of Mum last night."

Mansaku paused his singing, hand stilling in clouded rice water. "And I dreamt of happy things, like ducklings and world peace."

"Liar."

"Big brother is making breakfast, so let big brother have his lie." Mansaku kept his back to Hyo. Rare for him, he'd tied up his hair for chores, baring his neck where the stark black lines of a tattoo drew a seal crowded with calligraphy: Kiriyuki's seal, still as dark as when their mother, Hatsu, had inked it on him. "What was the dream?"

The Hakai sons weren't born with their weapons.

Hatsu had needed to transfer Kiriyuki out of Hyo's uncle to lock it into Mansaku. She'd had to do it before Hyo's uncle died from Kiriyuki eating at his spirit and took the nagigama with him.

In a way, it made Mansaku part-ghost, and he was sensitive to ghosts, spirit and dream in a way Hyo wasn't.

The talisman over the doorway was unchanged. No ghost had come by during the night.

Hyo said, "I let her comb my hair like a good daughter."

"Oh, that's scary, being a good daughter," Mansaku said dryly. He swept his hand over a length of spring onions and they crumbled instantly into a finely chopped pile. "Dreams are different here from in Koura."

"How so?"

"The spiritual plane's busy." Mansaku set the spring onions aside in a sieve. "I've felt things watching. Mostly they just swing close, take a look at us then leave, but some have tried the metaphorical door to your dreams and mine. It's the gods. They're nosy."

"I didn't feel anything," Hyo said. But the shadows of her dreams were already dissolving against the daylight. She couldn't be sure. "Are you all right? You're up early."

"I'm fine. Had a couple of loud knocks, but that's about it." He grinned but sobered quickly. "Just be careful. These gods get their power through musuhi. Through ties with humans. They *want* to connect with us. Dreams are another chance for it." He set the rice on the stove and wiped his hands. "And I can't defend you in dreams. Wait, O'Hyo, are you going out now?"

"I had an idea."

"It's not even six; it's too early for ideas."

"And you're stress-cooking before six because the gods kept you awake in the night." Hyo tightened her monpe hems and laced her boots over them. She didn't want to sit around thinking about shoals of gods drifting through the spiritual plane, eying up her dreams for occupying. "I think I've figured out how to make a privacy talisman against the gods."

At sunrise, Hikaraku's residents were mostly sleeping. A couple of windturtles wobbled at their mooring points, hydrogen veins pumping them full to flotation to offload goods and supplies. The hellmakers' seal on Hyo's palms was three fingers faded. Unluck hovered between buildings in broad, smoky bands, drawn to align with the north-east to south-west flow of jaki, malevolent energy, across Onogoro.

The day before, Nagakumo's tour had taken them past the Shin-Kaguraza Bridge. It had been cordoned off for repairs, and the crater left by Todomegawa's arrival was still there. What had caught Hyo's eye was the Onmyoryo's talisman that had been pasted to the cordon. The talisman was designed to shut out things in the spiritual plane – humans, but mainly ghosts and gods. It could help Hyo invent her own talisman for keeping the gods out of her and Mansaku's home and dreams.

There was someone already on the Shin-Kaguraza Bridge. They stood where Jun had died. Their face was hidden in a hooded cape the blue of morning shadows.

They were swathed in billowing folds of unluck, the dark light of the particles clinging so thickly to their form that Hyo could barely see their shape.

"Hey!" Hyo called out. They looked up sharply.

Oh, shit. She hadn't planned on what to say next. "I'm Hakai Hyo, a friend of Jun's! Who are you?" They said nothing. On impulse, she added, "Koushiro, is that you?!"

They startled, then raised their hand in response. *Yes.*

Jun's brother, stage name Kikugawa Kichizuru. Hyo looked around them. There were no reporters, as far as she could tell, but as she hesitated, he pointed – at her? No, at something behind her – and jumped.

Light as a sparrow, he landed on the bridge's narrow handrail. The movement was graceful, easy. He sped away down the rail's length with the barest clatter of geta, skirting around the rope cordon to jump off at the other end and vanish into the shadows.

Hyo spun round, in time to see a tall shadow disappearing around a corner. By the time she reached it, there was no one there. The walkway was empty.

But snagged on the branches of a potted sakaki tree were several strands of extraordinarily long hair.

"We've got him, Mansaku." Hyo laid flat a blank paper doll on the table and ground the nub of white ink into the tray. "He thinks he can get away from us now, but let's see him try."

"How about finishing breakfast first?" Mansaku said, returning from the kitchen with rice and a bowl of clear seaweed soup, made fragrant with mizuna and spring onions.

結界使用中!!

"Almost done." Into the ink, Hyo tipped the ashes of the hairs. She'd burned them in the entrance with the door open, and Mrs Meguro, their teahouse neighbour and the landlord's wife, had raised her eyebrows at her. Hyo took up the brush she'd brought from Koura, swept its familiar tip through where the ink was the right consistency, and wrote the charm down the doll's front. "There."

Hyo breathed into it, giving the doll a portion of her spirit. The charm trapped and contained her spirit in the lines of its calligraphy, and the newly crafted shikigami stirred.

Peeling upright from her palm, it stood, balancing on the paper edges of its feet. It looked Hyo's way. She said, "You know what to do."

It leapt down and scampered past Mansaku towards the door, where it slipped out through the crack. Hairs, nail clippings, teeth – all of them held some signature of spirit that tied them back to the person who'd shed them. The shikigami would be able to use Natsuami's signature in the ashes of his hairs to find him, then return to Hyo when it had done so.

"Maybe they're hairs from Buru-chan's tail," Mansaku said, tucking into his rice. "It'll come back to its cruel mistress reporting where to find the butt of a ghost-horse." When Hyo ignored him to sip at her soup, he added, "I'll take that back. You're not cruel. That's not even something to joke about. Hatsu was cruel."

"I'm sorry I held on to that piece of her coat," Hyo said. Mansaku's expression when she'd taken it from her pouch for Jun had been as if ice water had been thrown at his face.

Mansaku gave her a long look, then laughed.

"It's fine," he said. "It made me think that, if I died young and suddenly, you might carry around a piece of me too, even if everyone else around us said I wasn't worth it."

"No one would say that." Hyo paused, a question coming to mind that she hadn't asked before. "Mansaku, when did you stop hating me?"

He lowered his bowl, thinking. "I don't think I ever did. There was a long time I hated who I thought you'd turn out to be."

A clear knocking sounded at the door. A figure could be seen through the windows with a kerchief folded over their face. Hyo went to open it as Mansaku cleared away their food.

It was Ritsu, the robe-folder from the theatre. "Good day to you, Hyo-san. Is now a good time?"

"Ritsu-san." Hyo dipped her head in greeting. "Please come in."

"This is for you," Ritsu said, as soon as Hyo and Mansaku were both sitting opposite her. Declining Mansaku's offer of tea, she held out a small paper packet with both hands. "Kichizuru-san wanted to thank you for the kindness you showed his brother on the bridge, for covering his eyes. This is a gift from him."

Hyo took the packet, checked it out of habit for curse-work and opened it. Inside was a silk ribbon the colour of yellow mountain rose, about the width of Hyo's palm. When she took it out, the ribbon flowed between her fingers like water. "It's ... very fine."

Ritsu reached over the table, closing Hyo's hand over the ribbon. "Don't think about it too much. Just accept it."

Hyo thanked her inadequately and Ritsu turned to Mansaku. "Those stellaroids of Jun-san, how did you come by them? What do you – both of you – know of the curse that took his life?"

Hyo and Mansaku shared a look, then Mansaku sat forward and recounted their first night on Onogoro, their meeting with Todomegawa and their discovery of the stellaroids on Jun's shrine shelf.

"We were hoping that Koushiro could tell us what was going on with Jun," he finished.

Ritsu shook her head. "The first any of us heard about Jun-san's curse was when his curse-mediator came looking for him the night before he died."

"Do you know when Koushiro last saw Jun-san?" asked Hyo.

"It was in Fourthmonth, just before we noticed that Kichizuru-san's luck had soured. Kikugawa Troupe Leader Matsubei then asked Jun-san to stay away from the theatre for his own safety." Ritsu closed her eyes in thought. "Bad luck is known to spread across strong ens. As Kichizuru-san's last remaining blood family, Jun-san was vulnerable. We all knew that if anything were to happen to Jun-san because of his luck, Kichizuru-san would have been..." The corners of her mouth turned down. "Well, Kichizuru-san now *is* ... very distracted."

"How is Koushiro?" Mansaku asked quietly.

"He's the best shin-kagura performer of his generation. He knows how to make others *feel* when he's upset," Ritsu said with bleak pride. "It doesn't help that all the performances have been cancelled now. That Ukibashi girl insisted. All bar the one last performance that'll be on Jun-san's birthday – and that Kichizuru-san had to *beg* for on his knees – and he isn't receiving any visitors any more, except the ones he needs to do his job."

Mansaku blew out his cheeks. "Damn."

"If those stellaroids of Jun-san are genuine, as you say –" Ritsu's gaze was a challenge, boring into both Hyo and Mansaku – "then Jun-san was cursed before Kichizuru-san's luck rotted. Kichizuru-san *didn't* ultimately cause Jun-san's death by placing him in an unlucky situation with the wrong god at the wrong time."

Hyo replied with a solemn nod. "That's what we think."

"What makes you say a god cursed Jun and not a human, Ritsu-san?" Mansaku asked.

"You saw the shrine shelf in his home. Jun-san was watched over by the Paddywatcher, the Great Snake of the Grain. If he was cursed by a human, she could have stepped in and ended it, but his curse continued. Except for the curse-mediators, the gods don't interfere when other gods curse their followers. They don't want that sort of in-fighting. Hyo-san, this card you gave me." The Hakai hellmaker business card appeared from a pocket on Ritsu's apron. "Am I right in understanding that it says you can inflict bad luck upon people?"

"It's more about unluck but..." Ritsu squinted, confusion settling in, so Hyo went for the simplest answer. "Yes, it's true."

"Then you're an expert in bad luck?"

"You could say that."

"Then would you meet with Kichizuru-san and see what's wrong with him?" Ritsu said in a rush. "Could you tell us why he's so unlucky? Could you help him?"

Hyo winced. She was meant to be a source of misfortune. The hellmakers' curse would never allow her to directly pull unluck away from someone.

"All the major gods agree with the Wavewalker that Kichizuru-san isn't cursed," Ritsu continued, apparently taking Hyo's silence for reluctance. "They say that the bad luck has simply *naturally* gathered on him – that he's attracted it, somehow."

"So, they're saying that Koushiro's unlucky enough

to be ... very unlucky?" said Mansaku, stroking a non-existent beard. "Huh."

"If you can't actually do anything about his bad luck, that's no trouble," Ritsu went on tentatively. "You are quite young. I'd understand if you didn't want any en with Kichizuru-san. The extent of his bad luck *is* frightening—"

"I didn't say I couldn't do anything about his unluck and it doesn't frighten me," Hyo said sharply, then regretted it when Ritsu shrank away, a hollow hopelessness draining her features.

Back in Koura, Hatsu had owned an enormous paulownia wood puzzle box, adapted from a chest of drawers. Without locks and keys, its parts had opened up only after a secret combination of touches to the design on its sides to move the intricate karakuri mechanism within.

"*Puzzle boxes and people are the same*," Hatsu had said, whilst extracting Hyo's fingers from another booby trap. "*The right pressures in the right places in the right order are all you need to unlock them. If you want their secret, everyone has their mechanism.*"

Ritsu was weary, nervous, afraid, and the hellmakers' en was pulling the web taut, signalling to Hyo that this old robe-folder was a *chance*.

"I'm not frightened of Koushiro's luck," Hyo repeated in gentler tones, then continued, "I'll only know if I can help him if I meet him."

Breathing in slowly, Ritsu let out a low, uneasy laugh. "He won't meet you without proof of your skills, even as Jun-san's friend. We've made him meet too many diviners since this started, who've turned out to be frauds and the worst kinds of people."

"If proof is a problem –" Hyo turned the Hakai family business card around on the table, so that it faced Ritsu again – "you're welcome to test me."

Ritsu looked up from the card. "What are you offering?"

"Don't you have any enemies you'd like to see disappear, if only for a day?" Hyo leant forward. "From outside your theatre?"

Ritsu sat up with a jolt. She fell silent, contemplating both Hyo and Mansaku with an expression that could have been cut from stone.

"An unlucky day for every one of those filthy leeches from the weeklies on the theatre doorstep," Ritsu said at length. "How much would that cost me?"

Hyo brought up Ritsu's candle in her eye. Her flame of life was a short thick candle with a steady, healthy fire, but under Hyo's eyes, as if sensing her gaze, the flame wavered. "One week of your lifespan per leech."

"My *lifespan*?!"

"Or ten thousand tallers each, and an object of value to you – something you've kept close for many years, that's absorbed your love and life." Hyo watched her words sink in. "To curse them with a day's mild unluck. Or half a day of intense unluck. Your choice."

Ritsu raised a hand to where the protective talismans were stitched to her vest, then gripped the cloth tight. "Six of them. For a day, of the mild stuff. Come to the box office in three days – on the twenty-fourth, after ten. I'll leave your payment there for you."

"I'll need the names of the six and reflectographs of their faces."

"Their birth names?"

"Or the names they know themselves by." Hyo took the pad of paper and stub of a pencil Mansaku handed to her. She wrote out the order. "Could you sign here, please? With your full name?"

Ritsu shivered. She rubbed the spot over her chest where Hyo had looked at her flame of life and measured its remaining years. Then she took up the pencil. "How will I know when you've done your work?"

"You'll know. Would this be enough proof of my skills for Koushiro? For us to meet?"

"It would. Then once you think 'I know'," Ritsu echoed Hyo dryly, "come by the Shin-Kaguraza second floor's west side. Any day between six in the morning and two in the afternoon, and ask for me at the Plum Door. I'll take you to Kichizuru-san."

She wrote out her name and gave the order to Hyo.

TEN

縁切りの神様

Getting a divorce? Leaving your job? Removing those polyps? Then why not consult an en-giri god? These righteous fate-cutters will see that rotten en cut as cleanly and painlessly as possible – although who keeps the dog is down to you!

From "Don't Worry, They Can't Kill You Unless You Ask for It: A Beginner's Guide to Co-existing with the Earthbound Divine"

One day passed.

The shikigami didn't return. Hyo schooled herself to be patient. It was a little paper man roaming Hikaraku on no more power than the spirit Hyo had given it in a single breath. It would take time.

She finished her privacy talisman against the gods, modifying what she'd seen of the Onmyoryo's talisman on the bridge, and stuck it up over the doorway beside the ghost detector. Instantly the air felt lighter, as if Hyo had finally escaped a crowded walkway. The ghost detector remained spotless.

Two days passed. Hyo and Mansaku took matters into their own hands.

Whilst Mansaku tried Natsuami's name around the local shops, Hyo found Natsuami's publisher's address in *The Human Sideboard* and went looking.

She discovered two floors of office space emptied for refurbishment. An open window had let the sparrows in to hop across the desks. The faded notice by the door said the company was undergoing restructuring.

Hyo thought she felt eyes on her, turned quickly, and saw something white slithering out of sight – but that was all.

"I didn't find anything either," Mansaku reported over lunch. He slurped down his soba. "Nobody's heard of Ryouen Natsuami in the shops. They knew his pen name, but nobody remembered seeing anyone like how you described him either. You'd think someone who's basically bespectacled hair with feet would be memorable."

Three days after Ritsu's visit, when they were due at the theatre, Hyo woke to a steady drizzle of blood rain that turned into a haze of nauseatingly mineral fog by the late morning.

"This wasn't forecast for today," Mansaku noted, opening his new "divine-phenomena-proof" umbrella, certified by the Onmyoryo to protect against meat, fireballs and root vegetables, as he stepped out on to an uncovered walkway. "O'Hyo, you should invent an atmospheric taint-detector. We'd make a fortune."

"I'll teach you talisman basics, and you can do it yourself."

They took a convoluted, circuitous route to the Shin-Kaguraza Theatre that led them past Natsuami's notice hut. Hyo peered into its shadows, looking for signs the en-musubi god had been there recently, and saw nothing.

There were fewer reporters skulking around the Shin-Kaguraza steps. The blood rain had put them off, allowing Hyo and Mansaku to reach the box office without hindrance.

The ticket assistant was waiting for them. Spotting them approaching, he put down his phone.

"From Ritsu-san," he said, holding out a blue-grey envelope addressed to "The Hakai Diviners". "Can you really help Kichizuru-san?"

"Depends on what help Kichizuru-san needs," Mansaku replied brightly. "If he needs a haircut, I could do him a stylish short back and sides."

The assistant sniffed doubtfully but said nothing more. Behind him, the box office walls were swathed in talisman slips for warding off bad luck. Many were liver-spotted, like they'd been sprayed in old blood. Hyo put Ritsu's payment carefully away into her waist-pouch.

As Mansaku stopped to haggle for a bundle of dried hawk's talon peppers, Hyo turned over the puzzle pieces she'd gathered following Jun's death.

A slow, creeping curse that had dragged out Jun's fear and suffering as it drained him dry from his eyes.

An en-musubi god who struggled to make ens himself but doomed those he connected with when he did.

The Shin-Kaguraza Theatre – the place Jun had been trying to get to when he died, to deliver one last message to his brother.

The message to Koushiro, to "burn everything".

And Ukibashi Awano, the shinshu heiress.

Or not. Hyo wasn't sure what the hellmakers' en had tried to tell her when she'd locked eyes with Awano across the towers. She might not be directly connected. Maybe she was incidental. Maybe the kidnapping was important, or it could be the Ukibashi Shinshu Company itself.

But every one of these was a piece with an en with Jun's murder, and so with his murderer.

“Whoa, O’Hyo, careful!” Mansaku pulled her back by the collar, just in time to stop Hyo stepping on a white snake that had zigzagged out of a gutter and disappeared into a crack in the wall. “It’s like the one that was in Jun’s letterbox.”

“You need to watch out for those snakes,” said the hawker from whom Mansaku had bought his spices. “Most of them are envoys of the gods. You step on one, it’s Good Reason for a cursing. And I wouldn’t want to give the likes of the Paddywatcher Good Reason ever.”

She hurried away, draped in bunches of chili. “Leave the gods alone and they’ll leave you alone too!”

Hyo huffed. “I *wish* the gods would leave us alone.”

Mansaku nudged her and pointed to their left.

A familiar headless horse stood beside them, swishing a dark tail that trailed green-blue flames.

Fire crackled from its neck, throwing up puffs of sparks.

Mansaku smiled at it. "Long time no see, Buru-chan."

Buru-chan lifted her front leg and gave Mansaku a sideways kick in the shin.

He let out a high-pitched wheeze of pain, then nodded slowly. "Guess we're even now for that cut?"

With a satisfied puff of fire, the headless horse shook out her withers and circled behind them, urging them forward with a cloud of sparks from her neck-stump.

The curved coldness of an invisible scythe's blade swept over Hyo's skin as Mansaku turned to the horse again. "Didn't you learn the first time…?"

"Actually…" Hyo stepped forward, and the headless horse's fire flickered approvingly. "Let's go with it, Mansaku."

"You know where it's taking us, don't you?" he hissed as they walked on, the headless horse herding them from behind. "O'Hyo, we're going straight to the Bridgeburner, and maybe to the Onmyoryo, and then…"

He trailed off as they came back to their home. Outside Mrs Meguro's teashop next door, two people were playing shogi. One, Hyo recognized from the morning as a teashop regular. The other was a figure in pink with a bascinet encasing the entirety of their head.

Hyo's heart climbed to her mouth. In a bascinet like that, Natsuami would be able to hide his face.

But on the crackle of the headless horse's fire, the pink player finished their game with a clack and stood. "I've got you at last!"

Hyo and Mansaku stiffened. That bottled-down air of barely contained irritation was unmistakable.

Todomegawa the Bridgeburner ripped off his bascinet and flung it to the floor.

"You pick that up this instant, young man!" his shogi partner barked, making them all jump. "Throwing objects around willy-nilly! Did no one ever teach you to take care of your things? For shame! Young people!"

Todomegawa paused, muttered, "Excuse me," and stooped to gather up it.

Buru-chan trotted forward, swishing her tail. She vanished with a trail of sparks at Todomegawa's shoulder as he straightened and cleared his throat.

"Hakai Hyo." Todomegawa held up Hyo's paper man, her shikigami charmed with Natsuami's hair ashes. "What's the meaning of this?"

Hyo blinked innocently. "It's just one of my shikigami on an errand. Thank you so much for bringing it back to me."

"There's nothing *just* about it! Not when it's looking for..." Todomegawa's eyes darted sideways and he lowered his voice. "Someone you shouldn't be looking for."

Hyo looked Todomegawa over. The shikigami flailed its tiny arms in his hands. "You seem to know a lot about this 'someone'."

Todomegawa's eyes flashed. "I know *everything* about this 'someone'."

"Really? Perfect."

"I'm sorry?"

"You're exactly the person I need to talk to." Hyo gestured to their flat. Mansaku unlocked the door and swept his hand towards the main room. "Please, come inside."

"Thank you," said Todomegawa, looking bewildered as Mansaku took the bascinet from him and propped it in the entrance corner.

Mansaku went up to the kitchen, calling back, "O'Hyo, I'll do tea."

Todomegawa, somewhat sheepishly, held up a paper bag. "I've, er, brought this for you – as an apology for my behaviour the other day. It's a small thing, but, er ... mackerel narezushi, from Maruyoshi in Hamanoyokocho. They're the best on Onogoro. Be grateful now for my apology. And for the narezushi."

Hyo took the bag, half-expecting it to burst into flames. Todomegawa still seemed to be expecting something more. "Did you come here to threaten us, interrogate us or apologize to us?"

"I have been encouraged to multi-task." Todomegawa went to the table and sat at it straight-backed. He looked around, alert. "You've warded your home to keep out the eyes and ears of the gods!"

"Is there a rule against it?"

"No, but your ward is powerful. I can't even feel the Pillars here." His frown deepened as he spotted the talisman over her doorway. "Who made that?"

"I did."

Todomegawa opened his mouth, then closed it with an air of grudging respect.

Hyo said, "So, where did you find my shikigami?"

Smoked seeped between Todomegawa's teeth. "Where I shouldn't have – and you are *not* getting it back, you will *not* make another one and I am going to see this one incinerated in the Onmyoryo furnace."

"Fine. What's your connection to Ryouen Natsuami?"

Todomegawa choked. "What's *my* connection? How do *you* still have an en with him? Do you know how hard I have been trying to severe it this entire week? How much overtime I've done?! I still have Makuni Junichiro's case to close, and I already have to deal with *you*."

"You're the reason Natsuami doesn't have any en." Hyo realized, feeling a sick pitching in her stomach. "You're the reason he's so lonely."

"He is certainly *not* lonely. He has a number of select close connections that are carefully managed—"

"He barely has anyone who even remembers his name. Why are you doing this to him?"

"I'm ... his case-worker. At the Onmyoryo. It's one of my duties to ensure he's isolated from others, for both his sake and theirs."

"Does Natsuami know that?"

Todomegawa reddened. "He can never know."

"What does that mean: 'isolated for both his sake and theirs'?" said Mansaku, returning with a pot of tea and cups. "How dangerous *is* an en with this Natsuami guy?"

"An en with Natsuami has, so far, proven lethal to all the humans I wasn't able to severe from him in time," said Todomegawa shortly, taking his tea from Hyo with a polite little bow.

"Pretty unambiguous then." Mansaku poured himself a cup. "You hear that, O'Hyo? We're doomed."

Todomegawa let out a long hiss of steam between his teeth. "This is nothing to make light of!"

Mansaku folded his arms. "And that's what happened to Jun, is it? En with this guy? You couldn't cut it? Death?"

"How did you know that Makuni Junichiro had an en with—?!" Todomegawa stopped himself quickly, but too late. He smacked the table. "*I'm* here to question *you* about Natsuami."

"Oh, yeah." Hyo set down the pencil where she'd been taking notes. "Our mistake. Whenever you're ready then."

"Thank you." Todomegawa went quiet, collecting his thoughts. "Hakai Hyo, where and when did you meet Ryouen Natsuami, why are you looking for him and have you done anything to make your en with him uniquely stubborn to my efforts?"

"We met in a notice hut near the Shin-Kaguraza on the sixteenth. We were sheltering from the wild rain. I've done nothing to reinforce any en with him."

"I know you asked for him at the Hikaraku Ujigami."

"I was curious, that's all. He seemed nice."

"'Nice'," repeated Todomegawa, grim.

"And like he could do with some friends," Hyo said pointedly.

"That's all?"

"That's all." Todomegawa regarded her with narrowed eyes. Hyo carried on, "How does an en with Natsuami kill someone, anyway?"

Todomegawa looked suddenly smaller than he was and weighed down, the shadows under his eyes etched deep. "Before I leave here, I am going to curse the two of you to silence concerning everything I tell you. Do you consent to this?"

Hyo's resolve was firm. "I consent to that."

"Me too," said Mansaku.

"As you should." Todomegawa haughtily sifted through the bowl of snacks, picking out the kaki-no-tane crackers from the peanuts. "Then I'm going to tell you everything I can about Ryouen Natsuami to impress upon you the seriousness of your situation. You're new to Onogoro, but have you heard of Three Thousand Three Fall?"

Hyo nodded, and Mansaku said, "Bits and pieces here and there. Something about a god who irreversibly fell and went on the rampage? Killed their own followers?"

Hyo recalled the Wavewalker's voice like sea foam in her ear. "*We erased their heavenly name from this world, and erased them.*"

Even as she spoke, she remembered Natsuami's words: "*Natsuami ... it's my earthly name.*"

He didn't give her his heavenly one.

"The truth is this." Todomegawa took a deep breath. "Ryouen Natsuami calls himself an en-musubi god. That's both true and not. He *was* an en-musubi god, but the god part of him – that which had a heavenly name and had true powers over en – was executed by the Pillars for killing the three thousand and three. What is left isn't aware of this. What is left ... well, we're still trying to understand what exactly *is* left. We call him the anomaly. Without a heavenly name, Ryouen ought to have dissipated, but here he is – still among us, and in his shadow, that god who killed the three thousand and three is still there too. Somehow, erasing his heavenly name from the world failed to kill the god. He's only been shut out."

"Then does that god-Natsuami, his shadow, still have powers over en?" said Hyo.

"A bare fraction but, yes." Todomegawa shifted nervously. "He can still, very subtly, manipulate the world's en-networks to his purpose. His purpose is, of course, to return. The ens easiest to manipulate are those directly connected to him – namely, to Ryouen Natsuami."

"So, what you're saying is –" Mansaku swilled his tea – "Natsuami's ens with people become the strings by which his god part can use them as puppets for finding a way to bring him back?"

"Insultingly simplistic, but yes." Todomegawa wrinkled his nose. "Every en with Natsuami is a thread by which that god has access to a pair of eyes and feet, and an en-network – by which it can search this world and place what it needs into Natsuami's hands."

"Then why do the people connected to Natsuami die if the god needs them?" Hyo asked.

"For the simplest of reasons." Todomegawa looked almost guilty. "He grows bored of them, so when an opportunity arises for them to suffer and die, he'll tie them to that fate."

Hyo felt faintly sick. "Natsuami said he was powerless."

"He might believe that. He has no conscious control of his abilities."

"Do you know what made Natsuami fall?"

Todomegawa hunched his shoulders. "We do have one theory. The two of you are familiar with hitodenashi, are you not?"

"You could say that," Mansaku replied.

"Then you'll know that when a human eats hitodenashi pear they become a demon. But no one knows what would happen to a god who does the same. Our theory is that Ryouen Natsuami is the outcome." Todomegawa blew at his teacup, and the cooling tea billowed steam again. "They become a god who can destroy their own followers and still survive, without needing musuhi, or even a heavenly name. In short, a god freed of humans."

Cold seeped through Hyo's skin. "So the thing that Natsuami is searching for, that he is manipulating people's ens to find is..."

"Hitodenashi pear. We think he believes that consuming more of it is the answer to his return."

Damn it. Hyo's cup burned into her palm. "And do they find it?"

"They come close, but no, they haven't. Not yet."

Hyo tried to keep her tone neutral. "Is hitodenashi pear being grown on Onogoro then?"

Todomegawa bristled with indignation. "On Onogoro? Of course it isn't!"

"But people have tried, haven't they?" Hyo's voice rose dangerously.

"Yes – a thoughtless, greedy few." Todomegawa drummed his fingers on his knees. He pressed his lips into a thin line. "All have failed."

Mansaku folded his arms. "Was Jun one of Natsuami's en-puppets?"

"I cannot rule it out."

Mansaku nodded, then said, "Great – now, are we looking for a way to destroy Natsuami himself?"

ELEVEN

大蛇の使者

Gods aren't built like we are. Their "bodies" in the spiritual plane are made of divine potential – in other words, how probable is it for that god to be found in a particular place at a particular time.

DAUGHTER OF TAIRA,
Sixth Hellmaker

Todomegawa smacked the table. Crackers jumped. "Destroying Natsuami is not an option!"

"Why not? If the god part of him killed three thousand and three and what's left is still adding to the bodies with that en—"

"It's unthinkable!"

"Buddy, if Natsuami's still looking to regain *actual god status*, he's probably easier to kill off now than if that happens, right? We've just got to find the right way to do it—"

The table shattered.

Or more accurately, one moment Todomegawa had one hand resting by his teacup and the next it had punched through the surface in a fist. "***Unthinkable!***"

"All right, all right! We get it. No thinking," Mansaku said from where he'd jumped up, clutching his teacup whilst peanuts and crackers scattered around his toes. "Poor innocent table. We've only had it for four days."

Todomegawa blinked. He unclenched his fist slowly. "I apologize for the undue destruction of property."

He looked so sad and sheepish that Hyo just sighed. Mansaku raised his hands in surrender. "Don't sweat it; I'm sure people smash tables all the time."

"The table will be replaced. I will make sure of it."

"That's appreciated. Real paulownia would be good. Maybe with a bit of lacquer and gold-leaf detail. Brass inlay. Some mother-of-pearl…"

"Let's clean this up," Hyo said, and went to the kitchen for cloths.

When she returned, Todomegawa was gazing at the broken table with a deep, self-reproaching disappointment and Mansaku was unpacking the god's gift bag.

"You'll feel better once you've eaten," Mansaku said, lifting the lid of the narezushi's wooden box. "Sounds like you've got a lot on your shoulders, with Jun, and with this en-puppeting mass-murdering ex-god you won't destroy."

Todomegawa rubbed his temples. "No one is destroying Natsuami."

"Right, right. Don't worry. O'Hyo and I won't even think of mortally wounding him a little bit. Pinkie promise."

Hyo tossed Mansaku a cloth. Once they'd finished cleaning, they rejoined Todomegawa on the floor. Mansaku handed round the narezushi box, and they each took a sushi and unwrapped it from its glossy reed leaf.

As they ate, Todomegawa said, "Is it clear now how important it is that you keep your en with Natsuami as weak as possible?"

Hyo nodded. Mansaku grunted something vaguely affirmatory.

"Do not speak of him. Do not think of him. Absolutely do *not* go looking for him." Todomegawa's pointed glare at Hyo might've been more effective if he wasn't chewing on salted mackerel. "As per my role, I will watch over both of you until your en to Natsuami frays and breaks on its own."

Oh, hell, no. Hyo coughed. "You really don't have to do that."

"I will stay by your side. Night and day."

"No, really."

"I might've failed Makuni Junichiro, but I will not fail you two. I swear it." Todomegawa took a vengeful bite of narezushi. "And I will not deliver you to the Onmyoryo either."

"Why the change of heart? Onmyoryo out of tea?" Mansaku's tone was just east of needling.

Todomegawa glanced back at the privacy talisman over the doorway, then said, "I was a war god for five hundred years before I was an en-cutter; I know a weapon spirit in a human skin when I see one. Sword, axe, whatever you are..."

"I'm not the weapon," Mansaku said calmly. "I carry it."

"... the Onmyoryo is a direct pipeline to the Harbourlakes' Cultural Collection. All bladed weapons the Onmyoryo finds that are old enough to have spirit are handed over to them. They'll call you a tribute –" Todomegawa spat out the word – "then box you up as an exotic fascination, silenced of your own stories, to display and use for their own myths of convenience about themselves.

"The same goes for you, Hyo-san. There are those at

the Onmyoryo who are paid to keep the Harbourlakes abreast of 'interesting people'. Your curse would be interesting enough. Your gaze too..." Todomegawa touched his front gingerly, brushing the place where Hyo had captured his god's silver-flamed oil lamp in her eyes and measured his mortality. "They would remove you from Onogoro, then through his en with you, Natsuami would have access to the en-networks of the outside. His chances of coming into contact with hitodenashi pear would explode." He lowered his hand and shivered. "In fact, I would advise that you avoid anyone from the Onmyoryo, bar myself and my superior, the Wavewalker – until I can be sure of something."

Mansaku frowned. "Not going to share what that something is?"

"No," said Todomegawa with finality. "I am under some pressure to close Makuni Junichiro's case, despite the god responsible for the curse being still unknown. The argument is that, since no significant taint accumulation has been detected in the area, Makuni must have been cursed with Good Reason."

Hyo looked up over her narezushi. "And you've got a reason to think he wasn't?"

"As I said –" Todomegawa finished his narezushi and neatly folded up its leaf – "there is something I have to check. Gods, however, must be made to feel the weight of their ill-judged actions as much as humans."

A knock at the door. Todomegawa startled. Mansaku leant back to shout, "It's open!"

"Good afternoon," said the Onmyoryo officer from the doorway. "I'm looking for Todomegawa Daimyoujin. His divine signature was last detected entering these premises?" His gaze landed on the back of Todomegawa's head. "Sir is required back at the Onmyoryo."

"Now?" To Hyo's surprise, Todomegawa's voice wavered. "What for?"

"Your scheduled disciplinary proceedings."

"This is earlier than scheduled."

"The disciplinary level has been raised." At the word "raised", something slipped in Todomegawa's face. He stiffened. This wasn't missed by the officer. "You're responsible for the destruction of the Shin-Kaguraza Bridge and several fires in the area, risking a number of major hydrogen veins. If you'd please. Sir."

"Yes, of course." Todomegawa stood.

Hyo stopped him. She wasn't finished with him yet. "Your hands are dirty; don't you want to clean them?"

The officer looked into their apartment. Not seeing a back exit, he nodded. "You can have a few minutes."

He shut the door. Todomegawa went to wash his hands of the narezushi's stickiness in the water closet, and returned.

He removed a black lacquered seal stamp and red ink-pad from his waist-pouch. "Hold out your hands."

Hyo asked, "Are you going to be all right?"

"As he said, this is all scheduled," Todomegawa replied without meeting Hyo's gaze, "and as *I* said, gods must be made to feel the weight of their ill-judged actions. Both of you –" he lifted his stamp, leaving the briefly glowing lines of a silencing curse on their hands – "I know you're curious about Makuni's death and want to see retribution for it. Do not go investigating it yourselves. You are humans. There is a god on Onogoro who, so far, thinks they've got away with making Makuni suffer without penalty. They'll think they can get away with it a second time too."

"Noted," said Mansaku. "What does disciplining mean for a god?"

"I've no doubt that you will meet Natsuami quite soon," Todomegawa said, clean ignoring Mansaku's question. "When you do, don't tell him we've met. A replacement table will be sent. Thank you for the tea."

Todomegawa bowed, then he jammed the bascinet over his head and opened the door, saying: "I apologize for the delay, Officer Oike – I am ready to go now."

The officer gestured for Todomegawa to go ahead of him, bowed to Hyo and Mansaku, then the two walked out of sight.

Mansaku gasped and tapped Hyo's shoulder. "Look!"

On the ghost detector talisman over the doorway was a dark red blot, like old blood. *When did it appear? When the officer opened the door? When they were divvying the narezushi?*

Hyo jammed her feet into her zouri and rushed out into the walkway.

"Jun-san?" she shouted, startling the tea-drinkers outside Mrs Meguro's shop. "Jun-san, are you there?"

Nothing. No heaviness on her shoulders. No whisper in her ears. No sudden chill.

"I can't sense anything." Mansaku craned his neck around the doorway to look left and right. "He's gone. Again. Or not again, if it wasn't Jun this time. Could've been this flat's last resident, deciding he's going to haunt it, after all."

"It was Jun-san."

"You sure?"

She felt a tug of the hellmakers' en, tying hard and close. Hyo looked around wildly. "I don't know. But it was someone I have to talk to."

"O'Hyo, wait – shit, watch where you're walking!"

White flashed. A snake no longer than Hyo's forearm had streaked out across the walkway. As Hyo's foot came down, it lifted its frightened head and gaped to defend.

The icy curve of Mansaku's scythe swept around her, swung invisibly but lifting the ends of Hyo's hair with its speed and cut the snake in two.

The tea-drinkers fled as its head bounced over the boards and landed by their feet, fangs bared to the sky.

There was a dry rustling like straw sweeping across a floor, and Mansaku cried out.

Hyo turned to see white snakes swarming out of cracks in the walls to pile on Mansaku where he'd stepped out from their doorway. "Mansaku!"

He collapsed, vanishing under the snakes. Then just as quickly as the snakes had gathered, they scattered, and where Mansaku should have been was one human body's worth of sun-ripened grains of wheat, topped by a white envelope with four symbols down its front in stark black ink:

授呪布告

"A General Declaration of Cursing," said the booming voice of a stranger. "As Mansaku-san's closest family member, that's for you to accept on his behalf."

Next to Hyo was an Oblivionist priest – or at least, a man dressed as one. He was bald, bearded and built large and thick-waisted like an old camphor. His eyes were bulbous and his priest's robes were ill-fitting.

He hitched up the shichijo-gesa along his shoulder, eyed Mansaku's pile of grain and pressed his hands together in prayer. "Hmmm, how does the sutra go? Namu Amida?"

"Mansaku's not dead!" Hyo heard her voice pitch higher than normal.

"A chant in advance never hurts," said the priest. "Take the letter, Hyo-san. This one won't bite."

The way he said that, it was as if some letters did. Hyo's hand shook as she picked up the envelope.

The snakes swarmed back again. She tried to sweep them off. "No!"

"Let them be." Large hands landed on her shoulders and lifted Hyo, so that her feet dangled in the air. She struggled, but the priest was strong. "They're just collecting your brother to take him somewhere safe."

"Safe?"

"Safest. With the Paddywatcher, who Mansaku-san gave a Good Reason to curse him. They'll be taking him to her nearest shrine to explain himself," the priest said with a merry matter-of-factness. "And as it was all an accident, he'll be let go and un-cursed in no time. He was only running on a weapon spirit's instincts to protect their master, after all."

"That's not it at all." The priest's flame of life flickered in Hyo's eyes. A black pool of oil gleamed. She frowned. "You're a..."

"An Oblivionist monk with the Pure Land Sect." The priest – who was a god – put her down and clapped his hands in prayer again. "Namu Amida. And all that. Praise be to the Amida Untethered. You can call me Hatamoto-san."

The snakes gulped Mansaku down, not missing a single grain. In seconds, the pile was gone. The snakes, some knobbly with their swallowed mouthfuls, turned away as one to disappear into the walls again.

When Hyo made to follow the snakes, Hatamoto stopped her with a single finger to her shoulder. "Oh, no. Only Mansaku-san needs to visit the Paddywatcher today. You can spend time with me, old Hatamoto Yaemon! I'm here as a friend, I promise. Yours – as well as the Paddywatcher's."

Hyo stopped trying to shrug him off. "Did the Paddywatcher *trap* Mansaku into giving her a Good Reason to curse him?"

"She *did* think it might incline you towards cooperation." Hatamoto gave her a beatific smile. "Naturally, she hopes you'll think well of her when she, very reasonably, reverses the curse on your brother and returns him to you. I'm here on her behalf. Greetings, from Yamada Hanako. Otherwise known as Ohmononushi'no'Ohkami the Paddywatcher. She wishes to extend an offer of friendship to you."

Yamada Hanako. An earthly name, not a heavenly one, the kind Hyo might have found counting fruit in a maths textbook. "If she wants friendship, why doesn't she come and see me herself?"

"She hoped you'd appreciate her effort to remain ignorant of your face, so that you didn't feel pressured to accept her offer." Hyo tried to reply but Hatamoto raised his hands placatingly. "I'll make it simpler: the

Paddywatcher has your brother, Hyo-san. Listen to what she has to say and offer you, and Mansaku will be returned."

Hyo ground her teeth. She forced herself to calm down. "What does Yamada Hanako want?"

"She thinks you could help each other."

"How?"

"My dear, she was Makuni Junichiro's guardian god. She couldn't interfere with his cursing – but that another god has killed him without declaring themselves or their Good Reason is deeply insulting to her. She wants to find the who and why as much as you do." Hatamoto stepped closer, and lifted one hand to stage-whisper behind it. "If you're also looking for who cursed Makuni Junichiro, hellmaker, don't you think you could be allies?"

At Hyo's uneasy silence, Hatamoto chuckled. His chest shook and his rosaries jangled. "Let's continue this over some noodles. I know a place nearby. I've got coupons!"

"I met my first hellmaker about seven centuries ago. She was a goze, travelling with a foreign priest of the Pater-in-Pieces. Called herself a 'woman of misfortune' rather than a hellmaker, but it was the same curse – that same seal as yours on her palms." Hatamoto slurped through his third bowl of "moongazer-on-the-beach", an udon pile topped with a float of mozuku, shirasu and a raw egg. "She had four weapon spirits of the original seven with her.

The hammer, the saw, the sasumata and the nagigama."

"Not weapon spirits. Her brothers."

"I stand corrected. Her brothers, yes. Poor souls." Hatamoto sprinkled so much sansho pepper over his noodles that Hyo's nose stung. "Are you looking into Makuni Junichiro's death for ... what my goze friend would've called it ... a 'special case'?"

"A special commission. Yeah, I am."

Hatamoto beamed. "Yamada-san will be glad to hear it! Have you made much progress?"

"Some." When Hatamoto continued to look expectantly at her, Hyo said, "If Yamada-san was Jun-san's guardian, she watched over him the whole time he was cursed. What could I know about the curse and Jun-san that Yamada-san already doesn't?"

"I see your point. Yamada-san certainly knows more about Jun-san's activities before your arrival on Onogoro than you." Hatamoto slapped Hyo on the back. "But that which happens out of her sight or her immediate en-networks, that's as much a mystery to her as to any of us. Or, at least, any of us without that wondrous chaos compass that is the hellmakers' en."

"Where did Jun-san go to on Fifthmonth the thirteenth?" There were two days unaccounted for, before Jun sheltered in Natsuami's notice hut.

"Ah, yes, the day he left his home. He went to the Bridgeburner's Hikaraku shrine, in the next tower." Hatamoto pointed his elbow towards the neighbouring block. "Unless they've a sub-altar there, a god cannot exercise their power within another god's shrine – hence shrines usually turn away the cursed – but as the Bridgeburner's a curse-mediator, him sheltering Makuni wouldn't be considered 'interference' in a god–human dispute. It would've paused the progress of Makuni's curse – until Makuni stepped out from behind the shrine gates."

"Does Yamada-san know why Jun-san left the Bridgeburner's shrine?"

"Sure she does." Hatamoto grated a snowstorm of sesame over his second bowl of udon, grunting as he ground the mill. "Makuni lost faith in the Bridgeburner's ability to protect him. That's how it always is with gods and humans. Otherwise, two or three steps outside of the Bridgeburner's protection, when he started feeling that curse again, he would've known better." Hatamoto shook off the last flakes of sesame from the mill. "Don't suppose the Bridgeburner might've mentioned why Makuni stopped trusting him, did he? When the little river-on-fire was visiting you?"

"No." But it added up, if during his days at Todomegawa's shrine, Jun had learnt something that shook his trust in the en-giri god.

"I was a war god like the Bridgeburner, once upon a time." Hatamoto pushed the spring onion around his bowl. "Re-skilling after the Hell-on-Earth, though – it wasn't for me. You've seen my flame of life with those hellmaker eyes of yours, haven't you? How divine am I, these days?"

Hatamoto's oil lamp was different from Todomegawa's. The oil had been congealing in its dark dish, growing into a lumpen stem of cold translucent wax. The flame had an orange flickering smokiness, and was buffeted by luck and circumstances in a way that was more human than divine.

A god's oil lamp was hardening into a human candle.

Hyo looked away before she ended up staring. "What's happening to you?"

"The fate of all gods who were once humans: reverse deification." Hatamoto put a huge fist over where his flame flickered. "Instead of dissipating, we go back to what's left of our human lifespans – then death. There are a few of us in-between abnormalities around."

"Like Natsua—"

"Stop right there," Hatamoto snapped. "Don't say that creature's name. I lost eight followers to its madness on Three Thousand Three Fall. For the sake of those left, I'm not risking an en with it."

The noodle chef behind the counter quietly continued slicing udon dough as if he heard this sort of thing in his shop every evening.

Hyo nodded. "I won't say his name."

"Thank you." Hatamoto stirred his bowl. "So. You've met it."

"I have." Something made Hyo ask, "You?"

"Once. Two years ago. It heard that I was losing my divinity and came to 'compare notes' on the experience. It had the cheek to claim no memory of Three Thousand Three Fall at all." Hatamoto let out a mirthless chuckle. "And it had no idea how different we were.

Is *it* –" Hatamoto looked quickly over his shoulder, as if Natsuami might appear at the udon stall that very moment, then lowered his voice – "connected to Makuni Junichiro's death?"

"He could be," Hyo said and relished the way Hatamoto quivered. "You still think Yamada-san and I could 'help each other'?"

"Oh, yes. Very much so. Especially if *that* is involved." A fourth and fifth bowl of udon were set down in front of Hatamoto. "You've your ways of gathering information. Yamada-san has hers. You can go places and make connections with those she, er, may prefer to avoid."

"And what can she do?"

"Well, let's see ... your brother, now. There's the small issue of the nagigama parasitizing his spirit, isn't there? Dooming his spirit to nothingness like all the other hellmaker sons? Our friend Yamada-san might, for one thing, know of a way to split them apart." Hatamoto nudged Hyo amiably in the side. "That'd be a great help to you, wouldn't it? You two could finally be real family – none of this confusion about whether you're weapon and master, or brother and sister."

Hyo ignored his last words. They were family, without question. But the rest of it... "Yamada-san knows a way?"

"Maybe, maybe not." Hatamoto dabbed at his chin with a napkin. "If she did though, it would save your brother's life, wouldn't it?"

It would spare Mansaku the fate of their uncle, and all the boys before him.

Damn it. "That would help us."

"Thought so! Good. This all brings me nicely to the particular task she had in mind," Hatamoto said around the toothpick he was digging between his teeth. "There's someone Yamada-san is keen to hear from. Someone very close to Makuni Junichiro's death. Unfortunately, they're shy of a Pillar God's sheer spiritual power."

"All right. Who are they?"

"Makuni Junichiro's ghost, of course."

"Of cou— What?"

"Tonight the Hikaraku Onmyoryo are running a ghost-baiting exercise. They do them on occasion to count and catalogue the ghosts in the district. A god is offered up to the ghosts for four nights, and the ghosts come. They're always hungry for a god's pain, since ghosts tend to arise from humans let down by luck and fate." Hatamoto stood up. He held out a hand. "And tonight's ghost-bait is the very god who Makuni died believing had betrayed his trust. It's our fiery friend, the Bridgeburner."

TWELVE

霊餌

For those who enjoy ghost-watching,
around two o'clock in the morning
on clear nights around Uran Festival
or anniversaries of disasters is a good
time to see ghost lights – your local
hitodama, the souls of the restless dead.

From "Don't Worry, They Can't Kill You
Unless You Ask for It: A Beginner's Guide to
Co-existing with the Earthbound Divine"

Hikaraku Ivy Plaza was shaped like an ivy leaf's spade and hung from three thick cables between the towers, with its stem forming a walkway. A large rock stood at its centre, which, in the wan evening light, had the silhouette of someone very old and hunched sweeping outside their home.

Hikaraku was readying for the night. The lilac lanterns, strung along bridges and walkways like pearls, were starting to glow, but nearer the Plaza, the lanterns were dark, the shops were closed early and the windows covered. The Ivy Plaza stayed in its own well of

shadow, within which the blue-green floating spots of ghost lights shone.

Trailing flames as they materialized in the air, each ghost light was roughly the size of an apple. On the Plaza walkway, they formed an orderly dotted line of blue fireballs, floating silently before a desk where an Onmyoryo officer was sitting with a clipboard and a tally counter.

As Hyo watched, a ghost light stopped in front of the officer, hovering as he read off a few questions. Hyo heard no answers but the officer nodded and took notes, and the ghost light flew on into the Plaza to bob around the central boulder.

"This line for the living; this line for the dead, please!" called out a familiar voice, and then: "Hyo-chan?"

"Nagakumo-san?" Dressed in a green uniform with the blunt hilt of something strapped to her hip was Hyo's hancho, Nagakumo Masu. That uniform – Hyo had seen it out and about on patrols in the evenings. "You're a police officer?"

"By daylight – and, on these occasions, by ghost light! I come to ghost-baitings to find ghosts who could help with the force's unsolved files. Sometimes they remember enough to testify for their own cases. Sometimes they point me to a body we didn't know about." Nagakumo pushed up her headband to peer more closely at Hyo then at Hatamoto. "You're here for a ghost, I take it?"

"That's right," boomed Hatamoto.

"Join the line for the living. I'll come back and help in a moment," Nagakumo said, hurrying towards a man and a woman in the Plaza who were clutching smoking sticks of incense and surrounded by a cluster of bobbing ghost lights.

Human figures were dotted about the Plaza. Each carried sticks of incense, a box of which was on the Onmyoryo's officer's table, for which he was accepting, strangely, a payment of fresh leaves or sprigs of star anise. Each figure was looking about the Plaza with faces hollowed by hope, waiting for a ghost light to recognize them and drift their way. Of Todomegawa, there was no sign.

Hatamoto paid the Onmyoryo officer with a branch of star anise. He'd broken it off a potted plant on the way. The officer took their names and that of the ghost they hoped to meet that evening, then handed them their sticks of incense.

"What are these for?" Hyo asked.

"So that the ghosts can hear you if you call for them, even if they're not listening," the officer replied, before setting a lighter to the incense ends and waving down the flames to a smouldering glow. "Speak quietly and make no sudden movements. The ghosts will be more likely to approach."

Spotting Hyo and Hatamoto entering the Plaza proper,

Nagakumo came over to them again. "All sorted?"

Hyo glanced back at Hatamoto, who silently put his hands together. *Useless.* "How do we know if the ghost we want is here?"

"It's simple. You see the smoke coming off your incense?" Nagakumo pointed at the pearlescent stream of smoke wisping off their ends. "Say their name into the smoke, and if they're here, that smoke will point you to them. If they want to talk to you, you'll see the incense end light up. When that happens, me or one of the other officers here will come and find you. We're all –" she struck a pose – "professionals in possession. They don't call me Special Constable 'Witness Box Masu' in the force for nothing."

"No one calls you that but you," said the Onmyoryo officer.

"We can lend the ghosts our bodies to talk to you," Nagakumo continued. She indicated the incense stick again. "Usually for however long it takes for the incense stick to go out completely. That sound good to you?"

"Yeah, thanks, Nagakumo-san."

"A little white snake came by earlier, by the way. She said to expect you and be ready to lend a hand if there's trouble." Nagakumo patted Hyo on the shoulder, her gaze one of consideration. "You be careful now."

"Yamada-san is the patron god of the police force," Hatamoto explained as Nagakumo left to help a woman who was waving for assistance, a ghost light darting around her ankles. "If she asks the police to help, they don't disobey her."

Hyo brought the incense tips to her mouth. The smoke stung her nose. She whispered, "Makuni Junichiro."

The strands of smoke wavered, wove together, then flowed towards the boulder at the Plaza centre. Hyo's heart did a painful twist. Jun's ghost was really here.

Hatamoto said, "Let's go to him."

They walked towards the rock. Ghost lights were settling on the boulder's top, crowning it in burning snow. It was a teetering thing, wider at the top than the bottom. Its foot was obscured in mist, but brightly lit, crowded as it was by the flames of eager ghosts.

"Good evening, Ame'no'Iwaba-no-Mikoto," Hatamoto said, bowing deeply to the rock, because it, too, was a divine body. A god occupied it. A slender rope looped its girth with shide ornaments. "And to you, Todomegawa Daimyoujin."

There was a groan, then Todomegawa replied, "Good evening, Yatsuhata-no-Mikoto."

Todomegawa was pinned beneath the massive rock. What Hyo could see of his hands, neck, sides – every bit of him but for his face – was covered in talismans that were blocking off his divine powers. If he'd been human, he'd have been crushed and dead.

Todomegawa raised a hand to tap the underside of

the boulder above him. "Would madam please recite quieter?" The rock was silent, but then Todomegawa raised his voice. "I said, could you do that *quieter*?"

"What's she doing?" Hyo had to ask.

"Ame'no'Iwaba-no-Mikoto is currently reciting the full rulebook of acceptable godly conduct with regard to consideration for human safety," Hatamoto replied, an amused gleam in his eye. "And she will be doing this all night and day, without stopping, until the end of Todomegawa's disciplinary period."

Todomegawa shut his eyes. "I can't hear myself think!"

"That's the point, young river," Hatamoto said, consoling. "It's in part a refresher, and in part to take the human side of your mind off the fact that your earthly body is currently being crushed by a boulder. Would you rather she ... stopped?"

"Who's there with you, Yatsuhata?" Todomegawa tossed at them, expertly side-stepping the question. "I can't see with all these ghost lights in my face!"

"It's me," said Hyo, crouching.

"Hakai Hyo?" Todomegawa's gaze was unfocused, his face pale. "What are you doing here?"

"Does that hurt?" She had to know, because where the rock met Todomegawa's body there was a narrow crust of glowing divine blood. The ghost lights were dancing about it like they would lap at it if they could.

She didn't like the shadow of helpless resignation in

his face. She'd seen something too similar in the villagers' expressions that winter.

"It has to," Todomegawa said, through his teeth. "It's the suffering of the god that attracts the ghosts here."

"Physical *and* mental," Hatamoto added helpfully. "Todomegawa was human once. The body doesn't forget that a boulder could've killed it. The psychological self-torment of ex-biology is rather brutal—"

"Shut it." Hatamoto closed his mouth with a pout. Hyo returned to Todomegawa. "Makuni Junichiro's ghost is here."

His eyes widened. "I said *not* to investigate him."

"By ourselves – but you're here, so it's fine, isn't it?" said Hyo. "I'm not going to miss this chance to talk to him."

Todomegawa's hand clenched on the floor. "Then you didn't come here to see me suffer?"

"Why would I?"

"For your own satisfaction." His voice shook. "You're angry with me. I was responsible for your friend Makuni's life, and I failed to save him."

Hyo closed her eyes, then opened them slowly. "The only one who really deserves any anger is whoever cursed Jun-san in the first place. That includes all the anger you're hurting yourself with too."

Todomegawa snorted and looked askance. "Call him out. I bet he's close."

Ghost lights hovered around them. Hyo glanced at Hatamoto, who put his hands together and began to drone a sutra under his breath. No help from him then.

She held up her incense again and eyed the glowing red lines of fire eating their way down each stick.

"Makuni Junichiro," she spoke into the smoke and imagined her words threading into it, taking on its fragrant shapes. "We want to talk to you about who cursed you. Will you answer our questions?"

She paused, listening. Nothing; no change in the ghost lights dancing about them.

She tried again. "Jun-san, it's Hakai Hyo. From Koura, Occupied-Ukoku. We made it to Onogoro at last. Thanks for letting us stay at your place when you were out." Ghosts weren't the people they were in life. They were echoes. Their loudest screams, still ringing in the world. Hyo swallowed down a wash of nausea at the thought. "Can we talk?"

A ghost light detached from the nearby swarm. It drifted nearer, slowly, as if sizing them up from a distance.

"Not going to come any closer?" Todomegawa goaded it. "You're already dead. What have you to be afraid of any more?"

The ends of Hyo's incense remained stubbornly grey. Hatamoto looked on, running the beads of an enormous rosary through his fingers.

"Do you have anything on you that would've been important to him?" Nagakumo had returned, a clipboard under one arm, and assessing the situation in an instant. "Some ghosts just need to have their stakes upped."

Hyo thought quickly. Then it came to her. Passing the incense to Hatamoto, she opened her waist-pouch and found Jun's last letter to Koushiro.

Todomegawa stared, eyes on the splattered calligraphy. "Where did you get that?"

"I'm ready when you are!" Nagakumo tossed something to Hyo.

The gas lighter for the incense. Hyo caught it with both hands. Putting the lighter in her left, the blue envelope in her right, she switched on the lighter with a sputter, and set its flame to the envelope's corner...

"*Don't!*"

The incense exploded in Hatamoto's hands.

Cold metal struck. Pain shot up Hyo's wrist. The lighter went flying out of Hyo's hand to clatter on the boards at their feet, the ghost lights scattering like a shoal of fish. The living Plaza visitors fled from the rock.

Nagakumo stood over Hyo, breathing heavily, a jitte drawn from her hip and held high above her head.

Only, it wasn't Nagakumo. Her eyes were burning ghost light blue. When she opened her mouth, her tongue was wreathed in ghost light flames.

"*Don't,*" she repeated in a young man's voice, but scraped thin, as if heard from a distance. "*Must be delivered.*"

Todomegawa shivered. "That's him!"

"Jun-san." Deliberately slowly, so that the ghost could see, Hyo put the letter back in her waist-pouch. She patched together a smile. "Yeah, I'll deliver it. I promise."

"*O'Hyo.*" Nagakumo's mouth moved with Jun's voice. "*On my side? Or his side?*"

The jitte pointed downwards, to Todomegawa under the rock.

Hyo stepped between the god and the ghost. The tip of the jitte pressed against her breastbone. "What makes you think the Bridgeburner's not on yours?"

"*If O'Hyo were on* my *side, she would let me hurt him.*" Jun cocked Nagakumo's head. "*I would answer the questions of O'Hyo on* my *side.*"

"Let him come at me," Todomegawa said roughly. "You heard him, Hyo-san. If that's the price for answers, I'll pay it."

Hyo's guts twisted. "There is no way I am going to—"

Hatamoto's hand closed around her arm. "My dear, come this way."

"Mrrf!"

With one hand over Hyo's mouth and the other trapping her against him, Hatamoto drew Hyo aside, allowing Jun-in-Nagakumo to crouch down by Todomegawa.

The incense sticks smoked between Hatamoto's fingers, red smoulder consuming them at a steady pace. The grit of smoke stung Hyo's eyes.

Todomegawa looked up at Jun-in-Nagakumo. "Do

your worst. It is your due."

The ghost was silent. To Hyo's surprise, he set down the jitte, then, slowly, covered Todomegawa's ears.

It wasn't instantaneous. There was a second of confusion, the lines on Todomegawa's brow deepening as Jun blocked out the voice of the rock god, then Todomegawa jerked, cracking his head against the rock's underside. He gasped, eyes wide and unseeing as human panic and instincts took hold.

"Help me, please, it hurts; I don't want to die. Aniue!" Jun-in-Nagakumo flinched. *Aniue. Big brother.* Half-whimpering, half-babbling, Todomegawa's fingers – hooked to claws – raked the Plaza boards. "Aniue, where are you? It hurts, please. Aniue!"

Abruptly, Jun-in-Nagakumo released him. Todomegawa slumped, dropping his head to the floor and breathing hard.

"*This god has a brother too?*" Jun-in-Nagakumo regarded him coolly. "*Then this god understands why he should suffer.*"

"Did Todomegawa do something to Koushiro?" Hyo asked, wrenching Hatamoto's hand from her mouth. Hatamoto released her. At the name of his brother, Jun-in-Nagakumo stilled. "Is that what made you leave his shrine?"

"*Yes.*" He turned to her, eyes glowing green-blue. "*Yesyesyes. O'Hyo unDErstANds. This goD is NOT on*

mY side. Lying. Double-dEAling. Two-tongued! BeCausE of This god Kou is iN dAnGER."

His words warped and splintered in Hyo's ears, in a twisted kaleidoscope version of Jun's voice. "What did he do?"

Todomegawa spat out blood. "I've never lied to you!"

"*He pretends!*" Jun snarled. Nagakumo's face contorted. A dark stripe of blood ran down from her nose. "*Iheardhim IheardhimIheardhim. At his shrinE. Speaking with. Colluding with. He is NOT on my side. They were sCHEMING! Together! To hurt my brother, after me! For his pictures. My reflectographs!*"

"Scheming? We were doing nothing of the kind!" Todomegawa slapped the boards beneath him "Of course I'd speak to the Wavewalker about Koushiro's reflectograph collection! He's your brother's guardian god! He was concerned about his luck!"

"When was this?" Hyo asked quickly. "*Which* reflectographs?"

"The Wavewalker came to my shrine the evening before this fool left it!" Todomegawa glared daggers at Jun-in-Nagakumo. "He wanted to discuss Koushiro's luck. We spoke at the gateway only. I didn't let the Wavewalker in."

"*You didn't want to be overheard*," Jun-in-Nagakumo snarled.

"I didn't want you to feel unsafe!" Todomegawa closed his eyes. "Koushiro had a reflectograph collection we thought could've caused his bad luck. The Wavewalker had it destroyed. It seems that Makuni overheard and completely misunderstood—"

"*LiaR!*" Hyo dropped to Todomegawa's side, just in time to catch the jitte Jun swung down at him with her hand. "*There is no MISUnderSTANDINg. I KNOW what I SAW. COLLUDER. CO-CONSPIRATOR. You GaVE me HOPE. You APPEared WHen I nEEDed you. But yOU were NEVer on my side and you FOUnd NOTHING to help ME.*"

"Jun-san!" Hyo clenched her teeth as Jun bore all of Nagakumo's strength down on the jitte. "Who cursed you? Can you tell us that?"

Todomegawa said, "He can't; he's still being silenced; that curse is still on him."

"There's a violent possession over here!" At the frightened shout, Hyo remembered the other visitors on the Plaza. "Officers, help!"

"You're wrong, Makuni Junichiro," Todomegawa said, speaking quickly as the officers looked their way. "I was always on your side. I colluded with no one. And I *did* find something on the day you died."

This made Jun-in-Nagakumo pause. "*The day I died?*"

"Too late, I know. But it was evidence to suggest you weren't cursed with Good Reason." Todomegawa sounded exhausted. His words were slurring together. "Perhaps. I'm not certain of it yet. I am sorry, Makuni Junichiro."

"*What value has an apology to the dead?*"

"For letting you down." Todomegawa's voice softened, growing weaker. "And, perhaps, so it seems, for failing to see ... what was under ... my very nose..."

Something white fluttered over Nagakumo's shoulder.

It unfolded in mid-air – into a paper man, which stuck itself to Nagakumo's front. And then from behind them came chanting.

"*Rin, pyo, to, sha, kai, jin, retsu, zai, zen.*" The Onmyoryo officer from the desk was running towards them, cutting the air with the fingers of his right hand in the sword sign. "*Rin, pyo, to, sha, kai, jin, retsu, zai, zen! Rin, pyo, to, sha, kai, jin, retsu, zai, ZEN!*"

Jun-in-Nagakumo went rigid. He dropped the jitte and fell to Nagakumo's knees.

"*Soku, baku!*" The officer moved his fingers through the hand seals. "Come on!"

Dark lines ran from Nagakumo's nose. The glow dimmed from her eyes. The flames died to smoke from her tongue, then spinning like threads on a spindle, they coiled about the paper man on her chest and disappeared into it.

"*Ketsu!*" The officer sliced the air. "*Fuu!*"

A symbol appeared on the paper man's front: 封.

Sealed.

"Got him," the officer said with satisfaction. "Is everyone all right here? Nagakumo?"

"Fine..." Nagakumo sat up, rubbing her head. She sneezed. "Aww, shid. There's blud on my yuniform."

"What happened to the ghost?" Hyo asked. The paper man the officer was peeling off Nagakumo's front was still. "Is he..."

"He's sorted, so no need to worry." The officer held up the paper man. "We've caught him. Per protocol for violent vengeful spirits, we'll be taking him back to the Onmyoryo. You can be assured that he won't come back to haunt you."

The hairs rose down the back of Hyo's neck. "What the hell do you do with the ghosts?!"

"Before we get into that –" Hatamoto raised his hand and sniffed the air – "can anyone else smell something ... sweet?"

They paused. Ghost lights drifted.

Then Hyo caught it: a whiff of something tart and

syrupy that went straight to the back of her mouth, and tasted of salted apricots and last snows.

"Damn it!" Nagakumo gagged and spat at the floor. "It's yashiori!"

"You sure?" said the officer.

"Positive. No mistaking it. The incense version."

"In which case, this is where I take my leave." Hatamoto's voice was muffled behind a kerchief he'd pulled out of nowhere and tied about his face. He bowed to Hyo. "Hyo-san, thank you for your help! *Our* friend Yamada-san will be in touch."

He picked up the hems of his robes and ran from the Plaza like...

Like he'd seen a ghost, Hyo thought.

"We've got to protect the god. Hyo-chan –" Nagakumo pressed a kerchief into her hands – "tie this to the Bridgeburner's face. Don't let him fall asleep. Iwaba-no-Mikoto's a rock and doesn't have a nose. She won't be a problem."

"What's yashiori?"

"Divine drug. Doesn't do anything to us, but for gods –" Nagakumo's expression darkened – "it knocks them straight into the Under-dream. If you see any weird colours about his mouth, shout for me. You'll know what I mean if you see them. Quickly."

Hyo went to Todomegawa, kneeling by his head. With a jolt of alarm, she realized how quiet he'd been throughout the capture of Jun's ghost, and how still he was now; how he was breathing in thin little sips, as if he was trying to hold his breath but failing.

"Hey." She shook him by the shoulder. "Todomegawa! Wake up!"

A ghost light circled closer. Its pale flames lit up Todomegawa's face, revealing a green-gold discolouration at his lips and spreading twisting veins around his eyes.

"Nagakumo-san!"

"You're kidding me," said Nagakumo, rushing back. She examined Todomegawa herself. "No one reacts this quickly to yashiori, not unless they—" She cut herself off and shook her head. "Whatever. Just mask him up. Miura! The Bridgeburner's half-under!"

"Already?!"

"Keep him awake." Nagakumo squeezed Hyo's arm, then she stood and went. She and the two officers were searching for something in the vicinity of the rock.

Hyo tied the kerchief over Todomegawa's mouth and nose. As her fingers brushed over his scalp, to knot the cloth securely, his eyelids fluttered, then snapped open, focusing on Hyo.

"Hey." He looked so afraid. Hyo held out her hand to him. "Want something to hold on to?"

To the shock of them both, Todomegawa took it, gripping her hand in slippery fingers, torn nails digging. He breathed in shakily through the cloth then coughed.

"Hyo-san…"

"Don't talk."

"I must. Listen!"

"There!" Nagakumo pounced, snatching at something under the rock. It was small and nimble and evaded her fingers easily. "Agile little bastard!"

A straw doll darted out past Todomegawa's shoulder, skirting around Hyo's knees to scurry out into the open.

It trailed smoke from a gash in its chest. The bar of burning incense stuffed inside it caught the glow of the ghost lights with the same sickly colour as that sliding over Todomegawa's skin.

The Onmyoryo officer, Miura, blocked its way, hands ready in a sword sign. It changed tack.

"Do not pursue Makuni Junichiro's case without me," Todomegawa said. His grip tightened. "I mean it. His case is mine to resolve, not yours. I am your caseworker. I am *meant* to protect you. Wait for me to return – then we will confront them."

"Return from where?" The abrupt clarity in his eyes frightened Hyo. "Confront who? You've worked out Jun-san's curser?!"

"Remember this: my shrine at Hamanoyokocho." Todomegawa was flagging, Hyo realized, slipping fast. She leant in to catch his whispers. "Natsuami mustn't go there."

"Why?"

"Never mind. Just keep my brother safe. From hurting others. He never wanted to hurt others."

"I don't understand."

"I told you to avoid Natsuami where you could. I retract that. Hyo." Todomegawa breathed her name as if he were blowing out a candle. "My earthly name is Ryouen Tokifuyu. Call me by it, and he'll know to trust you. Don't tell Natsuami ... don't tell my brother ... that I'm the one who's been destroying all his precious en..."

His head sagged.

"No." Hyo shook Todomegawa again. "No, you don't! You think you know who cursed Jun-san. *Who did it?!* Hey!"

"Oh, no you don't!" Nagakumo's foot came down. She stamped the doll into the boards, grinding its body and the incense into the Plaza. "That's for ... every ... god ... we've lost to this damn ... life-wrecker!"

Nagakumo's stamping shook the boards. It didn't even make Todomegawa twitch. He was out cold. The green-gold shimmer of the drug was even in the whites of his eyes – in the thin slivers of them Hyo could see.

"What the hell is this?" Nagakumo picked up the mangled doll and turned it over, but the doll was nothing more than a crushed knot of straw. No charm, Hyo noted; no ink nor blood to bind breath; no sign of a maker.

"How is he doing?" Miura came to Hyo and Todomegawa. His face clouded as soon as he saw Todomegawa. "Damn it."

"He must've been a smoker. He reacted *fast* to that yashiori." Nagakumo joined Miura in looking down on Todomegawa in the rock's shadow. "Do you reckon ... someone knew? That the Bridgeburner had a habit? Maybe someone wanted him out of the way for a while. If they knew he'd be so easy to drown in the Under-dream..."

"Nagakumo," Miura said warningly.

The ghost lights rose.

They lifted from the crown of the rock, from the Plaza, from around Todomegawa's form, like a startled flock from a field, and vanished into the shadows between the towers.

Hyo waited a moment, listening to the darkness that the ghosts had melted into, then said, "Was that normal?"

"Could be a new normal." Nagakumo scrubbed off the blood from under her nose. "They like to spring that on us occasionally."

Miura raised his hand in the sword sign.

The other officer had been dispatched to the Hikaraku Onmyoryo. They were the only ones remaining on the Plaza (who were awake and not a god rock).

The moon shone brighter; the shadows darkened deeper.

The headless horse jumped into view, tossing the flames of its neck, and the long dark hair of its rider streamed like smoke behind them.

THIRTEEN

丸薬製造

The gods of fortune can give and take away good luck, but not the bad. To touch bad luck at all would reject the wishes of the humans who named them to exist.

SENA,
Twentieth Hellmaker

Ryouen Natsuami dismounted on to the Plaza.

"Evening, there," Nagakumo called out good-naturedly, but the knuckles on her jitte were white. "What can we do for you?"

"That's the Bridgeburner's horse," Miura said, and he wasn't wrong. Hyo could see the scar on Buru-chan's flank from when Mansaku had nicked her. "Who are you?"

They were tensed, and Hyo knew why. That crouching heaviness she'd sensed in the notice-hut shadows was there. It was immense and poised, and it was centred on Natsuami.

"I'm sorry to trouble you, officers." Buru-chan vanished with a swish of her tail. The moon slid out from behind a cloud. In its light, Natsuami seemed to glide as he approached. "I'm looking for my brother. You may know him as Todomegawa the Bridgeburner? I heard him calling for my help. But, perhaps ... his horse brought me to the wrong place?" His tone turned silkily icy. "Surely, with an officer from *both* the Onmyoryo and the police here on watch, my little brother shouldn't have come to any harm."

"We apologize!" Miura bowed at the waist. Nagakumo followed suite. "Our supervision here was inadequate! Please be assured that this incident will be treated with the utmost gravity! He's right here, sir."

"Thank you." Then Natsuami spotted Hyo in the rock's shadow. He stopped mid-step. His monstrous presence hovered on the moment's claw-tips.

"Ryouen Natsuami," Hyo said, naming him, wishing him there, before he could run. "From the notice hut on the day of the wild rain."

"Hakai Hyo," Natsuami said in an awed whisper, disbelieving. "You remember me."

He balled up his hands and strode the remaining distance.

"Toki? Toki!" he said, dropping to his knees, by Todomegawa – by *Tokifuyu*. The green-gold of the yashiori had deepened to a swirling iridescence colouring Tokifuyu's cheeks and forehead. A glowing red ribbon of blood threaded down from his hairline. Natsuami cupped Tokifuyu's face. "This green colouring…"

Miura approached them warily. "Is sir close to his brother?"

"He's the youngest and the last of my eight little brothers, and we've lived with each other for nine hundred years."

Miura turned away with Nagakumo. They began talking in lowered voices.

Natsuami glanced at Hyo. "I met you the day you'd been with Jun when he died. Now I meet you again with Toki when he's been poisoned. What am I to make of you?"

Hyo replied, "That I'm someone with an en with you."

"The humans with an en with me—"

"Have died, I know. But you can't run from me, just as I can't run from you – in which case, we may as well make this work." The hellmakers' en tugged, its tie closing. "Don't you want to know who killed Jun and drugged your brother?"

Natsuami paused. He pushed the hair out of Tokifuyu's eyes. "I wish you were more afraid of me."

"I'll never be afraid of you."

He looked at Hyo oddly, but it was true. Hyo wasn't afraid of Natsuami, and she never could be. It surprised her how unquestioning it was, but the more she thought about it, the more obvious the reason why.

Unconsciously, Natsuami manipulated the en-networks to, maybe, bring him to hitodenashi, and the hellmakers' en did the same to bring Hyo her commissioners. In a way, Natsuami wasn't so different from another hellmaker.

"Besides," she said, before the quiet got too long, "Tokifuyu asked me to keep you safe."

"*Me* safe?" he spluttered. "What a ... what a thing to ask of a human! And after chasing you all about Hikaraku, has he no shame? What was he thinking?!"

"Not much, or that deeply."

"Yes, that's probably true," Natsuami conceded. "Toki gave you his earthly name, then."

"Yeah."

"He chose to trust you." Natsuami tucked a handful of his hair behind an ear, revealing half of his face to the moonlight. "Very well. I can honour that."

"Sir," Miura said. He and Nagakumo had returned. "I'd like to ask sir to come back to the Onmyoryo and answer some questions, if possible."

Natsuami blinked. "I don't quite follow. What have I got to do with—?"

"It's just procedure, sir! Please understand." Miura held up his hands as if in surrender. "The dose of yashiori your brother was exposed to shouldn't have affected him like this, and we want to know why. The sooner we do, the sooner we can treat this incident as an attack on an Onmyoryo officer."

"I see. Then... Yes, I'll comply."

"That goes for you too," Miura said to Hyo. "We'd like you to give us a witness statement."

"At the Onmyoryo?"

"That's right," Miura replied, apparently oblivious to Hyo's unease. "Tonight would be best, whilst it's still fresh."

"No."

"Understandable, but our cafeteria does a decent curry udon. You'll get a free dinner, we'll pay for your taxicraft back—"

"I will take these two for questioning, Officer Miura." Footsteps sounded on the Plaza, accompanied by a wash of spiritual power, like invisible breakwater. "Neither of these darlings are for you to handle lightly."

The Wavewalker had arrived, dressed in Onmyoryo purple, his face masked and trailing ribbons with bells from his headdress. Under the edge of his mask, his green teeth were bared. With each step, the boards seethed with movement, as crabs, hundreds of them, poured out of his clothes.

Rage roiled off him. It chilled Hyo's skin.

Confusion and indignation warred on Miura's face. "But, sir—"

"One of my rivers has just been **drowned in the Under-dream under your watch, Officer Miura Takayoshi,**" the Wavewalker's voice crashed and echoed. The cables suspending the Plaza creaked. "**I will not see these two wasted by your incompetency – nay, to the incompetency of all the officers responsible for this ghost-baiting! Give them to me! This is a small price for my mercy!**"

Miura dropped to the floor, bowing his head to it. "Yes, Wavewalker, sir!"

A crab waved its claws at Hyo. In its pincer, there was a black pill.

She heard a voice in her ear say, "Take one of these and give those nosy eyes and ears of yours a rest, little darling."

"Or what?"

"Or I'll leave you to the good officers of the Onmyoryo, after all. You don't want that, do you?"

Hyo took the pill and swallowed it dry.

Heavy footsteps crunched through snow.

"Why won't the pear infect you like the rest of them?" The demon gazed down at Hyo. Her greatcoat swayed heavy with frozen blood. "Must we really repeat the winter again? All I want to see is the blossoms growing from your spine and breaking apart your body. It's not too much to ask of a human girl."

It wasn't. Hyo had seen it happen to everyone else. They'd rooted, sprouted, peeled open.

She flicked the trigger on the gas lighter. It clicked and clacked, sputtered, then died. She tossed it away. "Damn it!"

In front of her, Old Man Watanuki's empty eyes were following her movements. They were still visible through the growths of bark on his face.

She was glad he couldn't speak, that the hitodenashi had cracked apart his jaws. He couldn't say, "Stop!"

Couldn't say, "Do it!"

Hyo pressed her forehead against the bark. She needed more tinder to burn Old Man Watanuki down anyway. Maybe it was time for the hellmakers' archives – they were dry enough.

"Namu Amida Butsu," she said, just to break the silence, to defeat the demon. The silence in the village seemed to belong to it.

The demon laughed. "You invoke the Amida Untethered before me*?*"

To name a god was to wish them to exist in this world.

To refer to an Untethered One was to wish that someone did not: that they could escape this world's tethers.

The fat clusters of hitodenashi blossoms twisting up from Old Man Watanuki's body spat petals over her even in winter, and Hyo thought that spring was a good time to die. Yes, it was worth surviving all these winters to end it all in spring.

"Well, now, little darling, it should be about time."

The room Hyo woke to smelled of herbs and apothecary's honey, the binding ingredient in pills. The Wavewalker was working the pump and pedal on an old pill-rolling machine. Amidst its rhythmical clunk and clatter, perfect spheres of medicine pills were pattering into a tray.

It would've looked a familiar scene to Hyo – if the Wavewalker hadn't shed his humanish guises for one more obviously divine, with a twelve-tined crown of red coral antlers, strings of agate and pearls around his neck; and hakama that seemed knitted from sea urchin spines, if the machine's tray wasn't on the back of a giant blue crab, and if the pills in the tray weren't a fresh, summery green with an eerie starlight shimmer.

"How is little darling feeling?" the Wavewalker said without looking. "Energized? Well rested?"

"Yeah, I am," Hyo said with some surprise. That dream should've left her in a cold sweat. It had before. "What did you give me?"

"I call it the Nightmare Burner," the Wavewalker said with some pride. "It burns up a nightmare's negative energy as fuel for healing body, mind and spirit instead. It should have sufficiently re-energized you to tell me what happened on the Plaza."

"Whilst knocking me out for long enough that you could take me wherever you wanted."

"Neither you nor Natsuami should be brought into Onmyoryo premises. You'd muddle half the experiments being conducted there –" the Wavewalker stopped pedalling and picked up the tray from the crab's back – "and the Onmyoryo's full of officers who are too certain in their own goodness to appreciate the ... uncertainties you'd present."

Hyo sat up. She'd been laid out on a low couch by a table. "Am I not in the Onmyoryo?"

"You're at my shrine in Minami-Kanda. It specializes in my healing aspect. My main medicinal workshop is here." The Wavewalker sat cross-legged on the crab and snapped open a fan. "As is the island's best ward for treating the gods who overdose on yashiori."

Hyo remembered the drug's marbling patterns

spreading through Tokifuyu's skin. "What's going to happen to the Bridgeburner?"

"He'll be kept here until he wakes. I'll do everything in my power to speed his recovery. Everything. Yes, everything." With a curl of surprise, Hyo realized that the Wavewalker was shaken – rattled even more than perhaps she was. "We've yet no knowledge of the rhyme or reason for when these gods wake up. Some wake in days. Some in years."

"Years?!"

"We can't afford that with Todomegawa. As I'm sure little darling is already aware, Onogoro needs him. There are other en-cutters, yes, but only one en-cutter is Ryouen Natsuami's brother. Only Todomegawa has an en strong enough with that strange creature that we can rely on to be a leash in a crisis. Here, little darling, water."

"Thank you." The glass that appeared on the table was made of ice. Hyo didn't touch it.

"Start from the moment you arrived at the Plaza." The Wavewalker sipped out of his own yunomi, propping his head on his elbow. "No details omitted."

Hyo put her hands on the ice cup and focused on its smooth coolness. The short of it was that the Wavewalker had spirited Hyo away and there was nothing to stop him keeping her here until he had everything he wanted from her.

She told him what happened, and watched the

Wavewalker's reactions as she did so. But he was unreadable, as inscrutable as the sea, as tangled as a river, one expression flowing into another before she could get a grip on it.

Hyo told him that she'd gone to the Plaza in the hope of meeting Jun's ghost. She said his name, Makuni Junichiro, hoping to see how the Wavewalker responded as both the Shin-Kaguraza's and Koushiro's guardian god. He nodded, listening intently, and showed no obvious feeling until Hyo came to the moment that Hatamoto had smelled yashiori incense, when the fan cracked in his grip. By the time she'd described finding Tokifuyu already succumbing to the drug, and the destruction of the animated straw doll, the fan had been pulverized.

"Your account matches all the officers'." Hyo bit down on a breath of relief. The Wavewalker swirled his drink. "There's one thing little darling may know that they didn't. Did Makuni Junichiro say anything to Todomegawa?"

"He did, but..." And then it hit her. *Colluder. Co-conspirator.* Who Tokifuyu had been talking to. Who Jun couldn't name. Hyo faltered, then feigned confusion. "I couldn't hear everything."

"What did you hear?"

"Something about reflectographs. A collection." Hyo kept her eyes on the Wavewalker. "Jun said he overheard Todomegawa and you talking about it when he was hiding at Todomegawa's shrine – that it might've caused Koushiro to be unlucky."

"Ah, that would be Koushiro's collection of ghost pictures." The Wavewalker flicked away a splinter of fan. "I did visit Todomegawa's shrine to discuss those recently, yes. Junichiro often gifted Koushiro reflectographs showing spiritual phenomena. I wasn't aware of this until the end of Fourthmonth as Koushiro had kept it hidden from my eyes. After I identified it as a possible cause of Koushiro's bad luck, it was meant to have been destroyed. Todomegawa was raising the idea that Koushiro disobeyed me and kept some pictures to himself – hence Koushiro's continued unluckiness. Is this really what Junichiro's ghost wished to talk to Todomegawa about?"

"It's all I heard." Thunder rumbled low outside. Hyo breathed deep. "How did you find out about the collection?"

"Todomegawa brought it to my attention. He found it tracing an en between the collection –" the Wavewalker stretched a lock of green hair, making a thread of it – "and our anomalous friend."

"Natsuami?"

"That's right. For three years, I've been Todomegawa's supervisor and partner in his management of Natsuami's affairs and organizing Natsuami's world. Todomegawa reports to me everything he finds regarding Natsuami's ens, and I play all the roles needed for a minimal en-network that keeps Natsuami unsuspecting and mostly harmless. I'm Mr Funawa his editor –" a ripple of power and a mousy-looking man in glasses sat on the crab – "Mr Sato the bathhouse receptionist –" another ripple, a jovial face with crow's feet – "Ms Sawada the paper seller –" a mole, kerchief, friendly eyes – "and her cat, Ankoku-Kishi-Gokiburi-Crusher –" a petite tortoiseshell kitten – "and more."

"That's ... a lot of work."

"It's necessary, to keep people safe from him. Well, Todomegawa discovered that there was a reflectograph of Natsuami in Koushiro's collection, one which Junichiro had taken and given him, as a curse curiosity." The Wavewalker expression clouded. "Now, little darling, you know how easily en can form – at a glance, at a touch, at a word. A reflectograph was an all too powerful seeder for an en. Todomegawa reported it to me to get it out of Koushiro's hands. As Koushiro's guardian god. I was perfectly placed to do it. And then, it *just so happened* that Koushiro's luck turned. Suddenly, he was a lightning rod for unluck. I thought, *Now I have the perfect opportunity to get rid of Natsuami's reflectograph without drawing Koushiro's attention to it and strengthening that en.* I told Koushiro that his collection was a possible cause for his unluck attraction – and it *was*, this wasn't a lie – and had him burn the whole thing. But, as you know,

Koushiro's bad luck has continued." The crab bubbled. The Wavewalker patted it absentmindedly, gaze far away. "I went to Todomegawa to ask him to see Koushiro's en-networks, to check if Natsuami's reflectograph was truly gone or not – and, by extension, if Koushiro had disobeyed me. But it was futile. Todomegawa couldn't see anything."

Hyo narrowed her eyes. "And that's all you and Todomegawa talked about?"

"I'm telling you only what I can – my truth." The shells and pearls woven into the Wavewalker's sea-green mane of hair lifted in a breeze that Hyo couldn't feel. "You aren't satisfied by a god's word?"

"I've no proof it's true."

"Proof!" The Wavewalker laughed. He had a humanish face – the "ish" was that it seemed too sharp, his eyes too black and his laughter too bright. "Proof that I did what I did at the when and the where that I say, little darling, is for humans! We gods are both everywhere at once and one somewhere at a time! We could be anyone or anything and any voice and any sound. We have and leave no fingerprints, in more ways than one. It's why gods must confess to their curses and accept their taint!" He laughed again, sipped his drink – which Hyo began to suspect wasn't tea – then took an envelope from his robes. "Deliver this to Koushiro, and I'm sure he'll be only too happy to confirm his part of what I said."

"That's..." Hyo touched her waist-pouch where Koushiro's letter to Jun should have been. "You searched my things."

"Only for yashiori traces, so that little darling isn't suspected of being the straw doll's master." The Wavewalker tossed the envelope on to the table. "Make sure that Koushiro sees it. Last words are once-in-a-lifetime creations."

The flap was open and cool where the Wavewalker had touched it. "You could give it to Koushiro yourself, sir?"

"No. It has to come from you. He's heard that same advice too often from me, and he's not forgiven me for having his reflectographs burned. How did you come by it, by the way?" When Hyo hesitated, the Wavewalker said dryly, "Off Junichiro's corpse, perhaps?"

"Yes."

He laughed. "As expected of a hellmaker."

Hyo folded the letter away in her pouch. She checked that everything else inside was as it should be. Ritsu's envelope from the box office was also opened, but the Declaration from the Paddywatcher was untouched. The Pillar Gods really didn't interfere with each other.

The Wavewalker heaved a heavy sigh. "But the question now remains as to who brought the yashiori to the Plaza. It wasn't the ghost; it didn't have the presence of mind for that. It wasn't you, little darling, as you don't have the skills to animate the doll like the officers described. Which leaves, of those there –" the Wavewalker twisted his hair between his fingers – "Yatsuhata-no-Mikoto. That fading war god."

"He was by me the whole time. I don't think he could've done anything," Hyo said, which was true. Hatamoto's hands had always been busy and in view.

"So Ame'no'Iwaba-no-Mikoto says. Oh, yes," said the Wavewalker when Hyo's eyes widened, "we've spoken to her too. She's hard of hearing but she has keen vision and never looks away. All Plaza accounts flow to a single conclusion – that the one who dosed Todomegawa in yashiori is elsewhere, somewhere in Onogoro's shadows." The Wavewalker pursed his lips and winced. "What to tell his brother, if we're to tell him anything at all?"

"Why wouldn't you tell him something?" Hyo didn't like it. Natsuami had a *lot* kept from him. "He's hardly a suspect. He can't animate that doll—"

"I am more aware of Natsuami's abilities than you are, hellmaker, and more knowledgeable of his mind and nature," said the Wavewalker with a storm-cloud prickle of charge. "Tell him that the god – or perhaps human of unknown abilities – who poisoned his brother is somewhere on the island, and what do you think Natsuami would do, little darling? He'd look for them! Go out into Onogoro! Meet people! Make ens! We couldn't stop him. Our best and strongest leash on his behaviour is gone into the Under-dream."

A machine in the corner of the room chimed. The Wavewalker vanished and reappeared beside it, removing a tray of freshly dried pills. "Perfect."

"Without meaning sir offence..." Hyo cleared her throat and finally voiced what had been at bothering her, "Hatamoto-san wouldn't even say Natsuami's name because he thought it'd put his followers in danger. But you..."

"But I've thousands of followers, and name Natsuami without fear? Yes, I do," said the Wavewalker with pride. He shook the dried pills in their tray. "I don't say his name without thought of risk. I say it, little darling, because there *is* no risk. I'm the Pillar Water God of Onogoro, not a fading war god. I can shoulder one fallen anomaly – and, when they're all that remains of an old dear friend, I'll do so gladly – even if, as far as he is concerned, we're perfect strangers." He suddenly stilled, looking Hyo's way. "But you and he are not."

"Sir, I've met Natsuami *twice*. We're not friends or anything." The considering look the Wavewalker gave her made Hyo want to duck and hide. "Where is he?"

"In the ward with his brother." The Wavewalker stroked his chin. "He said he would wait for little darling to finish giving her statement so you could take the return taxicraft together. We're currently coming to the first hour of the tiger – three o'clock in the morning."

"Oh."

"We've supplied him with tea." A blink, and the Wavewalker was on the couch beside her, lifting Hyo's chin with a new fan, apparently materialized for this purpose. She had no choice but to look him in the eye, into an old deep darkness that was sometimes sea, sometimes river, and all water that had hewn rock, drowned lives and carved fates. "As a god of fortune, tasked with the protection of thousands on this island, some might say that I'm duty-bound to hinder your hellmaking, Hakai Hyo, in the same way that you are duty-bound to perform it. Wouldn't you agree?"

Hyo forced herself to hold his gaze. "What do you want?"

"Hellmaker, I'll give you free rein to investigate Junichiro's curse however you please, and to choose any special commissioner you need to avenge him, but in exchange you will perform one task for me." The Wavewalker tipped her chin up higher. "Your en to Natsuami isn't going anywhere. We may as well make use of it. I'm a busy god, a Pillar, as you can imagine? I can play many parts – but I need someone to step into Todomegawa's."

Hyo recoiled. "I'm not going to be a *leash.*"

"No, you're going to be his temporary home. His shelter." The Wavewalker spoke as if bestowing upon her a gift. "Natsuami needs to be watched at close quarters, and distracted from this doll incident – and you with your

nose in Makuni Junichiro's case ... it'd be the perfect diversion for him, wouldn't it?"

"Diversion?!"

The Wavewalker's scaled face filled her vision. "Does little darling agree to this exchange?"

FOURTEEN

お線香

Our gifts are those of the gods of misfortune: like the creeping gods of disease, and the faded gods of poverty and misery, we manipulate unluck.

TAMA,
Twenty-Second Hellmaker

"Make yourself at home."

"Thank you." Natsuami bowed. He set his things down in the entrance. "I place myself in your care."

On the way back, the taxicraft had stopped by the Ryouen brothers' tatenagaya. A mixed team of Onmyoryo and police officers had been waiting at its door, ready to search it for yashiori. They'd watched Natsuami closely as he'd bundled up his bedding and things, and had begun opening cupboards and closets as soon as he'd finished.

A new table had been delivered in Hyo and Mansaku's absence. Natsuami unpacked it whilst Hyo swept the remains of the old one into a basket. He said, "I do hope the Wavewalker offered you something worthwhile for this."

Hyo hesitated. Both Tokifuyu and the Wavewalker seemed to think Natsuami was oblivious to their schemes; it seemed that was not the case. "What is 'this' to you?"

"The kindness of hosting me, a near stranger, whilst the officers search my and Toki's home," Natsuami replied deftly, but his eyes were flicking around the room, taking in the talismans, the width of the floor, the door, the locks, "and I imagine something else will come up that will mean I have to extend my stay, likely until Toki wakes up."

Hyo winced. He definitely knew he was being handed over to a new warden.

"It was worthwhile," she said, making her decision – she'd tell Natsuami as much as she could. "The

Wavewalker's going to stay out of my work and let me keep looking for the god who killed Jun-san."

His head shot up. "The god who killed Jun...?!"

Hyo closed the door of the water closet on him. When she'd washed her face and emerged, she found Natsuami by their makeshift altar to Jun. It embarrassed her now, a little. It was no more than a dog-eared paperback and an incense burner.

Natsuami picked up the paperback. "This book..."

Hyo hurried to explain. "It's for Jun-san. We didn't have anything else to remember him by, so... He had a copy when he came to my village. You're the author, aren't you?"

"I was." His mouth creased into an unsteady line. "I never thought Jun truly liked them."

"He did readings for the kids. He roped me and Mansaku into acting out the gory bits. He loved them," Hyo said with absolutely certainty.

"Mansaku?"

"My brother. He's ... never mind." Hyo had hoped Mansaku would be at home when she'd returned. He would've known what to do to put Natsuami at ease. Hyo wasn't so good with the living. The dying, she knew how to work with those.

"We smashed a lot of vegetables for the sound effects," Hyo continued. Hatamoto had said that the Paddywatcher would return Mansaku if Hyo cooperated, and that she'd be in touch. Hyo could wait. She had no choice. "But nothing was wasted. The kids took it all home for dinner."

"Ah."

Natsuami continued to gaze at the book, expression hidden. Hyo said, softer, "I don't want to be your jailer. If you ask something, and I can answer it, I'll try."

"I didn't actually expect you to tell me anything." Natsuami lifted his head, letting her see his face. "I suppose ... you wouldn't be able to tell me why I'm under watch? If it has anything to do with why I can't keep my ens any more? Or why the few human ens I do make end so ... poorly for them?"

Hyo held up the back of her hand, where Tokifuyu's silencing curse stamp had lit up under her skin, like a warning. "No."

"Oh, a stamp curse. Bother." Natsuami extended his fingers. He didn't touch her but Hyo felt something graze the back of her hand, like teeth. "Only breaking the stamp itself would break this, and I don't know where Toki keeps his." He lowered his hand. "What is your work, Hyo-san?"

"Just Hyo is fine. Here." She found the old packet from Koura and gave him a business card. At this rate, maybe she should make new ones.

Natsuami read it. "Artisan hells?"

"An artisan hell's a curse," Hyo told him. The walls creaked with the turning of a nearby wind turbine. "I put a tatari on the target that turns the whole world against them."

"What makes it ... artisan?"

"They take some skill to craft. The unluck particles have to be directed into the right shapes to change the luck landscape, and the shapes I'd need to make are different with every commission. I can't reuse them."

Natsuami said uncertainly, "Where does Jun fit into this? You said before that the en brought you to those who needed you?"

"Sometimes the hellmakers' en brings me a death, then it ties me to someone who'll commission me to avenge on the dead's behalf. Jun-san's one of those deaths." Hyo showed Natsuami the seal on her palms. Three fingers on each were faded. "The hellmakers' en is a part of this curse. It brings me chances to undo this seal, and use the powers of the old gods of misfortune. If I don't use them, these powers wear through the seal, and get out of my control."

"Then a commissioner is someone who unlocks those powers for you?" Natsuami stared at her intently. "For vengeance?"

"Yes," she said. "But I can't go to the commissioner empty-handed. We need to know who we're cursing. I need a culprit and motive, before I can ask them to commission me."

Natsuami adjusted his glasses. "Are you sure I'm not your commissioner? For Jun?"

"I'm sure."

"How can you be?"

"I'd know if you were, and so would you." She offered him the box of incense sticks. "One for Jun-san?"

"One for Jun," Natsuami agreed, taking a stick of incense. Hyo struck a match and lit them both. They waved the flames out together, filling the room with the smell of sandalwood. "You heard what happened to Jun's ghost then."

Hyo set her incense in the stand. "The Wavewalker told me the Onmyoryo officers had 'disposed' of him."

"No specifics?"

"No." Hyo put her hands together. *Jun-san, I'm sorry.*

"Me neither." Natsuami planted his incense in the stand too. "Just thinking about it makes me feel sick, then I remember what happened to Toki and..."

Hyo opened one eye. He actually did sound queasy. "Are you going to—?"

"I'm sorry – in two minutes, I'm going to make use of your water closet and throw up in it."

They stood in quiet, hands together in front of a cheap paperback and a couple of incense sticks.

Then Natsuami went to the water closet, and Hyo was left to her own thoughts; to the rhythmic high-pitched creaks of the wall from the nearby turbine that sounded as if the tower was crying softly through gritted teeth. She had spoken to Jun's last echoes. Now they too had been forcefully silenced.

Her chest felt too tight. She went quickly to the water closet, for something to do, anything, and settled on bundling back Natsuami's hair into a thick braid, out of his way, so that he could swill his mouth clean of vomit and wash his face.

He said, "Thank you."

"Don't mention it." Hyo wiped her eyes on her arm. Then wiped them again. "Do you want tea?"

"I'd *love* tea."

"It won't be as fancy as the Wavewalker's," she warned, and slipped away, to get a grip on herself.

The clock in the kitchen pointed to ten to five in the morning – the end of the second hour of the tiger.

"What were you questioned on?" Hyo asked, once they'd settled at the new table and were both warming their hands on their cups.

"Yashiori, and whether I'd seen any sign that Toki might have been habitually using it. It's illegal to possess it, after all, so the Wavewalker was quite persistent. He went through a list of 'potential signs'." The corners of Natsuami's lips turned downwards. "But strange sleep patterns, restlessness and an unpredictable temper? These are simply my brother's personality quirks on a good day."

Hyo stifled a snort. "Has he always been like that?"

"For nine hundred years."

"You must have asked Tokifuyu why you're under watch?"

"Many times. He says that it's in case the god of destruction who caused Three Thousand Three Fall returns." Hyo nearly spat out her tea. Natsuami didn't seem to notice. He'd spotted the narezushi left over from Tokifuyu's visit. "Is that Maruyoshi's mackerel narezushi?!"

"Help yourself." She took one too when Natsuami offered her the box. "So, er, what's the god of Three Thousand Three Fall have to do with you?"

"According to Toki, I fought the god, valiantly and righteously!" Natsuami swung an imaginary sword with his free hand. "But I lost, and lost all my shrines and followers as a result – and hence much of my memories as a god. He and the Onmyoryo seem to think that, if the god came back, it would seek me out first to kill me in revenge."

"When you say, 'according to Toki'...?"

"I remember none of Three Thousand Three Fall myself." Natsuami directed his gaze down to the scars criss-crossing his hands. "I only have what Toki tells me."

"And do you believe him?"

"I'll believe it for his sake. I've some sense that I came very near death, and that it affected him deeply." Natsuami traced the line of a scar at his knuckles. The width of it matched his own finger. "I don't want to be a source of any more pain to him. But I recognize that I'm ... strange. For a god. For instance, I can exist comfortably without a heavenly name when no other god can. Toki hasn't been able to explain that."

"Do you want your heavenly name back?"

"To be called by it to help those who need me? Surely, it's only natural that I should?" A delicate pause. The lights dimmed, then brightened again, like a slow blink. Hyo opened her mouth to change the topic but Natsuami beat her to it. "I have Jun's letter to me."

She sat up quickly. "You do?"

"I picked it up from my apartment on the way here. If you still wish to see it?"

"Wouldn't this mean we 'share a turning point'?"

"I suspect we've already shared such an event now." Retrieving his basket, Natsuami extracted the blue-grey envelope with its blotchy security seal from its depths. "I tried to avoid you to keep you from harm – and we met anyway. If I cannot protect you and your brother, as Jun asked of me, by keeping my distance, then I've no option but to stay close to you. And if that's the case, I must help you."

He took out the letter. The blue paper had been folded in three. It started in pencil, then as the writer's dexterity diminished, he had switched to a white crayon before finally ending in white ink and brush.

The hellmakers' en tightened. All the threads tied by it sang.

Fifthmonth 15th

Natsu-san,

My friend, I know you are a god. I'm sorry; I think you didn't want me to find out, but you were such a good puzzle. I couldn't help myself.

You've no shrines, no mention in the libraries, nothing but an earthly name to go by. You've been erased from Onogoro's records, if you were ever in them at all. You've some power, enough that the gods who I asked of you refused to say your earthly name for fear of it. You exist without offerings of human musuhi.

So in this last letter to you, I write in need of such a god:

One who won't need to be paid in prayers, because I won't be here to offer them to you.

And one who I know will never hurt those I care for – that's why you've kept your distance from me, isn't it?

Please: protect my brother Koushiro.

He is in danger. You must've heard of Kikugawa Kichizuru's bad luck. The gods are saying it's a natural phenomenon. It isn't. The gods are behind it, but I am silenced from naming a single one!

I understand everything now. Why I was cursed. Why Koushiro has been too.

It's all my fault. I gave him a reflectograph he shouldn't have seen.

Tell him that he has to burn what he's kept of his reflectograph collection. Tell him I'm sorry.

I said that I'd take you to the theatre one day. I'm sorry I can't keep that promise.

It is good that we only met once then never again. Everything that could've happened still exists between us. I can still feel everything for you, nothing disallowed, perfectly and selfishly full of heart for you.

My kind and beautiful cursed god, I pray we have better en in the next life,

Jun

P.S. I've friends arriving today from Occupied-Ukoku. They won't know anyone here, no humans let alone the gods. I've left them my keys, but if you could help them – protect them like a real Onogoro god, not one who'd pick favourites and watch the rest die – my ghost will be able to move on faster.

The older brother is Hakai Mansaku. The little sister is Hakai Hyo.

"If you will allow me to," Natsuami said, "I would like to help you find the god who killed Jun, poisoned Toki and is seeking to harm Koushiro, and see them brought to justice."

"Hellmaking isn't justice, Natsuami." Hyo folded the letter up carefully to pass it back to him. "No one will forget; no one is forgiven. It doesn't restore balance, and it won't make anything fair. It's a service people come to because they're hurt, and sometimes they've made that hurt into a bomb, and we take that bomb out of their hands and blow it up for them, because we can do it with no bystanders getting caught up in it. That's all. Don't mistake hellmaking for justice, ever."

"I don't mind if hellmaking is just or unjust." Natsuami stared down at the explosion of brushstrokes on the envelope that was meant to be his name. "I heard from Toki that the Onmyoryo wish to close Jun's case soon and treat it as a cursing done in Good Reason. Your hellmaking's the only way now that I can see Jun's pain being known to those who inflicted it."

The incense sticks burning for Jun trailed their cobweb strands of smoke.

Hyo swallowed the last of her narezushi and crumpled its reed-leaf wrapper. She bowed her head. "Then we can help each other."

Natsuami's eyes shone, turned glistening, then he hurriedly bowed back. "Let's help each other." Tears ran easily down his face. "I'm so glad for our en. I'm sorry, I know I shouldn't be – it could hurt you – but I am! I'm so glad."

Hyo wasn't sure when she fell asleep. She'd hoped to stay awake until Mansaku returned, but one moment she had her head rested on her hand, drawing out the Onmyoryo privacy talisman she'd spotted in the taxicraft from memory whilst Natsuami laid out his bedding and prepared to enter the semi-sleep of the gods who'd once been humans. The next moment, she was dreaming.

Her dreams were vivid.

Maybe it was like when a heavy thumb pressed on a soap bubble, creating colours that swirled and danced. Hyo was the soap bubble, distorting under the divine pressure that was bearing its whole weight on her in the spiritual plane.

She dreamt that a blood-coloured rope sprouted from her navel. She tugged it and felt the pull in her guts. The rope went through her robes, pierced skin, sank deep but didn't hurt.

The other end disappeared down a black pit sliced into the snowy ground. The rope creaked as something heavy reached up, dragging itself out from somewhere deeper than a dream. It rose with the smell of blood, blossoms and the heady sweetness of pear.

Hyo was its anchor. She waited. But the creature did not appear. It was endlessly clawing at the rope, unable to hold a form, to climb it.

And it asks you to name it.

It would never reach her because it was unnameable.

But how hungry it was to be named.

FIFTEEN

八塩折

... and they called this eight-fold distilled sake "yashiori", so powerful that one sip of it rendered the great eight-headed serpent unconscious...

FU-NO-MONO,
Third Hellmaker

Natsuami was singing in the kitchen. The melody might've been fashionable in the eleventh century.

And then Mansaku's voice joined in, surprisingly tuneful, if mangling the lyrics. Laughter followed. "So, how does memory work for gods? Do you remember all the thousand years you've lived?"

"For those of us who were human, no," Natsuami answered. "What happened to me one hundred years ago feels like a story I was told by a grandparent, and before that, like an orally told epic of which I only remember fragments."

Hyo peeled her face off the table and leapt up, shrugging off a blanket that had been put around her shoulders.

"Mansaku!"

"O'Hyo!" Mansaku looked up from the stove where Natsuami was smoothing miso into a pan of stock. "Ha ha ha, look at you with those bags under your eyes, like a proper raccoon dog. Didn't you sleep?"

"You're back. Are you all right? *How* are you all right?"

"Oh, that's nice. You'd rather I was still rice?"

"You were *wheat*. When did he get back?" she fired at Natsuami.

"About two hours ago," Natsuami replied.

"You didn't wake me up?"

He looked remorseful. "We did try."

"You missed me trying to kill our guest. I opened the door, expecting a warm, concerned welcome, and the first thing I saw was this tall, dark hairiness coming out of the water closet, so I swung ye olde scythe and nearly bisected him. I thought he was some kind of demonic burglar, but— Oof!" Mansaku dropped his dishcloth as Hyo threw her arms around him. He lowered his voice. "This is more like it, but ... it's too sweet. I'm scared."

She gripped the folds of Mansaku's robes at his back. He was warm, returned and slightly damp from bending over the simmering pans. She said, under her breath, too quiet for Natsuami to hear, "You're going to tell me everything that happened to you with the Paddywatcher. We deal with her together."

His arms around Hyo tightened; a silent *thank you*. "Natsu-san told me what happened to the Bridgeburner yesterday. You talked to Jun's ghost, huh?"

"He had stuff to say."

"When did he ever not?" Mansaku gave her one final squeeze, then let her go. "So I've been laying down the ground rules for Natsu-san. He can sleep, cry, get angry whenever he likes, but he helps with laundry, which is fun for all the family, and peels veg."

Hyo held up the back of her hand where Tokifuyu's silencing curse was stamped. "Natsuami, I'm going to take Mansaku out for ten minutes to tell him the things that I can't in front of you."

"That's fine," he replied brightly, slicing a sweet potato. "Thank you for letting me know when you're keeping secrets from me."

"Sing so you can't hear us," Mansaku instructed, and Natsuami bowed.

Hyo took Mansaku up to their room above the kitchen. When Natsuami dutifully started up the long, trailing notes of another song, Hyo said, "You think he's 'demonic'?"

"The way Kiriyuki senses him, he feels like *her* but worse. He's bigger and got more teeth." They both knew which *her* Mansaku meant – *the demon*. They shivered as one. "Have you looked at his flame of life?"

"No."

"Yeah, like the demon, then. You couldn't look at hers either. Don't look at Natsu-san's; you'll probably bleed out from your eyes."

"Noted."

"He told me you made a deal with the Wavewalker to keep an eye on him whilst Flaming Eyeballs is out cold. Is that true?"

Under the tones of Taiwa-style ancient love poetry being sung below their feet, Hyo quickly recounted everything after Mansaku was cursed, from meeting Hatamoto to Natsuami sharing his letter.

By the end, Mansaku's eyes were narrowed, his arms folded. "The Wavewalker really told you about him having Koushiro's reflectograph collection burned for free?"

"I know." That had bothered Hyo too. "He could've made me trade something for it, but he didn't."

"Or maybe we're just suspicious bastards and the world gives out more free lunches than we thought?"

They both shook their heads. "Nah."

"In the Wavewalker's words then, 'it just so happened', that Koushiro's luck went shitty *a little after* he found out that Koushiro's collection existed." Mansaku scratched his head. "Is he trying to sound suspicious or...?"

"Mansaku, I think the Wavewalker *is* cursing Koushiro," Hyo said, the pieces clicking into place. "And the weirdest part is, yeah, I think he *was* trying. He was *trying to tell me* he did it, in as roundabout a way as possible. He cursed Jun. He's cursing Koushiro. He wants me to know that."

Mansaku's mouth dropped open. "Why?"

Hyo held up her hands. "Beats me."

Mansaku shook himself and straightened his shoulders. "All right, let's finish this over lunch. There's no hellmaking on an empty stomach, and this part Natsu-san can hear, right?"

Hyo nodded, then: "Lunch?!"

"Yeah, it's midday already. Keep up, O'Hyo. You'd think being able to see the flames of lives burning up would mean you'd have a better sense of your own internal clock, ticking away to death—"

Hyo gave Mansaku a push that nearly toppled him down the stairs.

Outside the window, a new banner was being hoisted up the side of the Shin-Kaguraza Theatre: a full colour reflectograph of Kikugawa Kichizuru – of Koushiro, red-winged eyes gazing out between wisteria petals, the date of his final performance splashed across it.

Below it, on the theatre steps, Onmyoryo billboards had been erected. They read in large white letters:

DANGER, AREA OF EXTREME
LOW GOOD LUCK PRESSURE
AND HIGH BAD LUCK PRESSURE.
PROCEED WITH CAUTION.

EXPECT LOW PROBABILITY
INCIDENTS OF HIGH MISFORTUNE
BEYOND THIS LINE.

Between the three of them, lunch became steamed rice, an iriko-stock miso soup green with spring onion and mizuna, soy-mirin stewed sweet potatoes, radish pickles and the leftover iriko sprinkled with sansho pepper and soy sauce.

As they sat to eat, Mansaku announced, "By the way, Natsu-san, O'Hyo has something important to say that we're going to discuss, right now."

"Oh?"

"I think the Wavewalker killed Jun-san," Hyo said without hesitating, "and the Wavewalker wanted to confess that when he questioned me. But he can't, because he's been silenced about it. And he's going after Koushiro now, too."

Natsuami dropped his chopsticks. "The Wavewalker killed Jun?!"

"That's what Jun-san was telling us at the Plaza. He called Tokifuyu a 'colluder' and a 'co-conspirator' for talking to the Wavewalker. Seeing them together is what drove him out of Tokifuyu's shrine." Hyo could imagine it: the deep betrayal and fear, seeing your own curse-mediator and curser together, talking in lowered voices, far from strangers. "Jun-san's ghost got as close to accusing the Wavewalker around the silencing curse as he could."

Natsuami's eyes were wide and aghast. "Tokifuyu would never..."

"I don't think Tokifuyu did," Hyo said. His shock and indignation at the Plaza had been too real.

"Good," said Natsuami firmly. "But the Wavewalker's a senior Onmyoryo curse-mediator and a Pillar God! He knows all the rules for cursing civilly!"

Mansaku laughed. "You're saying it can't be the Wavewalker because Jun's curser didn't leave a receipt?"

"He wouldn't have cursed Jun like this." Natsuami glanced from Hyo to Mansaku then back, as if silently pleading for someone to declare everything so far a joke. When neither did, he lowered his eyes to the table. "The Wavewalker wouldn't need to kill a human in secret. Had he Good Reason, he could do it openly."

"Then he didn't have Good Reason, and he knew it."

Hyo picked clean her rice bowl, grain by grain.

"Jun-san would have known who cursed him," Natsuami said reluctantly. "The cursed always know, instinctively, who's cursed them. He would've recognized his curser when he saw him."

"Exactly. That night at Tokifuyu's shrine, Jun-san saw Tokifuyu with the Wavewalker, his curser. He overheard them talking about Koushiro's reflectograph collection, and maybe that's when it all clicked for him. Like he said in your letter, Natsuami: *I understand everything now.* He thought he'd figured out why someone might want both of them dead. The gods talking about Koushiro's collection gave him the hint." Hyo set down her chopsticks over her bowl. "And then because Jun-san couldn't trust Tokifuyu any more, he left Tokifuyu's shrine to do what he could for Koushiro himself, knowing the curse would catch up with him and kill him."

"I get that the Wavewalker killed Jun, but isn't Koushiro different? The gods are saying that Koushiro's bad luck is natural," Mansaku pointed out.

"The *Wavewalker's* the one saying that," Hyo said, recalling Koushiro's letter to Jun from their first night. "He's Koushiro's guardian god. Koushiro would probably trust his opinion."

"*Everyone* would trust it." Natsuami looked sick. "As a Pillar God, most gods would defer to him."

"Do you reckon Jun's right about the reflectographs

being the motive? That there's something in Koushiro's collection that got them both cursed?" Mansaku wondered. "I thought part of the Bridgeburner's job was working out the WHY, meaning that Jun didn't know. But if Jun overheard these gods talking and decided 'this is it', it feels like Jun had some ideas."

"I'm sure he was putting the pieces together," Natsuami said with a small smile. "He was Jun, after all. A puzzle like his own murder? He couldn't have helped himself."

"Jun got it right with the motive," Hyo said aloud what she'd been thinking over, testing how it sounded. "I think ... that's what the Wavewalker was clueing me in on, when he was telling me about Koushiro's collection, and his bad luck. Jun had figured out enough that listening to Tokifuyu and him talking just confirmed it."

"But what I don't understand, Hyo, is why the Wavewalker would wish to 'clue you in on' anything at all." Frowning hard, Natsuami asked, "Why would he want to confess to you? I'm not saying this to deride you, or your skill, but he has Onmyoryo officers at hand."

The hellmakers' en tapped, but offered no direction. Hyo shook her head. "I don't know."

Mansaku asked, "Did the Wavewalker *really* say that we can keep digging into Jun's curse for the hellmaking?"

Hyo nodded. "Yeah."

"Weird."

They fell into silence. For a few minutes, there was

only the sound of focused eating, but the silence seemed noisier, filled with thoughts.

Mansaku broke it. "Jun's ghost didn't actually name the Wavewalker at the Plaza, did he? What do we need to prove that the Wavewalker killed Jun or is killing Koushiro? *Can* we prove it?"

"We can't," said Hyo and Natsuami at the same time.

Natsuami went on despairingly, "Gods can only be penalized on their own confession."

"And if he's silenced, the Wavewalker can't confess," Hyo continued. She frowned into her soup. "But I can't tell if he silenced himself or someone silenced him."

"It would have been himself. The Pillars are forbidden from cursing each other, and no other god could silence the Wavewalker *if* –" Natsuami pushed his glasses up his nose – "the Wavewalker really was the culprit. Heavens, I don't want to believe it."

Mansaku pulled a face slowly as if he'd found the shape of something unpleasant in his mouth and the more he probed at it, the worse everything about it became.

There was a knock at the door. Hyo set down her soup and went to open it.

The Wavewalker flashed her a smile that was briefly full of green teeth then perfectly normal as he assumed his Onmyoryo-officer disguise. "Good afternoon, is Ryouen Natsuami in?"

Natsuami came to the door. "How can I help?"

“I’m afraid I’ve news to share. May I come in, briefly?” He looked to Hyo. The privacy talisman was stopping him from entering.

“Briefly,” she agreed. A sickening rush of fear-anger-shock had surged up in her at the sight of the Wavewalker, Jun’s curser, at her door, just as they’d finished speaking of him, but she bottled it down. The Wavewalker had broken his disguise for her. He’d wanted *her* to know it was him, but not the others.

Why? What did he want with Hyo? For her to feel she was in his confidence? She wouldn’t know if she turned him away.

The Wavewalker stepped into the shoe-space, closed the door and began. “Ryouen-san, this morning, the dog team uncovered a significant quantity of yashiori in your home.”

Natsuami stared. “Significant quantity?”

“Seven kilograms of yashiori incense, in a range of hidden panels and with a number of kiseru pipes with which to take it.”

“This can’t be true,” Natsuami stuttered. “It has to have been planted! Or perhaps my brother confiscated it from someone! That kind of quantity...”

“Would indicate a habit, yes,” the Wavewalker-officer said. “Todomegawa Daimyoujin drowned in the Underdream within minutes of exposure to one fifteen-minute incense cone. Either he took it regularly or he was being dosed with it. Likely by someone he shared his home with."

Indignation flashed across Natsuami's face. "I'd never...!"

"That can be answered easily. May I see your nails?"

"Of course, officer."

The Wavewalker took Natsuami's hands then pressed the nail bed of each finger in turn.

After a moment, Hyo thought she saw the Wavewalker's shoulders sag with relief. "If you'd been taking it yourself or giving it to him regularly, even if you'd handled it with gloves, we'd expect to see some yashiori colour. Apologies, Ryouen-san. It would seem that the stock in your home was entirely your brother's."

"My brother would never!" Natsuami ripped his hand away from the Wavewalker. "He knows better than most the dangers of the Under-dream! He's terrified of what's down there. I've heard him say as much; he'd never willingly visit it. Please, I'm sure there's a reasonable explanation for that yashiori, if you'd only wait until he wakes up..."

"That's just the trouble, Ryouen-san." The Wavewalker adjusted his officer's hat. "If we don't know how regularly he took it, and how much was already in Todomegawa Daimyoujin's body, we don't know how deeply he's drowned. If we don't know this, we can't say when he will wake up. Thank you for your time. You will be kept updated."

He bowed a little too low and with a flourish, as if he rarely got the chance to bow to anyone and enjoyed the novelty of it, then he left before Hyo could stop him without raising the others' suspicion.

She thought about telling them that the Wavewalker had just been by, and decided against it. She couldn't answer why the Wavewalker was in disguise without exposing his part in Natsuami's en-management conspiracy.

Natsuami buried his face in his hands. "Oh, I'm a fool. If Toki's terrified of what's *in* the Under-dream, I practically implied that he'd taken it before, and that wasn't what I meant!"

Hyo said gently, "Leave it alone, Natsuami."

Mansaku tapped Natsuami's rice bowl with his chopsticks. "Finish your lunch."

Natsuami flicked out his sleeves as he sat down. "If they just looked at Toki's work history, it'd all make sense! Toki worked on the first Onmyoryo operation to see yashiori off the walkways. He interrogated the gods caught taking it! That's why he knows how dangerous it is!"

"When was Toki doing that?" Hyo asked.

"When he first joined the Onmyoryo – three years ago, just after Three Thousand Three Fall. It was a difficult time to be a god. Shrine attendance and musuhi offerings had never been worse. Yashiori use peaked, as a rare means of escape for gods from this unkind world and its humans." Natsuami picked at his rice. "He knows all the risks!"

"And all the highs that make them worthwhile," Mansaku added.

Natsuami shot him a look, but it didn't last long. "Indeed."

"You've never been tempted to take it yourself?"

"Never. But not out of any moral standpoint." Natsuami laughed. It faded quickly. "I lost so much of myself in Three Thousand Three Fall that I don't dare try. I could go into the Under-dream, but, without my heavenly name or any ens to people or places, with only a few threadbare memories as anchors, I fear there isn't enough of me left to find my way back out."

"What is the Under-dream?" Hyo asked.

"It's a place where I can't reach Toki," said Natsuami heavily, and sniffled. "I'm utterly powerless to help him."

Powerless. The feeling of being your own cage, incapable of helping anybody you cared for. Hyo knew that feeling.

She found her kerchief, pushed it towards Natsuami to wipe his eyes and nose, then stood. "We've got Ritsu-san's payment for her commission. If we clear the table, you can both help with it."

*

Katashiro dolls were substitutes. When a name was written down their front, they could attract misfortune and absorb curses on behalf of the person whose name they shared.

Hyo remembered making her first katashiro when she was four, but she had to have started earlier, because her fingers, in her earliest memories, had already known what to do.

An hour of cutting, stitching and stuffing, and between the three of them, they had six katashiro dolls, lined up on the floor, blank-faced and variously sized. Beside each doll, Hyo laid out a reflectograph with a reporter's face. Ritsu had supplied one per reporter, and two had clearly been taken from the theatre windows with a stellaroid camera. On the back of each reflectograph, she'd written a name.

Natsuami stopped grinding the white ink-stick and pushed the tray over. Dipping her brush in the ink, Hyo wrote a name down the front of each doll: *Hatta Kengo, Inoue Atsushi, Nozawa Kasuga, Matsumae Rikitoshi, Banba Suzu, Yamamoto Izumi...*

"... that's distinctive calligraphy."

Mansaku shushed him, and Natsuami covered his mouth with a sleeve.

Names done, Hyo took out the cash from Ritsu's envelope, along with a pair of old nigiri scissors. The scissors had obviously been looked after well. When Hyo held her hand over them and focused hard, she felt the warmth of human life and spirit that had seeped into them from being treasured.

Hyo swiped her right hand over the steel. When she'd gathered up all the residue of Ritsu's flame of life from the scissors, it flashed at the tips of her fingers with a soft golden flame, briefly visible even to non-hellmaker eyes.

She heard someone's breath catch. Probably Natsuami; Mansaku had seen their mother do this often enough that it never impressed him.

She repeated the process with her left, sliding her palm

over the wad of cash and collecting the flame of life with which Ritsu had imbued them. Another golden flame lit up then vanished, and with it went four-fingers' worth of talismanic symbols from each hand, as the hellmakers' seal melted.

Not completely – but enough for Hyo to seize the unluck, shimmering darkly around her, with her bare hands and shape it as needed.

She could hear herself chanting, words pouring up her throat that she felt on her tongue like seeds – poppy, dandelion, windflower – that were part sutra, part

something understood only between Hyo and the unluck at her command. But she could never write them, never know them to use for herself.

In one hand, the unluck coalesced into six nails. In the other, a hammer of the same back-lit shadow. Hyo knew the moment the others saw them when Mansaku stiffened and Natsuami shifted forward.

Hyo took one nail and poised it over the heart of the first doll. *Hatta Kengo.*

"*Here is the seventh hour of the ox, seven times risen, one strike known*," she heard herself as if through water. Human words at last. She raised the hammer. "*Hatta Kengo.*"

Hyo brought it down. There was a dull noise like a distant bell. The impact of hammer on nail juddered through her bones, and the nail of unluck sank into the doll.

She picked up the next nail. "*Inoue Atsushi.*"

One strike, then the next. "*Nozawa Kasuga.*"

When all six curses were cast, Hyo's head ached with effort. Sweat was running down her face and dripping down her neck.

"*Onoue Ritsu*," Hyo said, and felt the windflower-seeded words in her own voice. "*It is done.*"

Hyo dropped the hammer. It dissipated back into the unluck she'd called it from, and just like that it was over. The unluck faded out of her vision.

"O'Hyo?" Mansaku shuffled over on his knees. "How are you feeling?"

She picked up the taller bills and flicked through them. "Maybe like we're sixty thousand tallers richer?"

Mansaku cuffed her over the back of her head, then handed her a kerchief and went to put away the cash and Ritsu's scissors in the safe.

Natsuami drew close. "May I see?"

He was holding out his hand. It took Hyo a moment to understand what for – her own.

She put her hand in his and he turned it over to see the scrawl of the seal already reappearing on her fingers, darker than when she'd patched it over with sutra-copying, locking her abilities again.

Natsuami traced the seal on her palms. Hyo felt that heaviness in the shadows, looming over them both as he studied it. He said, "How will we know when the curses have taken effect?"

"The katashiro will tell us when their unlucky days begin and end." Hyo tipped her head towards the dolls, lined up on the floor. "Ritsu-san will simply know. The cursed, though, they won't know that she's behind their curses. She pays for her anonymity by taking on the curse recoil in my place."

"And will the cursed know that it was *you* who made their days unlucky?"

"I used Ritsu-san's spirit from her flame of life in the casting, so, no."

Natsuami looked as if he had more questions, but then he smiled, and layered his hands with hers. "You'd be a formidable enemy."

Hyo huffed. His hand was cool. "Only if someone commissions me to be."

Natsuami hesitated then said, "Mansaku-san told me that avenging Jun would be a special commission. Is there something different about a special other than the avenged being dead?"

"The number of years I'd need from a flame of life to complete the commission," she told him, remembering her promise to answer his questions when she could – to be less of a jailer to him. "For a special, it's everything that the commissioner has left to offer."

She braced for Natsuami to withdraw his hand, to treat her like something tainted, but he didn't. "The commissioner dies too?"

"I don't actually know how it works." Hyo looked away from him. "Jun-san's my first special commission. I don't know what happens at payment. The Records of the old hellmakers make it sound like that I'll know at the time but I won't get a choice."

"Are you nervous?"

Creaking from above said that Mansaku was upstairs and beyond earshot. Hyo was ready to admit it – but she still couldn't say it louder than a whisper: "Hell, yeah."

Natsuami closed her hand between his own as if she

were a pocket hand-warmer, bowed his head to them and shut his eyes. "It makes such a nice change to be told things."

Hyo smiled. "Even things you don't like?"

"Especially those. I feel as if I've come out of a long dark winter, one only I could see, where I was buried under ice and numbed to the world for everyone's safety," he said. "It makes *such* a nice change to have my questions answered."

"Yeah." Hyo covered his hands with hers, feeling the ridges of his scars under her seal. "Spring is a good place to be."

SIXTEEN

泡沫

… and the god told me this: people made their worlds from meaning, and meaning was a dream. This shared world was a dream bubble-foam raft floating atop Oblivion. The Under-dream lay below the raft, just before nothingness – raw thought and imagination, the bubble liquid.

"There's peace in the Under-dream," said the god. "I don't have to be anything any more."

TAMA,
Twenty-Second Hellmaker

Mansaku passed his finished picture to Hyo. "That's what Yamada Hanako looks like when she turns up in my dreams."

They'd agreed to talk about the Paddywatcher in public by her earthly and less godly sounding name. Leaving Natsuami watching over the dolls in the flat, eagerly awaiting the curses to take hold, Hyo and Mansaku had come to the coin laundry on Iris Hill's twenty-second floor.

Mansaku had described his cursing to Hyo. To Hyo's relief, he hadn't had to *feel* that he was grains in a hundred snake bellies. As Mansaku remembered it, he had been put to sleep, and when he'd dreamt, the Paddywatcher had come to him.

Mansaku had drawn a sketch of the god in pencil on the back of a flyer. Hyo took it and studied it. It was a decent portrait. "'Dreams'? You'd seen Yamada in your dreams before she cursed you?"

"She showed up when we stayed over at Jun's on our first night here," he said. "Then she was there at the edges of my dreams every night until you put up your privacy ward."

"What did she do in them?"

"Just looked on, from a distance." Sharpness flickered at Hyo's skin then disappeared, a rare nervous slip of Mansaku's scythe's edge. Anger shot through Hyo at the Paddywatcher. "I think she was scoping us out, both of us. Stalking, but being creepy-tasteful about it."

His picture of the Paddywatcher showed a humanoid figure in an ichime-gasa hat. Her face was hidden under a black veil, but her eyes were large and glowing under the brim. Her robes were boldly patterned, and she'd given herself an extra half a shaku of height with boxy pokkuri.

The washing machine chimed. Hyo folded the picture and went to unload it. "Did Yamada offer you anything when you were cursed?"

"Yeah, she did," Mansaku said, keeping his voice down. The radio was covering most of what they were saying, but the rhythm of their Old Tiger, non-Standard dialects had already got them looks. "She said she could keep me cursed with her as long as she liked because she had Good Reason. Either I listened to her, cooperated and got to go home, or I was going to stay put and start sprouting."

"She didn't force you to agree to anything?"

"No. She didn't want to get on our bad side."

"Too late for that." Hyo scrunched their mesh bag of mukuroji in her fist, the soap-nuts cracking. "So?"

"She wanted to know what we were up to behind our privacy ward, how far we'd got with Jun's curse and whether we had a commissioner to avenge him yet. I said, 'just trying to sleep in peace', 'far enough' and 'nope'. Then she grilled me on the hellmaking, like about how the commissioning works, the katashiro, your seal, *my* seal and the old seven weapons of the First. All of it."

Mansaku cracked a lopsided grin. It was a little strained. "Luckily for you, I've got the charm and charisma to talk through things with my curser like an adult, so here I am. Un-cursed and not food for birds. Imagine if it'd been *you* she'd caught in a dream-space."

Hyo flicked a damp sock at him. "And you can tell me all this freely?"

"Yep. No silencing curse stamp. Like I said, she doesn't want to be an enemy." So anything that came out of Mansaku's mouth would be what Yamada Hanako had predicted he'd tell and wanted Hyo to hear. He stood to carry the under-robes Hyo passed him to a dryer, then paused, hand on the machine door. "O'Hyo?"

"Yeah?"

"After I gave her all the answers, she offered to find a way to split me and Kiriyuki."

Feeling rose up Hyo's throat like a fist. "Yeah, I bet." Briefly she considered saying nothing, then thought of Natsuami, locked up with silences. "Yamada made me the same offer."

Mansaku tensed. "In exchange for anything?"

"Helping her when she needed it, like talking to Jun's ghost on the Plaza. But I don't think that was enough. She's going to ask for another favour soon. You?"

"Yeah." He added delicately, "She wanted something."

"Mansaku." The back of Hyo's mind conjured images – Mansaku's back smaller, his neck thinner, and

Mum's cold determination as she inked Kiriyuki's seal on to him. "I'm not going to tell you to refuse her offer when it's your life on the line. I don't care what she's asked you to do for it. Difficult, dangerous or terrible, just tell me when you need me."

Mansaku's eyes glittered with a scythe's crescent gleam. He turned to the lint tray. "She asked me to consent to being cursed one more time in the near future, with what curse, where it'll happen and when to be confirmed."

A chill swept over Hyo's skin. "You said 'yes' to that?"

"Yeah, I did. But it's fine! She wants us hellmakers around, for some reason. Whatever her curse does, it won't kill me."

Hyo didn't like it. But it wasn't her call. In the corner of her eye, she saw Mansaku's flame of life: the golden drop of his own human one, its ordinary wick, and then the vicious blue, hotter, wilder flame of Kiriyuki the nagigama spirit, which ate voraciously at their shared candle, strangling it with its spiralling wick.

Kiriyuki was nothing but an especially sharp flea, hopping through Hakai sons, becoming sharper, deadlier, more draining every time.

"The demon didn't give us a deadline. I don't know how long it's going to take to prove that they are or aren't growing hitodenashi here," Hyo said, under the laughter on the radio. "If it takes a lifetime, I need you to have a lifetime too."

Mansaku put his arm around her shoulder, then pulled at her ear until it hurt and she yelled for him to stop.

The six katashiro dolls hadn't changed when they returned. Mansaku took over watching them, then waved Hyo and Natsuami out of the flat to go to the baths.

"When the commission kicks in, we'll go to the theatre," said Hyo, when it was the two of them in the tower lift. "And you should come too."

"Are you sure?"

"Jun-san asked you to protect Koushiro in his place, didn't he?" Hyo noticed Natsuami absently petting the ends of his hair. "What's wrong?"

"Just contemplating the possibility a Pillar God might've killed Jun and drowned Toki in the Underdream, and got away with it, without any detection of accumulated taint." Natsuami's gaze darted about the lift, as if something might be listening. "Which suggests that, perhaps, Onogoro's means to detect taint accumulation may have been sabotaged."

"I hadn't thought of that."

"If we can't detect taint accumulation, we cannot detect a god falling," Natsuami went on in a rush. "And a Pillar God falling ... they're called Pillars for a reason. We need them. Any one of them falls, and Onogoro society will fall into chaos with them." He turned to Hyo with wide eyes. "What happens to Onogoro if you curse a

Pillar God with an artisan hell?"

"Nothing. They're *personal hells*, Natsuami. Only the one cursed feels it. No one else will suffer for it," Hyo told herself as much as him. "If it helps, I'm not asking you to believe the Wavewalker killed Jun. Only that Jun accused him of it, in a roundabout way. So that's our hypothesis, which I can't yet reject."

"You mean 'prove'?"

"No. Reject. No easier way to be wrong than wanting to be right."

The lift juddered to stop, and Hyo stepped out, Natsuami behind.

A duck-billed water god working the bathhouse's front desk flashed green shark's teeth when Hyo handed them her bath pass.

"Enjoy!" The Wavewalker stamped off the trip from Hyo's monthly slots before taking Natsuami's. "And hello, handsome, take all the time you need. Yes, little darling?"

Hyo waited for Natsuami to duck behind the noren of the gods' baths, and said, "How's the Bridgeburner, sir?"

The air seemed to rapidly cool and thicken; the shadows deepened. The music

週刊文葉
フロント
秋祭の前に
の健診に
行こう!!
あなたも、
毛穴に
悩んでいませんか?
肌に
やさしい
低刺激シャンプー

flowing through the radio broke up into a monotonous gurgling noise.

"He is unresponsive to everything I've tried for him so far," the Wavewalker replied in a whisper at Hyo's ear. The duck-bill lips of his form behind the counter didn't move. "Forget about Todomegawa for the time being, little darling. Focus on the hellmaking. On finding your commissioner and avenging poor, unfortunate Makuni Junichiro."

"Sir must be very busy," Hyo said carefully. "What with Kichizuru's bad luck and all the questions about Ukibashi Awano ever since her kidnapping, and now the Bridgeburner's yashiori poisoning to deal with."

"And the Midsummer Great Purification Rituals to arrange for the Sixthmonth too, since it won't organize itself. Yes, I am quite busy," said the Wavewalker with a self-pitying sigh.

"Great Purification Rituals, sir?"

"I forget. You're new to Onogoro. Every end of Sixthmonth, all shrines come together for rites to cleanse gods and humans alike of all the taint they've accumulated over the year so far." The Wavewalker propped his chin with his elbow. His gaze bored into Hyo. "I'm sure you'll enjoy it. Do come along to my Fugaku shrine. My Awano's arranging it to have the biggest reed wreath on the island. Your taint, my taint; it'll all be washed away."

"That's good to know, sir," Hyo said, trying to read his intent, but it was impossible. "Thank you for telling me."

"I'm a god of fortune, little darling. What am I here for if not to help humans, especially one who's accommodating our anomalous friend?" The Wavewalker snapped open a copy of the *Weekly Bunyo* magazine and sat back, kicking up his webbed feet. "Go on now, hellmaker. You'll find a friend in the baths tonight, and luckily for you, it's quieter in there than usual."

Hyo had to ask: "What would happen to sir if Koushiro – Kichizuru – died because of his bad luck?"

"Whatever I deserve," the Wavewalker replied, hidden behind his magazine. "But until then I'll be doing everything I can to maximize his chances of survival. Absolutely everything. If I do not protect his life, I'd have failed him."

Hyo left him be. This god, she didn't understand him. She walked through the noren for the baths for humans. There was only one other there – someone sitting in the main bath with a towel folded on their head.

They looked up as Hyo tripped on a shinresin basin with a clatter and waved. On their arm was the blurry blue tattoo of a wind god. "Hyo-chan! Come and join me!"

"Nagakumo-san." She waved back then got to sluicing the sweat off her shoulders.

This bathhouse was tattoo- and scar-friendly, in part

owed to the large offices of local "moneylending clerks" nearby. That suited Hyo fine. It meant no one complained about the scars on her arms.

Three cycles of winters in, Hyo and Mansaku had discovered they could ease the villagers' pain and slow the hitodenashi growth by feeding them their blood. Both their arms were an array of irregular scars where the villagers' teeth had sunken deep. They were ragged, rough, faded to pink.

Small crescents from the children, larger bites from the adults. Days of blood and snow, gnawed into Hyo's skin.

She ran her hand over them, and remembered where she came from: Tsukitateyama in Koura, from the Ukoku abandoned by the gods to the Occupiers, and now on Onogoro with a mission to confirm with her own eyes and ears whether hitodenashi was being grown in an orchard on Onogoro or not.

"Nah-uh. No more 'Nagakumo-san' from you." Nagakumo shook her finger at Hyo as she clambered into the bath. "After what went down the other night, you'll call me 'Massan' or 'Big Sister Masu' or nothing. We shared an Experience. How are you doing? The Wavewalker didn't go too hard on you, getting a statement?"

"No. You?"

"Nothing I didn't expect. He was pretty upset about it all, though." Nagakumo said, "I heard the Onmyoryo disposed of your ghost friend. What's his name?"

"Makuni Junichiro."

"Makuni Junichiro, right. Junichiro," Nagakumo repeated, as if consigning it to memory. "He wasn't the best house guest, but I wish him all the best."

Hyo sat back against the wall. "Do you know what happens to the ghosts the Onmyoryo capture?"

Nagakumo let out a breath that stirred the clouds of steam. "The paper man's burned in a ritual that totally cleanses the ghost of their angers and regrets and forces them to move on. Or, well, that's the theory. In practice, the ghost just disappears. We don't really know where they go. It's not as if they come back to tell the Onmyoryo."

Hyo swallowed down a sharp-edged lump. "What was it like, being possessed by him?"

"Hard work. I'm exhausted to the basement of my souls. I've taken leave for the rest of the month." Nagakumo turned her eyes up to the ceiling. "Any ghosts looking to possess me, they can get in line and wait."

"How long have you been able to...?"

"Let the ghosts in? It took some practice. And some help. My body's roomy, in the spiritual plane. Things blow in and out of the house of my souls like I've got all the windows open." Nagakumo settled her head against the tiles. "I must've been, hmm, three or four? When I first got possessed. By the ghost of a cat no less." Nagakumo bunched her hands into paws and mewed. Hyo smiled. "My mum took me along to the wind god in the second year of middle school. Got his protection." She lifted her forearm from the water, showing the scowling face amidst streaming clouds. "He showed me how to blow away the ghosts before they got in, so that's how I got a handle on it. But it's all still something I'm working on. I can't stop the ghosts from coming to find me or close my ears to them."

"What do they come and talk to you about?"

"Things they think will hurt their living loved ones mostly. Stuff they think the living are ignoring. But sometimes those are things like, 'There's a five-hundred-taller coin stuck in the vent on this or that walkway.'" Nagakumo hummed under her breath. "Did you see the Bridgeburner at the Wavewalker's place?"

When Hyo and Natsuami had left Tokifuyu in the yashiori ward, he had been alarmingly semi-transparent, which the Wavewalker assured them was normal. "Yeah."

"How'd he look? Oh, wow." Nagakumo saw Hyo's expression. "That bad, huh? Figures. Smoker like that."

"You're not surprised?"

"There were rumours. Police worked with the Onmyoryo on the first yashiori operation, and, well, word went round that the Bridgeburner got taken off the Onmyoryo side for dipping into the confiscated goods."

Hyo tried to imagine Tokifuyu indulging in rest and relaxation, and failed. "What did he want the yashiori for?"

"Escaping his problems into the Under-dream, probably. That's what yashiori is all about. There's supposed to be some messed-up stuff down there, but sometimes a god comes to a point where they'd rather handle that than humans. A really low point." Nagakumo wrapped her arms around herself. "You friends with the Bridgeburner, Hyo-chan?"

Hyo thought about it. "I guess."

"Hope he comes back soon then."

"Thanks."

"And maybe keep it vague like that. Maybe-friends. Not friends. If the god's not a work colleague, it's better to keep a distance. You don't want to be a god's favourite human, ever, like ... you remember Ukibashi Awano? Think of her and the Wavewalker." Nagakumo skimmed her hand under the water's surface, making waves. "He sends her a gift to help her get away from her kidnappers. She hasn't been right since. A weird eye, sick, tied to him for ever with those pills of his, whatever they do. Strong ens with gods never end well for humans."

Too late, Hyo recalled that the Wavewalker was just a changing room away and possibly listening. She glanced uncomfortably at the bath water as if it might suddenly turn into pinching crab claws, and Nagakumo laughed.

"Don't sweat it! Baths are warded. *They* want to

relax over there. No prayers, no curses, no human noise gets past that." Nagakumo pointed at the wall beyond which the gods had their own baths. "So we can say whatever we like in here. Fuchiha'no'Utanami'Tomi-no-Mikoto!" She cupped her hands around her mouth, so that the Wavewalker's heavenly name echoed. "You should've left your Ukibashi princess on the kidnappers' ship! The whole island knows there's been something fishy about her ever since, and we're not talking about your smell!"

Water gurgled. Hyo held her breath.

Nagakumo lowered her hands. "See."

"Have you ever asked ghosts to find things out for you?"

Nagakumo looked amused. "If I could ask them to listen in on everyone and tell me the goss, the police would pay me better. No, they only ever tell me what they're interested in talking about. But they do know that I'm one of few ghost-sensitives they can count on not to get them exorcised by the Onmyoryo when they're interested in … interesting things."

Hyo felt it: the brush of a thread coming close in parallel, catching at the tie of the hellmakers' en. "Is there something you know that you probably shouldn't?"

"Oh, you bet there is. Don't pass this on to anyone, all right?" As if just waiting for the moment, like some seal had been broken, Nagakumo whispered with a glee

reserved for gossip, cupping her hand around Hyo's ear, "Apparently the taint-detectors at the Onmyoryo haven't been operational for the whole past month, so if divine forecasts have been bullshitty lately, it's because they really are just bullshit. Broken or sabotaged, they can't tell which, but the ghosts have been livid about it."

Hyo pulled back. "You haven't told anyone this?"

"I'm not telling anyone who's going to tell the Onmyoryo." Nagakumo winked. "But my guess is you're not going to do that."

"Why don't you want the Onmyoryo to know?"

"The same reason I don't work for them. They can go to hell. They gave *me* hell when I was a kid. Besides, the Great Purification Rituals are coming up in a month, so whatever taint has accumulated will be cleansed away then anyway." Nagakumo stood, flicking water off her arms and pulling the towel from her head. "You should be careful around the Onmyoryo too."

"I've been warned."

"Good. You still got Makuni Junichiro's letter to his brother?"

"I'm taking it to him tomorrow."

"You'd better. It was weighing on Makuni's souls." Nagakumo extended her hand to help Hyo out of the water too. She spotted Hyo's scarred arms, and raised her eyebrows.

"Demons," Hyo lied. An easier answer than humans.

Nagakumo accepted it with a nod. "Well, at least you won't find any of those on Onogoro."

SEVENTEEN

大凶

The gods of fortune have their rules.
To curse a human, they need three
things: a name, a face and Good Reason.
Hence the saying: "If you don't disturb
the god, the god won't disturb you."

SENA,
Twentieth Hellmaker

The next morning, Hyo's seal was still dark and clearly inked over her fingers. Her vision wasn't obstructed by bands of unluck, and there wasn't a single trace of its shimmer over the Shin-Kaguraza Theatre. Fresh off of Ritsu's commission, the pressure to use her abilities had settled. Hyo's seal, for once, didn't need any patching over.

Hyo got to cooking breakfast whilst Natsuami folded up his bedding and Mansaku went up to the bathhouse. Outside, wild rain was falling, depositing quivering bodies of jellyfishes over handrails and draping their tentacles off cornices. She'd woken to the announcement from an Onmyoryo windturtle, warning citizens to stay indoors and apologizing for the unexpected weather.

"There *must* be some quantity of taint in the atmosphere," Natsuami said, looking out from the kitchen window to the ghostly jellyfish floating down between the towers. "If the Onmyoryo taint-detectors are as your friend says, how can it have gone unnoticed, or unmentioned ... or ignored?"

"Maybe someone at the Onmyoryo's telling them to keep quiet, so that people don't worry and their reputation doesn't take a hit." The Wavewalker could do that. He could probably come up with reasons to delay getting them fixed too. She saw the way Natsuami's face clouded when he'd thought the same as she had.

The lid on the rice rattled. Hyo lowered the

temperature. "And if they think Sixthmonth's Great Purification Rituals will clean up all the taint on Onogoro anyway, maybe they've noticed, and don't care."

"If the Wavewalker were to tell them the detectors could be fixed after the Ritual, as an authority on curses and healing, yes, his opinion would count for something." Natsuami hissed under his breath as his glasses steamed up over a pot. He took them off to wipe. "But surely the Wavewalker would have known Nagakumo would tell you this. And yet..."

And yet, the Wavewalker had urged her into the bathhouse at exactly the right moment – when Nagakumo, one of the few on Onogoro with an ear to the ghost-vine, would be on her own. Where no one else could overhear them; somewhere Nagakumo would be relaxed and open to sharing gossip.

Did he really want to be caught? A Pillar God? Why?

The Wavewalker was a mystery to Hyo, a puzzle box with no patterns or marks, no clues for how Hyo should press to figure him out.

But in the pill-making room, the Wavewalker had called Natsuami 'all that remains of an old dear friend'. Maybe, to Natsuami, even with his impaired memories, the Wavewalker might have been less mysterious.

"What do you think of the Wavewalker, Natsuami?" Hyo asked. "Do you know anything about what he's like as a person?"

"I have a feeling that once I knew a very good deal. But he was distant when he questioned me about Toki and the yashiori. I doubt we were close." Natsuami put a thumb on his chin and furrowed his brow. "He'll have his two faces though, like any god. His peaceful face is the water that drives a wheel. His wild face is the river that floods. Without a festival like the Great Purification Rituals to burn off taint, his wild side would be dangerous for Onogoro even if it wasn't completely fallen."

The door clattered open and shut. Mansaku called out, "I'm home!"

When the rice was done, Hyo and Natsuami took down the food to the living room, and found Mansaku crouched over the six katashiro dolls of Ritsu's commission on the table. "O'Hyo, take a look at them!"

The name written on each doll was warped, the brushstrokes twisted out of shape and blotchy as if they'd been exposed to rain.

Somewhere on Onogoro, six reporters had woken up to one day of mild unluck, as commissioned by Onoue Ritsu, for a cost of sixty thousand tallers and an old pair of scissors.

"What does mild unluck entail?" Natsuami asked.

Hyo pointed at the doll labelled "Hatta Kengo". "This one had a windturtle ramp block his flat door." She pointed at Inoue Atsushi. "This one's allergic to natto and jellyfish stings. He can't leave his house today either."

"How do you know?"

She shrugged. "Professional secret?"

The door flew open without any preamble. Mansaku looked up, and immediately a cold sense of sharpness hung in the air, invisible, but Hyo could see that the new arrivals felt it in the way they froze in the shoe-space. "Can we help you?"

"Which one's the new private diviner in the tower?" There were three men in gaudy patchwork robes, tattooed and missing fingers like other people missed buttons. The one who'd spoken had a piece of piping tucked into his belt, was chomping on a toothpick and was big, hairy and scarred.

"That's me," said Hyo. "Meatfist Kumataro, I presume?"

As soon as she said his name, one henchman muttered, "Aniki, I'm having some bad feelings about this..."

Meatfist Kumataro bit through his toothpick and the henchman shrivelled. "You've heard of me.

Then you'll know that we here are reputable, friendly, honest moneylending clerks from your local Ohne branch of reputable and friendly moneylenders." He cracked his knuckles and glowered down at Hyo. "You'll be coming with me."

She set the weight of her gaze on the three men's flames of lives, measuring their wicks and the rate at which they burned, the shadow of it holding their flame in a suffocating fist.

"No, I won't," Hyo returned. "Say what you want, right where you are."

"Or else you'll lose your noses," Mansaku said lightly, and the two henchman whimpered, feeling the invisible scythe edge press just above their upper lips.

Meatfist Kumataro experimentally lifted his piping in front of him. Its end dropped off, Mansaku's edge soundlessly slicing through the steel. Hyo watched a drop of sweat run down the side of Meatfist Kumataro's corded neck.

"We've caused a god who patrons our rival moneylenders some displeasure," he said, settling on an awkward, safe formality. "Our own patron god has announced a twenty-four-hour suspension of her active support of the group's good fortune. We want a diviner for the day at the office, who can keep track of our luck in real time and readily supply us with talismans to protect us from our rivals."

"Who's the god you ticked off and what did you do?" Mansaku asked.

Meatfist Kumataro shuffled, his henchmen shuffling with him like back-up dancers. "The Wavewalker thinks we might've been making and supplying dreamdunker to one of his river gods lately. Yashiori."

The shadows in the room deepened. Natsuami sat up straight. "And did you?"

"Absolutely not," said Meatfist Kumataro.

"I mean," a henchman said, not quite under his breath, "everyone in the friendly moneylending circles knew that the Bridgeburner was the one to go to if we wanted Onmyoryo-grade privacy talismans, because all we had to do was trade yashiori for it, which is dirt cheap—"

Hyo stuck out her arm and hit Natsuami's chest as he walked straight into it, hair bristling like snakes. She gave him a gentle but firm shove backwards, then said, "Who's the god who's abandoned you for twenty-four hours?"

"The Paddywatcher, but," the other henchman said quickly, "she's not abandoned us! She recommended we come to the Hakai diviners for help."

"A god's recommendation. Wow. What an honour. What do we get for supplying you with twenty-four-hours' worth of protection from spiritual threats?" Hyo pushed at Natsuami again, but he'd planted his feet on the tatami and wouldn't budge. He glared over her arm at the three gangsters. "Local businesses, we should support each other. We don't do special discounts for moneylenders, especially one-hundred-per-cent discounts."

"Oh, yeah, our lady the Paddywatcher said we should give this to you, if you helped us out." Meatfist Kumataro held up a little white tube, the size and shape of a forefinger and covered in scales. It was tied with a twist of wheat-yellow paper. "But only after."

Hyo looked to Mansaku. They both knew what it could be: the Paddywatcher's promised payment for their cooperation – a clue for cutting Mansaku free of Kiriyuki. They couldn't let it escape them. Mansaku signed against his chest, "I'll go."

"Hyo," Natsuami said, and she felt something like an enormous hand hovering over all their heads, ready to fall, "you should turn these people away; they don't deserve your help."

"Hey!" a henchman said, indignant.

"I won't go with you," Hyo began, and when the three gangsters clutched at various hidden weapons, as if a screwdriver and a bean-stuffed sock might change her mind, she continued. "But my brother will."

The gangsters looked, as one terrified unit, at Natsuami.

Mansaku waved at them. "She means me, by the way."

They looked marginally less terrified.

Hyo went on. "Mansaku's got better spiritual senses than me and some skill in the craft. For talismans, I'll sell you all the talismans and katashiro we've got in stock right now. That should do you for thirty hours. So, how about it, gentlemen? My brother and talismans for that note from the Paddywatcher and cash. Do we have a deal?"

The Ohne gangsters left with sleeves, belts and bags bulging, arms laden with katashiro dolls, and escorted Mansaku away into their vehicle like a prince, bowing and scraping as they opened the windturtle doors for him.

In the half an hour it took for the Ohne to go and return with cash for the talismans, Natsuami disappeared to the kitchen, and Hyo quickly taught Mansaku how to manipulate a shikigami. Their mother would never have allowed it. She'd have called it a waste of time for a scythe.

Mansaku had seen Hyo make shikigamis many times over. The craft came naturally to him, and in only fifteen minutes, he had three little paper men running across the tatami doing acrobatics.

"If you get into trouble, send a shikigami to tell me where you are," Hyo told him. "The more of your spirit you put into it, the further it'll go and the more it can show me."

"Got it." Mansaku slid a handful of pre-cut paper men between the layers of his belt. Natsuami was silent in the kitchen, so he switched to hand signs. "I'll make sure we get that tube from Meatfist."

Hyo signed back, "Don't risk your life for it."

"Never. I know what my life's worth."

She watched Mansaku climb into the Ohne gang's windturtle with some trepidation, then when the vehicle was gone, Hyo went to the kitchen.

Natsuami was sitting on a stool, pinching off the roots from a bowlful of beansprouts in sullen silence.

He didn't acknowledge her, so Hyo said, "When did we get beansprouts?"

She'd counted on him being too polite to ignore a direct question. Natsuami said, "A green-vendor came by last night whilst we were at the bathhouse."

"Let me help." Hyo thought Natsuami might refuse her. He seemed to think so too, but then he shuffled along the stool and made room.

She squeezed into the narrow space between the wall and stove to perch on the stool, ending up in an awkward near back-to-back. Hyo dipped her hands into the beansprout bowl and got picking. "What would you have done to those gangsters if you could've?"

"I'm fairly confident I had Good Reason to curse them," Natsuami said. "I don't know what I would've done to them though. I'm not very good at thinking up curses. I don't think I ever have been. But I suppose I could've..."

"What?"

"Scolded them. With some very bad words," he said darkly, and Hyo had to laugh. He looked briefly pleased with himself, then added, "But why go to the trouble? All three of them have some en with me now, and that might be enough."

"I promised Tokifuyu that I'd keep you from hurting others."

"I knew it! I knew he was protecting others from me, and not me from them! Oh, Toki. He did try. Does," Natsuami corrected hurriedly. He shook a sprout in water to float off a root fragment. "I can't be sorry about meeting you and Mansaku at all, though."

"Your ens don't end well for humans you care about. My ens bring in the bodies. Neither of us are good company for others. We might as well be company for each other," said Hyo. "And remember, I went looking for you. I wanted the en with you, for my own reasons."

"True."

"I'm not sorry to have met you at all."

Natsuami searched her face then looked away, but she thought he was smiling. "If Mansaku-san hadn't gone with those men, the Paddywatcher would've broken her promise of protection to the Ohne gang and accumulated taint. Advising them to hire you helped her get around that."

Hyo clicked her tongue. "Gods and all your loopholes."

"Yes, they've had all of human civilization to figure them out." Natsuami looked down at his bowl. "I didn't think about what to do with all these sprouts."

They made a simple soba heaped with beansprouts,

grated ginger and handfuls of spring onion for lunch, then Hyo packed the katashiro dolls of the reporters and Jun's last letter into a satchel. Enough time had passed for Ritsu to confirm what had become of her reporters, for Hyo's skills to have been proved real.

Hyo locked the door behind her and Natsuami, and headed for the Shin-Kaguraza second floor's west side.

It was time to see Makuni Koushiro.

The walkway of the Shin-Kaguraza's second floor was draped in a canopy of Kikugawa Kichizuru reflectograph banners. Emblazoned in large white symbols, they read:

FINAL PERFORMANCE!
LAST CHANCE TO SEE THE YOUNG SENSATION BEFORE HE LEAVES!

The front of the theatre was disconcertingly empty without its roving pack of reporters, and Hyo and Natsuami made it up the stairs unobstructed. The box-office assistant recognized her. This time, he gave them careful instructions to the Plum Door on the second floor.

It was opened by a weary stagehand, who took one look at them and the yellow silk ribbon Hyo had used to tie back her hair and shouted for Ritsu.

She appeared, tapping her long robe-folder's ruler over her shoulder. Heavy bags lined each eye.

"Not one of those six reporters made it to their office this morning, let alone here to darken the Shin-Kaguraza's doors." Ritsu rubbed her face as if to erase the dregs of a bad dream. "Unlucky days. I felt all of them. Missed trains, twisted ankles, food poisonings, bad news. The other reporters got wind of what happened to their ringleaders and stayed away today. They're going to be writing next week that Kichizuru-san's bad luck is spreading to them."

"Is this good enough as proof to see Koushiro?"

"Heavens, yes, I'll take you to him. He's in a mood, but I'll make sure he sees you." Ritsu's gaze was piercing. "And then you'll know if you can help him?"

"Then I'll know," Hyo confirmed.

Ritsu's gaze went past her to Natsuami. "Who's this?"

"My assistant. He's a friend of Jun-san's too."

Ritsu peered up into the shadow of Natsuami's rain hood. Natsuami cringed back, but at length Ritsu nodded. "Yes, you look exactly Junichiro-san's type, like you've a story to tell, if only Junichiro-san could solve the mystery of you first. Nosy, overcurious boy, always spotting the things that other people didn't."

She took a pad from her apron. "Sign this, both of you, and I'll take you in to see Kichizuru-san."

On the blue paper was a list. Hyo asked, "What is this?"

"A waiver of responsibility," said Ritsu. "If anything

unlucky happens to you on these premises, you're solely to blame, and you won't hold Kichizuru-san accountable in any way whatsoever."

"Including 'dismemberment' and 'disembowelling' – on the theatre premises?"

Ritsu presented Hyo with a short white pencil. "Yes, that would be very unlucky."

There were talismans everywhere, glued to the ceiling, the walls, plastered over doors to make-up rooms and instrument storage. Most were protection talismans, repelling threats from the spiritual plane and warding off bad luck. Privacy talismans were stuck over every door.

"We get through talismans like flypaper," said Ritsu.

Backstage smelled like sawdust and a cloying sweetness that Ritsu explained was robe glue, the hard rice-based varnish used to set the brightly coloured paper robes that the robe-folders made for the shin-kagura actors.

Stagehands rushed between rooms with rolls of artificial wisteria, instrument cases and the intensity of Occupied-Ukoku travel-checkpoint officials. A girl left a room with rows of people bent over glossy bundles of hair. Paper rustled as costumes were wheeled back and forth from storage.

"If you could enter quietly." Ritsu opened the double door, and the long note of a flute threaded out like a moonbeam.

Kikugawa Kichizuru danced at the centre of the stage. He was dressed in his rehearsal robes, in subdued shades of warbler greens and indigos. Rather than the limp cyclocloth of everyday wear, his robes were glue-stiffened to mimic the paper costumes of performance. The hems of his trousers trailed behind him, accentuating powerful gliding steps. His hands moved with forceful purpose. Three young men brandished tufted spears at him, and an older actor with a fierce scowl and rolling eyes shook a halberd, but Hyo only had eyes for Kikugawa Kichizuru, because the moment she saw him, she knew.

This was the figure who'd been wrapped in a cloud of unluck on the bridge, who had run along its handrail over an eighteen-storey drop to the bottom of Onogoro.

Makuni Koushiro, Hyo was sure of it.

At the sight of him, the hellmakers' en sang, all the threads tied by it thrumming as one.

EIGHTEEN

カミモドキ症候群

You'll know your commissioner when you find them.

TAMA,
Twenty-Second Hellmaker

A creak sounded. The actors paused. Their gazes went to the bell swaying gently over the stage. It wasn't the metal of a real temple bell, but it was still the height of two men, and weighed enough that it would crush an unlucky man if it fell.

The man currently centre stage was the unluckiest on Onogoro.

The bell swayed, its rope creaked.

Then stopped, silent and still.

The actor with the halberd turned on his heel.

Koushiro gritted his teeth. "I'm not finished yet, Matsubei!"

"No, you're not. Your hands are too stiff! Graceless! What are you trying to be? The fairy of a mochi mortar? We want lightness! The supple pliability of a vine! The sinuous strength of a snake!" Matsubei opened a small door in the stage corner with the butt of his halberd. "I'm going to go and take a shit now, so that these pants stay clean until the rehearsal's end. Everyone, take a half-hour break. Let's get some fresh air in here. Clean up the jaki a little."

Five minutes and a scramble later, the stage was empty but for Koushiro, who was gazing up at the bell and the red and white rope attached to it.

Ritsu cleared her throat. "Kichi-san, you've visitors."

"There's a paper cutout of me in the foyer; they can visit that."

"You *will* see these ones," she said. "This is Hakai

Hyo, Junichiro-san's diviner friend from Occupied-Ukoku." Koushiro stiffened. "She's the expert in bad luck I told you about, and she's the real thing – you've her to thank for the empty theatre-front today."

"I know who she is." Koushiro turned sharply. "But whether it was really her curse or the wild rain of jellyfish clearing the steps of those parasites remains to be seen. Hakai Hyo, Ritsu seems to think you can help me. Can you really do what no god has done?"

Hyo studied the actor. Jun had the same vividness in his expressions but Koushiro was all sharpness where Jun's edges had been rounded. His eyes were no less fierce for lack of make-up. "Are you going to give me the chance?"

"I could give you a good deal worse than a chance, if my bad luck's as catching as all those reporters are going to say in their next deep, highly necessary think-pieces."

"Then I *can* do what no god has done." Hyo held up three fingers. "For three reasons."

"Confidence is arrogance that's learnt its place. Do you know yours?"

"One." Hyo lowered one finger. "My abilities give me control over unluck, a particle the gods of fortune can't touch without consequence. Two, I don't think your bad luck is as natural as the gods have said. Three, I *know* that you didn't burn the whole of your reflectograph collection."

She didn't but the bluff worked. Koushiro blanched and Ritsu gasped. "Kichi-san! Really?!"

"No!" Koushiro flung his hand down. "You saw me burn everything – it's gone!"

Hyo held up Jun's letter. "Your brother didn't think so."

Koushiro came down the hanamichi. Hyo let him snatch the envelope from her. He tore it open. His eyes roved over the page. "Where did you get this? When?!"

"It's the last thing Jun-san wrote," Hyo said, standing her ground as Koushiro glowered down at her. "He was trying to bring it here when he died."

His gaze turned dangerous. "You stole it from his body?"

"Yes," said Hyo, so straightforwardly that even Koushiro was speechless. "I had to know what

my friend's last words were to make sure they actually reached you."

"Please." Natsuami stepped up beside her. "However it might sound, I assure you that Hyo meant no ill will by it."

"Assurances mean nothing to me, but if she meant me trouble, she's had ample time to do it already." Koushiro put the letter from Jun away, pressing it carefully between the folds of his robes. "I suppose I can't be surprised that an 'expert in bad luck' would *happen* upon my brother as he died. I did wonder then whether it was *too* lucky for the friends Jun had made on his expedition to be at his side in that moment." He looked her up and down. The cool suspicion diminished slightly. "You're wearing my ribbon."

It was the candle-flame ribbon he'd given Hyo, to replace her mother's haori scrap. "It's good material."

"The best," Koushiro agreed. He turned to Natsuami, then stopped and squinted. "Hold on a moment."

Pulling up his trailing trouser hems, Koushiro sprang from the stage to land next to Natsuami as light as a shadow.

"I know you." Koushiro drank Natsuami in with large eyes. "You were in a reflectograph that Jun gave me! And ever since Jun died, you've been following me around whenever I leave the theatre. I thought you were haunting me."

"I meant to protect you from a distance." So that's

what Natsuami had been doing when Hyo had seen him at the Shin-Kaguraza Bridge – he'd been stalking Koushiro about Onogoro's walkways. Natsuami looked vaguely embarrassed. "I apologize for causing you fear. Your brother left me this."

Natsuami offered Koushiro his own letter. Holding the letters side by side, Koushiro compared the two.

"Paper from the same notepad," Koushiro concluded. "The same cheap notepad he had on him at his death. Yours is definitely in my brother's handwriting. Mine ... I can still tell it's his, even deteriorated this much. Not fakes, then."

"Koushiro-san," Hyo addressed him.

He held his head high. "So long as I'm in this auditorium, you'll call me by my professional name."

"Kikugawa-san then," she said, and he nodded imperiously. "Did you keep some of the reflectographs that the Wavewalker told you to burn?"

Koushiro fell silent, but then he raised his eyes to the ceiling and said, "It didn't make any sense to burn everything. I've had that collection for years. I'd never had any trouble with it. Why would it all suddenly change in Fourthmonth?"

Ritsu sighed and shook her head. "We are going to burn what's left of that cursed collection *tonight*. Hyo-san, do you think it's the source of his bad luck, after all?"

"Of course it isn't. You heard her, Ritsu! She says my

bad luck 'isn't natural'. My collection being a 'natural magnet for negative energy' has nothing to do with it." Koushiro rounded on Hyo and Natsuami, eyes shining. "But the collection *is* why I'm being cursed, isn't it? That's why my brother's asking me to burn it. Like it says in..." Koushiro looked to Natsuami for a name.

"Natsu," Natsuami supplied.

"Natsu-san's letter," he finished. Hyo thought about it, then the shivery touch of the hellmakers' en confirmed it with a nod. Koushiro laughed. "What a hopeful fool!"

"Kichi-san!" Ritsu chided him.

"What? If a reflectograph in my collection's the problem, just burning it is never going to persuade the god to let me go! I'd have seen it, and whatever it showed, I'd have an eternal copy of it in here." Koushiro tapped the side of his head and bared his teeth. "I'm going to be unlucky until it kills me, whether I burn my collection or not!"

"Do you have to do this final show?" Hyo asked, and Koushiro twitched as if stung. "You know that everyone around you – your troupe, your audience – they're all in danger from your luck too."

"Perhaps you could seek sanctuary at a curse-mediator's shrine, as Jun did?" Natsuami suggested, then perked up at his own idea. "Yes, until we've found a way to negotiate with the god to give up their campaign!"

They'd agreed beforehand to keep quiet that Hyo suspected the Wavewalker. Hyo had no proof to offer to

Koushiro that it was him, and with Koushiro so close to the Wavewalker, Hyo had worried that letting Koushiro know would make the Wavewalker feel threatened, and work to kill him faster. Natsuami hadn't liked it, but he knew that silence could be a powerful tranquillizer.

"You don't understand," Koushiro said. He bunched his hands in his robes. "It's the promise of my final show that's helping me hold off my bad luck the most. It's keeping me alive."

Hyo narrowed her eyes. "How?

"Have you ever heard of Idol Syndrome, Hyo-san?"

"No."

Koushiro held up his hand and with Jun's letter he matter-of-factly gave himself a paper cut across his thumb.

It healed instantly. Hyo and Natsuami stared.

"Idol Syndrome. It doesn't work so quickly on larger injuries," Kikugawa went on, basking under Hyo and Natsuami's stares. "A rare but not unheard of phenomenon for those of us on stage. It works like this: whilst I still promise my audience there will be a show, this theatre acts as my shrine. My stage name of 'Kikugawa Kichizuru' acts as my heavenly name; 'Makuni Koushiro' as my earthly. I get musuhi from my fans as the gods do from their followers. They wish me alive. I've absorbed enough musuhi that, so long as I perform here, I'm very difficult to kill, nearly invulnerable. But as soon as I stop performing, if I step away from this theatre with no promise of return, I will lose all this – no audience, no altar, no heavenly name spoken, no musuhi. This bad luck will crush me and I'll probably die. I cannot cancel my final show."

"But then what about after it?"

"I'll find out if I survive to see it. You mentioned sanctuary," Koushiro said to Natsuami, "but that isn't an option for me. A shrine would give me shelter from a god, but not bad luck."

"He *has* been invited to perform at the Great Purification Rituals next month, for a special show," Ritsu chipped in with some pride.

"But in order to have enough musuhi to tide me over until then, to protect me from my luck, this final Shin-Kaguraza show and audience is my last chance to get it," Koushiro explained.

"Or," Hyo cut in, her tone low, "if someone wanted to take away your Idol Syndrome's invulnerability, your final show would be their best chance to kill off all of your most loyal audience – the ones who'd risk your luck to see you. Have you thought about *their* lives?"

Ritsu simply looked tired. She'd clearly heard this argument in the theatre already. Koushiro clenched his jaw. "I am going to perform, and you can't stop me."

"I'm sure we could try to make shrine shelter work," Natsuami tried again. "Just to give us and you more time—"

"The Shin-Kaguraza Theatre simply can't afford it. We

need this show," Koushiro said, his voice ringing. "And *I* will not be chased off *my* stage by anyone – god or human, but especially a taint-rotten, murdering god who cursed my brother, and would curse me. Will you help me, Hyo-san? If you're an expert in bad luck, helping me survive my last show should be easy, shouldn't it?"

"Show me what's left of your reflectograph collection," Hyo said, refusing to be cowed by Koushiro's sneering and posturing, "and then I'll know what I can do for you."

Someone tested the skin tension of a hand drum with a light *pop* of the heel of their hand. The troupe was returning from their break.

Ritsu whispered, "Kichi-san?"

Koushiro straightened. "Stay until the end of the rehearsal, Hyo-san. I'll show you what's left of my collection. Maybe we'll find this reflectograph that was worth Jun's life – and now mine."

Koushiro's dressing room was crowded. It was part office, with a desk overflowing with paper and a tray full of newspaper cuttings, and part dormitory, with a futon folded and stacked in the corner.

The rehearsal had ended early. The strings of every shamisen on stage had snapped, and the musicians had left with cuts on their cheeks. No one blamed Koushiro for it.

From his room's detritus, Koushiro pulled out a small chest of drawers. "I had hundreds of reflectographs. I've

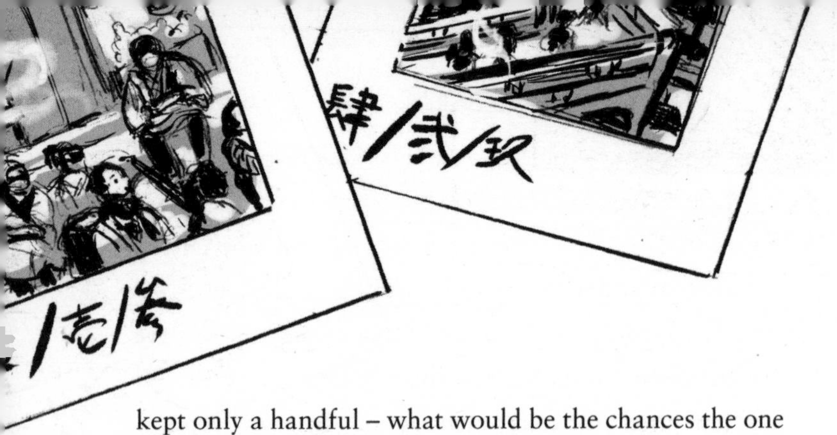

kept only a handful – what would be the chances the one that got Jun killed survived?"

"You were already unlucky when you burned them, weren't you?" Hyo pointed out.

Koushiro let out a bark of laughter. "I guess my chances are higher than most."

They weren't simply higher – Hyo was certain it would be there. She could feel it in the way the hellmakers' en was closing like a noose on the moment, but she said nothing as Koushiro opened the chest. It was black lacquer with a delicate golden detail of pines on the side, likely a gift from a fan. Its understated elegance was a stark contrast to the charred talismans slathered over the ceiling, and the bundles of amulets hanging from the walls.

The chest itself had half a dozen privacy talismans pasted over its surface. Koushiro took out a handful of stellaroid pictures and spread them on the table.

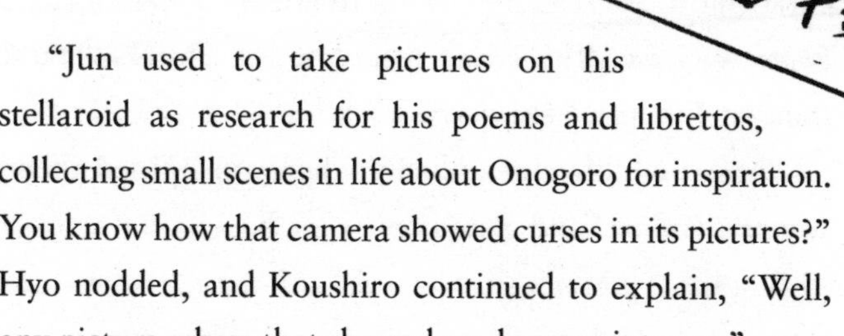

"Jun used to take pictures on his stellaroid as research for his poems and librettos, collecting small scenes in life about Onogoro for inspiration. You know how that camera showed curses in its pictures?" Hyo nodded, and Koushiro continued to explain, "Well, any picture where that showed up, he gave it to me."

"Did Jun actively look for cursed things?" Natsuami picked up one that showed a radio on a chair outside a hairdresser's. Shinrice farmers were gathering around it on a break from their pink-lit rooms, green-lensed goggles on their heads. Invisible to them, the chair was wreathed in wisps of green-purple curse. "Or people?"

"No – how could he? He couldn't see curses with his naked eye. But taking pictures around Onogoro, you're bound to stumble across a curse or two." Koushiro gazed down at the pictures. "I started collecting them because the curse colour fascinated me, but these ones

I kept because they were just beautiful pictures around Onogoro. I rarely find time to leave the Shin-Kaguraza to see ordinary stories like these for myself."

Ordinary for Onogoro. In every picture, someone or something was rimed in green-purple curse colour. The buraden train wound between warehouses, a spot of curse in its window. The black masts of the Harbourlakes' ships rose jagged behind schoolchildren on a ramp. Two children shared a curse by holding hands. Hawkers in Minami-Kanda sold fishcakes from backpacks, cooled with spinning fans, and a curse glimmered on an old woman's purse.

"Is it so wrong to think these beautiful?" Koushiro said softly.

Natsuami shook his head. "If they're beautiful to you, they are what they are."

"When Jun died of the curse, Matsubei said it was fitting that he should go that way." Koushiro seemed to curl in on himself. "Because I took such an indecent, improper interest in things that were sources of pain to others, and Jun fed my interest, it served me right."

He was different off the stage, Hyo noticed. He was smaller, lonelier and talkative – the way of someone who was rarely listened to, and didn't know when their next chance would be.

Everyone here listens to Kichizuru, Hyo thought, *but only Jun listened to Koushiro.*

Koushiro straightened a stellaroid. "This one's of you, isn't it, Natsu-san?"

"Oh. So it is."

Natsuami had been reflectographed exiting the very notice hut where Hyo had met him. His only visible features were his scarred hands, throat and a long sweep of hair, the rest of his face hidden by a half-opened umbrella. One hand was held out, catching sunlit drops of rain.

He was swathed in green-purple curse colour from which slim ribbons reached out to snag at passers-by with hooked ends.

Natsuami's lips twisted between a smile and a grimace. "May I ask ... why you kept this picture?"

Koushiro snorted, as if it was a mystery even to him, then he slid Natsuami's reflectograph over the table. "Have it."

"Oh, no, I couldn't possibly..." Koushiro locked eyes with him, and Natsuami relented. "All right. Thank you."

Hyo examined the reflectograph. It was tempting to wonder if this image of a cursed, murderous, fallen god had been the start of everything. But the date on its corner read sometime at the end of Secondmonth the previous year. Targeting Jun over a year after it was taken made little sense.

The Wavewalker and Jun had wanted the whole collection burned. The logical conclusion was that either neither had known which picture was the dangerous one or they'd known but hadn't been able to say. *Or*, Hyo thought, *they hadn't wanted to tell Koushiro which one it was.*

"Why do you think the gods got it wrong about my luck?" Koushiro asked conversationally, as Hyo pored over the stellaroids, following the tug of the hellmakers' en. "The Wavewalker's my guardian god. He's meant to be the best at identifying curses, and he's the one who said I wasn't cursed."

"The gods aren't all-knowing," Natsuami said with care. "Your situation is unusual, and they may have made a simple mistake. For the quantity of unluck attached to you, the god who manipulated that should be tainted enough for us to notice. They're not made to touch unluck."

"Is your situation unusual too?" Koushiro moved topics with less grace than he danced. "As a cursed god? What does your curse do?"

Natsuami looked queasy. "It does enough."

Hyo touched a stellaroid, and with an electric jump, a thrill ran up her fingers, the string tightened. The hellmakers' en tied *shut*.

The puzzle had a corner piece.

"This is it." Hyo held up the reflectograph. "This is what got Jun killed."

NINETEEN

射真

The trouble with the "Good Reason" limiter on the gods of fortunes' abilities is that most will curse first and find out if they had Good Reason later.

SENA,
Twentieth Hellmaker

The stellaroid was a beach view at night. It had been taken from somewhere high – a tower or a clifftop, perhaps. Moonlight drew the wave and tips of rocks in silver, outlined the small boats on the sea and lit the beach pale blue. To the image's right was a swathe of green-purple curse colour, covering a tall wall of rock.

In the midst of all that colour was a tiny pinprick of blue that Hyo would have overlooked if she hadn't, deep down, already known that somehow Ukibashi Awano, the Wavewalker's favourite, was connected to this.

"You can just touch it and tell?" Koushiro said, doubtful.

"As far as you need to know, yes." Hyo ignored his mocking eye-roll. "Did you really keep this picture just because you *liked* it?"

"Why else? It's beautiful; that curse-colour curtain looks like polar lights." *So he really hasn't spotted that blue spot of Awano's eye.* Koushiro's lips curled back, baring teeth. "A god would curse Jun and me for this? Ha! And they all let me think that *I* killed Jun with my bad luck. So is there any particular god you suspect, Hyo-san?"

"I'm investigating." She was reluctant to tell Koushiro about the Wavewalker when she didn't have the full picture yet. The Wavewalker had said at the bathhouse that he was trying to keep Koushiro alive. It hadn't sounded like a lie. Not telling Koushiro upped his chances of survival. "Why?"

"Ritsu said you were a hellmaker. A vengeance dealer." Koushiro's eyes gleamed cold and hard. "I'll commission you. I want whoever killed Jun – whoever's destroying my life – to pay!"

"No."

"You refuse me?"

"Only a special commissioner can avenge Jun's death. Right now, that isn't you. I'm looking for them, and I'll find them, but I hope you escape that fate." Hyo glanced at his flame of life, burning strong, and Koushiro's bravado fizzled under her gaze. "When's your final show?"

"This Skyday. The thirty-first."

"In five days? Cancel it."

Koushiro balked. "That's not an option!"

"You asked for my help as a bad luck expert. That's my expert advice. You said the Shin-Kaguraza can't afford it? Bullshit – they can't afford having an audience die. That kind of story sticks to a place for ever. You said you need the show to happen to survive your luck? The chances you're going to die after leaving are high anyway. Face it! You want the show to happen for your own stubborn pride, so you can go down fighting rather than running. Swallow it, cancel the show, don't give the god a chance to kill you *with* your audience and give us the time to stop the god trying to kill you." To Hyo's dismay, Koushiro was only looking more mulish and sullen as she spoke, and that rolled into a sharp spark of anger. "Your life is worth so much, and you'll throw it away to *dance*?"

"*Yes*," Koushiro said, in something between a breath and a scream. "On the Shin-Kaguraza stage, for my troupe-family, for my audience, *yes*! The Shin-Kaguraza is my *home*. Besides, why can't I commission Jun's vengeance? Ritsu commissioned you, and she's fine!"

"She wasn't avenging someone dead."

"What difference does that make?"

"The price band. You aren't ready to pay it, so you can't."

"Kichizuru-san," Natsuami broke in, as Koushiro reddened with anger. "Your brother asked me to protect you, so let me warn you about the special commissions. Hyo may ask you to pay with your life. Please," he said gently, "listen to her."

Silence.

Koushiro had kept the reflectographs the Wavewalker, his own guardian god, had told him to burn. He probably didn't have a good track record of listening to anyone, except Jun, who wasn't there any more.

"You're Jun's friend, Hyo-san." Hyo's heart sank as Koushiro crossed his arms. "Don't you want to see him avenged too?"

"I do." It was true. "But I can't do it myself. It's the rules of my work."

"Why do you do this hellmaking?" There was an elastic intensity to Koushiro's voice – the same as his movements on stage. He pushed to leave an impression, or tried to pull her into his rhythm. "Asking my life for Jun's? How's that even *fair*?"

Hyo thought of the Grandmothers' Records, read under torchlight, and the comfort of their ancient voices. She thought of copying talismans and reciting charms with Hatsu in the school holidays until her throat was hoarse and her wrists ached. All the katashiros she'd stitched and the paper dolls she'd cut, in the hands of villagers who'd put them up in their rooms and felt safer with their protection.

"Well, why do you dance, Kichizuru-san?" Hyo replied, holding his gaze. "And it isn't meant to be fair."

Koushiro paused then laughed, quietly, to himself. To Hyo it sounded almost pained, but then his expression softened. "You and Natsu-san have seen the same reflectograph. Aren't you afraid for your lives now?"

"You've seen Jun's stellaroids of us. Natsu-san and I are already too cursed for anything deeper than a silencer to get under our skins." She pointed at the beach stellaroid. "Do you know where this beach is?"

"On the south-west of the island: Hamanoyokocho," Koushiro replied, looking thoughtfully at it. "There are lots of beaches and small coves along there, but they're mostly inaccessible. They're all high cliffs and large rocks."

"*My shrine in Hamanoyokocho*," Tokifuyu had said, as he'd sunken into the Under-dream. "*Natsuami mustn't go there*."

"Can I take all the pictures?"

She thought Koushiro would fight her. His hand crept towards the corner of the shinrice farmers' reflectograph, flicking it miserably, then he shoved them all towards her. "Get them away from me."

Hyo thanked him and scooped up the pictures into her

waist-pouch. "How are you dealing with your unluck at the moment?"

She wanted to see what the Wavewalker was doing to keep Koushiro alive.

Koushiro showed her his amulets and talismans, the ones stitched on the walls and stitched into his clothes, then, from the same chest of drawers as the pictures, he took out several paper sachets of pills.

"The Wavewalker gives me these," he said, shaking out a black pill from one and a reddish pill from another. The black pill was indistinguishable from the Nightmare Burner the Wavewalker had given her. "This one's to help me sleep, and this one's to ward away bad luck and scatter what's already settled on me. He called it the Soot Shifter."

"Does anyone else take them?"

"Everyone's taking them, just to get through the day."

Whatever the Wavewalker was up to, his anti-unluck provisions were the real thing. Hyo borrowed a paper pad and wrote out some fresh talismans. A bloodstain-like splotch appeared on one as soon as she'd finished. She then made a set of thirty-three paper katashiro, tying strands of Koushiro's hair around the neck of each one and inscribing his name down their fronts.

"These are body substitutes," she told him. "They'll absorb the bad luck in your place."

It would have needed several thousand katashiro to

relieve Koushiro completely, and even then it would be temporary.

"Listen," said Koushiro suddenly. "Why don't we collaborate?"

"What do you mean?"

"I mean that you can do your investigation and find out who killed Jun ... and then once that's done –" Koushiro flexed his hands as if he were ripping something apart – "you tell me, and I'll go and avenge Jun myself, without a special commissioner, for all of us. I'll make them suffer with my own hands."

What would he do to the Wavewalker? Dance aggressively at him? Hyo made a show of considering it, and settled on, "Perhaps. If you cancel your show."

Koushiro's face was perfectly unreadable. "I'll think about it."

A knock at the door. Koushiro called out, "Yes?"

Ritsu pushed it ajar. "Kichi-san, Ukibashi Awano is here to see you. She's in the foyer."

"I'll be with her shortly." Koushiro rose. "Hyo-san and I are done here. You were right, Ritsu. She's been a great help to me, with her expertize – more than some gods, maybe."

He glanced back at Hyo before he disappeared behind a screen to change with a murky gleam in his eyes, and she realized with a jolt:

Koushiro had known all along what the stellaroid of

the beach showed. He knew it had the blue dot of his patron's eye. He'd waited and watched for Hyo to confirm it was the lethal image.

She could imagine the conclusions Koushiro was drawing about the heiress and her role in his brother's death – and the Wavewalker too.

"Don't."

"Don't what?" Koushiro replied innocently. "Don't worry, Hyo-san. What with all my rehearsals and simply trying to survive my luck, I don't have time to do anything confrontational before my final show." He came out from behind the screen, shrugging a haori into place on his shoulders, slate-grey hakama tied over his robes. "I don't intend to either. I'll show you both to the foyer."

In the foyer with Matsubei, the big man who'd wielded the halberd in the rehearsal, was Ukibashi Awano.

Her dayflower-blue robes had the weight of real silk. She exuded a presence, a calm steadiness, as if no amount of water could ever sweep her away. Her face was shockingly expressive in the way skulls were; the sunken pits made a lively gleaming beetle of her right eye, whilst the left was elegantly covered in the same scallop-shaped silk eyepatch she'd been wearing when she'd caught Hyo's eye through the telescope.

She was holding flying gloves cuffed in white lace in one hand, and with the other she patted what Hyo thought was a ceramic brooch before closer observation revealed it to be a familiar blue crab.

The Wavewalker noticed Hyo and Natsuami before Ukibashi Awano did. Hyo felt a churning in the air, as if an unseen current had suddenly changed its course to flow towards her, then Ukibashi Awano looked their way.

"Kichizuru, at last!" Matsubei flung up his hands. "Where have you been? You've kept our lady waiting!"

Koushiro bowed. "I'm sorry to have done so, Ukibashi-sama, troupe leader Matsubei."

"Kichizuru-san, would you introduce me to your friends? It's so rare to see new faces these days at our theatre." Ukibashi Awano spoke with the quietness of someone who'd never had to raise their voice to be heard. She put her heels together with a light click of her Harbourlakes-style ankle boots. "Unless they're press and rooting around for information that isn't theirs."

"They aren't press, Ukibashi-sama." Koushiro showed no sign of suspecting Ukibashi Awano of anything. If Hyo hadn't known better, she'd have thought he was genuinely glad to see her. His smile was charming; his body language said the cancelled shows were forgiven and that he was grateful for his last dance. "This is Hakai Hyo and her assistant Natsu-san. They're friends of my late brother. I invited them here to talk about my brother's unfinished libretto, the *Twelve Rings Project*. I was hoping to perform a section of it at the Great Purification Rituals."

"What a wonderful idea! Makuni-san was working so hard on it, it'd be a shame for it to go to waste."

"This is Ukibashi Awano, who needs no introduction," Koushiro said. Awano dipped her head to Hyo. "We of the Shin-Kaguraza value her and her access to the Ukibashi Shinshu Company's coffers very much."

"Kichizuru," Matsubei grumbled.

"Saving all your charm for the stage, as ever." Awano gave Koushiro a light flick on the chest with her flight gloves. To Hyo's astonishment, Koushiro laughed. "But I wouldn't have it otherwise. If you'd suddenly started tiptoeing around me like everyone else, I'd have thought someone really *had* cursed you."

Awano turned to Hyo properly. With the tip of her little finger, she lifted her eyepatch, enough for a brief, piercing glimmer of blue – the "jelly-eye" as Nagakumo had called it – in Hyo's direction.

She flinched and let the patch cover her eye again.

The little crab made bubbling noises at her collar. Awano tilted her head towards it, as if to listen, but then she covered the crab entirely with the gloves, blocking it from Hyo's sight and Hyo from it.

"You have something in your hair." Awano leant towards her. "May I?"

Hyo crouched so that Awano could reach her face. "Sure."

"Girl, do you know who you're speaking to?"

Matsubei spluttered. "This is Ukibashi Awano of the Ukibashi Shinshu Company! You should address her with the more appropriate formality!"

"It's all right, Matsubei-san. She doesn't know me; I don't know her. All we share is a lot of 'not-knowing'." Ukibashi Awano combed her fingers through Hyo's hair, tucking the strands behind Hyo's ear. Under the gloves and her other hand, the fragment of the Wavewalker bubbled in protest. "There. It's gone. Just a little something, but I couldn't let it go." Her hand slid down Hyo's face. "Candlewax, and the soot of life."

Hyo swallowed, her mouth dry. "Thank you."

"My pleasure." Awano lowered her hand from the crab and clasped Hyo's in both of hers. She was probably not much older than Hyo, but she was so painfully thin Hyo

couldn't say for sure. The thought came to Hyo's mind that she looked stretched – between sad and desperate. "Be careful."

In the shield of their hands, hidden from the Wavewalker, Ukibashi Awano flicked through rapid Harboursigns against her palms: "Please help me. The Wavewalker needs us."

She let Hyo go. "Kichizuru-san, I was hoping to see the rehearsals today, but Matsubei-san says they finished early?"

"They did," said Koushiro. "But I don't need anyone else around to give our lady a special preview of my solo dance sequence, and Matsubei knows I can do with the practice."

Matsubei shook a finger at him. "Damn right you do."

"Until we meet again, Hakai-san," Ukibashi Awano said brightly, as Koushiro led her away. "You and I are allies in this – I've seen it."

"In what?" Hyo called after her, but Awano only waved at her with her flight gloves and laughed.

The Wavewalker's little blue crab crawled on to Ukibashi Awano's shoulder. It stared back at Hyo until Awano rounded the corner, and they were out of sight.

TWENTY

巻物

To make a shikigami – a spirit familiar –
you need a vessel then spirit. For the vessel,
in the First Level, we may use a paper doll.
For spirit, we may use our own breath.
Think carefully of your intention
in their creation.

DAUGHTER OF TAIRA,
Sixth Hellmaker

The evening noises of Onogoro were muffled in the mist, but the police sirens were unmistakable, as was Mansaku, returned from the Ohne gang's offices, wringing blood out from his socks into the water closet sink.

"None of this is mine!" he said, as Hyo and Natsuami walked through the door. "I stood in a splash zone."

Hyo went to him in an instant. "Sit down. I'll finish that."

"I'm a big boy – I can wash my own bloodstains."

"Mansaku, just sit. Natsuami, can you do tea?"

"Of course."

Natsuami hurried away. Mansaku handed the socks over, washed his hands, smoothed back his hair, then slumped heavily against the living room table.

He held up the white tube tied with straw-yellow string. "I got the Paddywatcher's present."

"Never mind that." Hyo poured cold water into the sink, spooned salt into it from the pot Natsuami brought her, then left Mansaku's socks to soak. "You're not hurt?"

"You're kidding, right? As if anyone could touch me." Mansaku scoffed then softened, and held out his arms. "But I could do with a hug."

Hyo gave Mansaku just that. She held him and surreptitiously checked him for wounds whilst Mansaku recounted what happened with the Ohne gangsters ... ahem, "moneylenders".

It had been clear from the beginning that the Ohne were doomed. No number of talismans or private diviners they employed would've saved them, because the threat wasn't spiritual – it was human.

Mansaku made the Ohne a squad of shikigami to scout around the walkways, and in moments he'd discovered an army of the Ohne's enemies surrounding their main offices and businesses, who had united to settle old scores as soon as the Paddywatcher had announced her twenty-four-hour suspension of protection.

And settle those old scores they did, with some creatively wielded power and agricultural tools. The gangsters with the Wavewalker's blessing were especially vicious.

Mansaku had left when the head office was invaded. A white snake had guided him out of the Ohne's rooms whilst Meatfist Kumataro was distracted by an enemy gangster, helping Mansaku avoid the improvised weapons and flying fists in the corridors, until he was out and could escape down a walkway empty of both gangsters and police.

The little white snake had spat out Meatfist Kumataro's white tube into Mansaku's hand then disappeared. The message was clear. *The Paddywatcher keeps her promises. She expects Mansaku to keep his.*

Hyo looked at the white tube. "Have you opened it?"

"I was waiting until you got back. O'Hyo –" the

way Mansaku lowered his voice made Hyo's stomach sink – "at the Ohne's offices, someone was talking about hitodenashi pear."

Hyo's tongue turned suddenly leaden. "On Onogoro?"

He nodded, then Natsuami came down the narrow stairs with tea, so Mansaku closed his hand around the Paddywatcher's tube and secreted it up his sleeve. "Later. Tell me what happened with Koushiro."

Hyo let out a long sigh. "What *didn't* happen with Koushiro."

She and Natsuami filled Mansaku in, and when they finished, she set down the beach stellaroid on the table, the one Jun had been killed for taking and Koushiro would be next for keeping.

Mansaku hummed uncertainly, squinting at the dot. "Kidnapped heiress with her mystery eye, out on her own on a supposedly inaccessible beach at night. Yeah, the weeklies would definitely be interested. Especially considering this." He pointed at the curse-colour smudge all along the wall of rock to the image's right. "A curse that covers a whole cliff says to me 'ward'."

Natsuami set down his tea. "Do you suppose there's something hidden behind the ward? Perhaps within the cliff?"

"Hidden," Hyo agreed, "and shielded by a ward that will curse anyone who tries to go through it."

"Something hidden that's worth Ukibashi Awano

of the Ukibashi Shinshu Company paying it a personal midnight visit," Mansaku added.

Natsuami's glasses reflected the eerie colours of the curse. "What do you think that ward could be hiding?"

"At that size, it could be anything. A secret castle. Flightcraft dock. A giant attack robot." Mansaku stretched his arms luxuriously and folded them behind his head. "We could go and see for ourselves, of course."

"We could!" said Natsuami, brightening at the idea. "How about we go to Hamanoyokocho tomorrow? With the three of us, we'd easily find the beach that matches Jun's picture. All we'd have to do is follow the top of the cliffs to where he took it—"

Hyo cut him off. "We're not going to Hamanoyokocho. I don't want any of us getting hurt before Koushiro's last show at the Shin-Kaguraza. We've got to be ready in case something happens that night."

Mansaku stopped her with a finger. "You told Koushiro to cancel his show."

"I told him – but he's not going to listen."

Mansaku looked to Natsuami, who hesitated, then caved with a sigh. "All right. But I am very curious about Ukibashi Awano's left eye."

"Isn't the whole of Onogoro?"

"I don't know; I haven't been following the weeklies." Natsuami twisted the ends of his hair. "I wonder what that eye shows her."

"*Candlewax*," Hyo remembered Awano's voice in her ear, at the same time as she recalled how the girl had flinched, seeing *something* when she'd turned that eye on Natsuami.

Natsuami suddenly stood, pushing himself up from the table. "I'll do dinner! Please, leave it to me."

He wanted a moment to himself. Hyo and Mansaku let him have it. They waited for Natsuami to start singing, then Mansaku took out the Paddywatcher's white tube and undid the thread.

The cylinder didn't unroll. It twisted up tighter, turning thin and coiling with a tapered head, then the head split open, and the paper snake had a mouth. Its paper jaws opened wider, and wider, until the snake had opened its mouth so wide that it turned itself inside out and tore itself into flakes.

It regurgitated a scroll. Hyo grabbed it in mid-air. It was the length of her forearm, its cream paper backed in a deep purple silk that caught the light with a bronze diamond pattern.

Hyo met Mansaku's gaze. This could be the answer to freeing Mansaku from Kiriyuki. He nodded at Hyo to unroll it, whilst he scrunched up the remains of the snake in his hand.

The strong black strokes of the title appeared.

A Record of the Making and Sealing of Third Level Shikigami

"'Third level'," Hyo read aloud. Then something fell into place. "This is what we had wrong the whole time!"

"What? What was wrong?"

"We've been calling Kiriyuki a weapon spirit and thinking of it like a ghost that's possessing you." Hyo pressed the scroll into Mansaku's arms. "We should've been thinking about Kiriyuki like a *shikigami*."

"Like ... one of our little paper men?"

"They're paper bodies, animated by breath – containing our spirit. You're a shikigami, Mansaku, except with a meat body and your own spirit too, so Kiriyuki's spirit is eating you up inside." It seemed so obvious once Hyo had seen it. Mansaku wasn't *possessed* like Nagakumo could be. "We were looking in the wrong direction for answers. With this scroll, the Paddywatcher's showing us which way to look. It's a starting point to get you and Kiriyuki split apart."

Mansaku clutched the scroll, gazing at the black writing with a fragile expression of hope, as delicate as the end of his candle-wick.

He rolled up the scroll and handed it carefully back to Hyo. "You'll, er, have to read it for me. I can't read old cursive like you can. Could you...?"

"I'll write you a copy."

"Leave nothing out," Mansaku said firmly. "Not the ugly bits. Especially those. I can handle a horror story. *Human Sideboard* Fan Club Member Number Two, me."

"I'll copy it word for word."

Mansaku let out a breath. "This is a pretty hefty down payment for whatever curse she's going to put me under."

Hyo found a spot at the back of the closet and tucked the scroll away. She wished she could just as easily put away her worry about what price Mansaku would pay for this information – what curse the Paddywatcher would put on him, and for what.

She turned back to him. "Go on then – what did the gangsters say about hitodenashi on Onogoro?"

"The lower-ranking gang members were passing around a rumour." He paused, listened for Natsuami's footsteps overhead then continued, "They were warning each other that if they end up in a police cell or at the Onmyoryo, people like them might disappear – they were half-joking, but only half. They could all think of someone who'd suddenly 'moved districts' or 'gone into a centre' and hadn't been heard from again. And you know what they were calling the disappeared? 'Orchard-fodder'."

The hairs rose down Hyo's neck. A hitodenashi orchard on Onogoro would need living human hosts to grow from, to feed on their suffering. Human bodies had to be sourced from somewhere.

"They were scared, O'Hyo," Mansaku went on. "As much as they could be in the middle of a gang fight. I tried to ask them about it, but I was just an office guest for the day. They clammed up and jumped to looking busy."

"People are going missing from police cells?" Hyo repeated, aghast. "And from the Onmyoryo?"

"Yep – food for thought. And not the tasty kind."

The creaking overhead shifted to the stairs. Natsuami returned, holding a tray with bowls of rice and a sour pickled plum covered in hot green tea, dried horse mackerels and the leftovers from lunch.

He caught sight of Hyo's and Mansaku's expressions, and said wryly, "I see my cunning plan to allow you both time to scheme without being troubled by my presence was successful."

"No schemes yet – just top-secret info exchanges." Hyo rose to relieve him of the dishes. "Sorry we can't mix you in on it."

"*I* see that *our* cunning plan – to let you flex your

heavenly cooking skills in peace – was also successful?" Mansaku said.

"You do flatter me. And perhaps –" Natsuami bundled his hair to the side as he joined them – "it wasn't quite 'in peace'. I couldn't help thinking of how I looked in Jun's stellaroid ... and what that could mean to those who met me."

Hyo remembered the tendrils of curse-colour extending from Natsuami in his picture, hooked and clawed, stretching to passers-by – as if they could latch on to them. "Thinking about how cursed you are isn't going to make you less cursed."

"That may be so," Natsuami said tentatively, "but didn't you think that stellaroid of me was ... disturbing? Horrible, even?"

"Jun didn't think so. He saw that and he still wanted to be your friend." In Jun's camera-eye, Natsuami had been beautiful – curse and all. "And he's taken worse of me."

"He has?"

Hyo held up her hands for Natsuami to see the seal she'd been born with. "I'm very, very cursed, Natsuami."

"But at least you know that, and you know what you are. You are a hellmaker, and your knowledge of your curse lets you use it for others. Whereas I –" Natsuami's voice pitched higher, rising slightly – "I am a god without a heavenly name, whose own brother had to watch over *lest I hurt others*, like Jun. All I have is ignorance of myself. It'd be better for all if I dissipated and vanished like a normal god."

"Don't say that!" Hyo seized Natsuami by the collar. "Don't you dare, in front of *me*, wish your life away. Every flame of life, whilst it burns, can warm someone else and light a way for them, just by being there in a cold, dark world. Just by *being*. That flame of life is precious and beautiful, and I bet Jun and Tokifuyu both thought this world was more beautiful and precious for it."

"I wish I could agree."

She slapped Natsuami's chest, over his flame, which Hyo still hadn't looked at. Mansaku was right that it was like the demon's. Just as with the demon, every gut instinct screamed that Hyo shouldn't even *try* to look at Natsuami's flame.

"Being able to see the flames of lives is supposed to be part of the hellmakers' punishment," Hyo said. Natsuami's heart jumped against her palm. "It's meant to let us see with our own eyes how people suffer because of the bad luck we send them. Our gaze is meant to frighten people, because we make them aware of the smallness of their lives and the count of their remaining years, deeply enough to be able to give them to us as payment." She shook Natsuami by his collar again, just to make her point. "You've lived through nine hundred years, haven't you? You know what people do to things that frighten them? My grandmothers were called 'women of misfortune' and 'unclean things', banished from villages! Hated! It would've been so easy to hate those frightened people back. We could've become exactly the monsters of misfortune the gods wanted us to be."

"But you didn't?" Natsuami said, eyes wide.

Mansaku picked the meat off his mackerel and drank his tea, watching them both as he might a table tennis match.

"If we did, the gods who cursed us would've

won. And there hasn't been a hellmaker who doesn't hate losing. Hellmaking was put together by a long string of fuck-yous to the gods of fortune, and one of the first of those was to decide that although our gaze makes people feel death's shadow, we have to act remembering, honouring and loving people's brightness." Hyo let Natsuami go. "You don't deserve to vanish. *Refuse* that thought. It's a kind of curse too. All right?"

"All right." Natsuami was staring at her. "Oh, oh, no. I'm so sorry, Hyo, I didn't think..."

Hyo was suddenly aware of tears at her chin and her neck. *Springtime meltwater tears*, Jun might've described this kind of crying. Tears that fell after a long wintertime of the heart, after being packed down, compressed, allowed to freeze. The cracks they seeped through were unexpected, sudden and not always logical. She hadn't realized it, but she'd been rattled by Koushiro, by Kikugawa Kichizuru, and his disregard for his own life.

She didn't want Koushiro to be her special commissioner. She wanted to protect him as Jun had wanted. But the hellmakers' en, step by step, was starting to tie off the threads by which he could escape that fate. The thought weighed on her more heavily than she'd thought it would.

"O'Hyo..." Mansaku murmured. He reached over the table to poke her in the wrist. "Did Natsu-san make you cry? Say the word. I will punch his pretty patchwork face until he cries too. Tears for tears. I don't really want to, but it's big-brother protocol."

"Natsuami didn't *make* me cry. Stop embarrassing me."

And Natsuami was already crying, very freely.

"... is this flame of life really beautiful?"

Hyo wiped her eyes. Natsuami was touching his chest where Hyo had smacked it. She didn't know. She couldn't tell him after all this that she was afraid to look and meet the eyes of something so hungry to be seen it would eat her gaze and then her for looking.

But she could reply with absolute certainty. "Yes, it is."

TWENTY-ONE

海透眼

The gods cannot enter – by gaze or by form – the shrine of another god without permission, unless they have a sub-altar there. If asked by a god to trespass another's shrine, please contact the Onmyoryo for emergency advice and protection.

From "Don't Worry, They Can't Kill You Unless You Ask for It: A Beginner's Guide to Co-existing with the Earthbound Divine"

The red cord snapped, jerking with every attempt to drag Hyo closer. The mist swirled. Cloud frothed in thin white ribbons that curled around the cord, and Hyo was moving, slipping cun by cun towards the pit.

Here, it said with every tug. *I am here. Look at me – I am here. Fear me!*

"No," said Hyo. "I've never been afraid of ghosts."

She had brought them with her to Onogoro. Sometimes she saw them in the faces of the islanders she met. Here, they lived again. She had shouldered them to make that happen. She didn't chase them from her memories when they asked to be named.

At the next rough tug, Hyo pushed herself up on to her feet. Before the next pull could sweep her off balance and face down in the mist again, she squared her shoulders and ran towards the pit.

She snatched up the slack length and pulled, leaning her weight on her heels. "And I'll look at you without fear."

She pulled, and pulled, until something rose from the depths.

A forest of gilded teeth, a blinking crown of eyes, an expressive face striped with scars, and cradled amidst the teeth and eyes, almost lost in the fangs, was a small sleeping child in a green suikan, the clothes of the Taiwa era, hands clutching at the teeth like a comfort.

"Tokifuyu?"

The child stirred. The jaws closed around it.

Not yours, the hunger echoed. ***He is not yours to hurt.***

Hyo knew when she had begun dreaming of the rocks and that unseen thing endlessly climbing out of the pit: it'd started when Natsuami had come to live with them, invited within the privacy talisman's boundaries.

Mansaku, the lucky bastard, didn't seem affected by them at all, or perhaps he was but didn't remember. Hyo had seen him scratching around his navel a couple of mornings on waking, and when pressed about it, he'd had no answer to give her, just weariness.

He slept on, snoring softly, as Hyo crept down the stairs to wash her face and clear her head of dreams.

The morning's gloom shimmered slightly with unluck. It outlined Natsuami's sleeping form on the living room floor, allowing Hyo to tiptoe around the edges of his bedding to the water closet. The heaviness of Natsuami's shadow, which always seemed slightly more pronounced at night, filled the room with a crouched, watching presence, but Hyo had grown used to eerier things in her life. She ignored it and shut the closet door.

She'd splashed water on her face when she felt the movement behind her ear.

Hyo slapped it, and opened her hand. It was covered in water, then as more water dripped into it from her face and her fringe, the drops gathered together, coalesced and swelled into a single larger wobbling drop. When it was about the size of a goldfish, it leapt from her hand.

It splattered over the mirror, and the striplight's cold gleam lifted words out of the water.

Let me tell you what my left eye sees, Hakai Hyo.

In what felt like an extension of a dream, Hyo watched the water flow into the glistening shapes of a message.

No doubt you've heard already that this eye was a gift from the Wavewalker and that it helped me escape my captors when I was kidnapped in Firstmonth – this is all true.

This eye sees the world as water does.

Hyo bent closer to the letters. "What does that mean?"

Water divides the world into two things: containers, and container-escapes.

In the boat where I was held, this meant understanding my prison completely, then knowing the flaws that would let me escape it: a tired guard, a rusty nail, a captain under too much pressure, language barriers, resentment and suspicion.

With people, I can see what traps them in their lives, the things they carry on their shoulders that set them apart from others. For you, it is those candles you see already lit for everyone around you. As if they're all already dead.

Why am I trusting you, a stranger, with this?

Because I looked at you, Hakai Hyo, on the tower opposite the Shin-Kaguraza, and I saw in you an escape route for a dear friend of mine. I need your help to save the Wavewalker.

My water-eye lets me see that the Wavewalker has built himself a prison – he might be part of a scheme of which he can't cut free, made some promise he cannot break or has a secret he must keep.

Just as I saw your prison in candles, I see the Wavewalker's in taint.

You must have noticed the unforecast wild rains. I've heard things from the Wavewalker to believe he has damaged the Onmyoryo's taint-detectors himself. He means to go undetected in harming humans until the Great Purification Rituals, when the rites will cleanse him.

I am afraid for my friend, and what it means that he has accumulated all this secret taint, and what he still, maybe, means to accomplish before the Rituals. I want to stop him, in whatever he's doing, before he's beyond it. He could fall to destruction.

You are my means to stop this. I've seen it. Together, we can free the Wavewalker from his taint-gathering secrets.

I believe he's put himself under a silencing curse, so that he cannot share with me what he's done, even if he wishes to. I have tried to watch him and follow him to learn what I can of what he's hiding from me. The little I have, I will share with you, as a sign of trust:

The Bridgeburner found evidence of something the Wavewalker should not have done, and he has hidden it in his own shrine at Hamanoyokocho. Gods cannot enter the shrines of other gods, but the Wavewalker has been anxious to retrieve what the Bridgeburner found and destroy it. He's hesitated until now because the Bridgeburner has been able to defend his shrine, but the Bridgeburner is now absent.

Now all that stops him is knowing that breaking into the shrine of one of his own kin would add to his taint – but I don't think this will stop him for ever.

If you go to the Bridgeburner's Hamanoyokocho shrine, find that evidence and deliver it to me before the Wavewalker reaches it, I can confront him. I can force my friend to recognize his taint, end whatever he's doing and hold him back from a fall to destruction.

I am watched by the Wavewalker. There's little I can do without an ally on the outside. If you agree to help me, pour half of this message droplet down your sink. It will find its way back to me. Keep the other half for the future, upon your person. I'll be able to find you by it.

If you disagree, just wipe the glass clean.

Hyo stared at the glass. When she did nothing, the words flowed together, and began again from the top.

Hamanoyokocho. An incredibly mundane name for somewhere that seemed to be at the heart of Jun's murder.

With a tug at the back of her brain, Hyo recalled Tokifuyu, under the rock on the Plaza, pleading with Jun's ghost: "*I did find something on the day you died!*"

"'... evidence to suggest you weren't cursed with Good Reason'," Hyo repeated, feeling out the words with her own lips. Could it be the same "evidence" as what Awano wanted?

And, if hidden at his shrine, could this evidence be why Tokifuyu had wanted Hyo to keep Natsuami away from it?

The water droplets came to their final appeal again: *Agree or disagree.*

Hyo slid her hand down half of the glass, directing the beads of water into the sink. She collected the water from the other half on to her toothbrush then returned to the living room's gloom.

When she'd stood there for a few moments, toothbrush in front of her, stuck for what to do with a blob of animated water, Natsuami spoke up in a half-whisper, "You're holding that toothbrush with intent, and it makes me nervous."

"I need a home for a pet water drop," Hyo returned in the same kind of half-whisper.

Natsuami sat up and edged the closet open slightly. He rifled through his things, then found something and held it out to her. "My spare travelling ink-well."

"Thank you."

"If I were to ask about it...?"

"I'll answer." Hyo transferred Awano's drop into the well, sealed it, then lowered herself to sit on the bottom step of the stairs. "Ukibashi Awano thinks the Wavewalker is up to something bad that's causing him to gather dangerous quantities of taint, and he's sabotaged the island's taint-detectors to get away with it until the Sixthmonth Rituals."

"Ukibashi Awano says this? The Wavewalker's favourite?" Natsuami straightened, a dark shadow within the gloom, edges softened by unluck.

"I guess she'd know, as his favourite," Hyo echoed meaningfully. "Awano wants me to help find evidence for her – something she could use to stop the Wavewalker thinking whatever he's doing is worth the taint."

"Do you believe her?"

"I don't have to." Hyo held up the ink-well. The drop was too small to be heard when she shook the container. "It's still interesting to hear what the Ukibashi heiress and Pillar God's favourite wants us to hear."

"Are you going to help her?"

"We'll see." The tower creaked to the spin of its wind turbine. Hyo said, "Natsuami, when you sleep, do you dream at all?"

"I've not had a dream in three years – not even the feeling that I've dreamt and forgotten it." In the dark, Natsuami's voice seemed to come from all directions at once. "Why do you ask?"

"I wondered what Onogoro's number one mystery god might dream of."

"Number one!" He went on smilingly, "And what does Onogoro's *number one* hellmaker dream of that she's awake at this time in the morning, taking messages from shinshu heiresses instead of fitfully sleeping?"

"I'm not 'number one'; I'm the only one."

"What a coincidence! As am I."

"I dream the usual, then," Hyo replied, finding herself smiling "Nothing good. I've never had a good dream in my life."

"Never?"

"Never."

"Surely not; that would be too sad. Everyone should have a good dream, once in a while." Natsuami's tone was almost pleading. Hyo bent down and patted the part of him she could reach – his foot under the bedcovers. He said, "Hyo, what would need to happen for Koushiro to become your special commissioner?"

"He has to *want* to pay with his life to avenge Jun. Deeply." She drew her knees up to her chin. Heavens, she didn't know what she was doing. "It's right that he shouldn't."

"Jun asked me to protect Koushiro. Not stand by and watch him die." Natsuami sat still and shadowy. "Will the special commission make us enemies?"

"I don't know." The admission brought a soft chill of relief. Some things were easier to say in whispers in the half-light before dawn. "Stick around and you'll find out."

The shimmer of unluck in Natsuami's shape rippled in a nod. "I shall do so."

The flavour of wild rain that morning was slime. Thick, viscous and with a rainbow shimmer, it didn't fall in drops, but dangled in long trails from some impossible point in the sky, as if an open mouth were drooling a saliva chandelier over Onogoro. Cords of it hung between the towers in a slick curtain that Hyo parted with her umbrella on her way to the Shin-Kaguraza Theatre.

The reporters she'd cursed hadn't returned, and the number of their comrades had drastically reduced. She was able to go to straight up to the Plum Door, where the stage-hand opened it.

"Tell Kikugawa Kichizuru to cancel his last Shin-Kaguraza show."

"Or else what?"

"Ask Kikugawa. He knows." Hyo dumped a packet of talismans into the unsettled stage-hand's arms, because she could be nice like that, and left.

The following day, she repeated her visit, with the same message and another stack of talismans. No change.

The day after was the same. The wild rain had let up, leaving an unseasonable clammy coldness in the air, so that Hyo's breath lingered as clouds at her lips, and a pearly shroud wreathed the tops of every tower. Flightcraft had been grounded. The Onmyoryo had assured the public that they were doing everything they could to check atmospheric taint levels, whilst giving no specifics of what, in fact, they were doing.

The box-office man called out to Hyo as she made for the steps to the Plum Door. "Hakai-san?"

At the counter, he handed over an envelope of silky white paper, a far cry from the usual blue multi-cycled type. "These are for you from Kichizuru-san. We're all grateful here for your talismans – very few incidents these past couple of days! Very good value!"

"Glad to hear it." Hyo accepted the envelope, knowing exactly what would be inside, and what Koushiro had decided. "Tell Kichizuru-san thank you."

She opened the envelope at home, once Natsuami and Mansaku had returned for lunch. They'd gone to the Wavewalker's Minami-Kanda shrine to see Tokifuyu in the yashiori ward. Tokifuyu was as Hyo and Natsuami had left him: still semi-see-through, still patterned in yashiori's iridescent whorls, and sunken in a deep sleep.

If what Ukibashi Awano had said was true, Hyo now had some idea as to why the Wavewalker would've wanted Tokifuyu out of the way. And yet the god had seemed shocked by Tokifuyu's drowning. Maybe he hadn't known that Tokifuyu had had a habit and would have gone so deep into the Under-dream. Maybe he'd only meant for Tokifuyu to be set aside a few days, rather than indefinitely. A few days was all he needed to do something about the incriminating evidence in Tokifuyu's shrine.

The question then was why hadn't the Wavewalker done anything yet? He'd had a week since Tokifuyu had been taken out of the picture. Maybe he had, and no one knew, not even Ukibashi Awano.

But Hyo didn't think so. The pieces in this puzzle were still the wrong shape.

The envelope contained tickets to Koushiro's final show. They were printed with the floating bridge of the

Ukibashi family crest and silver looping lines traced an elegant motif of water.

The letter they were enclosed in said:

For the family box where Jun would have sat. It'd make him so happy to know that his friends were there, supporting me in everything I do, in his place.

"Could he still be persuaded?" said Natsuami, as Hyo put the tickets away and set the envelope amidst the three of them on the table. "Perhaps I could commission you for a little mild bad luck for Koushiro? To break a leg maybe?"

"What unluck I add to him now is nothing compared to what he's already dealing with. It wouldn't do anything." *Are there any other options?* Hyo buried her head in her hands, thought hard, but drew a blank. "It's no use. Koushiro wants to dance, so we'll watch the stubborn fucker dance."

Mansaku ground his teeth. "And be ready for whatever that unluck drops on us all. We'll have the best seats in the house for it."

"I should think that Ukibashi Awano and the Wavewalker will have the best seats in the house," Natsuami remarked, then a knock sounded at the door, and he looked up. "Is that an Oblivionist monk?"

Beyond the rippled resin slats in the door was the big, broad silhouette of a large "monk", who advertised he was such with a kesa slung over his shoulder and rosaries draped across his chest.

There was no mistaking Hatamoto Yaemon, even with the bascinet covering his face. He bowed when Hyo opened the door. "Hyo-san, we meet again!"

"What do you want?"

"Not 'what' – 'who'." Hatamoto pointed into the apartment, then crooked his finger. "Mansaku-san! Yamada Hanako would like you to come and help her, as you've previously agreed, right now."

"We just got box tickets to the theatre. Couldn't Hanako-chan maybe wait a day or two?" But Mansaku was swigging back his tea and rising. "I hope she can make up for it."

"I'm sure she will."

"Mansaku-san." Natsuami stood, stopping Mansaku with a hand. "Who is this man? Why did you flinch when he asked for you?"

"Shhh, save me some face. I twitched at most, like a dead frog."

Natsuami frowned at Hatamoto. "I feel we've met before."

"Us? No, young man! You've a memorable … hairstyle. I wouldn't forget you if we had." Hatamoto laughed nervously, and Hyo realized what the bascinet covering his face was for. He was hiding from Natsuami.

"It's all right, Natsu-san. O'Hyo knows what's up.

This is just a little challenge, that's all." Mansaku took a deep bracing breath, adjusted his neck kerchief, then faced Hyo. "Come back safely – and undramatically."

There wasn't enough spit for Hyo to swallow. "You too."

"That goes for *both* of you," he added, eying Natsuami as well. "Don't get killed by Koushiro's luck. Or, you know, horribly maimed."

Natsuami responded with a small nod. Mansaku put on his geta, Hyo stood aside to let him out and Hatamoto Yaemon bobbed his head and bascinet to them in a parting bow.

"If you'd come this way, Mansaku-san," he said. "Heavens, it does make a god's work easier when the humans are so agreeable!"

TWENTY-TWO

新神楽

Once, to dance a kagura meant to call down the gods that they could settle upon the dancer's bones and wear the dancer as their mask.

From "Don't Worry, They Can't Kill You Unless You Ask for It: A Beginner's Guide to Co-existing with the Earthbound Divine"

The chasm between Iris Hill and the Shin-Kaguraza Theatre was filled with solarcranes, parked above and below and jostling for roosting space like seabirds. The hiss of pressurized hydrogen and crackling of expanding flotation balloons echoed in the twilight, as the promise of Kikugawa Kichizuru's last show at the Shin-Kaguraza drew in one last crowd for one last time.

People risked a lot for "one", "last" and "time", Hyo thought as she climbed the steps. All around her, Onmyoryo-certified wild-rain umbrellas were hooked over arms and eyes were turning to the skies – perfectly clear, for the first time in many evenings, and all the more unsettling for it.

"Look at all these people," Natsuami said. He was wearing a face veil to hide the lower half of his face. "Even with the area luck-warning, they're still coming to see Koushiro."

"It's luck, after all," Hyo said. "Some people love to test theirs. They're called gamblers."

"The Hakai hellmakers, is it?" said the doorman when they showed him their tickets. "This way, please."

He led them up a quiet flight of stairs, away from the crowd, to a small box that smelled of real polished wood and had a view that directly faced the stage.

"Hakai-san?" Hyo heard as soon as she took her seat. She looked to their left and felt a cold jolt of surprise. Ukibashi Awano sat in the neighbouring box, apparently alone. The silk of her robes glistened in mother-of-pearl grey. She was putting away lace gloves in a clutch embroidered with shimmering silver fletchmarks.

Awano smiled, dipping her head in a bow, which Hyo returned. "Just my luck; we must have some kind of en."

"We must."

"Have you got my water droplet on you?"

"I do." Natsuami's ink-well was in Hyo's waist-pouch.

There was only a narrow wall and a handrail between them. Awano reached over it. Hyo took her hands, letting Awano's bony fingers clutch at her.

"I'm so glad for an ally," Awano said shakily, squeezing tight. "I knew I could count on you. My eye's not been wrong yet. May I call you Hyo-chan? I've always wanted a friend my age. You may call me Awano-chan, of course."

"Go ahead." Hyo lowered her voice, but she doubted they'd be overheard by the buzz of the audience anyway. "You said you wanted to free the Wavewalker from a prison he's trapped himself in. That goes for you too, doesn't it? You're trapped with him, as the only person who knows he has a secret he can't share. In telling me, am I a way out for *you* too, or are you trapping me with you?"

"You understand." Awano's eye shone. The left eye was hidden under a crimped fan today, painted with fish-scales. "You understand what it's like to be held captive and to have all control over your own fate stolen from you."

"You end up waiting," Hyo said, thinking of snow and

twisted bodies. "You've tried everything you can and you're tired. You're waiting for someone else to decide your fate for you – whether you're worth saving, or not. You're not even hoping any more, because the hoping hurts."

"We wait," Awano said, holding Hyo's gaze, "and, because we waited, nobody will let us be the hero of our own stories. No one wants a hero who is powerless. They want a hero who acts and never has to wait."

"Like the Wavewalker?"

"My hero *for ever.* What about you, Hyo-chan? Who saved you when you couldn't save yourself?"

"My own captor." Hyo looked at Awano's fingers, their tips whorled with the delicate prints of a human. "She trapped me to torment me for vengeance, then got bored, and let me go."

"And I was goods to barter. I'd have preferred vengeance." Awano pulled back and let Hyo go. "Kichizuru-san told me that you'd advised him to cancel this show."

"Did he say why?"

"Yes – for fear his bad luck will kill us all tonight."

"You don't think it could?"

"The Wavewalker is attending. If Kichizuru-san dies, here, in front of him, he'd have failed him as a guardian god, not to mention his other followers in the audience. He can't afford all that taint. Furthermore, I am here." Awano rolled back her shoulders, sitting up tall. "The Wavewalker certainly won't allow anything to happen that would risk my life too. That's what I'm betting my life on."

"You're a gambler?"

A slow smile spread across Awano's face. "I can't resist a bet."

It dawned on Hyo. "You think the Wavewalker is making Kichizuru unlucky."

"It's a plausible explanation for the Wavewalker's taint. I don't *want* to think it, so I'm betting my life tonight that it isn't so. Why would he want to? What's Kichizuru-san got to do with Hamanoyokocho or the Bridgeburner?"

"I've no idea," Hyo lied. She noticed then that Awano acted as if Natsuami wasn't there. "We can figure that out later."

"Ukibashi-sama!" came a voice, and Awano bowed, signing, "Later," to Hyo quickly, before turning to greet a woman in the box on her other side.

"It seems the Wavewalker isn't watching his favourite right now," Natsuami noted, without looking up from the pamphlet he'd been quietly skimming through. "Unusual."

That was true. There was no sign of any watchful crab about Awano's box or hint of ocean spray in the air. Hyo sat back. "Does that mean something?"

"If gods accumulate enough taint, they can no longer fragment themselves," Natsuami said. "He may need to keep himself in one shape to manage it."

"You don't want to believe the Wavewalker would hurt Koushiro either, do you?"

"I don't, but I'm surrounded by so many things I'd rather not believe, I've decided to pick one." Natsuami turned a page. "Or else my world feels as liquid as the Under-dream."

The auditorium filled. Somewhere, a rope creaked.

"Can humans access the Under-dream?" Hyo wondered aloud.

"Oh, yes," Natsuami replied with some surprise. "Not consciously, or by yashiori – but any creature that thinks, be they human or god or cat or cockroach, has a connection to the Under-dream somewhere. Like a rope and bucket that can go up and down a shaft to pull the water from an underground pool."

"And the water is ... thoughts? Dreams?"

"Everything that can ever be thought and dreamt and has been. Which is why gods *can* enter it, and with yashiori navigate it consciously – we're made in part of dream, when our heavenly names and appearances are imagined from it." Natsuami closed his pamphlet. "You asked me about dreaming before. Is something on your mind? Or ... in it?"

"I'm fine, Natsuami. My dreams are safe." Natsuami peered closely at Hyo. He didn't seem convinced. She had to give him something. "If the Under-dream's got everything down there that *can* be thought and *has* been thought of, that means your memories and heavenly name are down there too. I thought that might explain why Tokifuyu kept taking the yashiori to go there. That's all."

The pamphlet slipped from Natsuami's lap. "That's … all?"

"Well, not all. Then I thought about what would happen if *I* went down there. I've the powers of the old gods of misfortune, so maybe I could."

"Hyo." Natsuami grasped her wrist. His eyes were large and horrified. "Don't go into the Under-dream, not for me. *Especially* not for me. Nothing I've lost is worth losing both you and Toki for – not my name, my memories, nor who I was – and I don't want anyone else down there for *my* sake."

His rush of words were hushed and muffled by his veil, but the fear was clear, as was the answer to something Hyo had wondered for a while. "You know, don't you?"

"I don't know what you mean."

"About Three Thousand Three Fall." Hyo lowered her voice. "You know what you did, and you're running from it."

He knew. Hyo was almost sure of it. Natsuami *knew* that Tokifuyu was trying to keep him happy in blissful ignorance about what had happened in Three Thousand Three Fall, and was going along with it. It was easier than the truth. Easier than living with the knowledge that Natsuami had single-handedly killed three thousand people in a night, and that Tokifuyu was trapped with him as his minder, in case that murderous god returned in his brother's skin.

Hyo's tone turned hard. "Natsuami, get honest with yourself. You're not pretending that you know nothing for Tokifuyu's sake, but your own."

He let go of her quickly. "I don't know what you're talking about."

There was a hubbub from the surrounding boxes, a ripple of commotion as heads turned to Ukibashi Awano's box then quickly away, so as not to be caught staring.

The air had *unfurled*, peeling back and around from nothing, and the Wavewalker appeared, stepping down into the box out of the air. He was resplendent in sea-green robes and strings of red agate and amber, red coral antlers branching high and proud over his head, and masked with an oblong of pale cloth, green hair bunched on either side in glistening twine.

A swirl of unsettled pressure like a wave brushed against Hyo's face, acknowledging her without words.

The Wavewalker was whispering into Awano's ear. Hyo took out the straw doll she'd prepared and handed it to Natsuami – a katashiro for Koushiro, one upon which Natsuami could focus all his feelings of wanting Koushiro safe and protect him by it. It was a simple charm and one most humans could make work. Natsuami would have no trouble. Hyo had a pencil and a wad of paper katashiro, so that she could create katashiro after katashiro as Koushiro burned through them during his show.

Hyo tapped her pencil against the pad. Was this really the best she could do? Watch Koushiro from afar and try to absorb pieces of the unluck storm centred on him?

The depressing answer was … yes. It would be easier to root out hitodenashi rumours without being known to the police, so flashy options such as destroying the theatre were out. In hindsight, some Ohne gangsters on her side could've been useful.

Hyo glanced at the neighbouring box. The Wavewalker finished talking. He sat back. Hyo saw Awano's expression slide from blank to startled, then, as if waiting for the Wavewalker to take his seat, the lights dimmed.

An actor walked out upon the stage. It was the fierce-faced man with a halberd: Matsubei. He kneeled and bowed deeply to the audience.

"Good evening to all eyes and ears, to those in cyclocloth, and those in silks, and to the lice and fleas that jump magnanimously between you both." The man's booming voice effortlessly reached the rafters. Laughter came from up there, in ripples of power churning about the myriad god cabinets. "Welcome to the Shin-Kaguraza. I have an announcement to make. There has been a change in the programme. Tonight, for Kikugawa Kichizuru's final performance at this theatre, we will be presenting a new play! Dedicated to his late brother, and to our dear patron of this season: the Ukibashi Shinshu Company!" Matsubei gestured towards Awano and the Wavewalker, and the audience clapped for them. Awano smiled and inclined her head. "It is of Kichizuru's own making," Matsubei continued. "Please forgive Kikugawa Kichizuru and the Kikugawa Shin-Kagura Troupe this one final indulgence. We present to you *The Koga Brothers: Hunting of a Nameless God.*"

The theatre rustled with interest.

"That's not what they were rehearsing the other day, is it?" Hyo asked Natsuami.

"It isn't," Natsuami replied, after a weighted pause, then in a whisper, "The tale of the Koga brothers is a shin-kagura staple. This seems to be a new variation."

"What's the tale about?"

"The assassination of a shogun's aide at a hunting party, by two brothers, to avenge their father, and what follows when they succeed. Vengeance, in short."

The chorus began to chant, the drums popped and the two Koga brothers appeared.

"*Little darling.*" Hyo felt the smallest pinpricks of claws against her left ear, hidden in her hair. The tall figure of the Wavewalker had vanished from the neighbouring box with the fall of the lights. Awano appeared alone again. "*Don't speak. Write your answer upon your palm. I will see it.*"

The audience and Natsuami clapped loudly. The elder brother was Kikugawa Kichizuru – Koushiro – sharp eyes intensified with make-up. The younger was another young troupe member, who was talented, but beside Kichizuru looked a work in progress – perfect for his role. Their blue and white robes had been folded against their shoulders and waists. The ties on their vambraces and greaves were the striking vermilion of autumn leaves. They burst on to the stage with white faces, reddened eyes and ferocious energy.

Hyo opened her hand and traced her pencil over it. "*I'm listening.*"

"*Fifteen minutes ago, a fire broke out to the south-west of the island, in the district of Hamanoyokocho.*"

Hamanoyokocho! Hyo tensed.

The crab pinched her earlobe. "*What do you know of it?*"

"*I don't know anything.*"

Its pinch tightened and Hyo winced. "*Where is your brother tonight?*"

"With the Paddywatcher" didn't feel like a good answer. Her palms were clammy. "*I don't know.*"

"*Surely the hellmaker's weapon should either be at her side or acting on her orders?*"

Matsubei followed the Koga brothers on to the stage in heavy gold and black robes. He was the shogun's aide who'd killed the Kogas' father. The brothers swore vengeance upon him.

"*He's my brother, not my weapon,*" Hyo wrote. "*He can act for himself.*"

"*He was seen at Todomegawa Daimyoujin's Hamanoyokocho shrine.*" The Wavewalker's whisper cut through the shamisen and flutes with ease. "*He appeared to be looking for something, before he set the shrine on fire.*"

Mansaku did WHAT? It took all of Hyo's restraint not to say that aloud. Beside her, Natsuami was sitting forward, eyes shining. Koushiro's new play had introduced its twist. The Koga brothers weren't successful in killing the shogun's aide. They had stumbled upon a horrifying truth. The shogun their enemy served was a red-maned, gold-fanged demon – Matsubei, in a second role – to whom loyal attendants offered the chubby limbs of small children.

The two brothers fled, taking with them the secret of what they'd seen.

"*Do you know what your brother was looking for?*" the Wavewalker pressed her, unseen eddies buffeting at Hyo's spirit. "*What were his intentions?*"

"*I don't know.*" She kept her eyes on the stage. "*Where's Mansaku now?*"

"*That is what I was asking you. He is hidden from me.*" The crab let go of her ear. "*Whilst Todomegawa is away, his shrine is under my protection. I must report your brother as a suspect for arson and for attempting to steal holy treasures from the shrine, or else accrue taint.*

Did you send him to look for something there?"

"If you let Tokifuyu's shrine burn, haven't you already picked up a lot of taint?"

"Answer the question!"

Koushiro stamped his foot on the stage. Hyo jumped. The glint of Natsuami's glasses' frames showed he'd looked her way.

"*No*," she wrote on her palm.

"If you've lied to me..."

"I haven't."

The Wavewalker, she felt, had more to say, but with a clack of his claws, he withdrew. *"I hope you find your special commissioner soon."*

The lights rose for the interval. The crab in the corner of Hyo's eye vanished, and the Wavewalker was there in the Ukibashi box again, clapping his hands at Awano's shoulder as if he'd never left.

Hyo's heart had picked up pace. Mansaku had gone to Hamanoyokocho alone. He had searched Tokifuyu's shrine and set fire to it. Why?

Had the Paddywatcher cursed him to do it?

But again: *why?*

"Heavens!" Natsuami's gasp brought her back to the present. The straw doll in his hand was smoking at its edges, charred. "Look at this, Hyo!"

Focus on the present. Hamanoyokocho was far away. Mansaku was beyond her help. Koushiro wasn't. She hoped.

"Good," Hyo said, examining Natsuami's katashiro, then her own. The paper man was splotched with old blood splatters. She scrunched it up and activated a new one. "It's working."

"Are you enjoying the show, Hyo-chan?" Awano said across the railing. Her smile was tight. She put her hands over the divider. "I like the idea of a demon shogun. It's horrible but the Koga brothers' story could do with a new spin. Oh – could you pick that up for me?"

She'd dropped a sea-green handkerchief. Hyo did as Awano asked, and found faint chalk-white pencil markings scrawled on the cloth: "Hama-yoko shrine, on fire, now. News from Wave."

So that's what the Wavewalker had been reporting to Awano on his arrival. Hyo dusted off the writing and handed it back. "I *was* enjoying the show. Until, er, the new twist."

"That's a shame." Awano had caught her meaning: *Message received*. "Never mind; the second act's about to start!"

The lights went down. Something creaked in the rafters. The audience stilled, eyes going upwards. When nothing dropped, they let out a collective breath and broke into laughter. Natsuami gripped his straw doll with renewed determination.

"Kikugawa Kichizuru, you will survive the night," he muttered, over and over again.

The second act opened with a comedic dialogue. Two courtesans were gossiping about a regular at their brothel. They talked about how he had developed an unusual fear for oil lamps, and what had happened when one of them had lit a lamp as a test. Her regular had jumped awake, shouting that it was the eye of a demon, and that the demon had found him. As the days wore on, his condition worsened. What began with lamps extended to the lanterns, then to the moon, until finally he shuddered and quailed under the bright eye of the sun.

To demonstrate her point, the woman covered her head in a newspaper and did a cowering dance under a burning spotlight.

Hyo froze. The woman's newspaper was folded into the same shape as the mask Jun had been wearing on the bridge.

Ukibashi Awano let out a loud laugh. The Wavewalker followed, and the surrounding audience with him.

Hyo swallowed down bile. She heard crackling beneath her hands. Her second paper man was breaking up into flakes. She stuffed it into her sleeve and activated the next doll with the strokes of Koushiro's name.

The woman in the newspaper hat ducked behind a barrel of shinshu. She emerged the next instant as the younger brother, who in a quick costume change became the brother's ghost, dark hair trailing down a milk-white neck.

"Why?" he cried, face turned up to the Ukibashi box. "Why needed I to die? I but saw evil, not dealt it! Why needed I to die by slow-fed poison of my own fear? Why needed I to end my life with my face hidden to the sun, in darkness? Why, gods, why?!"

Hyo's stomach churned. She looked to the Wavewalker and Awano for their reactions. Whilst Awano was eagerly following the actors' movements with an entranced smile, the Wavewalker's lips under his mask were downturned and thinned.

Then Awano took something small from her clutch and made a quiet rattling noise, shaking a pill into her hand.

Luminous green, spiced, smelling vital and fresh – Hyo recognized it instantly from the Wavewalker's shrine. Awano's famous medicine, to withstand the spiritual drainage of her water-eye. But the moment he heard the rattle, the Wavewalker slammed his hand down, covering the tin in Awano's lap. "Put that away!"

"Fuchiha!" Awano hissed. "What's got into you? It's just my medicine—"

"Must you take it now?" The Wavewalker's chin lifted,

and even through the mask, Hyo knew he was looking her way, past her, into the box.

And Hyo followed his gaze to where Natsuami had stood up behind her.

In the theatre's dark he appeared to melt into his shadow and become twice as tall, the gleam of his glasses trained upon Awano's fist that contained the closed tin of pills.

"Natsuami?" Hyo pulled at his sleeve. He didn't budge.

In his left hand, Natsuami clutched Koushiro's katashiro. He didn't even seem to notice the red-hot spots of embers burning between his fingers. Those white twists of smoke catching the spotlight weren't just from the straw doll.

"Natsuami," she said, more urgently. "Sit down?"

He ignored her. The light from the stage illuminated the side of Natsuami's face, enough that Hyo could see the strange look in his eyes. Not blankness. Far from it: a peaceful, eerie alertness. It was the gaze of something swift enough, strong enough, that it had no need to worry that prey would ever escape it. *Death*, Hyo thought, *would have eyes like that.* Infinitely patient and unhurried.

The Wavewalker had put Awano's stole around her shoulders and pulled her from her seat, her hushed protests going unheard. The nearby audience had noticed and were whispering amongst themselves.

"What do you think that means?" a woman was

saying from behind a fan. "For both Ukibashi Awano and the Wavewalker to leave before the performance ends..."

"Are they offended by the play?"

"Perhaps there's urgent business at the company?"

"It's her health, more likely," another remarked. "I saw her taking those pills. Bright as cat's eyes, they don't look right..."

Fear and fury roiled off the Wavewalker with every unkind word, every rumour that bubbled up around them, but none of it stopped him dragging Ukibashi Awano out of the box, looking back in panic, Hyo realized, at Natsuami.

Then the lights went up for the second interval.

Natsuami blinked and put his hand to his mouth. He pulled a face. "Hyo, could you get my kerchief from my waist-pouch? I've, er ... this is a bit embarrassing, but ... my mouth's watering. A lot." She saw a thick strand of drool run down his chin and catch in his hair. "I can't seem to stop it."

"Here." Hyo gave him her own kerchief. Natsuami lifted his face veil and covered his mouth quickly with it. She prised his katashiro from his hand, and nearly dropped it. It was searing hot. "Has this ever happened to you before?"

"No." Natsuami pressed the kerchief harder over his mouth. "Hyo, there's something wrong with me; I feel like I haven't eaten in days. I'm so hungry, it hurts." He glanced to the side. "Did the Wavewalker and Ukibashi Awano leave?"

"They've probably just gone for the interval." But Hyo didn't believe it. The Wavewalker had looked as if he was fleeing, corralling Awano to safety, and as if taking permission from them, others in the audience were putting on their jackets and stoles and hurrying to leave too. For these gamblers, they'd tested their luck enough. "Sit down, don't move – I'll get food."

The boxes were catered for and Hyo had only to open the door for an assistant to glide over with an interval-ready bento and tea-set.

"This is so undignified," Natsuami murmured, whilst Hyo poured tea for them and laid out the lacquered boxes. She undid his veil, so that he had one fewer clinging piece of cloth to think about. "Thank you."

"It looks better already." By "it" she meant Natsuami's drool control.

"It *is* better, considerably. And I feel hungry but it doesn't hurt so much." Natsuami looked away from her. "Not one bit of this makes sense to me."

They ate in silence, and with an urgency Hyo couldn't justify. Natsuami moved red-bean rice shakily into his mouth. Each bite he took seemed forceful and deliberate, as if he were laying down, stroke by stroke, a talisman to ward something invisible away.

By the time they'd finished, the drooling had stopped.

Natsuami dabbed at his front, cleaned off his hair and said, "Hyo, were you following the play?"

"I was a little distracted."

"In the second act, the younger brother was haunted to death by his memory of the demon shogun's glowing eyes. It was strongly implied that the shogun's aide called upon the sun god to curse the brother," Natsuami explained. "The powerful demon shogun and the aide who serves them! Kichizuru-san isn't being subtle."

"He isn't trying to be." Hyo cursed under her breath and rued not following Koushiro's play closer. "He's accusing someone, or both of them even."

"The Wavewalker – *and* Ukibashi Awano," Natsuami mused. Hyo took their bento boxes and stacked them at the back of the box. "But who's the shogun and who's the aide? Should we follow them?"

"We're staying until the end of the show," Hyo said, even though a part of her wanted to do exactly as Natsuami suggested. *Yes, leave, go to Hamanoyokocho, find out what the hell is going on tonight, find Mansaku.* "We're here for Kikugawa Kichizuru and his bad luck."

Hyo picked up Natsuami's straw katashiro and pressed it back into his hand. He gripped it with renewed determination. Hyo did the same with her paper man as the lights went down.

Light conjured Kikugawa Kichizuru on the hanamichi. The older Koga brother was disguised as a woman, hiding her face under the broad brim of a lacquered hat, and fleeing to an Oblivionist temple for shelter from the sun god. On the main stage, the rest of the cast were monks, trying to turn the brother away.

The bell swung gently over the actors on its red and white rope. Kikugawa Kichizuru danced, demanding that the monks let him in.

"My brother was murdered by a god to protect a demon's secrets!" He turned to the audience, eyes rimmed in red and black. He tossed out his words like stones. What remained of the crowd stirred like the surface of a pool. "They murdered him with no good reason! And now you fear to help me lest they forsake you too!"

A spark flared in the face of the straw katashiro. Natsuami stubbed it out with a thumb.

"I curse you! All of you!" Kikugawa's movements became wild. The cast on the stage took up his script. Strings plucked shrill and striking with his steps. "I will have my vengeance – I will make a god of my own vengeance, my own pain, my own fury, and let it sit in my heart! And I will avenge all of us who the gods would kill, and from whom all of you would look away and call it for good reason!" The monks made one last aborted attempt to cast him from the temple. Kikugawa twisted away from them, coming to stand beneath the bell. "I would be a demon upon you all!"

The bell dropped.

TWENTY-THREE

千秋楽

If lucky, the humans who eat hitodenashi pear die.

If not, they become gaki, starving demons, who must eat pear or human flesh to keep their minds.

HATSU,
Thirty-Second Hellmaker

Which was as expected.

The bell falling was a popular climactic set piece.

Applause burst from the audience. The monks continued, as scripted, to discuss in a comedic back and forth what was to be done about the elder Koga brother, who had sealed himself under the iron bell.

"Hakai Hyo," said a voice from behind her. "I trust you've read my shikigami scroll?"

The smell of sun-warmed grain surrounded Hyo, clearing away the bitter smoke-musk of Natsuami's katashiro. She said, without turning, so that the god wouldn't have her face, "Yamada Hanako, I presume?"

"Indeed," said the Paddywatcher.

Natsuami bowed. Hyo swallowed down a surge of feeling. "Did you send my brother to burn down the Bridgeburner's Hamanoyokocho shrine?"

"Now is not the time," the Paddywatcher replied. "My scroll. Well?"

"I've read it."

"Learnt it?"

"In theory."

"That'll have to do. That katashiro you have there." A hand came into view. The nails were lacquered red. White scales trailed up the wrist in diamond patterns to disappear in a dark brown sleeve. Bronze threads glistened in the glare of the stage lights. "Offer it to me."

Natsuami pulled it close. "I'm afraid, madam, that I can't do that."

"He is no longer the human that doll can protect." A cold trickle went down Hyo's spine. "If you wish for fewer deaths in the next three minutes, you will do as I say. Now!"

"Give the katashiro to her, Natsuami," Hyo said.

The bell creaked.

Natsuami held out the katashiro doll. The Paddywatcher snatched it from him. "Be ready."

A flute shrilled. There was a swell of power, a smell like hot summer grasses, then Natsuami's katashiro crumbled into a pile of yellow grain that spilled through the Paddywatcher's fingers to the floor.

A cable snapped, dangled, a spark jumped from its end.

With a crackle, the bell – with Koushiro still inside it – burst into flames.

"No!" Natsuami cried, and placed a hand on the edge of their box as if to vault down from it.

"Stay!" commanded the Paddywatcher. "This is how you will help him best! He will come to you."

The actors and musicians were fleeing, leaving Koushiro to burn beneath the bell. Flames jumped from it to the ceiling, dancing along ropes, tearing down walkways, through curtain cloth. Heat flooded the hall, and the audience rushed for the doors, with the throb and wail of alarms in their ears.

The grains the Paddywatcher had scattered at their feet sprouted. Green shoots of rice grew from the floor of the box.

They shimmered with iridescence that burned in the corners of Hyo's eyes – a protective charm, holding the smoke, flames and crumbling theatre walls at bay. It spread down into the audience, shielding those as they fled behind it.

"Be ready!" the Paddywatcher warned.

The bell collapsed inwards, chunks of charred wood thudding to the stage, and like a bird pushing free of its eggshell, Koushiro emerged.

His varnished robes were ablaze. His hair had faded to the pale colour of blossoms. His eyes glowed gold. He had a sharp crescent-moon beauty that stopped a few of those in the fleeing crowd, transfixing them amidst the flames and thickening smoke. When he opened his mouth, even from this distance, Hyo could see the golden fangs bared in his black gums.

"*A demon's hunger is a million teeth ripping apart your body*," the demon in Koura had told Hyo that winter, smiling with the same sunlit fangs as wood cracked apart rib and spine in the snow.

"What's happened to him?" Natsuami breathed. "What has he become?"

Koushiro looked down over his audience. The few stragglers gazed back, then he jumped from the stage, landing nimbly on the back of a seat to perch like a bird.

It brought him face to face with a musician, who didn't move, not even as Koushiro seized him by the hair.

"I can see them." The words were a stage-whisper, but

reached Hyo through the crackling flames and creaking walls. The demon at the village had the same kind of voice. "Your gods, at your shoulders. So clearly! Oh, but I can hurt them now. Just by hurting you!"

He ripped the musician's head from his body.

A plume of blood shot up from the stump, and as if released from enchantment, the last of the audience unfroze, screamed and scattered.

"His demon's gift forces a human's pain upon their guardian gods," the Paddywatcher said thoughtfully.

"A demon?" Natsuami's voice shook. "Is that what he is?"

"Hakai Hyo," said the Paddywatcher, as Koushiro set down the head of the musician – licked clean of flesh – and searched the room's sea of fire for more prey. "You came to Onogoro surviving a demon's attack. I trust you know what to do."

"Some god you are," Hyo snapped, and at the sound of her voice, Koushiro looked up, eyes gold on black, and leapt.

He landed on the box balcony and crouched there, poised as on the handrail that morning on the bridge.

"Koushiro..." Natsuami murmured.

Koushiro's lips parted. Black gums glistened.

And Hyo grabbed the demon's long needle-coated tongue when it emerged from his mouth, and yanked him down by it, throwing him into the green stems of rice that had grown from the floor to tickle her shins.

Koushiro writhed, black and gold eyes flashing, claws slicing through the rice. Hyo wrapped his tongue around her fist. She tried to pin him down with her weight, but he kept sliding free. Her blood was running from her torn fingers down his tongue, towards his open mouth.

She just needed him to keep still, for another moment! "Natsuami, help me!"

"Me?! What could I do—?"

Koushiro lunged upwards to swipe at Natsuami, and, in a heartbeat, that alert peacefulness, still close to the surface, slid back into place.

With two sharp cracks, Koushiro's arms dropped limply to the floor, broken where Natsuami had caught them, and Natsuami had Koushiro's hands trapped under his knees, Koushiro's head shoved against the boards.

Natsuami blinked. "What—?"

"Don't move!" Hyo pressed down on Koushiro's neck to keep him still. She waited for her blood to reach his snarling mouth. "Just a little longer."

Hot winds whipped Natsuami's hair about them, getting into Hyo's face, so she didn't see when the black and gold bled out from Koushiro's eyes. She felt the change when the needles of his tongue shrank away.

The rice stems of the Paddywatcher's ward stretched tall around them. Hyo let go. Koushiro coughed, gagged.

"Remarkable," said the Paddywatcher appreciatively. "A temporary restoration of a demon's mind. This is unheard of."

"Hakai Hyo? Natsu-san?" Koushiro gazed up at her then at Natsuami, utterly lost. "What happened?"

"We don't have much time. I'm sorry, Koushiro, this isn't a cure; it's just temporary." Hyo turned to the Paddywatcher. "Help us! Get us all out of here, before this place burns up!"

"Even a hellmaker should refrain from commanding a god." The Paddywatcher's eyes flashed beneath the black veil of her ichime-gasa. Her small face, her glowing eyes, her red pokkuri shoes; she was exactly as Mansaku had drawn her. "But I will forgive it in this instance. Have the anomaly follow me with the demon. Walk where I walk and you will share my path."

In an instant, Hyo found herself in the Paddywatcher's arms and shielded from the flames by the fluttering black veil. The Paddywatcher took what seemed a torturously slow step, sliding her pokkuri out and in with a weaving motion. It left a glowing shape in the floor; a mark that Hyo couldn't decipher, like no symbol on any talisman or in any Grandmother's Record she'd seen. It was gone from her memory as soon as Hyo looked away.

Another weaving, sliding step, and they'd left the box. They were in the foyer.

The theatre collapsed around them, chunks of ceiling crashing down in torrents of sparks. Hyo finally felt the flames' searing heat. Natsuami held Koushiro tightly against him, stepping on the marks the Paddywatcher had made.

Another step. The foyer was gone.

Open-mouthed faces stood on the plaza, eyes turned up to the Shin-Kaguraza's front. Reflectograph banners burned and snapped in the wind. There was a low rumble then a *pop* – the sound of a hydrogen vein for the flightcrafts rupturing, then exploding as they caught alight.

The Paddywatcher took another step, and dropped into the chasm between the two towers.

They plummeted down, giant mirrors streaking by as brilliant ribbons, catching firelight and reflecting the orange glow between the towers. The Paddywatcher landed precisely on the tip of a bamboo stem. Under her careful control, it curved gently downwards to kiss the ground of the forest. Pale blue ghost lights scattered between the stems, trailing flames.

"This is the Zero Floor – Reikai, the bottom-most level of Onogoro, where the lost spirits gather in its shadows and quiet." The Paddywatcher set Hyo down on her feet. The boom of an exploding hydrogen vein echoed between the towers. "They will speak nothing of what happens here. Proceed with the demon as you need. I will observe you."

She vanished, and Hyo felt a smooth coil loop around her neck, heavy and solid with lean muscle. A white snake's head entered the periphery of her vision. "Go on."

Hyo rushed to Natsuami. He'd landed not far ahead of her, carrying Koushiro in his arms, but as he straightened, he adjusted his hold on Koushiro, moving one hand to the back of his neck like he might handle a venomous snake, and with the other clamping Koushiro's wrists together.

Koushiro was already struggling, gold and black slipping back into his eyes, the colour leeching out of his hair. Natsuami shot Hyo a helpless look as she neared.

"Hold on." She squeezed her wounded hand in a fist. Blood welled up between her fingers, which she dripped straight into Koushiro's mouth. "Better?"

Koushiro's eyes cleared. "What's wrong with me?"

"A demon's hunger."

He let out a shocked, incredulous laugh. "I'm not a demon!"

"It hurts, doesn't it? Like you're being eaten inside out by your own guts? And it's only for a short time, but my blood settles it, and makes it go away, as if all that pain was a dream." Koushiro's smile shrank. Hyo held up her forearms, baring the pale half-moons and stripes from tongues and teeth. "You're not the first demon I've met."

"A demon?" Natsuami repeated, aghast. "But how, Hyo? How could this happen?"

"There's only one way humans become demons." Hyo crouched to look Koushiro in the eye. "They eat hitodenashi pear. The lucky ones die. The unlucky ones survive as demons."

"And I'm unlucky," Koushiro said flatly. His eyes flicked down at himself, at the burned remnants of his varnished paper costume. He snorted. "To think, I could be too unlucky to even die. But I haven't eaten anything that could be pear."

"It only needs a little bit of pulp, not even half a fingernail's worth. Someone could have slipped it into a drink or your rice."

Koushiro let out a long breath. "The pills."

"Which pills?"

"The ones I showed you before, to ward off bad luck. We passed a basket around the cast before the show began, like we always do." He closed his eyes. "All someone had to do was mix it in there, and I would have been unlucky enough to pick it out before anyone else did." He trembled. His face flickered through an array of emotions too fast for Hyo to pin down. "There's no place for demons on Onogoro."

"What will happen to him?" Hyo asked the snake at her collar.

"He will be destroyed, as far as he can be." The Paddywatcher fluttered a pale tongue. "He will be beheaded at the Onmyoryo, his consciousness sealed away with five nails – of ice, clay, anise, iron and sunlight – piercing his skull, then submerged in molten iron, and the process repeated until his body fails to reassemble."

"No!" Natsuami drew Koushiro back, shielding him in his sleeves. "That's too cruel! He isn't a mindless monster to be ... melted away to nothingness!"

"I'm only *not* mindless because I still have Hyo-san's blood in my mouth." Koushiro laughed again, and it was ugly.

"Is demonification really irreversible?" Natsuami's gaze went from Hyo to the Paddywatcher, pleading. "If it's a curse, can't it be undone?"

"Koushiro's not cursed to be a demon. He's become a curse itself, cast upon the world. That's what hitodenashi pear does to people." Hyo repeated what the demon had told her and felt hollow for it – as if she'd lost a game she hadn't known she'd been playing. She said to Koushiro, "You changed the play tonight. What were you hoping to achieve?"

"Just personal satisfaction," Koushiro said and grinned with golden fangs. "I wanted to rub it into the Wavewalker's and Ukibashi Awano's faces that I knew they had something to do with Jun's death, somehow. I wanted to show them they could be laughed at."

Natsuami smiled. "Jun would've loved every bit of it."

"Obviously – I'd have had him at the kid-eating shogun." They all froze, as from above echoed the Onmyoryo's sirens, their windturtles soaring between the towers high overheard. Koushiro said, "I'd like to sit."

To hide his shaking legs.

Natsuami lowered himself and Koushiro to the long grass, so that they sat back to chest and it looked less like an arrest. Hyo joined them, and revelled in the cool touch of the dew and damp earth against her skin.

Natsuami let go of Koushiro's hands and neck to put his arms around him. "There must be some way to help you."

"I daresay there isn't." Koushiro coughed, and licked his lips. Hyo leant forward and wiped her torn hand over his mouth again, grimacing when his spiked tongue chased the edges of the wound for her blood. "My brother is dead, my theatre is ashes, my guardian god, the Wavewalker, who I've prayed to for as long as I can remember, has abandoned me." He dug his golden claws into the ground. "Was it really the Wavewalker who cursed Jun for that stellaroid? Is he behind my luck? Behind *this*?"

"I think so," said Natsuami with bitter disappointment. "I'm still an en-musubi god, even if an odd one – I can see when an en breaks, and the recoil to the one who meant you harm. The Wavewalker engineered your fate at the theatre tonight, and your en broke with unspeakable violence."

Koushiro asked, "Where does Ukibashi Awano fit into all this?"

"That I can't say." Natsuami held Koushiro tighter, as if he could keep him away from a demon's hunger. "The en-networks are too tangled for me to see everything at once."

"If I use my demon's gift I could avenge myself on the

Wavewalker," said Koushiro. "I could hurt Awano and that way hurt him too."

"An underfed demon wouldn't last a night on Onogoro," the Paddywatcher hissed at Hyo's shoulder. "All it'd think of is feeding. It would forget ambitions of revenge, and be easy pickings for the Onmyoryo."

"Then what can I do?" Koushiro snapped. "Why save me from the theatre, if you can't help me?"

Something landed on Hyo's forehead – a scrap of burned paper, one of many that were drifting down from the fire above. It was a piece of a talisman, blotchy from the absorbed bad luck. Its shredded shape wasn't far from a paper doll.

Hyo caught it between her fingers, and the hellmakers' en plucked.

She recalled the Paddywatcher's words in the theatre. "*I trust you've read my shikigami scroll?*"

The god had been giving her a hint.

The Paddywatcher's coils slid about her throat.

"I can help you," Hyo realized as she said it aloud. She looked up from the scrap of paper. "If you give me the permission, I could hide you for as long as you need and spare you the demon's hunger."

"Permission?" Koushiro repeated, as if looking for a catch.

"That's right." Hyo settled in front of him and pressed her bloodied hand to his mouth, because she needed him to have a clear mind, to be as human as possible for this.

"Makuni Koushiro, on behalf of the dead Makuni Junichiro, would you like to commission an artisan hell?"

TWENTY-FOUR

餓鬼

The law is a public vengeance. It spreads thin vengeance's burden upon the conscience, deliberately depersonalized. We offer what the law does not.

ZAKURO,
Twenty-Seventh Hellmaker

"If you were human, the price of a special commission would've been all the rest of your life years," Hyo explained. "But a demon's life is eternal. I can't measure it in the same way. To take a special commission from a demon, I'll need a different price."

"What would you have me give?"

"The whole of your eternal present. Your body, your souls, your spirit. The whole fire that's keeping you alive –" Hyo laid down the terms, feeling them to be true – "until we find a way for a demon to die peacefully, or we can change you back."

Natsuami said with a hushed horror, "Hyo, you can't ask that of him; that's eternal servitude – his life *yours*, until you decide it isn't!"

"He'll be a shikigami," Hyo said, and the Paddywatcher squeezed her throat. Thanks to the god's scroll, she understood what this entailed now. "Third level. Like Mansaku is."

"Like the paper messenger men of the Onmyoryo," Koushiro scoffed but his face was white. "Fuck you all; I'd rather die."

"Difficult as a demon," Hyo noted wryly, and Koushiro was silent. "I won't use you, if that's what you're worried about. I could keep you asleep for as long as it takes. But as a shikigami, when you're awake, for a short while, I could probably stop you feeling the demon's hunger."

Koushiro was breathing quickly. He looked up, to

the shards of sky caught in the canopy, glowing red and violet with fire, occasionally punctuated by the stubborn searchlight of the moon and the wheeling silhouettes of firefighter flightcrafts.

He said, "Remind me what an artisan hell is."

"It's a tatari that turns the whole world against the target," Hyo replied. "An inescapable moment. Nothing goes right for them. Worst secrets are uncovered. But no one uninvolved is hurt."

"Does the hell go on for ever?"

"No. Only for as long as is necessary. I don't make the rules."

"He must decide soon." The Paddywatcher swayed under Hyo's chin, flickering her tongue. "There are people looking for Kikugawa Kichizuru; they will come this way."

Natsuami shot her a sharp look. "He is being asked to part with everything he has – do not make light of it, madam!"

"It's all right, Natsu-san. It's all right now." Koushiro reached back to pat Natsuami on the side of his face. His fingertips left red lines of blood. "I've always earned my keep, hellmaker. I don't want to be kept asleep for ever. If you're going to shelter me as a shikigami, then I will help you – but I've conditions."

"What are they?"

"You can wake me whenever you need my help, then

you will give me the choice of whether to help you or not. That way, I won't be at your beck and call." Koushiro raised his head. "And you'll wake me as soon as you know what the Wavewalker and Ukibashi Awano have to do with Jun's stellaroid. You can't keep me asleep in ignorance."

Hyo nodded. "Is that all?"

"For the price of my body and souls? Not nearly. I expect the Wavewalker to hurt when you curse him, to have his secrets discovered by the worst people to discover them, to grieve and have no name for that grief. Yes – end it with an unnameable pain." Koushiro gripped Hyo's sleeve. She felt the pinpricks of his claws. "Can you do that?"

"I can."

"Then take it." He took her hand and guided it to below his collar, where his heart beat too slowly for a human and the sickening brightness of a demon's life put black spots in Hyo's vision when she looked directly at it. "Spirit, souls, body, all of it – I give you permission to make me your shikigami, and commission you to make hell on the Wavewalker for my brother and me!"

Hyo glanced once at Natsuami, who looked at her over Koushiro's shoulder, eyes shiny with tears.

He gave her a small, accepting nod. *Do it.*

Hyo rested her fingertips over the warmth of Koushiro's flame. "Then with your eternal present entrusted to me as payment, Makuni Koushiro, I accept your commission."

She didn't need to look at Koushiro's flame of life to take it because she was taking the whole thing, not several tens of years. She sought it out by its heat, plucked it from the dark and set it to her seal.

The talismanic symbols vanished from her palms, unluck flooded into her vision in a flurry of dark stars and the power of the old gods of misfortune flowed through her veins.

The spells in the Paddywatcher's shikigami scroll had been complicated as a sequence, but its parts simple. Hyo pushed her hands through the seals, her breaths through the sutras, and felt the words on her tongue with the burr of unluck's language, its wildflower seeds of shadows.

"Hyo," said Natsuami, "Hyo, it's done. Look."

Koushiro was gone. The grass where he'd sat was already bending back into place, erasing his imprint.

Natsuami was holding out a moon-silver bright paper man. The symbols down its front were dark, burned into it with fire: Hyo's own fire, if Hyo had done exactly as the shikigami scroll had said, but mostly Koushiro's.

The paper was warm. It didn't stain with the blood on her fingers. It carried an air of easy softness about it like a sleeper's breathing.

Hyo traced the seal on the body. "Goodnight, Koushiro."

"Kikugawa Kichizuru was an asset to Onogoro," said the Paddywatcher, uncoiling from Hyo's neck to nose the paper man. "Gods and humans alike were fond of him. He strengthened the ties between us and Onogoro was stronger for it." Unluck shimmered along her scales in a fine patina. "The Wavewalker has been secretive and strange ever since the return of the Ukibashi girl, but none of us ever imagined that the Wavewalker would harm Kichizuru."

Hyo pulled the Paddywatcher from her shoulders, and held her up to eye level. "Are you going to explain what you've done with Mansaku now?"

Natsuami lifted his head. "Mansaku-san? What's happened to him?"

"Nothing he didn't agree to," the Paddywatcher replied.

Hyo tightened her grip. The snake dissolved into a handful of grain that slipped free from her fist and scattered over the ground.

The Paddywatcher reappeared as the woman in the bronze kimono and ichime-gasa, stepping out from behind a bamboo stand, her eyes red spots of light in the shadow of her veil. "I cursed him to burn the shrine, yes, but he has disobeyed me. He salvaged something from it. He was meant to bring it to me, but he has hidden it near the shrine instead."

"You want me to find it?"

"He made it so that only you could do so. Bring it to me, and I won't deliver him to my police as their arsonist." Her red eyes glowed, unblinking. "I would've advised against taking this anomaly with you, but if your blood has such taming properties, perhaps in Hamanoyokocho that creature can be of some use to you when exploring the shrine's vicinity."

"There's something else at Hamanoyokocho, isn't there?" Hyo said. "Other than Todomegawa's shrine?"

"It has Onogoro's best mackerel narezushi," said the Paddywatcher, holding up her hand as if to show Hyo the back of it, and Hyo understood – she'd been silenced. "I take my leave. He is coming and it is best we don't meet." In a whisk of the wind that smelled of mud and young rice sprouts, the Paddywatcher was gone before Hyo could ask who "he" was, but she didn't need to.

As if waiting for the Paddywatcher to leave, the Zero Floor's bamboo forest swayed, bending against the swash of great invisible waves. Lightning flashed, thunder rolled, and when the burn of white light had faded, it was raining heavily, water pelting down in a rustling rush like a thousand whispering voices.

Gods of water were often also gods of rumours, stories and song. They were never meant for keeping secrets quietly. The air split above Hyo and coil after coil of a great body slid out of the shadows, as if something was being divulged, allowed free at last.

It should have been impossible for the Wavewalker's immense head to fit between the bamboos. Somehow, they curved around him, making space for the god and his red coral antlers, bristling eyebrow ridges, flowing green mane and trailing whiskers that crackled with lightning – the whole long face of the dragon three times taller than Hyo.

"Well, little darling." Hyo felt the Wavewalker's voice with her skin. The hairs on her arms caught it like bubbles. **"Have you found your special commissioner?"**

A thick coil overhead kept the rain off Hyo and Natsuami and cast them in shadow. The dark of the Zero Floor was suddenly much more pronounced, the only lights coming from the blue-white flickers of lightning at the Wavewalker's teeth, and the shine of his eyes.

"I have," she said.

"Then you've settled on your culprit?" The Wavewalker had many eyes, red and rolling, scattered throughout his mane and blistering his face.

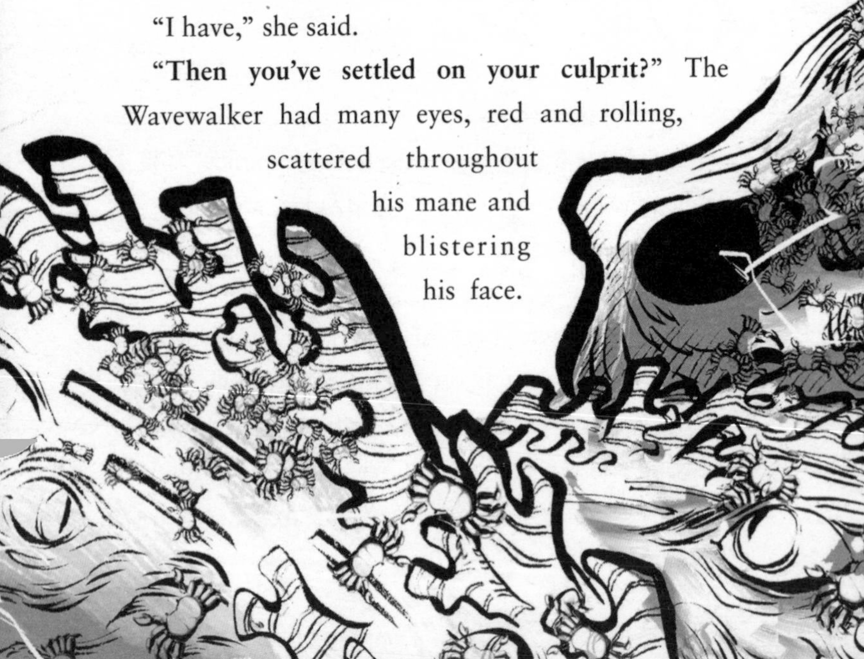

"Who deserves to pay for the life of Makuni Junichiro, which should never have been cut short? Come, tell me your conclusion."

"You cursed Makuni Junichiro," Hyo replied. "You never tried to hide it from me. You killed him because he had evidence that Ukibashi Awano had been out on that Hamanoyokocho beach. You owed Ukibashi Awano your life – so you acted to protect her."

"And then?"

"You worked out that Jun gave the beach stellaroid to Koushiro, to one of your own followers. You didn't want to kill him like you did his brother – but you still wanted to protect Awano, at all costs." Something dripped on to Hyo from the dragon's coils. It reminded her, smell and texture, of that gut rain. When she touched it, she pulled away a dead white crab, luminous even in the dark. "You cursed yourself to silence, because by then you were losing heart and your mind from taint. You knew that *you'd* become your own weak point. You had to make sure that *you* didn't confess what you'd done to, say, the Onmyoryo and cause trouble for Awano that way."

"Koushiro's one of my ujiko, my own, my protected." Something flickered in the Wavewalker's face; a hairline crack in a plate deepening, finally defining the shapes into which it would shatter. **"I only tried to do my best by him."**

"You got caught between protecting Awano or

protecting Koushiro. Fail either, you'd accumulate taint." Lightning flashed again, the boom of thunder following in seconds. The length of the Wavewalker's body was covered in open sores and pale cavities of dead flesh. Bleached bone peeked through whitened scales "Water hates being stuck. Then I came along, and you saw a way out."

"How were you my escape?"

"You figured you could live with whatever you did to Koushiro, and Jun, so long as you didn't get away with it. More importantly –" Hyo held up her hand to the Wavewalker's snout, and a tiny crab crawled on to it and clung – "the hell I'd cast on you would break you free of the secrets you were living with. You would never have to betray Awano. It would all be over because you were cursed by me. It wouldn't be your choice."

"It wouldn't," the Wavewalker echoed, the closest Hyo thought she'd get to a confession with his silencing curse.

Hyo took out the moon-silver paper man from her lapels. "Koushiro is alive."

The rain sighed. A gust of sea air caressed the paper. **"Good."**

"But I still don't understand." Hyo put away the paper man and stepped back. The Wavewalker's undulating river-grass mane smelled of deluges, of oily waves packed with filth and the pests of houses. Her eyes were watering. "What's so important about Ukibashi Awano being on that Hamanoyokocho beach?"

"I owe her my entire existence." The Wavewalker let out a long hiss through his row upon row of teeth. **"And this you do not need to know."**

"There's one more thing."

"What's that?"

"Why aren't you trying to protect Awano from *me*? You let her talk to me."

"I am the tide that breaks, the rain that crumbles mountains, the river given kingdom over all rivers, the endless chain between the water of sky and sea – but for all my power, there's something an old friend of mine always used to say that I've come to believe to be true." Those rolling eyes peppered over the Wavewalker's face looked past Hyo to briefly alight on Natsuami, then away. **"Gods cannot save humans – not in the way they really need."**

"You think *I* can save Awano? From what?"

The Wavewalker's face was half-rotted, half-fallen and taint-bitten, but Hyo thought she saw a final smile.

"To ask for the answers and expect them to be simply given to you?" he said. **"Not even the gods have that privilege. Why should a fledgling woman of misfortune? Enough, little darling, enough. You've been commissioned. You've a job to do."**

Thunder rolled. Rain danced over the Wavewalker's face, glittering with every spark of lightning that jumped from his jaws. Unluck came easily to Hyo's fingertips, collecting and weaving in threads and patterns her normal mind would have never been able to comprehend or replicate.

Koushiro's flame of life tugged at her. She had taken it as a price. She must do as she had been commissioned.

Hyo held out her hands. In one hand, unluck coalesced into a hammer that was longer than her arm, its head larger than her own, but weightless. In her other, a nail.

She let go of it, and it hung in the air, its tip poised at the centre of the Wavewalker's face.

"*Here is the seventh hour of the ox.*" It didn't matter if something didn't sit right with her. This curse was meant for the Wavewalker, and Hyo had been commissioned to deliver it. "*Seven times risen; one strike known.*"

Hyo raised the sledgehammer of unluck in two hands and set its face to the nail. "*Fuchiha'no'Utanami'Tomi-no-Mikoto.*"

She swung. The hammer struck. There was a hard, distant, dull noise, and Hyo thought she saw the nail sink – plunge into the Wavewalker's scales between his eyebrows – but she blinked and it was gone, not even leaving a shadowy nail head.

Everything felt so light and easy. Her head was clear, so clear, summer sky cloudless. This nail, she realized, was a pin in the map. Threads of en would tangle around it. The map itself would bend around it. Until her seal returned, the world would revolve around the Wavewalker so that nothing went his way.

Unluck settled in a design that Hyo knew but couldn't describe, reshaping the luck of the world into a labyrinth just for the Wavewalker.

"*It is done.*" Hyo let go of the hammer, and it vanished.

"**Thank you.**" The rolling eyes closed. "**There now. That wasn't so hard, little darling, was it?**"

Lightning flashed, and when Hyo's vision cleared, the Wavewalker was gone, and the grass was littered with the pale bodies of hundreds of little dead crabs, caught in the dark stems like stars.

TWENTY-FIVE

社

One famous example of a god who nearly disappeared is the Wavewalker: Formerly a god of far north-western Ukoku, so few of his followers reached Onogoro before the divine bombs fell that, come the present Ansei era, he was known to only one octogenarian married couple and could barely manifest as a thumbnail-sized crab. This was until, by chance, his shrine was rediscovered by Ukibashi

Awano, aged ten, who adopted him as her guardian god and resurrected his name.

Gods are just as vulnerable to luck, fate and bad en as humans are. Let's all work to take good care of them!

From "Don't Be Afraid: A Guide to Neighbourly Behaviour with the Divine"

It was past midnight when Hyo cursed the Wavewalker – the end of the first hour of the mouse.

The way the world would turn against the Wavewalker revealed itself to Hyo in touches of certainties.

A little after, an Onmyoryo officer would be at the theatre, assessing the likelihood of dangerous ghost appearances. She'd remark to a colleague that the Wavewalker should have accumulated a lot of taint that night, from the destruction of the Shin-Kaguraza, the deaths of the audience and the – as yet to be confirmed but widely believed – death of Kikugawa Kichizuru. She'd muse that it was strange that the taint-detectors had barely registered any change in the atmosphere.

Her colleague would recall that they'd seen Todomegawa Daimyoujin asking for access to the taint-detectors, not long before he'd drowned in the Under-dream.

Surrounded by the dead and the smoking remains of

the theatre, they'd decide that, perhaps, it could be worth checking the taint-detectors themselves, without their seniors, if only the Wavewalker wouldn't be there to stop them.

Towards the second hour of the ox, a journalist at the *Weekly Bunyo* who so happened to fall asleep at his desk would be there to take a call from a collective of Onmyoryo whistle-blowers, regarding defective taint-detectors, revealing how atmospheric taint levels were worse than had been released to the public. He'd remember the feeling of his hands as crab claws and would pick up his pen against the Wavewalker with glee.

Tokifuyu's Hamanoyokocho shrine was still burning. Police were combing through its pieces, and somewhere nearby, Mansaku had hidden whatever it was that both the Wavewalker and the Paddywatcher thought was trouble.

The Wavewalker's accumulated taint had already made him volatile – body, spirit and souls, he'd feel everything slipping from his control.

Hyo could see it all. It wasn't seeing the future. It was seeing the present, built in networks of en; how they crossed, connected and disconnected, or tore apart. It was reading the moments for when the chain reaction of other people's tiny, apparently inconsequential actions produced an inescapable outcome.

The rain came down in the bamboo forest. When it

hit a hovering ghost light, it wrapped them in a halo of sparks.

Hyo and Natsuami took shelter in the doorway of Iris Hill's ground floor, where Natsuami held out his hand. "May I see?"

Hyo thought he meant her palm that Koushiro's tongue had shredded open. Instead, Natsuami peeled back her sleeve to the first scar on her forearm, from where Hyo had fed a villager her blood.

"You've met demons before?"

"This bite didn't come from a demon," Hyo replied. "This was one of my neighbours – Yamagoshi-san. She liked to make wind chimes out of the god-killer glass she found out in the forests. My blood worked on the hitodenashi-infected too – it slowed the growth of the tree. The way hitodenashi changed their bodies was less violent and painful for them."

He lowered her arm and said sadly, "Did you and Mansaku come to Onogoro to escape the hitodenashi you saw in the world outside?"

Hyo almost laughed. Wasn't that Onogoro's problem in a spoonful? It split the world into an "inside" and "outside". It acted as if its actions – past, present and future – could continue as a parallel bubble world to an "outside" without consequence. Hyo thought of how little she'd thought of the mainland since arriving, how little she'd read of or heard news about other places, how often she'd been told that demons weren't a problem here, because this was *Onogoro*.

Instead of laughing Natsuami off, her throat tightened. There was a small fearful thing that huddled at the core of her. It shivered at the slightest chill that reminded it of endless winter, of being trapped and powerless, except for the flame of life's power to burn, endure and survive. She'd cursed the power at the time, but her fearful thing had clung to it.

She held on to that fearful thing now, wishing she could say that Natsuami was entirely right: *Yes, Hyo had come to escape hitodenashi, so, yes, please, let her run in the opposite direction from all this. From Koushiro, from the Wavewalker, from everything.*

Natsuami put an arm around her. Hyo was silent too long. She let the rain cloud of him hold her and the dread of his shadow numb her panic, and was absurdly reminded of sweet ice and its simple coldness and sweetness.

Then there was a soft rattling in Hyo's waist-pouch, and the bamboo forest beyond the doors lit up with the blue-white light of a solarcrane's searchlight.

"That's our ride," said Hyo, straightening.

"We were waiting for a solarcrane?"

"I need you to know something." Hyo took out Natsuami's portable ink-well from her pouch, where it had been shaking and clinking against her pencil and coins. "You heard what the Paddywatcher said: Mansaku burned down Tokifuyu's Hamanoyokocho shrine. She wants me to go there to find something Mansaku's hidden for me."

Natsuami tilted his head. "At Toki's Hamanoyokocho shrine?"

"Right – now this is the part you should know. Before Tokifuyu drowned, he told me that I had to keep you away from his shrine. He didn't want you to go there. He didn't say why." Natsuami opened his mouth. Hyo held up her hand, and he closed it. "But Tokifuyu isn't here right now, and I need to go there. I can go alone or with you. Be honest with yourself, Natsuami, and don't think about what I or Tokifuyu want. Do you want to come with me to Hamanoyokocho?"

A ladder dropped down outside the doorway, scattering raindrops. Its steps were lit up by the solarcrane above. Natsuami looked at them.

He said slowly, "I might be a hindrance if I react like I did in the theatre. If I blank out for no reason."

"I wouldn't have been able to handle Koushiro tonight without you," Hyo told him. "We're friends. That means if you blank out, I'll keep you safe through it. What's it to be?"

Natsuami paused, then he set his hand on the door and pushed it aside. Rain-chilled night air smelling of smoke blew in, and the stepladder up to the belly of the solarcrane was a straight, still line of steel.

"Of course I'll go with you. I consider both you and Mansaku-san as my friends, and I've too few of those to lose even one." He took off his glasses and folded them into his waist-pouch. When he turned to Hyo there was a glint in his eyes. "And what big brother passes up the chance to do exactly as his younger doesn't want him to do? Especially when it relates to a whole secret shrine."

"*Secret* shrine?" Hyo stopped at the foot of the ladder.

"Well, yes." Natsuami said, "Because as far as I know, or thought I knew, Toki doesn't have a shrine at Hamanoyokocho." He met Hyo's gaze. His smile slipped. "Oh, heavens, now suddenly I'm quite scared."

The solarcrane turned out to be flown by none other than Ukibashi Awano.

"Hyo-chan!" Awano greeted her, as soon as Hyo and Natsuami entered the cabin. She was dressed for flight, the blue sleeves of her robes tied back with black ribbons, flight gloves on, left eye covered with her scallop eyepatch. The ladder folded up and interlocked behind them to make a hatch. "I'm so glad you're alive. When I heard about the Shin-Kaguraza burning I wanted to come back and find you immediately, but the Wavewalker insisted that we went home. I sensed my droplet was down here in the Zero Floor – I had to come and find you!"

"Where's the Wavewalker?" Hyo buckled into the seat behind Awano. Natsuami took the seat beside Hyo.

"A meeting with the other Pillars. About the Bridgeburner's Hamanoyokocho shrine apparently." As before, Awano barely acknowledged Natsuami's presence, but for a flex of her fingers on the yoke as he clipped in. As soon as Hyo was settled, Awano was expertly lifting the solarcrane up and between the towers, smooth despite the rain. "This is it, isn't it, Hyo-chan? This is our chance! We can go to the Hamanoyokocho shrine. Find what the Wavewalker doesn't want to be found before he does." Lightning flashed to the south, and Awano gripped the yoke with resolve. "And then I can save the Wavewalker from his secrets."

"The thing the Bridgeburner hid might've burned with the shrine," Hyo pointed out.

"But it didn't," Awano replied, and shot Hyo a knowing look in the mirror. "Otherwise why aren't you telling me to stop?" When Hyo said nothing, she smiled. "I heard about your brother."

"What about him?"

"That he burned down the shrine, or is the chief suspect for it anyway." Awano went on, in sing-song tones, "Did you send him to the shrine to find what the Bridgeburner left there? Whilst the Wavewalker was distracted by Kichizuru's last show?"

Rain drew branching trees on the windows. Hyo said, "More or less."

Natsuami pretended to be interested in his seat-belt mechanism.

Awano let out a coo of delight. "Hyo-chan, you

sly thing – you didn't give anything away earlier. I underestimated you!"

"Good."

"Should I change course to wherever your brother is hiding?"

"No, he had to make himself scarce fast. He left what he found near the shrine."

"Then we can retrieve it?"

"That's my plan."

"And mine."

Thunder rolled. Awano guided the solarcrane between the towers, following the sleek spine of the buraden rail, with deft touches on the controls. She flew the flightcraft southwards, evading weaving bolts of lightning, which, when Hyo saw one fall to the east, moved as though *alive*. It looped and twisted *sideways* before swimming on to a nearby lightning rod.

"This shrine at Hamanoyokocho, is it really the Bridgeburner's?" asked Hyo. A shrine that his own brother hadn't known about.

"It is – but it's a peculiar sort of en-giri shrine. It's where people go to cut en with gods if they want to stop following them for good." Awano braced herself as the solarcrane juddered against a gust of wind. "Or if they die, their relations can take their old god cabinets, relics, talismans – anything that connected them to the god they don't need any more – and leave them at the

Bridgeburner's Hamanoyokocho shrine. The artefacts are exorcised and the en between god and human severed."

"It sounds a bit sad."

"It's a glorified rubbish dump," Awano said. "People also deliver what could've belonged to gods we've forgotten – the dead gods. That shrine's just there so that people can feel better about throwing out god-related trash."

"How long has the shrine been there?"

"Three years," said Awano. "They built it to handle the clean-up from Three Thousand Three Fall. There were so many shrines for gods nobody could name any more."

Natsuami's face fell. Hyo reached over, prised open his hand from the armrest and held it firmly as Awano adjusted the yoke and the solarcrane dipped downwards to bank between the towers.

They approached the Hamanoyokocho shrine in the shadow of the towers along the cliff tops.

"I should cut the wing lights," Awano said. "The police will see – or the Onmyoryo..."

"Keep the lights on," Hyo said. "No one will see us, and we won't be stopped."

Awano gave Hyo a questioning look, but she did as Hyo said, and, just as Hyo said, they were neither seen nor stopped. All the luck of the world was bending against the Wavewalker, so was on Hyo's side. Police combing through the Hamanoyokocho ruins happened to turn and look in the other direction as the solarcrane neared. A stray ribbon of lightning jumped in the face of another, blinding them and disguising the sounds of the solarcrane parking at the nearby craft-roost.

The Hamanoyokocho shrine was unmissable. Its shrine gate was charred but still standing, and its top lit up with a blue-green glow. It resembled ship fire – the kind that flickered around the tall masts out in a storm. Eel-like ribbons of lightning swam about between the burned-out halls and smoking altars.

It stood at the top of a cliff, over which edge Hyo had only to look over to know that in front of Tokifuyu's shrine was where Jun had taken his stellaroids.

Below her was the stellaroid's grey beach, with its sheer wall of rock to the right, and a curving arm of black rock to the left that shielded it from sight by the sea. The moon lit it bright, its shadows dark. The curse that had been visible in Jun's stellaroid was invisible in real life.

Natsuami recognized it too. He put a hand on Hyo's shoulder as if to steady himself.

Awano gave the beach barely a glance. She'd hurried to the shelter of a large boulder near the gate and was watching the officers going back and forth about the shrine's ruins, their round lanterns held high in the sea of smoke.

"They're a joke!" she said, when Hyo and Natsuami joined her. "They're not going to find anything in this storm, and they know it. They're here just to make a show of showing up. Otherwise, everyone would complain. What happens now, Hyo-chan? How do we find what your brother left for you?"

In the solarcrane, Hyo had found one of the unused paper men she'd made to be Koushiro's katashiros in her waist-pouch. Now, she applied the paper man to her lips where they'd cracked in the heat of the theatre, set her blood to it and infused the figure with her breath and spirit.

When the shikigami fluttered its sleeved arms, Hyo set its feet on the ground. "Go find."

The shikigami scurried away. Awano pursed her lips. "A paper doll won't survive the rain."

"The blood makes it hardier than just normal paper; it's a piece of my body as well as spirit." Hyo looked around her quickly. "Where's Natsuami?"

Awano sniffed and pointed to the shrine gate. "That creature you insist on keeping close is over there."

"'That creature' is someone with an earthly name, which you can ask for when he gets back here," Hyo replied coolly.

"Do you know what that thing looks like in my eye?" Awano stopped her, grasping Hyo by the arm. "Teeth and the nothingness of hunger, dipped head to toe in blood,

mouth golden like it would swallow all light if it could. A body rebuilt and reshaped on the bones of a curse. A great forest of pain. A shadow that casts itself."

Her fear was real, but Hyo didn't have time for it. She shook Awano off and went to Natsuami. The rain had

briefly, let up. Natsuami was staring through the gate, straight ahead at the smoke-draped hulk of the shrine. One hand had risen to his chest, pressing it as if hurt, whilst the other rested against the shinwood column of

As Hyo drew near, Natsuami stuck his hand through the gate, wafted it this way and that, then retracted it.

"I shouldn't be able to do that," he said wonderingly, examining his hand. "Gods can't enter the shrines of other gods."

"Maybe the gate's broken, from the fire."

"Whilst the gate still stands, so do the shrine rules." Natsuami lowered his hands. "What does this mean?"

Hyo shook her head. "You'll just have to ask Tokifuyu when he wakes up."

"So many coincidences and chance happenings, working our way." Natsuami stood at the centre of the gateway. Police officers went this way and that, apparently oblivious to them. "Even I can feel the inescapability of it all. It's horrible. I truly hope never to commission a hell from you."

"I hope the same," said Hyo sincerely, and felt a tugging at her hem. Her shikigami had returned. "What have you found?"

It beckoned at something out of sight, hiding apparently in a crack in the wall bounding the edge of the shrine complex. Hyo went towards where it pointed, Natsuami following.

As soon as she was close enough, three paper-man heads emerged from the various cracks in the wall. One slipped out entirely and touched Hyo's hand. It felt like the blunt edge of a blade.

“Mansaku!” Hyo held out her hands. The three dolls dragged out something hidden in the stone wall, tossed it into her palms then jumped after it. Mansaku’s consciousness fluttered, spread across the three shikigami. A small guttering flame of life lent warmth to each shikigami’s heart – a splinter of Mansaku’s. “Thank you.”

Their object delivered, Mansaku’s shikigami crumbled into flakes, their tiny flames of life spent. Hyo touched her own shikigami to dispel her spirit from it too, and examined what Mansaku had defied the Paddywatcher to rescue from the fire.

It was a bamboo tube. Its side was cracked from where Mansaku’s shikigami had tried to cram it into the wall. She moved to open it, then Natsuami’s hand landed on hers, closing her fingers tightly over the tube.

“What’s wrong?”

“Don’t open that where I can see it.” In a flicker of lightning, his face lit up sickly pale. “I don’t know why, but … whatever it is, I want it too much. You can’t let me touch that, Hyo. If you do … do you remember how hungry I felt in the theatre?”

“Yeah?”

“It’ll win.” Natsuami shut his eyes, like a child in the dark wishing away monsters. “That hunger. It wants whatever you have.”

He spoke those last words with such terror that the

hairs on the back of Hyo's neck lifted. But then she saw Awano looking out from under the boulder, and the hellmakers' en *pulled*.

"Put your arms around my middle, cross them, and hold your elbows."

"Excuse me?"

"It's to restrict your hands. Don't let go of me." Hyo spotted Awano losing patience and heading their way. Natsuami, with some hesitation, hurried to do as she said. "And when I tell you to close your eyes, do it, and keep them closed."

He breathed through his mouth in thin sips. "Yes."

"Is that what your brother left for you?" Awano spoke in a whisper, creeping past the gateway to them. Her eyes were fixed on Hyo's fist containing the bamboo tube. Her eyepatch had fallen apart in the rain. The water-eye shone piercingly in the shadow of the shrine wall; a window into a distant sea. "Is it the same as what the Bridgeburner hid from the Wavewalker?"

Through the crack in its side, Hyo had seen what was in the bamboo tube. A corner piece to the puzzle. "I'm sure of it."

"Perfect," Awano said, her eyes bright. "Let's go back to my craft and open it there."

"No, let's open it somewhere closer."

"Closer?"

"Yeah. Like down there." Hyo tipped her chin to

the beach below. Together she and Natsuami shuffled backwards to the cliff's edge. "I'll see you at the bottom, Awano."

Natsuami's arms wrapped around Hyo, pulling her to him as she jumped and took him with her, over the edge of the cliff and down to the sands of the grey beach.

TWENTY-SIX

呪浜

Hunger is the real curse for demons. It steals away their minds.

The only way for a demon to satiate their hunger and regain their human minds is to eat human flesh or the pears that have been grown on it.

HATSU,
Thirty-Second Hellmaker

Natsuami turned in the air, facing the sea as they fell. He bundled Hyo up to keep her feet lifted, so that when he landed, she didn't feel the impact – only how Natsuami braced against it when he dropped on to the sand, sending visible ripples spreading through it.

He set Hyo on her feet. "Are you all right?"

"I'm fine." Hyo looked around for signs of Awano following. None yet. "You?"

"I just need a moment." Natsuami drew in a shaky breath. "I didn't like heights when I was a human. My body remembers that."

Hyo winced. "Thanks for following my lead, then, even when you were scared."

"You said my life was beautiful, just for being there. I trust you. I feel that if I follow you, I'll remember how to trust myself too. Enough to shoulder all those secrets others have been keeping for me." Natsuami raised his head. "What now, Hyo?"

Hyo faced the tall wall of rock to the north of the beach. "We find out what that cursed ward is hiding." She paused, noticing the patterns of the unluck currents, read what they meant, then lifted her hands to her head. "Cover your ears!"

Lightning slammed into the cliff face in a flash of searing light that warmed Hyo's eyelids and with a boom that shook through her body. The air smelled faintly toasted. Hyo opened her eyes, removed her hands from her ears and found herself knocked on to the sand by the force of the blast, Natsuami similarly on his hands and knees.

"Unluck is on the Wavewalker's side," Hyo said, picking herself up. "Which means luck is on ours."

The rain began again, each drop like a nail and ricocheting hard enough that the stone shrine gate – which had suddenly appeared at the base of rock wall – was outlined in reflected moonlight.

The lightning had left this stone gateway burned, the plaque at its top melted, and a piece of its arch had been blasted away. Beyond it, previously invisible and hidden by the cursed ward, was a path of stepping stones to a low, narrow cave-mouth, like a thin-lipped smile.

Hyo and Natsuami exchanged a look then ran towards it.

The shrine gate stood in two shaku of tidal water. A stone spire to the side was carved with the heavenly name of the god it was dedicated to: *Fuchiha'No'Utanami'Tomi-no-Mikoto*. The Wavewalker. On the other side of the stone spire, the charm for the cursed ward that had hidden the cave had been damaged in the lightning blast.

The ward was down. Whatever the Wavewalker had tried to hide here had been laid bare by a single – unlucky for him – stroke of lightning.

"I suppose there's no question of ... *not* going in there?" said Natsuami tentatively, regarding the dark smile opening of the cave-mouth with a grimace.

"You don't need to." Awano emerged out of the rain, pulling her rain hood close about her as the water sheeted off it. Her water-eye burned in its shadow. "It's just another one of Fuchiha's shrines. His smallest and oldest. There's nothing to see."

"Why was it hidden under a ward?" Hyo asked.

"Because it's our private one." Awano drew near enough that Hyo could see her soft smile as she stopped to look up at the shattered gate. "Just for him and me. This is the beach where I found the Wavewalker, all those years ago. I was small and he had so little power that I could hold the whole of him in one hand. I could take him home in my pocket. My pet god."

"How did you get down to this beach?"

"Back then? There's a way through the caves from the cliff's other side. A passage just big enough for a small and curious child."

"And what about now?"

Awano was covered in sand. It had pooled in the folds of her robes. Her left arm was set at a strange angle, which she yanked into place with a crack.

She spoke in a voice so low with anger it was almost a growl: "You came down here knowing full well that if I were as human as I look I wouldn't be able to follow."

"Natsuami, hold on to me and close your eyes," Hyo said. Then, when Natsuami had done just that, Hyo held up Tokifuyu's bamboo tube for Awano to see and broke it open.

An algacell evidence bag dropped out. A divine privacy charm had been painted on its front in vermilion, and the Onmyoryo's five-pointed bellflower crest stamped in a corner. It contained a handful of grey sand and teeth.

Human teeth.

No. If only it were teeth.

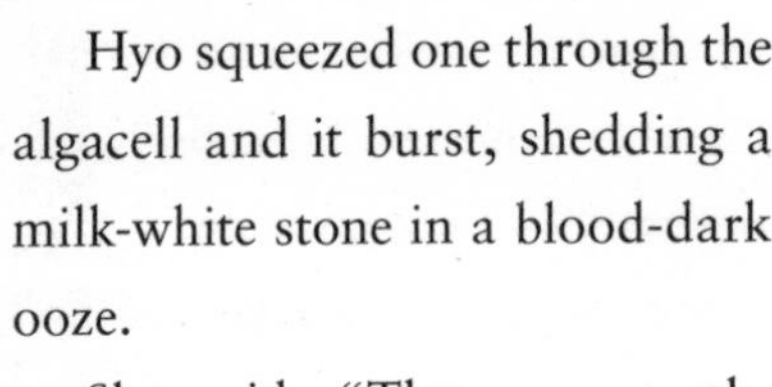

Hyo squeezed one through the algacell and it burst, shedding a milk-white stone in a blood-dark ooze.

She said, "These are teeth-seeds of the hitodenashi pear tree."

"I know." Awano moved closer, the intensity of her gaze making Hyo shiver. "I'm heir to the Ukibashi shinshu makers. I know everything there is to know about hitodenashi. After all, without hitodenashi, there would be no need for shinshu."

"The Bridgeburner found this here, didn't he? On the beach, near the Wavewalker's oldest shrine." Hyo let her eyes slide deliberately to the broken shrine gateway. "Hitodenashi seeds on Onogoro; I wonder what the Bridgeburner thought when he found them here."

Awano made a grab for the algacell bag. Hyo swung it out of reach, just in time, and she laughed. "Eyes on me, Hyo-chan. Yes, I wondered the same. Did the Bridgeburner jump to conclusions, and assume the worst and think we were growing hitodenashi here? Or did he worry that the Wavewalker was helping the smugglers, letting them land on this beach? But I thought he'd found more than this. It's just a few seeds!"

"How long have you been a demon, Awano-chan?"

"Ever since I escaped my kidnappers." She began to move in a slow circle, and Hyo mirrored her movements, Natsuami walking with her. "This is how the Wavewalker 'saved' me, Hyo-chan. He couldn't reach me himself, so he sent me a hitodenashi pear on the waves and bent my luck. It was a small pear, no larger than an azuki bean. It washed aboard the boat and made its way down to me, through the cracks in the boards and the ceilings. I'd never seen one so small, so I didn't know what it was, but I trusted that the Wavewalker would never deliver me something that would hurt me. I ate it. I got my demon's gift with this water-eye, to escape my cell, and then I had my demon's hunger, teeth and strength to tear apart my captors, save myself and return to Onogoro. What gave me away?"

Hyo pointed to Natsuami with a thumb. "My friend here had a reaction to your pills in the theatre. There's hitodenashi pear in them, isn't there?"

"Oh, that's right." Awano put a thumb and forefinger to her chin. "Your creature's strange episode was why the Wavewalker forced us to leave early."

"He's been fed hitodenashi pear before," Hyo said, and Awano's eyes widened, flitting to Natsuami then away again. "He's sensitive to it. The Wavewalker makes those pills for you. To curb your cravings."

Awano put her hands together and applauded. "Very good, Hyo-chan."

"Fed demons keep their human mind and can keep their human appearance." They circled each other again. Hyo kept her eyes on Awano's mouth, for any sign of a needle-covered tongue. "What do you want with these teeth-seeds?"

"I'm going to do as Ukibashi Awano of the Ukibashi Shinshu Company should do." Lightning flashed somewhere on the clifftop, turning Awano into a dark silhouette. "I'm going to destroy the evidence that the Wavewalker condoned hitodenashi pear on Onogoro. The Wavewalker guards our seas as Chief Water God. No hitodenashi seeds could have washed ashore on a beach without his knowing. I said I would save the Wavewalker from his secrets. I will do just that."

"A demon destroy hitodenashi teeth-seeds?"

"I was Awano of Onogoro first," she said in clipped tones. "I have access to the shinshu to do it."

"What about your pills? What about wherever the Wavewalker is sourcing his hitodenashi pear from to make them for you? Aren't those evidence that hitodenashi's been permitted on Onogoro too?"

"Step by step, Hyo-chan. I'm prepared for this to be a long and difficult trial for me – that I must endure, for the sake of Onogoro."

"I think you're lying."

"You can think what you like." Awano sighed heavily, as if Hyo was being unreasonable. "It amounts to the same thing in the end. I can't be seen, let alone caught, as a demon. I am the future of a shinshu company. Shinshu keeps Onogoro free, so my survival is equal to the continued freedom of Onogoro to live as we please."

"No, there's more to this than a packet of seeds," said Hyo. "You don't want anyone nosing around this private shrine of yours and the Wavewalker's. I wonder why?"

Awano straightened from the odd crouch she'd been curling into. "Fine then. When I heard that the Bridgeburner had been drowned in the Under-dream, I thought this was our chance to do something about what the Bridgeburner had hidden there. But the Wavewalker did nothing. Absolutely nothing. He dragged his scaly heels, made this excuse after that. Do you know, he wasn't even behind the Bridgeburner's drugging? He wouldn't lift a finger against his dear little river's shrine, so what could I do but take matters into my own hands? Now, I'm doing just that."

Hyo nodded. "And how do I fit into this?"

"I saw that you'd be able to get whatever it was the Bridgeburner had hidden, when I couldn't." Awano smiled. "And I was telling the truth when I said I wanted a friend my age. The Wavewalker told me you came here to escape the troubles of the mainland, and I thought, why not? Did you know I went to school in the Harbourlakes? That's where I learnt how they want us Ujin to be – a field of pretty de-thorned flowers for them to pick from without complaint, put on a shelf and show off how their custodianship has been merciful. I thought we might see eye to eye, Hyo-chan, both of us having witnessed the outside, and who know what they think of us here. You'd understand how Onogoro needs me." She held out her hand, lifting her tin in the other. "Now, why don't you tell your monster to stand down, and give those teeth-seeds to me? It's for the good of Onogoro."

"Dragging his heels?" Hyo clicked her tongue and shook her head. "Is that what you really think the Wavewalker was doing?"

"It's certainly what you're doing," Awano returned sweetly.

"Were the Makuni brothers' deaths on your orders too?"

"Orders? No. *Prayers.*" A dark band of blood poured over her chin and then pearls dribbled from Ukibashi Awano's mouth – her teeth were falling, scattering on the sand, and in their place, there was gold. "I don't care how far away Makuni Junichiro was, or how small I was in his reflectograph. He saw me here – he caught me in his picture – so he had to die."

"Makuni Junichiro and Koushiro both took weeks to 'die'. The Wavewalker could've killed them in an instant, he's powerful enough, but he didn't. I couldn't figure out why. Now I get it." The rain softened. Hyo was already feeling cold and numb, but it was a relief nonetheless. "The Wavewalker held back to give *you* time. He wanted *you* to change your mind about wanting them dead. Because you're special to the Wavewalker, Awano. Because you are his *beloved guardian human* who saved him – even when he made you a demon."

Awano lashed out, hand tipped with golden claws, but Natsuami pulled Hyo backwards, out of her reach. "I never asked to be his favourite!"

"Oh, poor you. Heiress to a shinshu company; loved by a god without ever asking for it."

"Hand over the teeth-seeds," Awano hissed through her teeth and held up her tin of hitodenashi pear pills, a thumb on its lid, "or I'll open this right under your friend's nose, and see how you deal with *two* hungry demons."

"Want to bet, Awano? I'm feeling lucky tonight." Hyo grinned, despite everything, and pointedly stuffed the algacell bag of teeth-seeds back in its tube, which she put away in her waist-pouch. "And I think, somewhere, that tin's lid might've come open when you weren't looking and dropped a few pills here and there, and you're not going to be keeping your mind or human face much longer."

"What kind of a bet is that?" But something made Awano stop and bring the tin up to her ear. She shook it. It was silent. "No. How? But I filled it earlier, it was full just... What did you *do*?"

"The Wavewalker is unlucky tonight, and by extension, apparently you," Hyo said coolly. "No one uninvolved is affected by an artisan hell – but it looks like you're involved enough to share in his one."

"He's a stalker! An obsessive! A creep!" Step by shaking step, Awano advanced upon Hyo and Natsuami. One eye blazed blue, the other sunk into black and gold. "I never asked for this water-eye either. I never wanted to be able to see with ... clarity! All the flaws in the world! All the weaknesses in the system! How fragile it is, so full of holes and cracks to exploit! It's a curse, not a gift! But now that I actually want something from him? He can't do it properly! He couldn't keep the beach clean or stop that Bridgeburner finding those seeds! Sloppy. Slapdash. Useless!"

And she lunged, jaws wide and golden, eyes rolling back in her head.

Hyo took the charmed paper of the sleeping shikigami from her collar to her lips. "Wake up. Will you help me, please, Koushiro?"

"*Gladly.*"

In an instant, Makuni Koushiro was there, trailing his burned paper actor's robes. He landed on his feet, light and lithe as a tiger, to catch Ukibashi Awano by her torso, and tossed her against the column of the broken shrine gate, so hard that the stone shattered.

"Ukibashi-sama." Koushiro cracked his knuckles. "So this is why you were so keen to come to my performances in person. The poor heiress for whom all the hearts of the island bled, and you were there checking the Wavewalker's progress in disposing of me and that reflectograph. Hakai Hyo, what do you need?"

Hyo looked over to where Awano's form twitched and jerked at the base of the gate. "Can you keep her distracted as long as possible?"

"Who do you think I am?" Koushiro smiled with golden teeth. "If Onogoro's foremost shin-kagura dancer can't keep a pair of eyes on him, what good is he?"

Koushiro stretched his legs, first one then the other, then his arms. His eyes shone in the gloom. He glanced at Natsuami at Hyo's back. His gaze softened. "Take care of Natsu-san."

He leapt, as lightly as he'd done on the bridge, seized Awano by a leg from the base of the shrine gate and slung her out into the rain.

Hyo tapped Natsuami's arms. "You can open your eyes."

"I'm not sure I want to," he said, as snarls, shrieks and wet ripping noises cut through the rain's hissing. But he opened one eye, then the other, and found himself and Hyo under the broken shrine gate's arch, standing on the first stepping stone.

"It's our chance," Hyo said, looking along the path of rain-slicked rock to the cave. "Are you with me?"

"Do you know what's in there?"

"... I've some idea."

"I do too." They both stood on the first stepping stone, rooted to it, as if the brine lapping at the rock was sucking down their ankles. "Do you think you could go in there alone?"

"No," Hyo admitted, her voice small. "Could you?"

"No, never." Natsuami jumped. He landed on the next stone and turned, offering a hand. "I'm with you. Let's go together where we wouldn't alone."

Hyo followed with a jump. He caught her fingers, and as they both passed through the gate, the crabs arrived.

Pale and tiny, their shells looked soft, barely formed, some bubbled with tiny blisters on their carapaces that opened to show red, round human eyes. They swarmed, surrounding the stone then piling up until they were an uneven column in the vague shape of a crumbling man.

"*Hakai Hyo*," said the Wavewalker, sounding distant and strained. "*Leave*."

"I can't do that."

"*Awano has prayed to me for your death*." The Wavewalker was covered in unluck, forming ghostly shapes that bent and mangled the luck landscape around him, accumulating in walls and tripwires. "*She wasn't meant to suffer too*."

"She wouldn't have if you hadn't been the knife and let Awano hold the handle. I'm sorry."

This time he appealed to Natsuami. "*You don't know the demon's hunger. It hurts her. I do this for her. You are kind; a kinder god than me. Leave this place. Let it go unknown. You never saw it*."

"I'm afraid I'm only the pieces of the better god you knew," said Natsuami forlornly. "And there are answers here that I'd benefit from too. I'm so tired of being chained with secrets. I think you understand that?"

The column of crabs crumbled with a heavy sigh, dissolving into bubbles in the tide. "*Good luck to you both*."

Water rushed in the distance, crushing stone and sand, and a dark grey wave swept in from the sea, up the shallow channel to the stepping stones. Hyo grabbed Natsuami, pulling him to the next stone, but then her feet were no longer touching anything. Spinning waves full of storm-sharpened debris had picked them up, carrying them sideways, up and down. Hyo could hardly think past the hard litany to hold her breath and the heady panic that she couldn't.

Then she saw the cliff rising towards them and the waves surged to dash their bodies against the dark rock.

TWENTY-SEVEN

... C has described the monster that pursued him in the Under-dream for three days as endless golden teeth and shadow. I would suggest further action be taken in exploring the Under-dream for Onogoro's continued safety.

From a report by RYOUEN TOKIFUYU
on an interview with God C

Hyo was at the pit in the mist, clouds flowing about her ankles. With some shock, she saw that the red cord was coming apart, thread by thread.

Dimly, she knew what had happened. She'd hit her head; she was unconscious. She had been, maybe, overconfident. Free access to all her powers had made her reckless.

She could die. She wasn't invincible. She could sink under the waves and drown.

And be another name on Natsuami's list of those he'd brought to a sticky end just by connecting to them.

Hyo snatched at the red cord, and gripped it. She spoke to the god in Natsuami's shadow. "Don't you dare undo our en now. This is what you did to Jun, and the others you connected to through Natsuami, isn't it? You tie our ens and manipulate our fates as you like, then when you're bored of us you throw us away. You're too cruel to stick with any of us to the end."

The hunger gave the cord a resentful yank, hungry to be felt, impatient for a change, to show proof it existed in the shadows. *See me, feel me, know I'm here, fear me!*

"Pull on me all you like. There's no crawling out of the Under-dream for you, not when you can't be named," Hyo told the unnamed god. "You need me as your monkey on the earthly plane to get that hitodenashi into your hands.

"Listen to me. I am here on Onogoro to look for hitodenashi. I *want* to find it. I *will* find it, and if you keep me alive now, you won't be bored. Could the others talk to you? Sense you like I can? Don't kill me off now."

The tugging stopped.

Then the red threads that had been fraying closed together again.

"Thank you." She tested her footing. "I'm coming down."

She took a running jump into the pit.

There was no sense of weight, nor time. She was at once too heavy for her own existence and too insubstantial. There was both agonizing pain as she tried to shed the iron of her body and euphoric promise of relief as the bubble of tension that she was in the universe's skin finally looked to break apart...

Something wrapped around Hyo, cocooning her before the Under-dream could pull her apart. She held up her hand and called up the flame of her life to see it.

Golden teeth. Hundreds and thousands of them, row upon row, curved and hooked and wickedly sharp. They dug and let go, dug and let go, in the way a cat's claws flexed on a favourite lap with a motion like slow breathing.

The shape of the whole couldn't be seen, just impressions. Vague shards of something that only existed in sense and instinct. She saw it in glimpses, as if through floating curtains. Sometimes there might have been a face like Natsuami's, rain-cloud-shadowed.

Sometimes there were crowns of branches in twisted gnarly claws, candles in the boughs, streaming ribbons of smoke.

There were eyes. She couldn't say where. Only that they were there, and more than could have ever fit into Natsuami's face.

That malevolence in Natsuami's shadow, that cold hunger and fury against everything at being unnamed, held her tightly. She was its way out. She could speak with it, fight it, bargain with it, amuse it.

The child in the green suikan from before was nowhere to be seen.

"You've got Tokifuyu down here, haven't you?"

The hunger did.

"He's missed. We'd like him back."

Little gods had come and gone, the stupider trying to kill it, as if it could be killed without a name, or as if something so vast and furious could die, but Toki never tried that.

Toki had tried to talk to it.

He had wanted the hunger to tell him what had happened the night it had killed the three thousand and three, how it had come to be so hungry. Toki was hungry for answers and the hunger had fed upon his hunger and given him no relief.

At first, the hunger had wanted to keep him for ever but it had learnt quickly that letting Toki go meant that Toki came back. Toki would look upon it. The hunger

yearned to be looked upon, because in its brother's eyes, it saw its name.

"Your earthly name?"

Its name of heaven.

"Tokifuyu knows it?"

Toki alone spoke it in the night-time of his heart. He had to remember it, to keep the en between it and the world cut. This was how the hunger lingered in the dream beneath dreams when it should have dissipated.

"Are you keeping Tokifuyu down here until he gives up your name?"

There was nothing in the world that would compel Toki to speak its name. No pain would make him any more truthful. No threat would persuade him.

"You were given hitodenashi pear on Three Thousand Three Fall, weren't you?"

The tree of curses freed us of humans.

"What would putting hitodenashi pear in Natsuami's hands do for you?"

The human in the god would be absolutely devoured.

It could be free of its own feeble earthly human heart at last.

"Don't put yourself down like that."

Don't put myself down?

"It isn't feeble. Anyway, I'm here now." Hyo tried to see all of it, every piece of it, the pieces of Natsuami that had been cut from him, and thought, *This is him too.*

Every god has two faces. En can trap and hurt as well as catch and save. "I can help you but I need you to let Tokifuyu go. There are things happening in the world that I need help with."

The teeth dug. Let go. Held.

Breathed.

I can help, if you wish.

Water roared. Rocks scoured at her limbs. Everything stung then numbed, moments shaped by breath after breath.

Then there was a sleeve shielding her head from the stones, debris, seawater and rage, divine rage and pain, flowing around her, a pillar digging into her back, and gradually, slowly, quiet.

The water lapped at Hyo's neck. She heard a distant echo of the wave splashing against a wall. She was in a cavern, a tall one, its corners deep. The Wavewalker's attempt to wash her and Natsuami away had delivered them both straight into the hidden cave.

Luck, it seemed, was still against the Wavewalker.

The back of Hyo's head where she'd collided with the pillar throbbed but her shoulders had taken the brunt of it. She sat up. Her nose and mouth filled with the smells and tastes of seawater and blood.

"Natsuami?" Hyo whispered. His outline beside her shone with the glowing vermilion of a god's blood. She saw him lift his head by the gash at his temple, which had spilled blood on his cheeks in a dripping mask, its eyes and mouth dark holes. "How badly are you hurt?"

One bloodied hand skimmed up her arm, drawing her into visibility. It came to rest on her face, then wiped a line over her right cheek, and left. Painted in his blood, now he could see her.

The other hand was clamped over his nose and mouth, thin threads of molten iron glow running between his fingers. He was gnawing on them, Hyo realized, biting deep into his own flesh.

"What's wrong?" said Hyo. "What have I missed?"

Hyo leant against the pillar to stand, then stiffened. It was bark – tree bark, with an oddly ridged, regular texture that would never cease to raise the goosebumps over her skin.

It dawned on Hyo that all her worst-feared ideas of what she'd find in the cave were correct, and with a hum, the room lit up.

The orchard of hitodenashi trees stretched their branches to the lights.

Natsuami's gaze rose to fix on the shadows of fruits above.

Hyo seized him by the shoulders before he could move. "Don't look at them!"

And she looked at Natsuami's flame of life, capturing its white-hot life that burned all on its own – no candle, no wick in oil, needing no musuhi or energy that Hyo could see.

Natsuami froze, just as Tokifuyu had done all those days ago, with the instinct of a small animal that had felt itself seen by something utterly inescapable.

Hyo's eyes blurred heavy with tears and something thicker. With one hand, she untied the sodden ribbon from her hair, locked her other arm around Natsuami's neck and pulled him close to tie the flame-coloured silk over his eyes and to press a scrap from her torn sleeves over his face.

He murmured through the cloth,

"Who told you that I'd had hitodenashi pear before?" Hyo tapped the back of his hand, indicating Tokifuyu's silencing seal. "Ah. I understand now. So, I was given pear, and became a sort of … demonic god of destruction for Three Thousand Three Fall, and then by erasing my heavenly name, Toki severed that god from me. And ever since, it has been looking for pear through me and the ens I make. As a way to return."

"That's what I think." Hyo looked away from him to study the orchard. "But you're not a demon. You're something else. Between god, human, demon and ghost."

"A little like you?"

"Yeah, let's go with that."

A cool vapour hung between the trees, threading through roots that arced out of their beds to sprawl across paths. Seawater lapped against stone walls and tree trunks. Hitodenashi pear grew in terraced basins, in shallow and flat-bottomed, low-walled pans. It didn't need soil, although Hyo had trimmed the roots off the toes of many

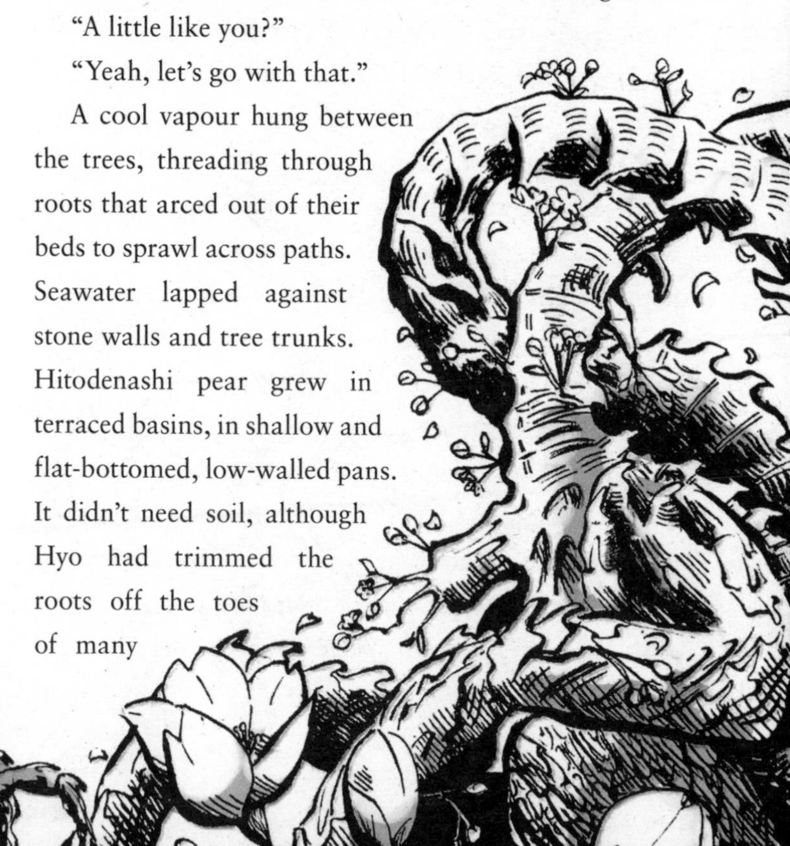

villagers' feet. Hitodenashi was opportunistic and hungry to grow, spread and reproduce. It would do whatever it could to speed up the process.

All hitodenashi really needed was a human host body to infect, like the one in whose lap Hyo sat, legs bent and cracked in the pan and still clothed in stiff folds of dark cyclocloth. Their torso had turned to bark. Their head was gone. Maybe it had dropped off when the rest of the tree had burst from the top of their spine. The bark looked like a thorny braid of silvery human vertebral columns. There were tattoos in the leather of human skin, the coin scales of a carp. The young Ohne gangsters had been right to worry. People who could be made to disappear without a fuss had been brought here to be *compost*.

Everything was covered in blossoms. Clusters of green-white petals sighed in the wind wending through the hole in the wall that the Wavewalker's wave had smashed into.

Natsuami said, "This is a hitodenashi orchard."

Hyo had a wild urge to laugh. "Yes, it is."

"I don't remember eating any fruit. Then again, I don't remember being the god of destruction who could kill three thousand and three." He paused. "But you're right that I do know what I've done. I do know I was responsible. The worst thing is that I feel ... nothing. No guilt, no remorse, no tangible feeling that I did it. I might be reading about a villain in a story."

"Come on." Hyo buckled down the feeling that suddenly welled up in her chest. "Let's get out of here quickly, for both of our sakes. If the ribbon feels like it's slipping, tell me."

Hyo guided Natsuami carefully out of the tree's bed, climbing from the shallow pan where the human host had been chained, and into the aisle between the terraces.

"A whole orchard just for Awano," said Natsuami wonderingly.

"No," said Hyo. "The Wavewalker sent her a pear to get her off the boat. He probably already had this orchard then."

Branches swayed, and petals fell, blanketing the water in a pale and ghostly raft. The petals covered the contorted bodies in the pans. Not all were dead. Faintly, Hyo could see the spots of their flames of life.

"I was thinking," said Natsuami, "that you'd never had a good dream."

"You're hung up on that, of all things?"

"Everyone should have a good dream at least once," Natsuami said wistfully. "I'm sorry that you came to Onogoro to escape the hitodenashi and had to find this. You're never going to have a good dream at this rate."

Pale petals, veined blue-green, floated between them.

Hyo said, "I didn't quite tell you the truth."

"Oh, good! So you have had a good dream?"

"No, that part was true." Something round bobbed by, wrapped in the crisp edges of an algacell bag. The impulse howled through Hyo, loud and clear: she wanted someone else to know. She wanted the island to hear her, for the gods to quake and be afraid, for all these shinshu companies to be jostled out of their curse-bought comfort and apathy for everything beyond the island's borders. Why should she and Mansaku have to carry everything

on their shoulders? Why shouldn't she tell someone?

"Mansaku and I came to Onogoro to find hitodenashi here, not escape it."

"You came to the world's sole source of shinshu, the cure for hi[illegible]denashi, to find hitodenashi?"

“That’s right,” Hyo said bitterly, sick and weary of hiding it. “Shouldn’t I be congratulated? I’ve found an orchard on Onogoro. Exactly what I came for. This is exactly what I wanted.”

“You didn’t want to find it at all. I can tell. How could I congratulate you?”

“Natsuami, you don’t know what I wanted. You don’t know the first thing about me.”

Pinching the algacell wrap on the bobbing pear, Hyo pulled it from the cold water and tossed it out into a nearby pan. Natsuami’s grip on her hand as she led him was so trusting. Hyo cursed herself. She had to keep it together. She couldn’t lose it over a few petals in the face or the perfume of pear hitting her pallet.

“*There’s a ghost at your shoulder*,” said Natsuami, lilting, “*it stands at your hair.*”

“Where did you hear that?”

“*And it asks you to name it, and tell it it’s there*. You’ve said it in your sleep.”

Hyo focused on the gap between the trees. *Walk on, Hyo.* She’d walked on many times before. “So?”

“So, I think it means that you know what it is to have a shadow on your shoulders, and although the shadow is a frightening thing, you would still spend time with it, listen to it and see it lived with rather than destroyed.”

“So you think ... what? That I won’t hurt you?”

“That you’re my friend and I trust you.”

There was no way for Hyo to wipe away the tears this time. They'd just have to fall, angry and unchecked by any kindness, bared as livid as wounds. "Trusting as easily as you do is probably how you ended up getting fed hitodenashi in the first place."

"I'm certain that would be the case," said Natsuami, without any hint of remorse.

Hyo picked up another fruit, twisting her fingers into the vine tendrils sprouting from its algacell wrap. Hitodenashi pears looked like human heads, down to their grimacing faces and the way their cheeks swelled and darkened when bagged, as if suffocated. The vines had the sleek texture of hair.

She slung the pear away. It landed with a distant splash. "Natsuami?"

"Yes?"

"I'm glad we have an en."

"Likewise."

The blossoming trees gave way to the fruiting. Seasons didn't dictate the life cycle of hitodenashi fruit. They grew and bloomed on blood and painful memories, and sucked dry all the curses a human had ever wished to toss at the world but sealed in their hearts. At the base of each tree sat a mound of cracked bone and flesh wrung to bark toughness.

Who had all these people been? Foreigners? Prisoners? Anyone who could disappear without anyone asking questions?

“Hyo.” She jumped. Natsuami stood still, head tilted, a petal caught on the yellow ribbon blindfold. “I can hear someone crying.”

Hyo could see clearly enough.

At the end of the aisle, Awano crouched on a mound of fruit, chewing into a pear with sobbing breaths. Unluck rose in towering, shimmering walls around her, trapping her in a corner of the Wavewalker’s hell.

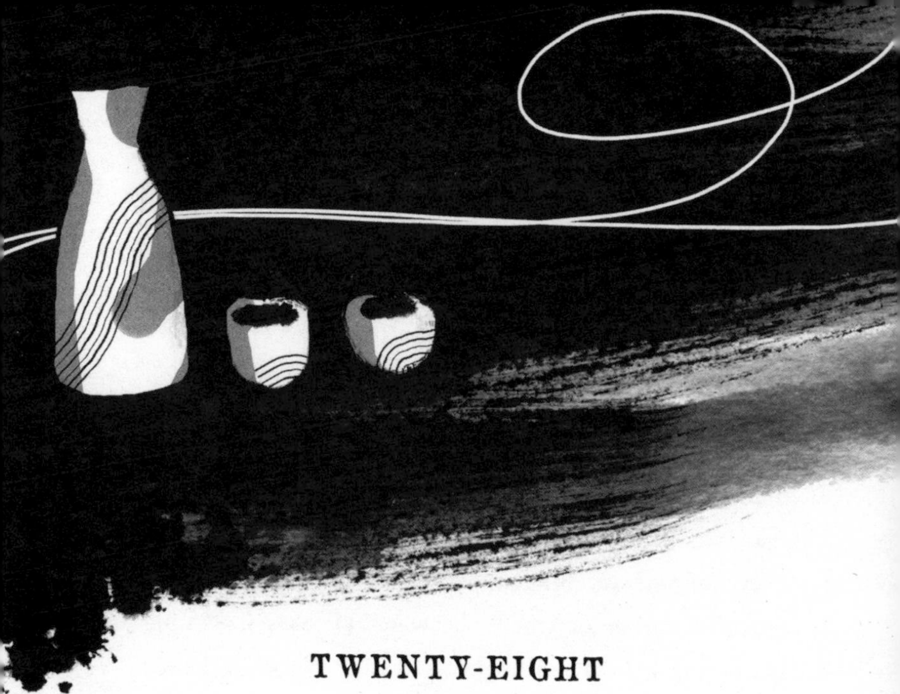

TWENTY-EIGHT

人手梨

Hitodenashi grows on human blood, flesh and all the curses upon the world that the human has cast and stored in their heart. It needs the pain of live, suffering humans. The curse acts to keep its human alive to sustain itself for as long as possible.

HATSU,
Thirty-Second Hellmaker

Awano held the fruit by its thick vine of hair. She ripped open its cheeks with flicks of her needle-covered tongue and wept.

Koushiro was with her. He looked up as Hyo and Natsuami drew near.

"Had enough?" Hyo said.

"We took off each other's limbs a few times. I hit her with her own leg. She returned in kind. Then she got hungry, and we came here and talked. I was performing at the Ukibashi New Year's Party when she was kidnapped. Everyone was watching me on stage. They weren't paying attention to her or where she was." He was frowning, examining his clawed fingers and their blood-darkened ends. "What happens to her now?"

"I don't know yet."

Koushiro narrowed his eyes, but nodded. "See this through for me, hellmaker."

He disappeared. When Hyo opened her hand, his paper doll nestled in her palm as if it had been there all along. She put it away in her robes and met Awano's gaze.

"Ukibashi Awano." The ripest pears tracked Hyo's movements. They had beady eyes with which to spot humans to bite and sink their teeth-seeds into. "I've an offer for you."

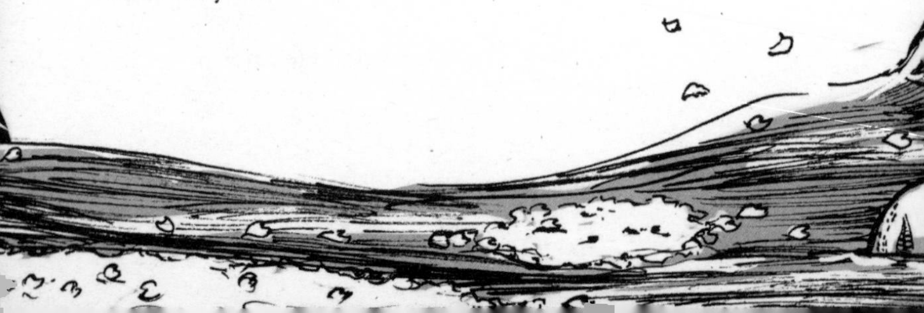

"I don't want to hear it." Awano lifted her chin. "Koushiro explained your hellmaking to me. You're lucky that Fuchiha's not with me right now – which means it's unlucky for him. Whatever you're going to ask of me, it'll only hurt him." She picked up another pear, which gnashed its teeth-seeds angrily, and bit into its forehead. "I should kill you and eat you. I could do it. And I would, if I could just –" her tongue sliced open the pear's face – "stop ... eating ... these ... fucking pears!"

Fuchiha. The Wavewalker. "This orchard, was it made for you?"

"No. He had it all already set up before he started harvesting from it for me. I don't know how long it's been here." Pear pulp dripped from Awano's mouth. She looked miserable. "He's finally had enough of me, hasn't he? I prayed to him. He should be here, killing you for seeing his orchard. For seeing me like this."

Hyo felt a sharp pinch. A small blue crab was perching on her wrist.

Go to her. The crab tugged at her sleeve, pulling Hyo towards Awano. *Gods can't save humans. Save her.*

It dropped into the water, vanishing under the petals.

"Awano-chan." Hyo waded closer. Natsuami followed. His shadow, heavy and hungry, the most terrifying thing in the orchard, wrapped around them both. "The Wavewalker held back from killing me for your sake. I think he saw, like you did with the water-eye, that I was exactly as you said – your way out."

Awano snorted. "I was wrong about that."

"I don't think so."

"Hah!"

"I can stop you hurting. I can make it so that you can stop eating." Awano stilled, a pear core between her teeth. Hyo met her baleful gaze. "I'm going to give you the benefit of the doubt and say that, back in the solarcrane, maybe you were telling the truth when you said you wanted to save the Wavewalker. I have him in my hell. You can still help to save him. You can put his fate back into his hands."

Awano gulped down the core and wiped her mouth on the back of her hand. "How?"

"By cutting his fate free of you. The Wavewalker nearly fell trying to keep you safe. He made those pear pills for you, mucked around with the island's taint-detectors for you and cursed the Makuni brothers for you."

"What do I have to do?"

"Pray."

"To the Wavewalker?"

"No." Hyo looked past Awano's shoulder to where bands of unluck had thickened and gathered. "To him."

With a deafening crack, the ceiling caved in.

Petal-crested waves jumped in all directions. The wind swept through, smelling of brine and blood, but still fresher than the sweetness of hitodenashi. There was smoke, blue lights, crackling flames.

A white headless horse in a red tasselled harness landed in the rubble. The god in the saddle had silver flames leaping from his mouth and eyes. He wore robes from the Wavewalker's yashiori ward, and fell off his horse on landing.

Natsuami cried, "Toki!"

Awano stared. "The Bridgeburner?"

Tokifuyu's shoulders heaved as he rose. "Hakai Hyo, you've no idea what you risked going into the Under-dream!"

"Welcome back. I've some idea, which is probably worse."

"Toki, please." Tokifuyu looked up so quickly that Natsuami might've shouted, "Calm yourself. I'm sure we'll all have our explanations later."

Tokifuyu's face, wan and still yashiori-green about the lips, unclenched like a fist. "But, Aniue!"

"Can you listen like the god the humans need you to be and help, or are you going to let that temper get the better of you?"

The last was spoken calmly, quietly even. The flames fizzled from Tokifuyu's mouth and eyes. "Are you angry?"

"Yes. But I've decided that it can wait. And you will do the same, and you will do what is asked of you ... or ... or..." Natsuami hesitated then drew himself up straight. "Or we will not be speaking after this."

"Aniue!" Tokifuyu gasped. "All right. I'll listen."

Hyo returned to Awano. "You're going to pray to the Bridgeburner to break your en with the Wavewalker."

"Break our en? I could do that myself!" Awano clambered to her feet, cradling a pear with the bloated face of a middle-aged freshly drowned man. "I just have to leave Onogoro. That's all I wanted from tonight, anyway! All you had to do, Hyo-chan, was give me those teeth-seeds, then I would've burned this orchard to the ground, taken my solarcrane and cut all en with all of you! I don't need you, or that minor god, to do that!"

"Minor god!" Tokifuyu fumed. "Just who do you think you are?"

"I'm Ukibashi Awano of the Ukibashi Shinshu Company." Awano's eyes shone. "And just imagine what the world would think if I revealed that Ukibashi Awano herself was made a demon on Onogoro and saw, with her own eyes, that hitodenashi pear was grown here. I could do that at any moment. Ukoku culture's reputation as shinshu-makers, rather than hitodenashi's inventors would crumble, and the world wouldn't let you forget it this time. I never would reveal this, of course, but you wouldn't know it. This tiny island will depend on my merciful silence for ever."

"That doesn't cut your en with Onogoro or the Wavewalker, it only reshapes it," said Hyo. "Tokifuyu, can you cut the Wavewalker's en with Awano?"

"Of course, but—"

"Cut it so it's as if they never had any connection at all, so that they forget they ever had an en?"

Tokifuyu clenched his jaw. "I have no such power."

"Toki," Natsuami said quietly, "I can tell when you're lying."

Rain poured through the hole in the ceiling. The drops landed heavily and smelled of iron. It was raining blood.

Fire crackled. Tokifuyu lowered his head.

"It can be done. If I cut a human's en to a god's heavenly name, they can be made to forget their en with the god in the past and present, and will never connect with them again in the future. They'd remember only a space, some feeling that someone must have been there once." Tokifuyu hunched his shoulders. "It's pathetically easy how humans can forget someone so strongly connected to them."

Hyo turned to Awano. "Choose to cut your en with the Wavewalker and *you'll* be saving *him* this time. He won't remember you, but he'll remember that someone stopped him from falling, when he couldn't do it on his own."

They shared a look. Unluck spun in twisting, tangling shapes.

"And he'll be free of me?" she said bitterly.

"Never. You'll be a ghost to him, Awano-chan. Always at his shoulder but he won't be able to name you and send you away."

"And I'll never be free of you, Hyo-chan, will I?" Awano bit into her fruit. Juice ran down her chin. "You'll be the one who saves me this time, when I couldn't save myself. That kind of en lingers."

"You're right," Hyo said, "and I'm sorry for it."

Awano was stunned into silence. Then she laughed. She laughed and laughed, first low and quiet in the shell of her throat, then louder, with her hands wrapped around her middle. "So what do I get for cutting my en with the Wavewalker?"

"I'm going to offer you an artisan hell."

Gone was the hunger pain from her eyes and its fog. Awano's mind was perfectly clear. "You'd get vengeance for me?"

"On the people who kidnapped you."

Unluck settled in its smoke-stain snow, crystallizing unseen on Awano's shoulders. "You'd make them hurt like this? Unable to escape? All their fate out of their hands?"

Hyo stared into the burning blue of Awano's water-eye. "I'll find out who they were or are and make them pay in your name. You'll be with me when they suffer, to see it yourself."

"Like Koushiro."

"That's right. You'll become a shikigami. You'll keep your mind. You won't feel hungry. And one day, if you still want to, you can kill me."

"Hyo..." Natsuami chided her.

"That night Makuni Junichiro took the picture of me,"

Awano said, "it was the first time I'd come to this beach since the kidnapping, and the first night I visited this orchard, to see for myself where the Wavewalker's miracle medicine pills were coming from. I saw all these people ... in these plant beds, all becoming food for me. And I was happy, do you know? I thought I'd never be hungry again, so I ran outside. Just to be joyful, instead of tired, hungry and scared, and you know the rest." Awano wiped her eyes. She blinked up at the blood raining through the ceiling and smiled. "It's a deal. Make your offer, Hakai Hyo."

"Ukibashi Awano," Hyo said, "would you like to commission an artisan hell?"

The moment the en broke between Ukibashi Awano and the Wavewalker wasn't obvious.

The blood rain continued. The storm blew wildly across Onogoro. Night on the island carried on.

But Hyo knew it had happened. She saw a blizzard of unluck swirl through the orchard and flow out of the orchard roof to pile upon the Wavewalker and burden him with an unnameable, inescapable ghost for ever.

For a god so used to the weight of a name, trapping him in a loss without one, which could never have its edge worn smooth for speaking of it, would surely be a quietly tormenting hell.

And then Awano was gone. A moon-white paper man was in Hyo's hand.

Hyo was left with the orchard and all that remained to be done was to burn it down. Otherwise, somebody else could find this, spread the seeds and grow it again from the pains of another abandoned people. She had to get rid of it. She had to see it burn—

"You will do nothing of the kind."

Little made sense before Hyo blacked out, especially the sight of a giant white snake, slithering along the orchard ceiling.

There was a knocking.

Hyo reached for the door, only realizing as her fingers pulled back dark cedar that this wasn't her Hikaraku flat. A wind chime turned in the eaves. A three-shaku high "*Die, Hag!*" was slashed in Mansaku's handwriting into the house's front.

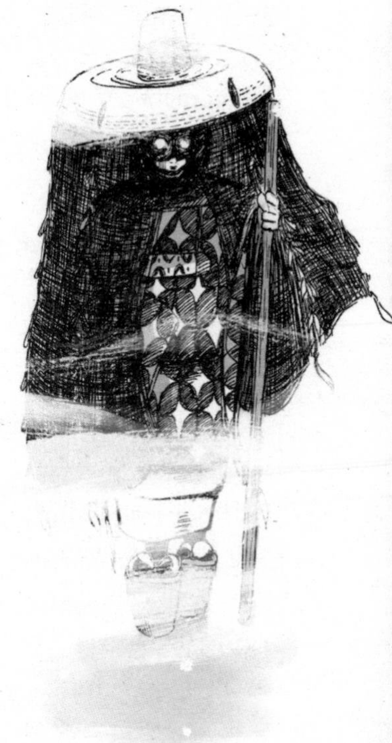

It was home. In Koura.

The Paddywatcher stood outside, wind lifting the dark veil of her ichime-gasa hat, towering over Hyo in pokkuri as red as blood on snow.

"Hellmaker."

"Yamada-san."

The Paddywatcher raised her eyebrows. "We have things to discuss before you wake. Let me into your dreams."

"Do you need my permission?"

"You are jealously guarded."

Hyo stepped back from the door. The Paddywatcher – Yamada Hanako – untied her ichime-gasa, gave it to Hyo to prop against the wall, then, in a blink, was kneeling on the tatami. "If you have any, I should like some eggs."

"Eggs," repeated Hyo, dumbfounded.

"Yes, you should have some." The Paddywatcher pointed towards the door that led to Hatsu's writing room. "In there."

Hyo slid it open. A black void of nothingness breathed its chill at her, and hanging within it was a basket of eggs, shells hot to the touch. She lifted six into her apron and carried them back to the god, who was waiting with a small black plate and a bowl.

"I am fond of eggs," the Paddywatcher

said, as Hyo heaped them in her bowl. Her fingers burned from the shells. "Once I was a mountain, first and foremost. I couldn't care less for eggs, but then I was a snake and I learnt that eggs were good. I was also the plentiful sheaf of wheat and bountiful harvest. I still am all those things, whilst also being a Pillar being – but I am also a Pillar for having been and still being all these things. Do you understand what I am saying, Hakai Hyo?"

Hyo kneeled opposite and took up an egg to peel. "I think you're saying that what you do isn't for a mere little human like me to understand, which makes that a trick question."

"Do not insult me with this lie that you think yourself a 'mere little human'."

"All right. Then there's nothing 'mere' or 'little' about being human. You cursed Mansaku to burn down the Hamanoyokocho shrine and tipped off your police officers about it." Hyo set the smooth white egg on the Paddywatcher's plate. "Where are you keeping my brother?"

"Hakai Mansaku is here."

"In his dreams? Or in the earthly plane?"

"Both. I, too, have a shrine in Hamanoyokocho, a little north of the Bridgeburner's. You and your brother are both there in a deep sleep."

"I got you the teeth-seeds from Tokifuyu's shrine."

The Paddywatcher bit delicately into the egg. The sunburst yolk oozed over her lips. "Indeed."

"Have you called off your police yet? Or is that conditional on whatever else you want from me?"

"Arrogant ignorant child. But astute." The Paddywatcher licked her lips clean. "Yes, I will quash all suspicion regarding Mansaku if you agree to maintain your silence."

"On the existence of the Wavewalker's orchard."

"Yes."

"But it's not just his orchard," Hyo realized. "It's your orchard too. You're growing hitodenashi with the Wavewalker." Hyo remembered something Awano had said, about the Wavewalker not being the one who had drugged Tokifuyu. "You're the one who sent the yashiori doll to the Ivy Plaza to drown Tokifuyu in the Underdream and get him out of the way of his shrine. That was *you*, not the Wavewalker."

"Yes, it was."

"You can animate straw. You had access to yashiori as patron god of the police officers."

"That is so."

"And now you're admitting all this to me because I'm exactly where you want me to be. Mansaku is in your hands, accused of arson. I've got hitodenashi pear teeth-seeds in my possession, which is probably illegal. We're not from Onogoro – we're from the *outside*. We'd be the perfect scapegoats for anything hitodenashi-related. So I'm not going to have any choice but agree to let you curse me to silence." Hyo handed the Paddywatcher another peeled egg. "And then I'll be a ready pawn for more of your schemes."

"Your awareness of the situation makes this discussion easier."

Hyo focused on the next hot egg in her hands, its heat numbing her fingertips. "Did the Pillar Gods plant that orchard?"

"We did," the god replied readily. "You weren't here for Three Thousand Three Fall, Hakai Hyo. You know nothing of what we all lost that night. Whatever you imagine, it cannot compare. Terror. Pain. Cruelty. These words are but dragonfly wings, a noise and a flicker. Kindness was destroyed that night. It has never returned. People remember it. In their hearts, deep down, they remember that their ens could be turned against them. I believe you know how the incident came about."

"A powerful en-musubi god was given hitodenashi pear," Hyo said. "By who?"

"All we know is that they were human. The god of destruction wasn't simply killing their followers. They were executing them, for betrayal. It knew that one of them had given it the fruit. We don't, however, know if it succeeded in finding the culprit." The Paddywatcher waved, and there was a tokkuri and two cups between them on a lacquered table. "We were to blame as well. We'd become complacent. We thought hitodenashi a problem of the 'outside', and knew too little of it to save our dear friend. So, in the aftermath, we determined that the means to study hitodenashi, and understand it, was necessary."

"To prevent it happening again?"

"There are many outside Onogoro hoping to find a way to get their hands on shinshu. Many who would like to see us collapse from the inside." The Paddywatcher's red eyes glimmered like coals. "They feel it would put us in our place, after Ukoku rebuilt on Onogoro and became prosperous, despite losing in the Hell-on-Earth War."

Hyo said, "I don't think the rest of the world cares as much about Onogoro as you think."

"Perhaps not. But this small island's people wouldn't be alone in thinking that they are greater in significance than they actually are." The Paddywatcher swallowed her peeled egg whole. "That the Wavewalker threatened the research orchard with his personal favouritism and private purpose was unacceptable. You served us well, hellmaker, in ending that business."

"How is the Wavewalker?"

"The Onmyoryo have been working to exorcise some of his taint before the Great Purification Rituals. For sabotaging the taint-detectors, we are arguing diminished responsibility from acute taint accumulation. We will win.

We cannot afford a Pillar to fall." The Paddywatcher's red agate eyes drifted around the room of Hyo's dream: the calligraphy over the doorway, the notebooks stacked by the walls, a window that looked out over a small yard to stacked logs and forest. "He has been significantly weakened since the Bridgeburner cut the en between his heavenly name and the demon." The Paddywatcher folded her hands in front of her. "His heart is broken."

Outside the window, there was a pale shadow of greenery under snow. It was spring. That took Hyo by surprise. "Does the Wavewalker remember Awano?"

"No, but his heart is broken nonetheless, even if that isn't the name by which he calls his pain." The Paddywatcher poured from the tokkuri into the two cups on the table. "What would a god have to pay for a hellmaker's artisan services?"

Hyo raised her eyebrows. "I thought Onogoro gods have the power to manage their own vengeance, so long as there's 'Good Reason'."

"I've never been human. For that, there's only so much I can understand of human pain and suffering," said the Paddywatcher. "You humans know how to hurt each other best, to make it personal. The likes of me and the Wavewalker, we can create calamities, but landslides and deluges are impersonal, meaningless things. Making pain *personal*, so that the human on the receiving end suffers, and is made to feel hopelessly lonely when no other can share in that suffering, is not my speciality."

"Who do you want to make suffer that much?"

"I want the human who fed my friend hitodenashi pear and created Ryouen Natsuami to be found and tormented," the Paddywatcher said smoothly. "I have been observing your work. The results satisfy me. I am interested in a commission. What would be your price, hellmaker, for me to learn if the culprit is alive or dead, and, if the former, to make a hell for them?"

Hyo considered it. "I'm afraid my prices are under review."

"Until when?"

"... until I've finished reviewing."

"I see. Then we shall have to see that your hellmaking business continues, and you've the time and space to relax and review." The Paddywatcher held out a filled cup. "We shall meet again soon, no doubt."

Hyo counted down until what felt like an appropriately nervous length of time had passed, then took the cup. "This is for my silence on the orchard that the gods of Onogoro grew, and you letting Mansaku go, his name in the clear?"

"You agree?"

"Just one last question."

"Yes?"

"If you knew nothing about hitodenashi here on Onogoro, who helped you plant the orchard and grow it in the first place?"

The Paddywatcher gazed at her with the unreadable steadiness of the mountain. “Who helped us is unimportant. There were many. Planters. Scientists. Students who rediscovered misplaced war documents in their libraries. There was no single advisor.”

“Documents by who?”

“Was it not your ‘one’ ‘last’ question?”

“Right.” Hyo raised her cup. “Fine. I agree to everything.”

“Good.”

They drank.

Hyo put the cup down, and woke.

When she opened her eyes, Tokifuyu was glowering over her. “Try to convince me, Hakai Hyo, that I don’t have Good Reason to curse you.”

TWENTY-NINE

兄弟

For a fortnight, the monster questioned T and E about whether they knew the monster's name.

From a report by RYOUEN TOKIFUYU
on an interview with Gods T and E

"You didn't know what could've happened to you in the Under-dream!"

Twenty minutes later, Tokifuyu was still pacing back and forth, repeating all his arguments as if repetition would hammer them home in Hyo's skull. She stayed horizontal on the bed and sighed at the ceiling.

"And to talk to *him* there! You could have lost your mind. You could have *given* him your mind. For all we know, he could've possessed you! And your hellmaker abilities! And then imagine what kind of danger Onogoro would've been in!"

"That shadow was going to tie me an en with a sticky death, right there and then in the water, just because it had a chance to," Hyo replied so calmly that Tokifuyu closed his mouth with a sheepish sizzle. "I'm not going to apologize for talking to it and convincing it that I should live and let you go."

"You're not going to apologize?!"

"Why should I? How were *you* planning on getting out from the Under-dream anyway?"

Tokifuyu clammed up at last. Smoke rose between his teeth. He faced the window, silently seething, and Hyo took the moment to study her surroundings.

She was in a narrow single-storey building, sectioned from the rest of the room by a screen, on which a poem in cursive script had been drizzled to float like seaweed. Lighting came from a window and a lamp enclosed in a square shade. A cone of incense was burning in a dish. Its woody smell was soaked into her clothes – which had been changed for dark grey cyclocloth sleepwear and a snug belt. Her hair had been washed and combed. The cuts on her limbs had been cleaned too, some uglier gashes on her forearm stitched.

The marks of the hellmakers' seal were already returning faintly to her palms.

Tokifuyu said, "It shames me that I cannot break your en with Natsuami."

Hyo almost smiled. "You don't need to take it personally."

"But I'm an en-giri god. I break harmful ens. It *is* personal to me." When Hyo laughed, Tokifuyu crossed his arms, scowl deepening. "Did I say something amusing?"

Hyo hastily turned her laughter into a cough. "Just something in my throat."

Tokifuyu eyed her suspiciously. Then he blew out a stream of sparks from his nose and resettled cross-legged. "You're the first human to speak to Natsuami in the Under-dream."

"I guessed as much." It was probably some effect of having the powers of the old gods of misfortunes sealed in her.

"You and I are going to have work closer together. From here on, whenever he speaks to you again – and he will do so – you will report it to me." Tokifuyu set his hands on his knees. His face reddened. "If I cannot relieve you of that en, then allow me to … listen, and share, in whatever may be too much for you alone."

Hyo studied him, letting Tokifuyu simmer. Then she nodded slowly. "I'll take you up on that."

Tokifuyu let out a long breath. "Good."

He seemed off-kilter. Hyo thought she understood. Personal hells were lonely. Tokifuyu had been in one, built by his secrets, for a while. Anyone would be caught off guard if they suddenly found it shared. She said, "Any starter tips?"

"Be careful if he ever directly asks you to do something for him," Tokifuyu replied. "The shadow's proud of his freedom from humans. He's trying to trap you in a chance to offend him. It's twisted logic, but he'll hold the fact that he ever needed help – especially from a human – against you." His expression darkened. "Should he ever return, I am due to suffer the most and be killed first. At this rate, you will be second. But do not be afraid. I will do everything I can to keep us all safe with him."

Safe "with", not safe "from", eh? thought Hyo, before saying, "Thank you."

"Yes, you should thank me."

"You call the Under-dream god 'him'. Everyone else calls him an 'it'."

"It's only natural they would," Tokifuyu said shortly. "He's a totally fallen god of destruction – an 'it' in the same way floods, quakes and storms are – a powerful force of nature, born of the world and without need of human thoughts."

"But it's different for you, isn't it?" Flames wavered at Tokifuyu's eyes. Hyo said, "He told me that you remember his heavenly name."

Tokifuyu froze. "He knows this?"

"Yeah."

"But he's let me leave the Under-dream countless times, without trying to force it from me." Tokifuyu stood abruptly, moving to the window. It was grey outside, the view blurred by a thin film of rain. A privacy talisman had been pasted over it. Hyo waited, letting the thin slide of rain on window rasp away at whatever Tokifuyu was thinking about. "It's true. I remember it. I have to, in order to be able to keep the en between his heavenly name and the world cut. The dream of the name still exists in the Under-dream. Someone might, one day, dream it up again."

"And call the god back?"

"It won't happen." Tokifuyu clenched his jaw. "I won't let it."

"You should tell Natsuami. Not his heavenly name," said Hyo quickly, when Tokifuyu sucked in a deep breath as if powering a fireball, "but that you remember it. That you're keeping it safe."

Tokifuyu deflated, cooling. "I'll consider it."

Hyo propped herself up. "Are you going to tell me where I am now?"

"You are in the Paddywatcher's south-western shrine. You've been under watch for hitodenashi infection." Tokifuyu sniffed then said in tones of clear disapproval, "You have been asleep for two days now."

"Two days?!" She didn't feel hungry or stiff enough for it to have been a natural sleep.

"Two days, ten hours, nine minutes," he said, as if this was much too long.

"And you've been here waiting the entire time?"

"Of course! I had things to say and you might've tried to flee!" Tokifuyu added, "Mansaku-san is here too, for your information."

"Have you seen him? How is he?"

"He awoke this morning. He is insufferable. He is fine. The Paddywatcher vouched for him to the authorities." Tokifuyu drummed his fingers on his knees. "He is keeping my brother company today."

Hyo groaned. "Let me guess. You haven't spoken to Natsuami since you were both at the orchard."

"He's been busy, and so have I and … what are you doing?"

"Some god you are." When Tokifuyu moved to stop her from getting up, Hyo fixed her eyes on the dancing flame of his life, fed with the dark oil of those who willed him alive, and he froze. "You've been avoiding him. No.

We're done with this, Ryouen Tokifuyu. Where are my clothes? Give me your haori."

"You dare order a god to clothe you..." Tokifuyu grumbled but he was already shrugging off the bright orange cloth and handing it over. "He wouldn't speak to me yesterday."

"How hard did you try?"

Tokifuyu hung his head, and to Hyo's shock he scrubbed his eyes fiercely on his sleeve. She smelled charred cyclocloth. Tokifuyu apparently cried tears of burning oil.

How lonely and young he looked. If the Paddywatcher was a mountain and a snake, this was a river and a human boy who had lost his family. Hyo asked without thinking, "How old were you when you became a god?"

"Old enough," he said. "I was a princess when I died in my river. If the war with the Ghost King hadn't happened, back then in the Taiwa, I would have been married at least five years previous to some saggy-breasted old middle chancellor from the court. If I was old enough to bear children, I was old enough to become a god."

"True." Hyo let him help her to the door. "Let's find our brothers then."

Police tape still fluttered in spots about the shrine ruins. Mansaku and Natsuami were alone, something which could only have been arranged by the gods. Curious humans should have been all over the place.

Mansaku's eyes lit up. He smiled wide, mouthing Hyo's name, then turned, saying something to Natsuami.

Natsuami didn't move. He stayed with his head tilted up to the shrine's ruined face, rain sliding down the slope of his umbrella. Mansaku left him to meet Hyo and Tokifuyu at the shrine gate, twirling his umbrella as he sauntered towards them.

"O'Hyo, really? I didn't think I raised my little sister to be a disrespectful slob, coming to a house of a god in the clothes she slept in."

"You didn't raise me at all."

"And that's why you turned out all right." Mansaku glanced at Tokifuyu, who was clutching his umbrella with white knuckles. Then he gave the god a not too gentle shove.

Tokifuyu's eyes and teeth exploded with fire. "Hakai Mansaku!"

"Go away, Toki. I want a touching reunion with *my* sister on whom *you* dumped *your* messed-up brother, and you're spoiling it."

Tokifuyu made a small jerky movement with his head that could have been a nod or a nervous neck spasm, and went.

Hyo reached for Mansaku, pulling him into a hug. "You're all right?"

"I should be saying that to you," he said, voice thick. "I heard from Natsu-san. Hitodenashi. On Onogoro."

Hyo nodded. "It's just as the demon said."

"You think she got the rest right too? About Akasakaki?"

"The Paddywatcher told me that useful documents just turned up when needed. Planters and scientists magically knew what to do. Someone helped the Pillar Gods make their orchard." Hyo shook her head. "I don't want her to be right."

"Me neither. We'll have to find out."

Hyo shuddered at the thought. "Are you really fine?"

"As fine as anyone who's been in a cursed sleep can be," Mansaku replied breezily, but he was wearing two neckerchiefs over Kiriyuki's seal, "and who missed out on his little sister's first special commission. Is it done?"

The seal on her hands had been becoming clearer by the minute. The stars of unluck had vanished from her sight. Hyo nodded.

Mansaku sighed. "Good. That's it then. Jun, you hear that? She got 'em."

"Jun-san's ghost is gone, remember?"

"But we still have his name."

Mansaku didn't let Hyo go. They watched Tokifuyu come to a stop behind Natsuami.

"Those two haven't spoken a single word to each other since I came to," Mansaku told Hyo out of the corner

of his mouth. "Not even at meals. I had to put my foot down when they tried to use me as a messenger pigeon."

They watched as Natsuami tipped his head to the great grey shrine. Tokifuyu stiffened, then gave a slow and heavy nod in response.

This was once my shrine, wasn't it?

Yes, it was.

"The Paddywatcher came up with a story for how the Wavewalker picked up all that taint," said Mansaku. "They're going to say it's because he failed to protect Koushiro from all that unluck, even though he was trying *so, so hard* to keep him alive."

"Almost true then. Does the Wavewalker believe it?"

"Either he believes it, or he's got to believe that all his closest god friends are liars, right? I'd take the lie."

And then Natsuami's voice echoed through the forecourt: "... it's a truth that wasn't for you to hide from me!"

"Oh, here we go," Mansaku said.

"I caused Three Thousand Three Fall. I killed my followers and those dear to them. I tried to kill you! I know I did! You dream of it! Mistaken? How so?" Tokifuyu interrupted quietly. It made Natsuami stare. "You ... you thought I was happy not knowing, and my happiness made you happy? Hear me now, Toki, loud and clear! I am ... *not* ... happy!"

"I KNOW!" The umbrella Tokifuyu was holding over his head went up in silver flames. He hurled it to the ground. "You haven't been happy for some time! I AM WELL AWARE!"

"You were cutting all en I might've had with people, but for those that you *allowed* me to pretend everything was normal, and, of those, how many were the Wavewalker?! I know that an en with me is dangerous. I know that everything you've done has been for my sake. But I've been so alone with everything I did, and what little I *knew*. I've been so alone with myself." Natsuami raised a shaking hand in a fist, wringing the air. "I've been ... so ... *lonely*! Do you understand this?" Natsuami dropped to his knees. The umbrella fell to the side as he raised his hands to his face. "I've been so lonely!"

"I know," Tokifuyu said, too quiet to hear but Hyo

could read his lips. The rain turned to steam when it struck him. "Aniue, I'm sorry."

He followed Natsuami to his knees in the rain-soaked earth, and folded over, pressing his forehead into the dirt.

Natsuami, who had been kneeling as limp as a spent paper doll, regarded Tokifuyu in steady silence, then reached out to put a hand on his shoulder.

"I've decided," he said, "I won't be angry."

Tokifuyu's response was lost in the rain.

"At myself, yes, because I took advantage of you, but never with you. I know you think you deserve it, and that's why I mustn't be." Natsuami took hold of Tokifuyu's shoulders and lifted him up from his bow. "I'm not the only one who's been unhappy for some time now, am I?"

Tokifuyu crumpled. Fire bubbled at the corners of his eyes. He shook his head fiercely, and wailed, "It can't compare!"

"Oh, Toki." Natsuami brushed away a falling bead of fire. "It doesn't need to compare."

"We've got to take that one to the theatre someday, O'Hyo," said Mansaku, as Tokifuyu continued to sob loudly, clutching at Natsuami's front, drops of liquid fire running down his cheeks. They rolled to the water and melted into ghostly ribbons of steam. "Tragedy, comedy – either way, we'll have fireworks."

THIRTY

大祓

Every old mountain, tree, river, road, island that has played a part in human fate and fortune has its god. The island of Onogoro has, itself, a very old god.

AN,
Twenty-Ninth Hellmaker

The shin-kagura play ended in an explosion of blue ribbons and silver petals of rice paper, and to the crowd's cheers.

"Thank you for your attention!" The actor bowed deeply to the audience. It was the younger Koga brother. "We will carry forward the memory of Kikugawa Kichizuru into the future of our craft! Please support the new Kikugawa troupe – I am Kikugawa Umezo; thank you and we'll see you again!"

As the crowd dispersed, the vendors emerged on the walkways. Their trays displayed inked prints of Kikugawa Umezo, paper fans and lucky charms with the Wavewalker's shrine blessings on them. Fortunes were being read

to laughter and tied to the potted pines and railings. Onogoro fluttered with blue-grey paper twists and ribbon decorations.

Hyo stopped a vendor with a handful of slim paperbacks. “How much for one?”

The libretto for the new shin-kagura had been published as part of the Great Purification Rituals festivities. The lilac cover depicted the two Koga brothers painted in white as moonlit figures. The story had changed since Koushiro had performed it at the Shin-Kaguraza. Now the two brothers spent a year on an island that was Onogoro in all but name, enjoying the turns of the seasons in the coming and going of the rains and the rice, meeting fishers, shinshu brewers, shrine-keepers, gods, old shogi players, students and dancers – until the ghost of their father appeared to remind them of their duty to avenge him.

The whole story was, in fact, a horror story. Whilst each of the twelve scenes depicted something recognizably loved in Onogoro, the father’s ghost would appear at the end of each as a glowering shadow at the brothers’ shoulders.

The librettist of *The Tale of the Koga Brothers: Twelve Moons’ Ghost* was anonymous.

“Natsu-san did Jun and Koushiro proud,” said Mansaku, paging through the booklet. “And he was so worried he wouldn’t finish in time.”

“Excuse me, dears,” said a voice from beside them, “but have you a moment? I’ve been on my feet all day. I’d like a little help finding a spot to sit down.”

The old woman was half Hyo’s height, bent at the waist, white hair scraped back from her face. Her hitoe was granite-grey cyclocloth, her haori patterned with tortoiseshell shards.

Hyo held out her arm. So did Mansaku, with a smile that the woman returned. “My! Candy on each arm, at my age! Thank you both.

“I do like a good festival,” she said, as they moved away from the plaza. “The noise. The drama. It’s a good purge of feelings. I like them very much, especially after a storm. In fact, they’re most necessary after a storm. Don’t you agree?”

“I’m always ready for a festival!” said Mansaku gamely.

“This one came at a good time,” the woman went on with an approving nod. She glanced sideways at Hyo. “Do you know the story of Nakihime, my dear?”

Hyo replied, “They say she tied the gods into the earthly plane, giving all their heavenly names to the humans to call them by.”

“That’s the one. She cursed the gods to be at the mercy of luck. And en. And fate. All that it means to be part of this world.” The old woman nodded slowly. “You could say she was a hellmaker of a kind, to us of heaven at least.”

Hyo smiled. "I think it's been since the Gateway Terminal, divine madam?"

"Hakai Hyo and Mansaku," said the god from the Gateway counter, a gleam in her eyes, "the hellmakers looking for hitodenashi on Onogoro, I've been watching with much interest. Yes, it's been fun. How do you like Natsuami? He's immensely troublesome, but I like that in a young god. Or whatever he is."

Hyo dropped her smile. "You're the one who tied the en between him and me, which Tokifuyu can't break."

"And look what it did for you!" said the god with glee. "You found a friend who opened the secret parts of the island to you – the worst parts of it. It's better to be disappointed earlier rather than later, hmm? And now

your hellmaking business is known by both gods and people. You should celebrate. Have a little plum wine on me; I'll arrange it."

"Oh, that'll be nice," said Mansaku, smiling a little too widely.

"Good; I'll send it to your new address. Hamanoyokocho, was it? A little office at Todomegawa Daimyoujin's shrine there. Yes, very good."

"There's one thing I don't understand about Natsuami." Hyo asked, "Why didn't you all just lock him away after Three Thousand Three Fall? You could've—"

"Oh, no, even if we could've, we wouldn't," said the god slyly. "Can you think why?"

"He was bait," Hyo said. "You were hoping whoever fed him hitodenashi pear would come back to finish the job."

"Oh, you are a suspicious girl. Maybe you do have what it takes."

"To do what?"

The god chuckled. "To live in peaceable harmony with everyone else on Onogoro, of course. What else would I want for Nakihime's little spit?"

"So you're *not* expecting O'Hyo to dig up what happened to Natsu-san on Three Thousand Three Fall night and catch the culprit for you?" said Mansaku pointedly.

The god patted Mansaku's arm, beaming. "Not unless your dear little sister wants to."

"Can I make one request?" Hyo said. They turned into a broad walkway that sloped and spiralled gently down a bridge's support column.

"By all means."

"Can I ask divine madam to never interfere with my en, or Mansaku's, or Natsuami's, or Tokifuyu's again? Or any of my friends'?"

The god let out a hoot of laughter. "Well, I could try, but I am an en-musubi god, Hyo-chan. To *not* interfere in the en of my islanders ... why, it's like asking the turtle not to carry its shell or the cedar not to grow tall. Sometimes, I won't be able to help myself and the en may be tied *just so.*"

Hyo sighed and resigned herself to future meddling.

"No long faces." The god reached up and pinched Hyo's cheek. "There's a lot of work to be done! There are ghosts who need to be named and seen. They all want to be seen, deep down. They may hide from us gods but might emerge for you."

Mansaku grinned. "In short, you're going to work us to the bone?"

She cackled. "I'll be watching closely."

They came out on to a wider walkway. White sparrows perched along the railings, fluffing their feathers against the wind. The curving length of boards was familiar. It led to a notice hut, one which the people were skirting around, despite their smiling faces and festive chattering, as if compelled on instinct to avoid it.

"Well, now, I think I can go on very well from here with just the one of you. Mansaku, will you be a dear?" said the god, batting her eyelashes.

Mansaku placed his hand over hers. "Of course, divine madam. See you later, O'Hyo. I'll pick up chicken skewers and sides on the way back. It's a party tonight – because I say so."

With that, Mansaku let the god lead him away.

The wind blew in. Changing direction, it came from the east. The spark of every flame of life wavered as if a giant hand had stroked through and played with their heat with its fingers.

There was someone in the notice hut. Hidden in the shadows, Natsuami simply sat and looked out. Nobody paid him any attention, or maybe the instinct that turned their feet away also turned their eyes.

Spotting Hyo, Natsuami lifted his hand in greeting, which she returned.

Hyo closed the door behind her, muffling the sounds of Onogoro's festivities to a soothing murmur. "Your play went down well."

"Did it, really? That's a relief." The tension in the shadows eased. "Are you enjoying everything?"

"I like it. There's so much going on, so many people out, but then there's also..."

"So much going on, and so many people out."

"Yeah." Hyo looked around the walls. Slips of paper

were tucked, tied and twisted into the gridded slats; so many people looking to make a connection, casting a message out to luck and fate. "You're not going to see for yourself?"

"En with me are still dangerous. There are too many people out there right now, who I could put at risk." Natsuami looked wistful. "There may be fewer people around the hour of the ox though."

"The cursing hour," Hyo remarked dryly.

He smiled. "Fitting for you and me?"

"And ghost lights probably. Yeah, I'll join you for that." Hyo suspected much of the festive stalls and events would have shut for the night, but it didn't matter. "In the hour of ghosts and curses."

"Who's the ghost at your shoulder, Hyo?" Natsuami said, after a beat of silence. "Is it the demon who destroyed your home?"

The people of Onogoro drifted by in front of the hut like creatures in a tank.

A lump rose in Hyo's throat. She gripped the folds of her sleeves and tried to swallow it down, but it stayed, stuck and sticking.

Natsuami placed his hand over hers, the one that had grabbed Koushiro by the tongue in a move she'd perfected on a demon before.

"Something haunts you," he said. "I've wondered what it might be. The weight of the hellmakers' duty, or the unluck you see, or the villagers you lost to hitodenashi pear. I should like to know the name of your ghost, Hyo. Let me see it too."

The Sixthmonth Great Purification Rituals were a series of good days. All the taint that had been pooling and festering in Onogoro was being burned out. A weight was lifting from it, rising like smoke. The sun's rays were bouncing clean and silvery from the mirrors to the paddies, and the sounds of repairs to the storm-damaged bridges and walkways mingled with the bells and flutes.

Hyo said wonderingly, in part to herself, "What good would it do?"

"I don't know," Natsuami said. "But we could find out together?"

Distantly, Hyo remembered that there were things about Natsuami to be feared. He had a bottomless hunger in his shadow that could not be trusted, that would manipulate her in order to climb out of its in-between world of dreams. Compared to it, her ghosts didn't seem so unspeakable.

"Wait a moment." She found a privacy seal in her sleeve, activated it with a brush of blood from her cracked lips and stuck it over the doorway. Hyo returned to the bench where Natsuami was waiting. "I can't do a silencing curse on you."

"I've no intention of telling anyone." The corner of his

lips turned up. There was a little darkness. "It'd be nice to have something I can keep from Toki for a change."

"Oh, is that why you want to know? Payback?"

"Perhaps," he said playfully.

"Perhaps. Right." Hyo let the moment settle, the shadows close in. She sat hand in hand with her friend and his shadow god of destruction. "The name of my ghost is Akasakaki Yotoku. Do you recognize it?"

"No. Who is he?"

"He was a scientist for the Ukoku Forces of the Hell-on-Earth War. He created hitodenashi. When the Fellowship closed in on his station, he released the experimental subjects, sending the infected out into the world, as a distraction whilst he escaped." Hyo closed her eyes, letting the muffled festivities wash over her. "The demon who came to Koura was one of his original subjects. She was looking for vengeance. She wanted me and Mansaku to suffer for it."

"You and Mansaku? But you weren't even alive during the Hell-on-Earth War. Why you?"

"Our father was Akasakaki Yotoku's grandson. We were his last remaining family and the closest the demon could get to making him pay. The way she saw it, whilst we lived, Yotoku lived on in us." Hyo took a deep breath. "Joke's on her though."

"I don't see any joke."

"She wanted to infect us with hitodenashi and watch

us suffer like that. But Mansaku and I –" Hyo laughed – "we're immune to hitodenashi. It can't grow in us. Akasakaki engineered it into my unborn grandmother before his wife could escape him, and we got it from our dad."

"Immune to hitodenashi?" Natsuami's eyes were huge. "But, Hyo, that's incredible; it's unheard of! You and Mansaku could be the keys to wiping that curse off the face of this world for good!"

"Exactly, and that's why the demon spared us."

"Why?"

"To end Onogoro's monopoly. They won't have the only cure. What do you think will happen when Mansaku and I tell them all that our blood can stop demons' hunger, and that we cannot be infected ourselves?" A flute trilled and Hyo shivered. "Onogoro's peace depends on being the world's only place that can make shinshu. We could end that, in a few generations."

Natsuami's voice shook, "But what does the demon have against Onogoro? If she was after Akasakaki..."

"She only came to the mountains for us, Natsuami, because she couldn't get on to Onogoro to kill Akasakaki Yotoku himself."

He looked at her sharply. "She believed that Akasakaki's—!"

"Still alive on Onogoro."

"But he'd have to be in his hundreds by now."

"I know," Hyo said. "But she was certain of it: that Akasakaki Yotoku was still alive, that he was being allowed to live here, happily helping the gods of Onogoro grow hitodenashi in secret, whilst the rest of the world suffered. She wanted Onogoro to suffer for hiding Akasakaki and letting him live, as much as she wanted Akasakaki himself to suffer. And she commissioned me, in the end."

"What did she ask of you?" Natsuami asked lowly.

Hyo smiled. "She didn't 'ask' us. I promised her. Her and all the villagers I burned. I promised I'd make hell upon the island if we found Yotoku here, if we found that they'd let him hide in silence as if nothing he did had ever happened. Then we'd reveal ourselves and our immunity to hitodenashi. Shinshu won't buy Onogoro's freedom any more."

Arms wrapped around her. A curtain of hair shrouded her in ink and incense smoke.

"It's a rotten peace and a cruel freedom. The en that 'peace' has tied between us and the outside is poisonous." Natsuami lowered his voice to add, "That Onogoro has allowed this monster of a man to shelter here is shameful. If it takes hell to find him and bring him out, then let there be hell on Onogoro."

Hyo breathed out slowly. "Your god of destruction is showing."

"Really? I thought it was my pseudo-hellmaker."

Natsuami sat back and so did Hyo. Sounds of a local parade echoed from another walkway.

"Where's Tokifuyu today?" Hyo wondered.

"Addressing his own water-god duties at his shrines. He's being a very busy river. Very responsible."

Natsuami tipped back his head, basking in the sunlight filtering into the hut, and, closing his eyes, smiled.

It was a smile without clouds, a summer night sky, as quiet and steadily hopeful as moonrise.

Hyo prodded Natsuami in the arm. "What's that smile for?"

"It's not every day a god of destruction discovers that he isn't the only time bomb ticking on this island. Both of us could destroy everyone here, in one sense or another, if the stars align. We're not alone. We're together, in this hell of ours."

This hell of ours.

Hyo liked the sound of that.

The east wind blew. It rippled through the flames: the candles, the thousands and millions of lives; of crawling, creeping things in the walls; of laughing, dancing and singing people; over the dark mirrored surface of musuhi feeding the gods' lamps; through the young green stems of rice in the paddies, and shinrice in their magenta hydroponic stacks. All lives wavered and adjusted.

There was a loud thud, and a body bounced off the notice-hut roof to slam down at the entrance.

The crowd stopped to stare, nonplussed, then panicked as the body burst into flames.

Hyo sighed. "And until then I've hells to make. Looks like my holiday's over." She held out her hand. "And yours too, if you'll help me. Ready?"

Natsuami took all of her in: Hyo and her ghosts; the ones she carried with pride, the ones she feared to name, the ones they shared.

"All right, hellmaker." He took her hand. "I can help, if you wish."

There's a ghost at your shoulder,
It stands at your hair
And it asks you to name it
And tell it it's there.

Hyo told it, "I'm here."

GLOSSARY

aramitama 荒魂: the wild face of a god.

azuki bean 小豆: a little red bean that makes an excellent paste for sweets.

buraden ブラ電: in this book, the abbreviation for "burakuri-densha", i.e. "dangling train", which is slang for the Onogoro monorail system.

cun 寸: a unit of measurement, about three centimetres.

en 縁: a fateful connection, made between people and whatever and whoever they might encounter in life. This includes other people, animals, plants, objects, landscapes, words and abstract concepts.

en-giri god 縁切り: a god who specializes in cutting and undoing harmful en.

en-musubi god 縁結び: a god who specializes in shepherding and tying together en. (You'd like to think they know what they're doing.)

Fellowship, the: the alliance of nations, including the Harbourlakes, against Ukoku in the Hell-of-Earth War.

First of Us 原初のもの: the first hellmaker.

gaki 餓鬼: in this book, a demon distinguished by extreme hunger, and someone who was once human, who ate hitodenashi pear and survived. The term is borrowed from Buddhism.

geta 下駄: a wooden footwear marked by an addition of wooden supports on the soles that lift the wearer's feet off the ground and out of puddles or snow on the road. There are many types of geta.

god cabinet 神棚の神殿: this isn't actually a cabinet – it's a small house/sanctuary/hall (a shinden 神殿) for the god on your shrine shelf. I was stuck for what to call it because I felt that 'house' might give the impression that there, on the shelf, is a god's home, and that's not quite right. I settled on 'cabinet' because often the shinden contains something that can be a shintai (神体), or a 'body' that houses a god, but it isn't ideal.

gomen kudasai ごめんください: this is said when entering a stranger's house. It's partly asking for permission to do so without actually asking, and partly apologizing without actually apologizing because what you're asking for is help getting around the house on your visit. In Nagakumo's case, however, she's saying it as a polite formality, because the tatenagaya follow a template design: she knows where things are, but she's got to pretend she doesn't as it's a stranger's house.

goze 瞽女: blind female travelling musicians and storytellers, who often played the shamisen.

hakama 袴: a type of trousers or overskirt that can be tied on top of your robes and belt.

han 班: in this book, a local community unit overseen by a hancho, who come together to clean their designated corner of the neighbourhood, grow food and keep an eye on each other. When elections are held, if one member doesn't go to vote, the whole unit gets fined.

hanamichi 花道: a catwalk stage in a kabuki theatre that runs through the audience.

hancho 班長: the han leader.

haori 羽織: a jacket, usually of mid-length, but some fancy long ones have been seen.

Harbourlakes, the: a large country notable for their worship of the Pater-in-Pieces, aka the Dismembered God, and their blackships, powered by the body parts of their god.

hitodama 人魂: the simplest type of ghost – the most basic appearance of a human soul detached from a body, looking much like a little long-tailed fireball.

hitoe 単衣: a kimono-type robe with no lining.

ichime-gasa 市女笠: a sedge-woven hat with a wide brim and a sticking-out part in the centre, mostly associated with upper-class Heian-era women, who often wore them as part of their travelling attire.

iriko いりこ: dried anchovies, good for stock and snacking.

jaki 邪気: malicious energy, likely to flow into the house from the demon door (鬼門 the north-east direction) or the back demon door (裏鬼門 the south-west direction). It can be radiated by things.

jitte 十手: a weapon carried by Edo era policemen, about forty-five centimetres long, with a hook section for catching blades and a baton section for hitting people with. ⊠

joubutsu 成仏: literally, to become a Buddha, but in less literal terms, for the ghost to give up lingering in this world and move on to their next life.

kagura 神楽: dancing, supported by music, in the worship and celebration of gods.

kaki-no-tane crackers 柿の種: rice crackers shaped like persimmon seeds.

karakuri からくり: a technology for mechanical movement that developed and became popular in the Edo period, which saw the creation of automata for entertainment.

katashiro doll 形代: a substitute body, used in the purification of people, when it can take on their taint, or used to give a temporary body to gods and other formless things.

kegare 穢れ: taint; a clinging, sticky uncleanliness. Its sources include sex, crime, death and those things adjacent to death, such as disease, butchery, childbirth and menstruation.

kiseru 煙管: a long-stemmed smoking pipe.

kumade 熊手: a rake, like in gardening – the iron version can be a weapon.

mizuna 水菜: a nice spicy green leaf; a bit like rocket but not.

mochi 餅: rice pounded into a plain silky dough that you can pat and dry into cakes. ⊠

monpe もんぺ: the common term for yamabakama, i.e. hakama where you can close off the hems around the ankles when you're working in fields, or in any environment where you'd rather that the cloth around your legs didn't catch on your surroundings. Often associated with the Second World War period.

mozuku モズク: a delicious, soft seaweed, like eating a little raincloud.

mukuroji ムクロジ: washnut, or Indian or Chinese soapberry; the skin of the fruit is rich in saponin and was used in the Edo period as soap for washing clothes. You can put the dried fruits in a wash net and it'll do its magic.

musuhi 産霊: in this book, the creative energy humans imbue into the naming of things, to make things be and wish them to exist. This is how the gods come to have actual forms and selves. It's based on the musuhi in the Kojiki: the creative energy by which all things were made between heaven and earth.

nagigama 薙鎌: a scythe – some examples have been found with curved and serrated edges, and there's some theory that it could have been used to cut seaweed, which is why in this book it's a water-scythe.

narezushi なれ寿司: salted fermented mackerel sushi, wrapped in leaves, packed tightly; tasty.

natto 納豆: fermented beans, sticky; good with egg on rice and a drizzle of soy sauce.

nigimitama 和魂: the peaceful face of a god.

niisan 兄さん: one of the many ways to address an older brother.

noragi 野良着: clothes worn for agricultural work.

noren 暖簾: a curtain; a hanging cloth divider.

noroi 呪い: the type of cursing more likely to be done by one person against another; also the general word for a curse. In this book, noroi work by turning the person's own self against them.

nukadoko ぬか床: fermented rice bran. You can pack vegetables and fish into it for pickles.

onigiri おにぎり: rice balls. Not doughnuts.

Paraisium States: in this book, a union of countries tied by a shared cultural history and allegiance to the Pater-in-Pieces. The Harbourlakes are derived from an extreme splinter group.

pokkuri ぽっくり: a type of geta made by hollowing out a block of wood instead of adding supports to the sole.

sakaki 榊: an evergreen plant used in offerings and rituals.

sansho pepper 山椒: Japanese pepper; it has a delicate prickly burn.

sasumata 刺股: a pole with a U-shaped end section, like ox horns, which can be used as a weapon to trap and pin down the opponent. Notably used in the Edo period by firemen to take apart burning buildings.

shaku 尺: a unit of measurement, about thirty centimetres.

shamisen 三味線: a three-stringed instrument.

shichijo-gesa 七条袈裟: a type of Buddhist priestly formalwear, brought out for occasions such as funerals. In this book, it's Oblivionist formalwear, and Hatamoto isn't wearing it appropriately.

shikigami 式神: a spirit familiar, often bound up in a paper form, and associated with onmyoji, who were diviners and exorcists employed from the Heian to the Meiji period by the imperial court.

shin-kagura 新神楽: in this book, a form of popular theatre developed from a mix of different kagura traditions, kabuki, noh and revue – cobbled together on Onogoro.

shinresin 神似非樹脂 (略してエセジュ): polymer made from shinshu-brewing waste products. It can be heated and moulded into a range of shapes.

shinwood 神似非木 (略してエセギ): a polymer made from shinshu-brewing waste products with the appearance and close texture to varnished wood.

shirasu しらす: whitebait, often baby anchovies. The poor anchovies don't get a break.

shiso しそ: an aromatic herb.

suikan 水干: a type of menswear, worn from the Heian to the Edo.

Taiwa 太和: in this book, an era about a thousand years ago. Heian-inspired, this era is associated with: poetry-driven advanced meme culture; upper classes put in charge of their own taxation; more aesthetic sense than actual sense; and male tears. Natsuami and Tokifuyu were both deified during it in the course of the Taiwa period war with a ghost king.

tallers タラーズ: in this book, currency based on the Harbourlakes tallers.

tatami 畳: a dried and compressed rice straw mat for flooring. Smell nice but beware black mould.

tatari 祟り: a type of curse associated with gods and ghosts, whereby great disaster is inflicted upon people. In this book, it's a type of curse where the world is turned against someone.

tatenagaya 縦長屋: in this book, a tall, very narrow apartment. They look like paperbacks on a shelf.

tokkuri 徳利: a sake flask.

Ujigami 氏神: a god responsible for the protection of a community, previously defining that "community" by blood, but these days it's more simply by membership to the god's presiding area.

ujiko 氏子: a person in the guardianship of a god. Loosely speaking, a parishioner.

yashiori 八塩折: in this book, a drug made from shinshu by-products that affects gods but not humans. It is usually smoked but can also be consumed as incense.

Outside this book, it was the super-sake brewed to knock out Yamata-no-Orochi, the eight-headed, eight-tailed snake of legends.

zouri 草履: a sort of woven sandal with a strap to stick your toes through. Flatter than geta.

AUTHOR'S NOTE

This book is not an anthropological treatise of Japanese culture, nor one for Japanese history.

It is a fantasy mystery novel, where I have had my fun with both.

The gods are fictional. Even if – like Ohmononushi'no' Ohkami – they share a name with real ones, they are different in their myth and features. The worldbuilding is Edo-inspired but not Edo-faithful to any particular portion of the Edo era. Shin-kagura, whilst inspired by kabuki, is not kabuki. The fashion and hair leans more towards Taisho, Meiji and the contemporary than Edo, and the cloth patterns are a mishmash. The cover, for instance, has Heian-wear with a non-Heian pattern – and that's all right, because whilst history gave me the skeleton to build on and springboards to work off, I am not bound to cling to it.

There has been a certain squeamishness by English

language academics in the past to call the Japanese kami "gods", as opposed to "spirits" or simply "kami". There's some argument that it's because they're "different" from ideas of gods more familiar to these particular individuals, but I don't know why there can't be different ideas of gods and for them to not still be gods. Sometimes I feel that calling them anything but "gods" in English gives permission to diminish their power in the Japanese landscape, to make them "lesser" to other gods of the world in cultural importance. This feeling will probably change in ten years, but, for now, I am deliberately choosing to call them "gods".

This story began with an idea of an en-musubi god who couldn't make his own ens. Connected to Buddhist ideas of pratyaya, en has its analogues throughout Asia where Buddhist influence can be found, such as yuan in China and yeon in Korea. En, yeon and yuan all share the same Chinese character, and, whilst are more similar than different, I do not know the particular nuances of 縁 outside a Japanese cultural context, so I cannot and do not speak for these.

ACKNOWLEDGEMENTS

Ah, the end credits. Well, in the immortal words of a nun who sings amidst sentient hills, let's start somewhere that isn't at the end.

Thank you: to my agent, Lydia Silver, who *got* the manuscript, who championed the book with all the energy I sometimes lack, and who believed that the time was right for this story; to Kristina Egan who's been putting the word out about Hyo abroad!

To my team at Scholastic, to Yasmin Morrissey and Lauren Fortune, for all your faith, vision and ambition for an odd project; to Polly Lyall Grant, who arrived in the middle of the editing Jenga rebuild; to Genevieve Herr, who dealt with a hefty manuscript, then with me returning the hefty manuscript in unpredictable chunks at 3 a.m. and with being the editorial constant throughout; to Jamie Gregory, who gently nudged me into actually sending the pictures – shocker – in order, and who put up very gamely with me over the cover; to Tierney Holm, who combed through two versions of the manuscript for the illustration brief; to Sarah Dutton, who kept the editing coordinated and gifted me with (much-appreciated) deadline extensions; to Wendy Shakespeare, who's taking good care of me during the last stages for the manuscript; to Harriet Dunlea, Hannah Griffiths and Ellen Thomson in publicity and marketing for all your excitement and ideas; to Catherine Coe – the WC question will never not amuse me; to Zhui Ning Chang, who left no stone unturned in the proofreading.

To Erika, who read the first draft chapter by chapter, when it was a mess – brave person.

To Maisie Chan, who pushed me to go for the WOWCON scholarship, and who has been a well of writerly wisdom and support since my first Facebook post; and to all you wonderful writers of the Bubble Tea Writers Group, for the advice, camaraderie, dim sum, encouragement, hugs and hopefulness when things are hard.

To Tariq, Akemi, Olivia, to my friends online and in person; to Grishma, Rona, Helena; Jamie and Kenichi; to Talia, who kept me writing through my master's by being a morning person; to Barbara and Gwenafaye, who saw the snippets and samples of the rewrite and got excited for me; to Rupert Dastur, whose writing trip seems to be running parallel to this one's. You guys all heard me at my highs and lows regarding this project, and thanks for getting me through it.

To the books, manga and noh stories that fed into the making of this; to the Onmyoji series by Yumemakura Baku and its movies; to Detective Conan (Aoyama Gosho) and its policemen pointing out that there's been an unplanned murder and the detective just happens to be there as a witness AGAIN; to the Yokomizo Seishi Kindaichi stories and their drama adaptations; to revenge service stories such as *Uramiya Honpo* and *Hell Girl*; and, I guess, *Sailor Moon*, because without being three and striking her magical girl poses, I don't think I'd have my own dark detective 'magical girl' now.

To the Great Shrine of Izumo and its surrounding mythology; to the gods of my family and house.

And lastly to you, reader, more likely to be a faraway stranger than not. Thank you for reading, and for sitting through these end credits. May you always find the right book when you need it. Take care.